SAMSON

K.B. KIRTLEY

First Edition

Cover Design by MIBLart

ISBN (paperback): 979-8-9898780-2-4
ISBN (ebook): 979-8-9898780-3-1

Published by Kirtley Books
www.kirtleybooks.com

Dedication

For my mom – Who started encouraging my love for reading and stories before I could even talk and never stopped. I'm sorry for not dedicating the first book to you and hope you can forgive me.

These stories wouldn't exist without you.

More in this Series:

Books

The
WHITE KNIGHT

Short Stories
(available for free at KirtleyBooks.com)

THE STREET RAT

EAGLESS

chapter

ONE

Wood and plastic cascaded to the floor, sending the room into silence. Sam jerked his hand back to his side, now fully awake, his heavy breathing replacing the ringing of his clock. Where the alarm had rested moments before now sat a crater. Shards of wood and plastic lay scattered at the foot of his nightstand.

Sam eased himself up on his bed, bringing his long legs up to his chest as he wrapped his trembling arms around them. Closing his eyes, he whispered a familiar refrain.

"Breathe. Just breathe."

After repeating the mantra four times, his rapidly beating heart began to slow. He gently placed his feet on the floor, then reached down and picked up one of the larger pieces of plastic to examine it. The clock was cheap, but he'd never had any issues with it before now. Certainly nothing that would explain it shattering.

How did this happen?

He used his foot to sweep the debris into a pile in front of his nightstand before gently using his hand to do the same on top of the table, collecting the remains together on the floor. With the remnants of the alarm now removed from the nightstand, the crater was even more pronounced. A perfect rectangular indention now marred the table. Holding his hands in front of him, Sam flexed them open and closed, examining them from every angle.

Everything looked the same. He did the same with his arms, poking and prodding at his muscles, unable to see a difference. The muscles didn't offer any more resistance than usual.

Sam got to his feet as lightly as possible and tiptoed across his bedroom to the already open bathroom door. The room was clean except for a pile next to the bathroom door consisting of a backpack, camera bag, and yesterday's clothes that he'd left there in a daze at 2:00 am after getting home from work. His bare feet barely registered the cold tile bathroom floor. Sam reached blindly past the shower curtain to turn on the hot water.

Crack.

He yanked his hand back, and the broken off shower handle came with it. His eyes widened in fear, and he dropped the broken handle to the floor. The metal clattered against the white tiles and his stomach clenched; his fingers had riddled it with deep imprints.

"Breathe," he repeated to himself again. "Just breathe."

His head swam as he tried to control his heart rate. The buzzing of the air conditioner grew louder, and the fluorescent lights of the bathroom glowed brighter. Gently, he turned on the sink, using one finger to barely pull at the knob. It turned on without issue and Sam let out a sigh of relief as he splashed cool water on his face.

He studied himself in the mirror, watching the beads of water roll down his face.

Everything looks the same, he thought, looking into his own dark eyes and searching for any clue as to what could be wrong with him.

His long black hair fell in the same way it always did, down past his broad, copper shoulders. His arms had the same muscle definition they'd had the day before. He was strong but not that strong.

He walked back to his nightstand to further inspect the damage. The imprint of his alarm was a quarter-inch deep on the table next to his lamp. The bottom of the imprint wasn't smooth—there were cuts and indentions within the rectangle where pieces had pressed into the wood. His phone was on the nightstand too, hopefully too far back to be impacted. He reached a hand out but stopped short of grabbing it.

"Hey, AVA," he called out to his phone.

"How can I help you?" the phone responded in a feminine, robotic voice.

"Call Hailey."

"Calling Hailey Hall."

His cousin was at her best under pressure. Sam was always reminding her that—no matter how good she was at handling pressure-filled situations—it was still healthier to take breaks and relax from time to time, advice she never heeded. But right now, he needed her ability to handle extreme situations.

"Hailey?" he asked, making sure she could hear him. "It's Sam. I have a problem."

"What kind of problem?"

"I'd rather talk about it in person. Can you meet me for coffee before work?

"Of course, Sammy. Is something wrong?"

"Maybe. It's probably nothing. I'll explain more when I see you."

"Okay…" worry seeped into his cousin's voice, but Hailey didn't press any further over the phone. "Fran's? Eight-twenty?"

"Sounds great. I'll talk to you then."

Sam waited for the phone to disconnect, not daring to try and hang it up himself. After Hailey ended the call, he buried his face into a pillow, letting out a low groan. Then he walked to the bathroom again and threw another splash of cold water on his face. He pulled his dark hair into a bun on the top of his head, then took a blue and orange checkered button-up shirt out of his closet and grabbed a brown pair of pants.

Once he'd finished getting dressed, he grabbed his camera from the pile. Slinging the bag over his shoulder didn't cause any issues, but he hesitated as he reached for his sunglasses. As gently as he could, he lifted the glasses by the temples and let gravity open them. Using both hands, he guided them to his face, applying as little pressure as possible and let out a sigh of relief as they came to rest unharmed. Once they were safely on his face, he headed for the door, only to stop again as his hand made contact with the knob.

"Breathe," he whispered to himself as he tentatively placed his thumb and middle finger on opposite sides of the knob and prepared to turn it. "Just breathe."

The door opened without any damage, and he felt a slight weight lift from his shoulders as he successfully managed to leave without breaking anything else.

It was supposed to be a light day. The Dutchmen, Duncan's professional football team, had played their season opener at home the night before, forcing Sam to stay out late covering the game. All he had on his schedule for today was a meeting with Barry Jenkins, the editor of the sports section, regarding when he was to leave for Sanders, New Jersey to photograph that weekend's game against the Pirates.

Still in his new hire training period, he wasn't getting many assignments beyond the football beat right now.

While he had taken photos of all types of events in college, the previous paper he'd worked at before moving to Duncan had pigeonholed him as The Sports Guy and early on in his tenure at the Duncan Daily, and that label had stuck. As such, he was only on staff part-time until a position opened up that would allow him to take on more commitments.

Hailey's schedule, though, was always hectic. She was given two articles a week of her own to start out, and she spent time helping research at least another two articles a day for other journalists. She also received a bonus article every time the White Knight made an appearance. With their history in college, she'd gotten that prized assignment when the White Knight moved from Franklin to Duncan shortly after she arrived. With him making the paper at least twice a week, her output was more than double any of the other rookies on staff. Sam knew that if he was going to talk to his cousin without scheduling at least a week in advance, it would have to be right before work and it would have to involve doing something she would be doing anyway. So, coffee at the diner next to the paper's offices it was.

The coffee shop was a short walk from his apartment. Sam's main priority when he'd gone apartment hunting in the spring was to find a place within walking distance of the paper. Given how his day had gone so far, though, he decided to hail a cab instead of risking more damage on his walk. The yellow car pulled up to the curb and Sam reached for the door as it came to a stop.

As soon as he pulled at the handle, he realized his mistake. The handle broke off effortlessly in his hand.

Sights and sounds flooded Sam's senses. He stood on the curb holding onto the yellow door handle of the cab, his heart picking up speed. A siren blared up the block. An OPEN sign blinked in the barbershop window in front of him. Two dogs barked at one another across the street. A bird hopped into the road, only to take flight again as a car approached. A mother pleaded with her child to stop whining as they passed by behind him. His senses were on overdrive, and the world seemed to be rocking underneath him as the uncomfortably familiar feelings of blood rushing to his head and a vomit-inducing nausea threatened to overcome him.

A gruff voice cut through the overwhelming sensations. "Hey! Are you getting in or not? You're wasting my time here!" the cab driver yelled through the rolled down window.

Sam slowly backed away from the cab without answering. He turned and walked the opposite way as the cab driver hurled choice words at his departing back.

"Breathe," Sam whispered to himself as he walked away from the scene. "Just breathe."

His eyes began to focus back in, and the distinct sounds faded into background noise as his heart rate slowed. He left the buildings behind and walked through the park that was a shortcut to downtown.

Walking is probably the safest call for now, he thought as he continued trying to calm his breathing, nodding to reassure himself that walking would solve his problems.

Sam didn't have to walk much further to get to *Fran's*. The diner sat on the first floor of one of downtown's oldest buildings, right across the street from the park. The food and coffee there were great, but that wasn't why it had become their go-to spot. *Fran's* was cheap, a two-minute walk from the building that housed the paper, and, even after just a couple months, Sam had really begun to feel at home with the workers and regulars at the diner.

He grabbed a table tucked away in the corner as he waited for Hailey to arrive, nervously watching each of his movements to make sure he didn't have another incident like earlier. He struggled, resisting the urge to tap the table or check his phone, for fear of what could happen, opting instead to fiddle with the door handle he still held in his hands. He looked down at the deformed piece of metal to find the paint had already vanished from where he'd been rubbing it. He lifted up two fingers as the young waitress brought over a pot of coffee and a couple of mugs to his table. She filled them with a smile before rushing back across the room to wait on another table.

He took a sip of the hot coffee as he waited, leaning forward to press his mouth to the rim without lifting it from the table. Scratching at his beard, Sam watched the clock on the wall as it hit eight-twenty. Not thirty seconds later, Hailey walked through the door. Hailey was five-foot-ten and had the same copper skin and Cherokee features as Sam. She kept her own black hair cut short and close to her head.

"Thanks, pal!" Hailey greeted as she sat down, dropping her bag next to her in the booth before grabbing her mug. "So, what's this big problem of yours? Did your editors like your photos *too* much and now your co-workers are jealous?" she teased.

"Not quite," he chuckled and tried to force a smile. He could tell it didn't work, though, when he saw Hailey's entire demeanor shift as she leaned forward and furrowed her brows.

"What happened, Sammy?"

"I, umm. I, uh… I think there might be something wrong with me. Physically speaking." Glancing around to make sure no one was listening, he leaned forward and continued in a soft, rushed voice. "I broke my alarm clock this morning, turning it off. It shattered, Hailey. It left a dent in my nightstand and shards went everywhere."

"I'm sure there's an explanation for that," Hailey answered, reclining back into the booth after Sam's hushed declaration. "It was probably just old or cheaply made.

You know how the quality of a lot of that stuff is. I'm sure people break their alarms all the time. It's nothing to worry about. You were starting to scare me."

"It wasn't just that. I also ripped off my shower handle turning it on this morning. Do you hear about that happening all the time? Or how about leaving a crater in an oak nightstand? Ripping off a taxi's door handle?" He dropped the handle on the table between them, the yellow painted metal crushed with the imprint of his hand. "Do you hear about those things all the time? Something is wrong with me, Hailey, and I'm worried. I have to be overly careful anytime I reach for something, afraid I'll break it. I take pictures for a living, Hailey. I can't even turn an alarm off without crushing it, how am I going to use a camera? Or edit the photos on a computer? I need to get this figured out ASAP. Look at this."

Sam put a finger on the table and pressed it into the laminate top. The table gave way as he pushed into it. He stopped after making a half-inch deep impression of his pointer finger.

"I'm sure these tables are just old. And you're a strong guy. Everything is going to be okay, Sammy. I wish I could stay and figure this out with you right now, but I have a meeting with Williams at nine and you know how he gets. Go talk to Barry about this weekend and then get out of the office for the rest of the day."

Hailey poured the coffee from her mug into a travel tumbler.

"You should go talk to Taylor," she said. "See if he has any advice for who you can talk to about this. He or his dad might be able to point you in the right direction. I'm sure there's a reasonable answer to all of this. Maybe it will just go away on its own. It could have been just adrenaline or something. You had your first regular season game last night and almost got trampled there at the end. You were probably just still amped this morning without realizing it. Whatever it was, I'm sure Taylor can help. Just hang out at their place and I will come by as soon as I get off and we can talk about it more."

"Okay, yeah, I'll do that." Sam nodded as he spoke. "Can you let them know I'm coming by, though? I can't really use my phone right now, and I'd feel better if they knew I was coming than if I just showed up at their front door."

"Of course I can," she answered, resting a hand on Sam's forearm. "Everything is going to be okay. I'm sorry I can't stay longer or help more right now. I know you're feeling anxious, and I feel bad blowing you off, but I'll see you this afternoon, Sammy. We're going to figure this out. I promise."

Lifting her hand off his arm she stood and grabbed her bag. He stayed sitting in the booth as she hugged him before heading towards the door.

"Thanks again for the coffee by the way!"

Sam closed his eyes as Hailey walked out.

"Breathe," he reminded himself, leaning his head back against the booth. "Just breathe."

TWO

Sam walked out of Barry's office and let out a long breath. He wasn't leaving for Sanders until Friday, giving him three days to figure out what was wrong with him and how to control it.

Taylor seemed like a decent enough guy, but Sam didn't know him that well. He had spent a few evenings in group settings around him, but only because Hailey and Gwen invited him to tag along. But Hailey trusted him, and he was Gwen's cousin, so that was good enough for Sam. Besides, it wasn't like he had much of a choice at the moment.

Sam groaned as he stepped out of the cool building and into the hot summer sun. It was going to be a miserable walk to Taylor's apartment across the city.

Sam loved his fifteen-minute walk to the paper, and rarely needed his motorcycle. He traveled so frequently for work, and when he wasn't traveling, his hours at home were sporadic at best, so he usually got things like groceries, meals, and other shopping delivered. The paper paid for a rideshare to take them to and from the airport as long as they left from and arrived at the office. In his few months in Duncan, he'd probably ridden his bike more to Taylor's apartment for the rare times he hung out with their group than he had for everything else combined. But the bike wasn't an option today. He and his father had worked tirelessly restoring that bike, and he wasn't about to risk hurting it with whatever was going on with him.

What would've been a fifteen-minute ride turned into an hour-long walk in the early-September heat of southern Missouri, but he made it to the apartment. Sam lifted his hand to knock after climbing the stairs to their unit but froze as his knuckles approached the door.

"Uh, Taylor," he called out, leaning his head against the door. "It's Sam. Can you let me in?"

A few seconds passed as Sam looked around the hallway. He cleared his throat to try again, but stopped as the door opened.

"Hey Sam!" Taylor greeted, squinting as the sun shone through the door. "I thought I heard a voice but couldn't tell. Did you knock?"

"Uh, I did not. But there's a good reason for that, which I'll explain in a minute. Is it, uh, okay if I come in?"

"Oh yeah, of course!" Taylor answered, stepping aside to let Sam enter the living room. Taylor was half a foot shorter than Sam, with the same pale complexion and sandy hair as his cousin. "Jason and Lance are at work, so we've got the place to ourselves to talk. Hailey didn't say exactly what the issue was, but made it sound like it was a medical thing, so I figured you'd like some privacy."

"Privacy is definitely appreciated."

Sam looked around the apartment that was similar to his, just with three bedrooms instead of the one he had. A small kitchen sat to the right, while a couch and two chairs were around a coffee table and pointed at the tv. Other than that, the room was bare.

"I do need to make sure you know that I'm not yet a medical professional, so I can't legally give you any diagnosis or anything like that. Just getting that disclosure out of the way," Taylor explained as they sat down, Sam on the couch and Taylor in the chair facing him.

"No, I understand that. This is an, uh, unique issue."

Taylor raised his eyebrows but motioned with his hand for Sam to continue.

"I know this is going to sound strange. I wouldn't believe it either. But this morning, I woke up with super strength." Sam raised his hand to stop Taylor from interjecting as he continued. "I know. It sounds insane. I know it does. But I went to hit my snooze this morning and crushed my alarm clock into a hundred pieces and left a crater in my nightstand. I went to shower and ripped the handle off when I went to turn it on. I tried to open a cab door, and the handle came off in my hand. I've been walking on eggshells all day trying to keep from hurting someone or breaking something else."

Taylor shook his head. "I'm sure there's a normal reason for this—" he started before Sam cut him off.

"There's not."

"Maybe it was faulty equipment." Taylor shrugged. "Or maybe you've gotten stronger recently and just swung a little harder than you're used to."

"Taylor," Sam fought to stop his tone from rising into desperation, "I'm telling you; something is seriously wrong with me. Let's go outside. I'll show you."

"What does that mean?"

"I'm not sure yet," Sam admitted, shaking his head. "Let's just go see what we can find, I just don't want to break anything in here."

Outside, they walked across the parking lot to the small park next to the apartment complex. Sam slowed to a stop in front of a tree at the back of the park, near the edge of a wooded area where no one else was around.

"Alright," he told Taylor as he took a stance in front of the tree, "stand back. This is the first time I've tried to use this on purpose and I'm not sure what's going to happen."

Taking a deep breath, Sam balled his hand into a fist and pulled back his arm. He swung forward, but redirected at the last second and whiffed on the swing, his momentum carrying him a few steps away.

"I got scared," he explained with a forced laugh, hopping in place. "Even though I'm pretty confident it's not going to hurt, my brain still won't let me just punch a tree."

"Maybe that's for the best. Again, there are other reasons that this could be happening. Our brains are usually right about stuff like this. It's how humans have lived so long."

"You don't get it, Taylor, it's not some other thing. It's super—"

"Think about this logically, you can't—"

"GahhHHHH!" Sam exclaimed, turning and punching into the tree as Taylor interrupted him.

Taylor stared with wide eyes, his jaw dropping, watching the splinters that showered off the tree where Sam had struck. Sam, though, felt horror rise in him as the bulk of the tree began to fall into the wooded area. His ears began ringing, and the sun shone brighter as his senses threatened to overstimulate him again. He forced the sensations down and sprinted under the falling tree, opening his arms to catch it. The force of the catch caused him to take a step backwards, but that was all it took for Sam to be able to hold up the tree. Gently, he laid the tree onto the ground as Taylor watched, unmoving, his mouth still agape.

"I told you," Sam whispered, returning to Taylor and sinking to the ground to lean against the trunk, his nausea coming back even stronger after initially pushing through the stimulation, "this isn't a normal problem. There's something going on here."

"We're going to run some tests and see what's happening to you. See if there's a reason for this, and if we can find the limits. I'm sorry I doubted you, Sam."

"Don't be. I don't really believe it myself."

Sam was quiet as they walked back to the parking lot. Taylor ran back upstairs to get his car keys while Sam waited at the car. Taylor opened Sam's door when he returned, closing it back behind him once he was in.

"Thanks," he said as Taylor got behind the wheel. "I'd rather not break a second car today."

"I'd prefer that too," Taylor laughed as he backed the car out.

"So here's what I'm thinking," Taylor said once he had merged onto the interstate, breaking the short silence without taking his eyes off the road. "There's a warehouse the hospital uses for storage and overflow. It doesn't have a ton of equipment, but it has enough for what we need, and I can get us in there without anyone else knowing what we're doing."

"Okay." Sam nodded.

"I'll pick you up tomorrow, and once we're there, I'll take your vitals, examine you as well as I can, and maybe try to do some bloodwork if we can to see what exactly is going on inside you. Then after we do the physical, we'll see exactly what you're capable of. There's some old workout equipment there from the hospital that we can use to see what changes you're undergoing. What do you think?"

"I think I want to know what's happening to me, and if you think these tests would give you a chance to figure that out then I'm down for whatever."

"We are going to figure this out, Sam. It's going to be okay."

Sam took a deep breath, breathing in through his nose and exhaling out of his mouth, looking out the passenger window. "I believe you."

Taylor pulled into Sam's apartment complex and parked in front of Sam's stairs. Opening the passenger side door, Taylor asked "Do you need me to come up to open the door for you?"

"No," Sam responded. "I think I can get that. I'm going to need to learn how until we get this under control anyway."

"I'll come by tomorrow around noon to pick you up to go to the warehouse. Just try and take it easy until then."

"I will. And hey, Taylor, thanks."

"Of course, Sam," Taylor answered, crawling back into his car.

Sam walked up to his apartment door as Taylor drove off. As carefully as he could, Sam pulled his keys out of his pocket and was able to unlock and push the door open without breaking anything. After shutting and locking the door behind him, Sam walked back to his room and fell onto the bed, lying diagonally across the mattress, face down in the pillows as his feet hung off the side. He groaned into his pillow without moving. With the adrenaline from the day wearing off, Sam drifted to sleep, not bothering to get comfortable or even take off his shoes.

A banging at his door startled him awake. Groaning again, Sam pushed himself up into a sitting position on his bed, wiping away some drool residue on the side of his mouth.

Maybe it was a dream.

Blinking his eyes open, he saw the imprint on his nightstand and that hope withered away. More banging at the door forced him up off the bed and into the living room to open it as gently as he could.

Hailey brushed past him with a bag in her hand as he stood in the doorway, smiling at the still-attached, not-dented-at-all doorknob in his hand. Closing the door with a light touch, Sam walked back to the living room, where Hailey was laying out a takeout dinner on his coffee table. Announcers chattered animatedly over a baseball game on the TV.

"You didn't answer the phone, so you didn't get a say in where dinner was coming from or what you were getting," Hailey said as she continued to pull containers out of the bag without looking up.

"Yeah," Sam answered, rubbing his eyes again. "Sorry about that. I fell asleep when I got back from Taylor's and I just sort of crashed. I slept really hard."

"I figured you were just asleep. Frankly, I'm glad you were. I've really been wanting to try that new Chinese restaurant near the paper, but I knew you would never give that the okay if you were awake."

"Oh," Sam sighed.

"I wish you could see your face right now," she laughed as she handed him the last box from the bag.

Sam breathed a sigh of relief as he opened it to find a burger and fries.

"I got it from *Fran's* after I grabbed my food. I explained their newest regular had a really rough day today and that I had brought my own box, so they relaxed their no takeout rule for me, and I quote, 'Just this once.' How was your day with Taylor?" she asked as she opened her own takeout container.

"It went okay. He didn't believe me at first. Like you, he said there had to be some sort of rational explanation. Then I made him go to the park with me, where I punched a tree and left only a stump as the rest fell to the ground. He believes me now and wants to run some tests tomorrow. He also drove me home, which was kind of him."

"I'm sorry, did you just say you punched a tree, and it fell over? Like you're Paul Bunyan sans axe now?"

"Something like that," Sam answered as he tossed a fry in his mouth. "Although I did exaggerate when I said it fell to the ground. It was falling then I ran over and caught it and gently laid it down so no one got hurt or anything."

"Sammy." Hailey reached up from her spot on the floor to touch her cousin's knee. "I'm so sorry you're going through this and that I didn't believe you. Please let me know if there's anything I can do to help."

"This is a good start." He smiled, lifting up his burger.

Their laughter was cut off as the TV cut from the baseball game to breaking news from the local station.

"We have just been informed that the vigilante known as the White Knight was involved in an altercation tonight after a carjacking threatened to become more violent as it neared Chester Park. More on how the White Knight's intervention likely saved dozens of lives tonight at ten."

Hailey looked from the screen to Sam, then back to the screen before turning her eyes back to her food.

"Go," Sam whispered to her.

"No, not tonight. I already had to cut coffee short on you today. After the day you've had, I should stay with you."

"Hails, go. Really. I am fine. I've got my burger, and even after my nap I still feel really tired. I'm going to bed soon anyway. I'll catch up with you tomorrow after Taylor runs his tests. You should go do your thing tonight."

"If you're sure that's okay."

"I am." He held her eye until she relented.

"Okay, I'll go. But I'm holding you to keeping me updated, Sammy."

"Will you go already?" Sam laughed. "You've got a job to do."

Grabbing her container, Hailey headed for the door, closing it behind her with a wave.

Sam finished the rest of his burger. Even after his three-hour nap and even though it was just now nine o'clock, he was drained. He walked to his room, turned off his lights, and crawled into bed. Within minutes, the weirdest day of his life came to a close as he quickly drifted off to sleep.

THREE

Sam hung the wet washcloth he'd used over the shower curtain rod to dry. Hailey had helped him submit a maintenance request for the shower handle, but until that was fixed, the washcloth and the sink would have to do. Sam finished his morning bathroom routine and got ready for the day.

Wednesdays were typically easy days for him, and this one was no different. With him working weekends, his days off came in the middle of the week. Sam preferred that schedule in general, but the timing now was even better since it gave him the freedom to work around Taylor's schedule to run the tests. It also meant that he didn't need an alarm set for that morning, which was good since he hadn't bought a new one yet and he still hadn't risked his phone.

It was only nine-thirty, but the air was already heavy with heat and humidity as he stepped out of his apartment and onto the sidewalk. Sam ignored the cabs driving by and started walking downtown. He hadn't had any issues so far that morning, and he wanted to keep it that way.

Luckily, he arrived at *Fran's* at the same time someone else was leaving and they held the door open for him. He had successfully avoided pull doors since snapping the handle off the cab, and was unsure if he could temper his strength enough to keep it from breaking if he tried to open one.

"Hey, Sammy!" Darlene greeted as he sat down at the bar.

"Morning, Darlene."

No one outside his family had ever called him Sammy. He didn't care for the nickname, and the only people he didn't make a fuss over using it were his grandparents, his mom, and Hailey. And now Darlene. It was hard to feel too upset with anything Darlene called you because it always felt like there was genuine affection behind any name she said. She was in her early sixties, had red hair piled on her head, and looked exactly like what you'd expect a diner waitress in southern Missouri to look like and she had the southern charm to go with it. The thing he loved most about her, though, was that she makes people feel like they're family when they're with her.

"Hailey came in last night and said you weren't feeling too good. She was even able to get Dennis to break his no takeout rule," she said, raising her voice to make sure her brother heard, and eliciting a grunt from the fry cook in the kitchen.

Fran, the restaurant's namesake, had been their mother. Now the two siblings ran the diner together on their own, along with the occasional college student they'd bring on to help out.

Lowering her voice back down to where only Sam could hear, she added, "I'm not sure if it was her charm or because it was for you, but I don't see him bend his rules too often, much less break them. At least one of you two must be pretty special to get that treatment. If not both of y'all." She smiled and patted his arm as she walked over to fill up the cup of another man further down the bar, but she continued the conversation. "How are you feeling today, honey?"

"I'm feeling a bit better today, Darlene. I'm not sure what it was, but I was just really tired yesterday and couldn't stay awake. I have more energy so far today, though. And I'll have even more after I get a cup of coffee and a breakfast sampler."

"Coming right up, sugar." She poured him a cup of coffee and gave him a smile before passing his order back to Dennis and taking her pot around to the other tables.

"Morning, Sam," a raspy voice greeted him with a slap on the back.

"Morning, Harry," Sam returned.

Harry was another regular at *Fran's*, though he had been a patron much longer than Sam. He was only an inch or two shorter than Sam, and his gray hair stood in sharp contrast to his black skin. Even in his older age, Harry had a gravity about him that could pull and entire room into his orbit.

"When Darlene got home last night she said your cousin got Dennis to break his no takeout rule." Harry whistled for emphasis. "I've known Dennis for a long time now, and I don't think I've ever seen anyone whose name isn't on that sign be allowed to get takeout from here. I am mighty impressed by that girl's gumption."

"If there's one thing Hailey has in spades, it's gumption," Sam laughed, taking a careful drink from his coffee.

"That was a big win we got this weekend," Harry told Sam, switching the topic to football. "I still can't believe you get to watch all these games from the field," he laughed.

Sam smiled back. "It's pretty crazy to me, too. Being a photographer isn't like watching as a spectator, I don't really get to enjoy the full fan experience at the games, but my experience is still pretty incredible."

Dennis brought Sam's food from the back while Darlene talked to customers on the other side of the diner. He hadn't bothered with coloring his hair like his younger sister, so his hair was almost completely gray. He was just under average height, and carried that characteristic as a badge of honor.

"The Highlanders are barely good enough to count as a win at all," he grumbled, resting on the bar as Sam started eating his eggs. "Much less a big win. The Pirates game will be a better test to see if the Dutchmen can make it over the hump instead of another year being a first round out."

"The Highlanders are a scrappy group, Dennis, you know that." Harry had lifted his hand to point at Dennis as he talked. "They're never an easy win. But you're right that this week will be a bigger test. That Pirates' defense is the best in the league again. You know us Sanders boys are tough as nails. Feels like this is a make or break year for Sparks. I like the kid, but if Dante doesn't show he was worth the number one pick the team used on him three years ago, it might be time to move on."

"Aye." Dennis nodded. "He definitely hasn't lived up to his billing yet. Wouldn't be as much of an issue if the defense would step up, though."

"You know that's right," Harry agreed with a laugh.

"Shouldn't you be cooking?" Darlene chastised Dennis as she came back behind the bar.

"I was having to do your job before the kid's food got cold," Dennis retorted, gesturing at Sam's plate, which already half-empty despite his caution with the fork. "I'm getting back to it now," he said, throwing his arms in the air as he walked back through the door.

"And you—" she turned towards Harry "—who do you think you are, distracting my cook with your sports talk?"

"How do you know it was me?"

"Well, it certainly wasn't Sam! He's just minding his own business, eating his hash browns."

Sam smiled and nodded along as she talked, his mouth still full of those hash browns.

"It's a good thing you're handsome," Darlene continued, "or your mama wouldn't have ever gotten me to get you out of her house."

"It's a good thing indeed," Harry laughed. "Now, can I finally get a cup of coffee? Or should I have married Dennis to get that service?"

"Watch it," Darlene warned with a point while Dennis hollered from the kitchen, "I'm out of your league, Harry," sparking a laugh from everyone at the bar.

"I wish I could stay longer this morning, but I have to go meet a friend." Sam stood as he got his wallet out of his pocket. "I'll be back by to see y'all soon, though," he finished as he put a ten on the counter and grabbed the last of his bacon for the road.

"Sugar, we appreciate it, but you know you don't have to explain yourself to us," Darlene assured him. "We know you've got better things to do than hang out with a bunch of old folks all day. We always look forward to your visits. Take care, honey."

"Will-do, Darlene. Y'all take care, too!" he called out as he exited the diner, timing his stride to follow a couple leaving so he wouldn't have to open the door.

Taylor's phone was pressed against his ear, and he was leaning against the side of his car when Sam walked up. He was parked on the side of the street right in front of Sam's apartment.

"Where have you been?" he asked, ending the call and shoving the phone is his pocket. I've been trying to call you for fifteen minutes. I banged on your door until I got yelled at by one of your neighbors."

"I was at *Fran's* eating breakfast. I thought we were meeting at noon?" Sam asked. He had started the fifteen-minute walk back at eleven-thirty so he knew he wasn't late.

"I sent you two texts letting you know I was going to come by at eleven-fifteen because my eleven o'clock meeting got canceled. Did you not get those?"

Sam looked around, lowering his voice. "Taylor, I can't use my phone. It's dead on my nightstand because I don't want to risk crushing it on accident and losing everything I have on there. That's why Hailey called you yesterday and not me."

"Oh. I guess that makes sense. We'll need to figure something out for you on that. You need to have some way to communicate with people."

"If you've got something that will fix that, then I'm in. Should we get going?"

"We should," Taylor answered, opening the passenger door. "Sorry for acting like a chauffeur. I just don't really want to risk it."

"You're fine. It's probably the right call."

Taylor walked around to get in the driver's seat and the two of them got on the road. The warehouse was a ten-minute drive from Sam's apartment complex, halfway between Taylor's place and the city center. There were other buildings around, but since they were the only car there, it seemed like the other buildings were either vacant or only being used for storage.

The building itself was just as nondescript: gray walls all around with a white roll-up door on one side and a white metal door on the front where they'd parked.

Taylor opened Sam's door before leading the way to the warehouse entrance. He unlocked the door and flipped a switch inside to the left. The lights buzzed as they flickered on, revealing the inside of the space. Floor-to-ceiling cloth dividers hung around the building, separating the large space into smaller areas. The only section they could see from the door had a collection of workout equipment crowding out a row of hospital beds that were pushed to one side.

Taylor seemed to read his mind. "The hospital owns this building, but they haven't used it for anything but storage in years. There have been a couple times in the past where they needed overflow space, but that's been awhile. Old beds make their way here whenever new ones arrive. The hospital gym got updated a couple years ago, and the old equipment was sent out here too. My dad is the Chief of Medicine, so he has access to all the facilities. I come here to study when I really need to be alone and focus."

"That's a pretty cool setup," Sam commented, looking around the bare warehouse at the gray walls and the dull green dividers. "What's in all the other sections?"

"Just a bunch of other random stuff that the hospital has gotten rid of," Taylor explained, leading Sam towards the divider with the beds along the wall. "Dad doesn't like getting rid of things that could be useful later, even when the chances they're going to be used are slim, so everything finds itself piled up here after a while."

Taylor pulled a bag out from under the bed at the end of the divider and placed it on the table next to them before pulling up his chair.

"Don't worry," Taylor assured him, "this is my equipment bag, not some throwaways left here. I came by on my way to class to drop them off and put a fresh sheet on the bed, so you can feel safe lying down there. It's all clean and sterile."

"That's a relief," Sam laughed as he sat down on the side of the bed.

"Now," Taylor started as his face hardened and he opened his eyes wider, "you can say no to the question I'm about to ask, and that's okay, but to get the best results from these tests it would help me to know what your previous results were before all of this happened from your last doctor's appointment. Those results are very well protected, but I have quite a bit of experience with both medical computer systems and hacking, and I can get those if you give me permission. Otherwise, I'll just go off what we learn today."

"Do whatever you need to do," Sam responded. He wasn't surprised by Taylor's familiarity with medical software, but his hacking expertise was unexpected. If it could help him get the answers he was looking for, though, Sam wasn't about to complain.

"Okay." Taylor pulled a clipboard off the desk. "Then let's get to it. Do you use drugs or alcohol?"

"I do not," Sam answered as Taylor's pen scratched on his sheet.

"What's your diet and exercise look like?"

"I work out four days a week regularly. My diet is pretty average. I eat at *Fran's* probably a bit too often, but every other meal is usually healthy."

"Are you sexually active?"

Sam stared at Taylor for a beat before responding. "Not recently."

"Is there any history of health issues in your family?"

"Like, in general? Or specifically if there's been something in my family where they woke up with a superpower? Judging by the look on your face I'm going to say in general. No, not really. A couple heart attack deaths on my mother's side. A case of diabetes here and there on my father's. Nothing more than that."

Taylor took that sheet off the top of the clipboard and put it below the other remaining sheets. "Alright, walk over here with me real quick so I can get your height and weight."

Sam followed him towards the nearest warehouse wall to a scale with a sliding measuring tool.

"Six-foot-three," Taylor said as he wrote down Sam's height on the clipboard. Moving the weights around on the scale, he found the balance. "Two hundred and fifteen pounds."

Sam followed Taylor back to the table and sat down. Taylor pulled out some of his tools. First, he checked Sam's blood pressure. Then heart rate, respiration rate, and temperature, noting the results on his clipboard as he worked in silence. Taylor examined Sam's nose, ears, and mouth, and then listened to his heart and lungs. Taylor tapped below Sam's knee with his reflex hammer, but nothing happened.

"Huh," Taylor grunted as he tried two more times before switching legs and finding the same result. "Interesting," he commented as he scribbled on his clipboard.

"With the exception of you not reacting when I struck your knee, I didn't notice anything off. Your heart might be doing a bit more work, but that could also just be how your body works. I won't know until I see your previous results. I'm going to run a few lab tests to see if we can find something there, so the next thing we'll do is take some samples. After that, we're going to do some physical tests to better gauge what you can do. Then I'll test your vitals again, and we'll call it a day. How's that sound?"

Sam nodded, glad he'd eaten before he came. "Whatever you think is best, Doc."

"We're going to run four labs," Taylor explained as he pulled out some containers from his bag. "Blood, saliva, urine, and hair will all be tested. I want to cover my bases since we don't really know what we're looking for."

Taylor pulled out a long cotton swab and Sam opened his mouth to allow him to get a sample. "How are you with needles?" Taylor asked as he pulled one out of his bag.

"Not the biggest fan, but I can manage. I'll look away while you do what you have to do."

Taylor rolled up Sam's sleeve and searched for a vein, applying a small amount of alcohol with a cotton swab to the place he would be sticking him. He carefully placed the needle against Sam's arm and pushed into the skin.

The metal clanged as the end of the needle broke off and fell to the floor.

"Well," Taylor sighed, "I guess we're not doing a blood test today. Let's move on to your hair." Taylor retrieved a pair of tweezers and secured a piece of Sam's hair between the tips. When he pulled, nothing happened. He tugged again, harder this time. The third time, Taylor gasped as the tweezers leapt from his hands while Sam's hair stayed in place.

"Did you even feel that?"

"I mean, I knew you were pulling it. I could feel something happen, but there was no pain."

"You try."

"What?"

"I'm not going to be able to pull your hair out, but you might be able to. Just grab a strand and yank it."

"Whatever you say, man." Sam shook his head as he reached on top of his head. Wrapping a piece of hair around his finger he yanked. With a yelp, Sam extended his hand to Taylor to give him the hair. "That better be helpful," Sam grumbled as he massaged away the sting.

"It should be," Taylor answered without looking up from his work of placing the hair in a container. Once finished, he handed Sam a cup from his bag. "To the left at the end of the divider, go for about two more dividers and there will be a restroom to your right. Pee in this—up to this line here in the middle—then bring it back."

"And that's the last one?"

"That's the last one."

Five minutes later, Sam returned from the bathroom, cup in hand.

"You can just set that on the table; I'll take care of it later," Taylor said by way of greeting. "Follow me over here to the workout equipment for the next part of the exam."

The two walked across the small area within the divider to where a makeshift gym was set up. There was a bench press, squat rack, treadmill, stationary bike, some free weights, and something that looked like the workout version of a multi-tool pocketknife with a seat and a bunch of wires hooked to weights with handles.

"I want you to start out on the treadmill," Taylor instructed, coming to a stop next to the machine. "We'll start you out on one of the middle settings and work up from there."

"I thought we were testing my strength?" Sam asked. "How does me running on a treadmill help us with that?"

"We're testing in what ways your body has changed. We want to see the limits of your strength, yes, but we also want to see what else has changed. For instance, we didn't know that your skin had hardened to where it couldn't be pierced until you broke my needle. I want to see if your muscular changes are affecting your speed and stamina as well."

"Whatever you say, Doc," Sam responded with a shrug as he stepped up onto the treadmill and began walking.

As Taylor increased the speed, Sam had to transition from a fast walk to a slow jog.

"Make sure to stay light on your feet," Taylor instructed. "We don't want you accidentally stepping through the bottom."

Sam nodded in confirmation while picking up speed again to match the treadmill as Taylor cranked it higher. Sam was at a full jog now. A few beads of sweat clung to his forehead but he felt no other sign of exertion. No heavy breathing or side pains. As Taylor continued to increase the treadmill, Sam increased his speed as well until Taylor motioned for him to hop off. Sam breathed a little heavier than normal but felt otherwise unaffected.

Taylor moved to the next machine. "We're going to do the bench press now. How much do you normally bench?"

"Two hundred and fifty pounds usually."

"Is that for reps or a max?"

"Reps. My max is three hundred and fifty pounds."

"That's where we're starting. Just remember to go as slow as you can while you lift it back up."

"No offense, Taylor, but should we maybe start at lower than my max for this? You're not exactly going to be able to spot me on this."

"I really don't think we need to be worried about that. Just try it."

"Okay," Sam sighed as he got in position while Taylor finished adding weights.

Super strength or not, it felt irresponsible to start with his max without a spotter who could help if he struggled. It went against every rule he had been taught about gym safety. With a deep breath, Sam lifted the pole up and slowly brought it down as his eyes widened. As slow as he could, he lifted the pole back up and set it down. Sitting up, he turned wide eyes on Taylor.

"I could barely feel any weight!" he exclaimed. "It didn't even feel like I was lifting the pole, much less my max!"

"That's what I expected," Taylor answered. "We're going to increase by a hundred pounds at a time until either you strain or we're out of weights."

"Let's do it." Sam smiled as he laid back down on the bench. Four hundred and fifty, five hundred and fifty, and six hundred fifty all went by without stopping.

"I could kind of feel some weight there," Sam said as he sat the pole down following benching seven hundred and fifty pounds. "I'm still not sure it really even felt like the bar used to feel though."

"Try this last one," Taylor instructed as he loaded more on. "This will be nine hundred pounds. We have a couple more weights but there isn't enough room for any more after this."

Sam lifted this one with ease as well. "That one felt more like the bar," he said, sitting up after laying the bar back down.

"So, it took about twenty times the weight for it to feel the same for you. Meaning now you could potentially bench a max of seven thousand pounds. Not too shabby."

"But we're not sure that it's linear," Sam argued.

"True, but this lines up with the force needed to break the tree. The math checks out. I think it's a fair estimate to work off of."

"You really think my strength has increased that much?" He shook his head at the thought.

Benching seven thousand would be almost like putting a truck on both ends of the bar. He thought getting more information about this strength would make it easier to understand, but numbers like that made it feel even more unbelievable that this was happening.

"At least. Sam, I've never heard of nor seen anything like this. You're hardly even breaking a sweat. It's going to take some time to figure everything out, but I have a couple more things I want to do to test your new abilities. We need to go out of the city to make sure no one sees you, though. I'm going to take my bag and do the post workout vitals on the road. You ready?"

"I told you, I'm down for whatever needs to be done today."

Sam needed to know what was happening to him. And if he'd had any lingering doubts about trusting Taylor being able to help find those answers, him being so right about the weights earlier had taken care of those.

"Then let's ride."

Taylor drove north out of Duncan for about five miles before taking an exit off the interstate. He drove another ten miles down a county road that took them through a small town and then into acres and acres of farmland. When he finally stopped, it was on a deserted stretch, still in the road.

"I want you to get out of the car," he told Sam.

"Are you abandoning me out in this field?" Sam laughed as he unbuckled and waited for Taylor to reach across him and push the door open before he stepped out of the car.

"Not if you can keep up." Taylor smirked as his tires squealed as the car took off, the sudden acceleration closing Sam's door for him.

"Hey!" Sam yelled as Taylor drove off, kicking up dust on the old road. "If he thinks I'm going to play his stupid game—" he muttered before trailing off.

Taylor had already driven a hundred feet and was still going, gaining speed as he went. Sam looked back at the miles of land stretching back between him and home before yelling, "Gah!" and taking off after Taylor's car.

Taylor watched the speedometer hold steady at twenty miles per hour as he checked his rearview mirror, waiting for Sam to give chase.

"Come on," he mumbled, tapping his wheel.

Then Sam started running.

Sam quickly started gaining ground on the car as Taylor increased the speed to twenty-five and then thirty miles per hour. And still Sam closed in on him. The car hit thirty-five, then forty, then forty-five miles per hour, and Sam continued to get closer and closer. He was only about ten feet behind the car when Taylor finally started pulling away at sixty-five miles per hour. A short sprint burst kept Sam close for a few seconds longer before Taylor pulled away for good.

Taylor slowly came to a stop before turning the car around and returning to where Sam waited, his hands braced on his knees as he sucked down air.

"You were running over sixty miles per hour right there!" Taylor yelled as he raced to him. "That's twice what world caliber athletes can sprint. And you did it for three miles! That might be more impressive than the strength!"

"If you… ever…" Sam panted, "pull a stunt… like that again… then… we… are going to see… just how far… I can throw… a human being… into the air."

"That's fair. You have my word I won't do that again. I just needed to push you in a way I couldn't with the weights. Here," Taylor jogged back to the car and returned with an unopened bottle of water. "Drink this," he said, tossing it to Sam.

As Sam drank, Taylor returned again to the car to rummage in his bag, then waved Sam over to sit in the passenger seat for him to test his vitals.

They went through the same process as at the warehouse, Taylor noted all of Sam's results on a new sheet from his clipboard as Sam's breathing returned to normal.

"I think that's about everything we need today," Taylor explained.

"Good. I could use a nap."

"I'm sure you could," Taylor laughed. "I want to see one more thing before we leave, though. But you'll have to cross into that field to make sure nothing happens to the road."

Sam climbed over the fence as Taylor instructed, "Now I want you to take one step and jump as high as you can."

Sam shrugged, but got in position. Taking one step forward, he pushed off the ground, and yelped as he shot into the sky. As he slowed at the peak of his jump, he darted his eyes around to see his surroundings, but other than when he looked down, there were none. White-hot panic shot through his chest as his body started its descent, before he closed his eyes tight and braced for impact.

He landed with a thud, and dirt flew into the air around him. He was standing in a hole six inches deep, but other than his still present panic, he was unscathed.

"That was incredible!" Taylor exclaimed from next to the car, his hands and clipboard behind his head as he stared at Sam with eyes wide open.

"Take me home," Sam demanded as he climbed back over the fence. His heart was pounding and his skin burned. Luckily there wasn't much out on the back road to give him sensory overload as he walked to the car.

"Yep, absolutely," Taylor answered, running around to open Sam's door. "We've got to get back so I can run these tests."

"Hmph," Sam grunted as he tried to knock off the dirt and dust that covered him after his impact in the field.

Breathe, he told himself as the car started to roll forward, his senses threatening to overwhelm him. *Just breathe.*

chapter

FOUR

Sam put a couch pillow over his head to drown out the banging coming from the front door. He hadn't even made it to his bed after Taylor had dropped him off earlier because he had been so worn out from the tests. He furrowed his eyebrows remembering how Taylor had sent him into the sky without warning after making him chase down the car. Sam hadn't spoken the entire trip back to his apartment. That had less to do with his frustration, though, and much more to do with how tired he was after exerting himself during the tests.

The knocking continued, forcing Sam back onto his feet to answer. Hailey and Taylor stood at the door, a bag of food in Hailey's hands and a collection of drinks in Taylor's.

"It's about time you answered," Hailey complained as she pushed past him into the apartment. Taylor waited until Sam stepped aside and gave him a nod. "I've been knocking for five minutes," she continued.

"I, uh, wasn't expecting company tonight," Sam answered as they all sat around his coffee table. Hailey and Taylor sat down on the couch while Sam took the chair, yawning. "I just woke up from a nap."

"Taylor texted since your phone is MIA because he wanted to let you know the results from everything earlier. I told him to get us some drinks while I got tacos and we'd make a party out of it. I'm excited to hear what you two found out today!"

"But only if you want that, Sam," Taylor interjected. "If you don't want to know yet or if you're uncomfortable talking about it in front of Hailey, that's your call."

"No, it's fine," Sam answered while taking his box from Hailey. "Let's hear about it."

"Include all the parts that I missed too!" she added while putting sauce on her taco.

"Okay," Taylor started, "I picked up Sam this morning and took him to one of the hospital's overflow locations. It's a warehouse mainly used for storage. I took his vitals and there wasn't much out of the ordinary other than a slightly stronger heart rate and the fact nothing happened when I checked his reflexes."

"He's always been a bit slow to react," Hailey interrupted, tossing a sauce packet at Sam. "Give it a couple more days."

"Then I tried to take samples for the labs," Taylor continued. "I took a mouth swab and got a urine sample without any problems. I couldn't pull a piece of his hair, though; he had to do that part. And then when I tried to take his blood, his skin broke my needle. And then it got weird."

"That wasn't the weird part?"

"Not even close. I had him run on the treadmill, but the speed wouldn't go high enough for me to learn anything. Then we moved to the bench. I put on as much weight as I could, nine hundred pounds, before he even felt like he was lifting an empty bar. By my estimate, he could probably bench seven thousand pounds if he had to."

"I'm sorry." Hailey's taco stopped halfway to her mouth. "Seven what now? You can't really expect me to believe that."

"Nine hundred is twenty times forty-five. So, if that felt like the bar, and his max is three hundred and fifty pounds, well, the math says it should check out."

"We still don't have evidence that increase is linear," Sam reminded Taylor as he crumpled up the taco wrapper before taking a drink.

"True, but it matches what he did yesterday with the tree. It takes a lot of force to do what he did."

"I can't believe you found all of that out today." Hailey shook her head as Sam worked on his second taco.

"That was still the warm-up," Taylor told her. "Then we drove out into the country where there weren't people around to see us testing him. I let him out of the car and then he ran alongside me as I sped up, and he hit sixty miles per hour, Hailey. And he kept that pace for three minutes!"

"That's incredible," Hailey gasped.

"It's also not the full story, is it, Taylor?"

"That part isn't really relevant here, Sam."

"Oh, I think it is."

"What happened?" Hailey asked.

"My tactics weren't completely transparent."

"He asked me to get out of the car and then peeled out and told me to catch up or I was walking."

"Ha!" Hailey squealed and covered her mouth, rocking back and forth.

"It worked, though!" Taylor insisted. "We found out how fast he could run and for how long. Then I had him jump and he went probably, what? Twenty feet into the sky, Sam? Twenty-five?"

"I'm not sure. I was preoccupied at the time."

"It was something like that. Then I checked his vitals again. I took the samples to the lab after I dropped him off here and called you when I finished up."

"Okay, so what are the results?" Sam asked.

"Your vitals the second time lined up pretty well with how they should've changed after a workout, with one exception. Your heart was beating much harder than it should've been. Fully exerting yourself seems to be overworking your heart. The labs came back showing, from what I can tell, that your cells themselves have increased in mass and density, and that's what's causing these differences. You've grown an inch and gained twenty pounds since your last physical. Your blood is having to work much harder to move through your body with the increased cell density, and the burden of that is falling on your heart. I can't really know much beyond that without much more advanced equipment and the ability to draw blood, but that's what we know for now. That your cells are changing in some ways, and that your heart is having to work harder to make it work. I'm not sure what any of this means, though, yet."

"So, is it reversible?" Sam asked after a pause.

He could feel his skin beginning to itch and his mouth drying out as he realized what the answer was going to be. What the answer had to be. He'd already gotten taller and heavier without doing a thing. That couldn't be reversed, so why would any of the other symptoms be able to? His face and arms warmed as the anxiety started giving way to fear.

"Not that I know of," Taylor answered. "But again, we're currently working with a very limited data set. We don't know what it is or how it happened. This clearly isn't some natural cause, and without more information as to both what your body is doing and how this happened, I think the chances of reversing it are slim. It seems to be something you'll need to try to learn to live with for the time being at least."

So that's it. Twenty-five years old, and my life is effectively over—at least any life I've ever known. Any life I may have wanted. Now I get to live in fear of breaking something, of breaking someone, every day for the rest of my life.

The ice machine in his freezer sounded like an avalanche as he spiraled into the panic's vice grip, and the LED overhead lights coming from the kitchen felt as bright as the sun.

"Are there ways to miti—" Hailey started before she was cut off.

"What if I don't want to live with it?!" Sam yelled, hitting the table, the shape of his fingers carving into the wood.

Sam put his head in his hands and leaned forward as his ears began ringing.

Breathe. Just breathe.

He grasped at the neck of his henley and unbuttoned it one further to try and help his breathing.

Much softer, he continued, "I don't want any of this. I just wanted to take photos, move to a new city, and make a life for myself. I don't want to be like the White Knight. I don't want to be a hero. I don't want to be some comic book protagonist or go on some sort of hero's journey. I don't want any of that. I just want to be a normal guy and live my normal life, a life

I loved. And now you're telling me that I just have to learn to live with this, this, this curse? That I have to go through the rest of my life afraid I'm going to break something? Break someone? What if I trip and grab someone's arm on accident? That person just lost their arm. What happens if I sneeze?"

He dropped his head into his hands.

"How am I ever supposed to have a meaningful relationship when I could break that person at any time? When I can't sleep in the same bed with them without fearing I might roll over and hit them in my sleep? How am I supposed to learn to live with this?"

"Sammy," Hailey whispered, resting her hand on the crook of his arm. "We're going to figure this out. Together. You're not alone. You're not going to be alone. I promise. Give Taylor and me some time to figure out where to go from here. We'll come up with a plan. In the meantime, just, take it slow, okay?"

"Okay. I'm sorry for yelling, Taylor. I'm not mad at you, I'm just mad in general. I'm also really tired. I don't mean to be rude, but do y'all mind heading out so I can get some rest? Today has been a lot."

"Absolutely, pal," Hailey answered as she and Taylor grabbed their things and headed for the door. "I'll come by tomorrow to check on you," she assured him as he closed the door behind them.

Sam walked straight to his room and collapsed on his bed. He was asleep before Hailey and Taylor had made it to their cars.

The next morning, Sam laid in bed staring at the ceiling. He'd been up for a while, but he hadn't moved yet. He wasn't sure how long it had been without his phone or clock, but he knew it had to have been at least an hour and a half. Maybe two hours. And still he laid there, unmoving save the occasional blink.

Learn to live with it.

The thought disgusted him. Everything in life could be going well and good, and then you wake up one morning to find you will live the rest of your life as a pariah, unable to be close to people or live a normal life.

How are you supposed to learn to live with that?

His parched mouth finally compelled him to get out of bed to refill his water bottle. On the way back to his bed, he saw his camera bag and his heart dropped. He still had to fly to Sanders the next day, though the thought filled him with dread.

How am I supposed to take pictures like this?

Sam walked to his closet, where he had a collection of cameras. He needed to practice before he left, and he needed to do it on a camera that wouldn't hurt him, or his bank account, if it broke. Obviously, he couldn't use his work camera. Not only did he need to use it that weekend, but the Blickon Z 2600 was his dream camera. He'd saved up for years to buy it, and was only able to finally afford it when he got his inheritance after his mom's death. His dad's old camera wasn't an option for practice. Neither was the instant. That still left four of his quality cameras, as well as a couple disposable.

The one he had used with his college paper had seen better days and wasn't anything fancy, but he couldn't risk losing it. The camera that he'd bought before he was on the paper, on the other hand, was a piece of junk and the reason he had to buy the second one before getting the job. He had looked into selling it, but could never find anything close to what he had paid for it, so he'd held onto it. His first post-college and his photo shoot cameras were in luck.

He walked that camera and the two disposables back to his bed and sat back down on the edge. Taking one of the disposables in his hand, he gently laid the other two down next to him.

Breathe. Just breathe, he reminded himself as he closed his eyes, slowing his heart rate as much as he could.

Then, in one smooth movement, he lifted the camera up to his face, focused on the framed poster on his wall, and put his finger on the shutter release. On the next exhale, Sam tried to focus on making an almost imperceptible movement with his finger downward.

Crack

Sam opened his eyes to find the camera broken. He'd managed to keep from fully pushing through like he had feared, but there was an indention in the camera and the shutter release had broken, cracked into three pieces.

Crap.

Sam got back to his feet, leaving the two remaining cameras on his bed, and walked back to his closet. Digging around, he didn't find anything he could use to soften his push. His bathroom and the rest of his room were no more helpful.

"Maybe," he said out loud to himself while looking around his kitchen, "maybe I could use a rag. Wad it up and push through that." He grabbed a wash rag and hurried back to his room, grabbing the disposable camera that was still intact. He piled the rag on top of the shutter release and situated his finger on top.

Breathe. Just breathe.

He again pressed as softly as he could. He heard the photo take but couldn't feel anything happen to the camera. Removing the rag, though, he found this one had also cracked.

With a sigh of frustration, he leaned forward and tossed the camera under his bed so he didn't have to look at it. It thudded into something. Sam crawled under to find a box he had forgotten about and as he pulled it out, he felt a sliver of hope. It was the box his newest camera lens had come in, filled with a special type of packing peanuts to protect it during shipping.

This could work.

Grabbing his camera from college, Sam once again focused on the poster. Placing a packing peanut on top of the shutter, Sam held his breath. He stared at the poster from his favorite movie in its wooden frame, the man dressed in all black, medieval adventurer's clothes, the woman in a soft pink dress, the swordsman and the giant standing behind them. Sam let out his breath and gently pushed again. The camera clicked as it took the photo. The packing peanut completely flattened against the camera, but when Sam removed it, the shutter was still intact.

"Ha!" he exclaimed, eyes wide. He laughed as he stared at the camera, and his eyes began to water.

This could work, he thought again. With two more packing peanuts, Sam succeeded twice more. Jumping off the bed, he retrieved his work camera and pulled out one more peanut.

Breathe. Just breathe.

He snapped the picture. Heart thumping hard, he removed the flattened peanut and yelped as the camera was still fully intact. He sat the camera down next to him and leaned back until the giddiness overcame him and he just laid in bed laughing. For the first time in days, he'd had some sort of progress, some sort of control.

It's something, he thought as he smiled.

chapter

FIVE

The next day, Sam packed his duffel and secured his camera bag inside his backpack before pouring all the packing peanuts on top of it for his trip to Sanders. His duffel bag was fuller than usual since most of the things he would typically pack had been displaced by all the packing peanuts. Hailey was waiting with her car at the curb when he walked out of his apartment building at 7:30 am. She opened the backseat door for his bags and then the passenger door for him to get in before walking back to the driver's seat.

"Thanks again for the ride," he said. "I know it's early, but I'm not really comfortable calling a cab with my condition yet."

"No problem, pal. Just know you owe me one." She winked at him before shifting the car into drive and rolling away from the curb.

"After this last week I feel like I owe you a few," Sam laughed.

"Speaking of which," Hailey started in a more serious tone, "how are you feeling after the other night? I know you were still pretty upset when Taylor and I left. I tried to come by last night, but you never answered so I assumed you were asleep."

"Yeah, I crashed early last night. Sorry about that. But I'm feeling quite a bit better today. I broke two disposable cameras yesterday trying to figure out how to take pictures, and then I solved it. My bag back there is overflowing with those little packing peanuts because they let me take a picture without breaking the camera if I'm careful."

This time, Hailey joined Sam in his laughter as they drove.

The drive from Sam's apartment to the Duncan Airport was just under twenty minutes. Most of that time Hailey filled Sam in on what all he was missing in the office by not being there every day.

"I'm just saying you're missing out on all the exciting gossip by only being in the building two days a week," she finished.

"And I'm just saying I prefer it that way," Sam laughed as they pulled into the short drop off line.

"You're sure you're going to be okay going to Sanders? With your condition and all?"

"I think I've gotten a bit better at managing it. I'm a little nervous, but I think it'll be okay."

"And there's nothing I can do to help?"

"You've done so much to help already, and I really appreciate that. I'm going to be okay though. I'll see you Sunday night and catch you up on everything on the ride home."

"And I'll catch you up on any new gossip at the paper," she answered with an exaggerated smile as they pulled up to the curb. Hailey ran around to open his door and help him get his bags. She gave Sam a quick hug while he held his arms out away from her, then she hopped back in the car to leave the drop off lane. Sam turned, steeling himself to walk through the airport, which was teeming with breakable things. With breakable people.

Breathe. Just breathe, he commanded himself as he walked to the entrance.

Sam walked through the airport doors and headed for security. The paper would pay for the flight, but not for checked bags, so carry-on was all he brought. He knew, intellectually, that he had nothing to fear going through security, but that didn't stop his mind from racing through all the scenarios where for some reason they knew about his abilities. He could just imagine stepping through the machine and then being pulled to the side and told he wasn't going to fly and that, instead, people from the government were looking for him and on their way.

Breathe. Just breathe, he told himself again.

Making it to the security line, he unconsciously tapped his foot as he thought through what all could go wrong. He looked down to see a small rut under his foot. He gulped and moved forward in line, hoping no one would notice.

If I could only get to the plane, he sighed to himself.

The plane.

He was about to get on an airplane with a hundred other people to fly across the country. Getting stopped by airport security was unrealistic, but him accidentally breaking something in the plane? Something that would bring him and everyone else on board to a fiery demise? The rational part of his brain couldn't just write off that possibility.

"For the last time," a tired voice cut into his thoughts, "put your shoes and bags in their own bins, along with anything in your pockets and step through the machine."

He had made it to the front of the line and was now receiving dirty looks for holding it up. He quickly followed the instructions, grabbed his belongings, and took off for his gate once his shoes were back on.

"Hall!" a voice called out to him as he approached his gate. "Over here!"

Brooklyn Jones waved him over. She was the paper's lead football writer and had been for the past five seasons. She was a foot shorter than him and had her brunette hair pulled back in a ponytail. She was talking to another journalist, who worked for a national company but lived in Duncan.

"Hey Sam!" she said as he walked up. "You've met Rick Lorenzo, right?"

"I've seen him at games, but I don't think we've ever been introduced," Sam answered. "It's a pleasure to meet you," he finished with a smile.

Rick smiled back. "You as well."

"I don't mean to be rude, but I don't love flying, so I'm going to go over there and try and relax before takeoff," Sam said as he excused himself to go wait in the chairs next to his gate.

It wasn't true; he actually loved flying, but he was far too anxious to make small talk right now. Networking could wait for another day when he wasn't worried about killing everyone around him.

Despite all of his worries, he boarded the plane, got situated, flew across the country, and landed on the east coast without any issues arising. Nothing was broken during the trip. Sam released a sigh of relief as the plane touched down in Sanders, New Jersey in one piece.

He exited the plane behind Brooklyn. The paper had grouped their seats together and their rooms were next door to one another's at the hotel. They took a shuttle from the airport to the hotel, where Sam declined Brooklyn's offer to get drinks with some other journalists, again blaming the flight for his need to be alone.

The room key shook in his hand as he unlocked the door and gave it the slightest of pushes. The door opened all the way and rested on the wall, but didn't slam the way he'd feared. Relieved, he walked in and dropped his bags at the foot of his bed and laid down. A week ago, he would have gone out with Brooklyn and met others in the business and had a good time. A week ago, he could have at least turned on the tv to watch something all night.

The peanuts!

Sitting up, Sam grabbed his backpack and opened the top the slightest bit. Packing peanuts spilled out onto the bed from the overstuffed bag. He took a handful that had spilled and sat them on the nightstand before closing the bag back. Taking one peanut and the remote he pushed the power button as lightly as he could through the foam. The tv clicked on and the squashed peanut fell away to reveal a fully intact remote. There was already a college football game on, so he didn't have to waste peanuts to find something else. He drifted off to sleep while the post-game show played.

Sam woke up as the early light streamed in through the window. He was still wearing his travel clothes and laying on top of the comforter. He rubbed at his eyes and found that the football game had been replaced with the local news.

"Coming up at eight," the anchor's voice rang out from the tv, "the homeless population in Sanders is rapidly declining as a result of the successful new measures put into place recently by the city."

Sam left it on as he got dressed, grabbed his backpack, and left his room. The team had a walkthrough at ten that morning, and he needed to get a couple pictures for Brooklyn's piece.

There was no shuttle for the practice, and Sam had not yet figured out how to control his strength with cars. The stadium was only three miles away, though, and with his new stamina, a jog wouldn't leave him too tired or sweaty.

He took off at as leisurely a pace as he could, but still made it to the stadium in just 12 minutes. With twenty minutes until the practice started, there were hardly any players on the field. Not enough to warrant wasting his peanuts, anyway, so he made his way to the bench, sitting on the visitor's sideline.

"How's it going, Hall?" Brooklyn asked as she sat down next to him.

"Can't complain," Sam lied. "Waiting for the rest of the team to come out to take some pictures."

"They'll be out soon," she answered, nodding along. "I was still down there when they closed the locker room. I didn't have a chance to talk to any of the returning starters today, but I was able to get some good time with a few of the new arrivals to build up those contacts. I'm supposed to interview Sparks after practice, so most of my article will be from that anyway."

"I'll try and get some good shots of him today."

"That would be helpful; I appreciate that. I'm going to head up to the press box for a bit, I just wanted to make sure you were handling the trip alright."

"Yeah, I'm fine. Thanks though!"

"Anytime," she answered with a smile and a pat on his shoulder as she walked away.

As practice finished up, Sam went to look for Brooklyn before she left for her interview, catching her just as she left the press box.

"Brooklyn!" he called after her as she walked towards the elevator.

"Hey Sam, what's up?" she asked as he approached.

"Two things. One, my computer was acting up a bit this morning and I'm going to need to spend some time on that this afternoon. Could I give you my SIM card with the photos so you can find a photo for your article?"

"Of course. What was the other thing?"

"I'm having a bit of trouble getting it out of the camera," he laughed and lifted it up towards her. "Usually, my giant hands aren't an issue because I have tools in my computer bag to remove it, but I don't have those on me since I left my computer in the room. Would you mind helping me?"

Brooklyn laughed with him as she pulled the card out of the camera.

"Blickon Z 2600? That's a good one, right? This is the one our last photographer used. He was the best, so I assume this is the best."

"I don't know if it's the best, but it was my dream camera, so I'm pretty partial to it. My dad always used a Blickon and he was the best, so I think your last photographer had good taste."

Brooklyn smiled and handed the camera back to him before looking at her watch. "I have to get going for that interview. Good luck with your computer!" she called over her shoulder as she raced towards the closing elevator door.

Sam breathed a sigh of relief as she left. He didn't like lying to Brooklyn. He didn't like lying at all. His mom's number one rule had been to always be honest with her, and he had taken that rule seriously. Not just with his mom, but with everyone. But now? Lying was going to have to become as natural as breathing. That might chip away at his sense of self even more than the changes to his body, but what choice did he have? His first day on the job with his new strength was complete without any major issues, but this was not a long-term solution.

SIX

"Look at you getting that front-page, above-the-fold photo, Sammy!" Hailey gave him a playful shove as they looked at Tuesday morning's paper. They were sitting in a booth at Fran's with their lunch in front of them.

"And I didn't break a single thing the whole trip. I'd call it a success," Sam laughed. He had gotten in at three in the morning after flying in from the game. The Dutchmen had beaten the Pirates 31-24. He'd just woken up an hour before meeting Hailey for a late lunch. "The only thing is, now I have to find more peanuts."

"More what now?"

"Packing peanuts." Sam pulled one of the few remaining from his bag and lowered his voice. "These bad boys are the only way I was able to take pictures without breaking the camera. I need to get more of them, and I'm not sure how."

"That's ridiculous."

"It's true!" Sam laughed. "I experimented the other night with some old cameras, and I wasn't able to take a picture without breaking the camera until I used these. I tried softening the touch in other ways, but these were the only ones that worked. Problem is, I have to use a new one for each shot because they get crushed."

"You should check with the camera store you ordered your last one from. I'm sure they have boxes of that stuff you could buy. Or at least point you in the right direction."

"That's smart. I'll go this week. I think I have enough for this week's game, but after that, I'm probably out. I won't be able to today, though. Taylor left a note under my door to let me know he is wanting me to come over to the warehouse to check on a few things when he gets out of class."

"Did he say what?"

"Yeah, he just wants to make sure that things aren't continuing to change with my body since this is so new. Make sure everything is consistent with how it was last week."

"Oh, that makes sense. Taylor's not, like, worried about you or anything, is he?"

"I don't think so, why?"

"I was just worried about you while you were gone. You can't call or text me to know how you're doing or to let me know if anything is going wrong. And with how this is affecting your body, I'm just nervous. I don't want anything to happen to you, Sammy," she finished, giving him a light shove to his arm.

"I think I'm okay." He smiled at her, reaching out his hand to return the shove before thinking better of it. "At least, I don't think anything is going to happen to me. I'm less confident that I won't accidentally do something that could cause a problem."

"Hopefully, Taylor has figured something out. Or at least has an idea to help you manage in the short term."

"I guess I'll find out soon." He shrugged as Darlene walked up to the table.

"Can I get you two anything? More coffee? Tea?"

"I think I need to be going, actually," Hailey answered. "I have a meeting in ten. Could I get a coffee to go?"

"Of course, honey. What about you, sugar? Tea to go?"

"I wouldn't say no to some sweet tea to go."

"Coming right up." Darlene smiled at them as she walked back to the counter.

"I'm going to come by tonight to check on you and to hear what Taylor has to say. I'll even bring dinner."

"Sounds good to me," Sam responded as they stood up out of the booth. They took their drinks from Darlene at the register and parted ways as Hailey headed back to the office and Sam left for the warehouse.

Sam slowed to a walk in front of the warehouse to find Taylor's car already there. He was finding that he could maintain a jog for a few miles without feeling winded as long as he didn't push himself to a sprint. It was six miles from Fran's to the warehouse, and Sam made it in less than twenty minutes, feeling like he had just warmed up. The downside to jogging was that he had to be careful with the routes he took, because if someone saw him running at twenty miles per hour for miles without stopping, it could spur some unwanted questions.

Taylor had left the door open to prevent any obstacles from being broken on Sam's way in. As he entered the warehouse and his eyes adjusted from bright sun to the dark interior, he saw Taylor, laptop open, sitting on a stool next to the bed they'd used previously.

"How was Sanders?" Taylor asked as he approached.

"I didn't break anything, so that's a plus," Sam laughed.

"That's totally a win! You didn't have any issues with taking photos?"

Sam went through the full explanation for Taylor as he had with Hailey.

"That's genius!" Taylor exclaimed when Sam had finished. "I'll see if I can find you some more of those and maybe some other materials that can help while we figure out what's going on."

"Speaking of which, you didn't exactly tell me what we were doing today. You said something about more tests, but there was more?"

"There is, but I want to check your vitals first. The other thing is something that needs to wait until it's time."

Sam shook his head at the deflection but sat down on the bed as Taylor readied his equipment. Going through the same process as he had twice before, Taylor jotted down the results of each test on his clipboard as he went. After finishing the vitals, he took a saliva swab before having Sam pull another strand of hair, and then finished by having Sam take a cup to the bathroom once more. He skipped another attempt at drawing blood.

"Alright," Sam said after handing Taylor the cup, his arms crossed and his fingers tapping at his bicep, "what did we learn?"

"Nothing yet," Taylor answered with a shake of his head. "All the vitals came back normal. The lab results should be more instructive, though."

"Okay, so where does that leave us?"

"I'm going to just be straight with you, Sam. What's going on with you doesn't appear to exist in the medical field. There's absolutely nothing that's even remotely like this anywhere. There is no way to know what's happening exactly or why. Meaning, there is no cure." Sam let his head drop as Taylor continued. "I'll keep looking and reaching out to experts, but it will be a while if something ever comes of that, and it's more likely not to happen at all. So now we need to move to the next best course of action: managing your new abilities. To that point, I know a couple people who are, um, well-positioned to help you learn to control your newfound strength so that you can live a somewhat normal life and not have to worry about crushing everything. What do you think?"

"When can we start?"

"Right now," Taylor answered. "Come on out, guys!"

Sam turned his head to follow Taylor's line of sight to where one of the curtains pulled back as Jason and Lance walked out.

"Sam," Taylor said as the two approached, "you know Lance Locke and Jason Morgan."

"I do," Sam answered, unsure where this was going. *Of course, I know them. Am I that inconsequential to their friend group that I need to be reintroduced to them?*

They came to a stop in front of him. Lance was a couple of inches shorter than Sam, but still towered over Taylor. He was athletically built and had recently cut his shaggy black hair shorter over his white face. Jason was about eye level with Sam. His black hair was shaved close to his brown skin. He was also athletically built, but in a different way from Lance. Lance was strong but lean like one of the slot backs, while Jason had a more buff physique like a linebacker.

"Well, today you're not working with Lance and Jason. Sam, meet the White Knight and Ironside."

OH.

"Wait, what?" Sam asked, cocking his head as he appraised the duo in this new light.

"That's right," Taylor answered with a smile. "Lance and Jason were the Franklin University heroes, and now they're Duncan's."

"We're excited to bring you in on the secret," Jason laughed with a slap to Sam's shoulder.

"We're also excited to see what you can do. Taylor's filled us in a little bit but assured us that we wouldn't really believe any of it without seeing for ourselves," Lance told him.

"Okay." Sam shook his head and lifted his hands. "Let's rewind a bit here. You two are the vigilantes? And you have been the whole time? Like, that was you that was there when the explosion on campus happened? And all the nights here in Duncan when the news would cover the sightings?"

"It's been us the whole time," Jason smirked.

"Does Hailey know? What about Gwen?"

"Negative on that," Jason answered again. "We didn't want to worry them, and we figured it was safer if they didn't know."

"This is all insane. I was just wrapping my head around my powers, but this is almost weirder. How does something like this even start?"

Taylor and Jason turned to Lance and raised their eyebrows.

"Alright," Lance sighed. "I guess if we're going to ask you to trust us with what you have going on, you deserve to know all of our side of it. Last winter, something happened to Gwen. I was supposed to be there, but I opted to study on my own that night. The guilt was eating me up inside, so the next semester, I started taking my dad's old nightstick out in my hoodie as I walked around campus, trying to prevent that from happening to anyone else. In doing so, I became aware of a drug ring happening in one of the fraternities, except these weren't normal drugs. They made people faster and stronger, and they weren't being sold off to students; they were being created specifically for one man." Lance's tone turned to pure vitriol. "Matthew Fox."

"WHAT?" Sam interjected, surprised at the billionaire philanthropist's involvement.

Lance nodded and continued. "I know. He was using them to help with some off-the-books research a professor at the university was leading. Anyway, I tried to follow them back to their fraternity one night, and they caught me. I fought off a couple, but there were too many. They ended up getting the best of me. I'm not sure what would have happened had they gotten the chance to finish, but Jason and Taylor ran up right at that moment. They helped me get better, and they joined my fight. I'm probably only alive because they did. Taylor would run the missions from the computer, help with any injuries, and get us the information we needed. Jason would give me support in the field and, more importantly, he designed and created all of our suits and weapons."

"Wait, really? That's incredible."

"It's nothing." Jason rolled his eyes and waved his hands. "Just some unprecedented creativity and engineering. No biggie."

"So," Lance went on, "after we had teamed up, we tried to figure out how to stop Fox. I ended up traveling to his house one night and got beat up pretty bad. Got beat up another time pretty bad when he showed up to campus one night, but Jason got me out of that bind. Then he blew up the building they had been experimenting in to cover his tracks."

"Fox blew up the building? I thought he was trying to help the campus? Were there not other ways to get rid of the evidence?"

"I'm sure there were, but he wanted a building named after him, and that was an easy route to get there. He also wanted to build trust in the public and look like a hero to pave the way for his future plans. That's not the worst part, though. The bombs were attached to students. I ran in and he told me where the bomb was, so I took off to diffuse it. When I got to the room, there was a student tied to a chair with a bomb in a chair in front of him. I got him untied, then I stuck the sword into the bomb and sent a shock of electricity through it as the timer neared zero. Then the building shook. There was a second bomb on the other side. He had played me. The suit Jason made me held up, though, and only one of the bombs had gone off so I was able to make it out, but there were a lot of students who didn't. And then we closed up shop in Franklin and moved up here to keep up the fight. And I think that's pretty much everything." Lance turned to Jason and Taylor. "Did I miss anything?"

"You left out all the other times I came in and saved your butt, but I think other than that you hit the high points," Jason answered.

Taylor nodded. "There was that incident with the hacker and with the fraternity's backyard operation, but I think it was a pretty good summary."

Sam sat back down on the hospital bed and stared wide-eyed at Lance. "I can't believe all these times when I've seen the White Knight on the news, or each time Hailey covered a story, it was always you. Or that you two were part of it, too. Or that Hailey and Gwen don't know about it. It's all a lot to take in."

"That's fair, man," Jason told him as he sat down next to him. "But we wanted to be honest with you from the jump. We know it's not some light thing for Taylor to tell us what you're going through or for you to accept us knowing. We wanted to show you from the very first moment that you could trust us, by trusting you with our secret."

"We know that if people find out about your secret, it will change your life even more than the secret itself has. We didn't want to just take that from you." Lance stood in front of the couch with his arms crossed as he talked. "Your secret could get you thrown in a lab somewhere. Ours would get all three of us thrown in jail for a very long time. We want you to know we're in this with you and that you can trust us."

"Taylor's told us a bit about what you can do," Jason continued when Lance had finished. "It sounds really cool, but we get that it might make everyday life more difficult. We may not have powers, but we've had to take on a lot since we started all this. No one can know exactly what you're going through, but we do have experience dealing with huge changes to our everyday lives and how we see ourselves. And we want to help however we can. Lance here has spent years learning discipline in various forms like yoga, martial arts, fencing, and meditation classes. He's going to help you better control yourself and your body to help you regain some normalcy. I'm going to craft you some new accessories to help you not have to baby everything. We'll run some tests, and I'll ask you some questions, and then I'm going to make you some things like a new phone case and camera case so you can do normal things without always being afraid you're going to crush something. It'll be a tough transition, but we'll be here with you through it all."

"That's all really nice, but I can't ask y'all to do that. It's too much. I can't pay for Lance to be my personal tutor, and I certainly can't pay for you to make me all of that stuff."

"You won't have to pay me. Fox Industries will be paying me. I have a bit of freedom at my job to experiment on things, and it's not too hard for me to sneak those things out. I'll be using their materials, their equipment, and the time that they're already paying me for. Nothing else goes into it."

"And I have a pretty flexible schedule," Lance said. "And Taylor is more or less subsidizing my White Knight career, so some pro bono tutoring is quite literally the least I can do."

"So, it's settled." Taylor smiled. "Jason will have Sam run a couple tests to see what needs to be made and get to work on that. Lance will help Sam with self-discipline exercises, and I'll continue monitoring your health and note any progression or regression throughout the process."

"I think I can make that work," Sam answered. "You said Fox's drugs were making people faster and stronger. Could that have anything to do with what's happened to me?"

"I don't think so," Taylor said, shaking his head. "Not unless you can remember getting injected or taking some sort of super strength pill. That was my first thought, too, but I don't know how Fox could have gotten that into your system without you knowing."

"Was worth asking." Sam shrugged. "When can we start?"

SEVEN

The tests and training would have to wait until the week-end. Jason had taken a late lunch to meet with them, but he needed to get back to work at Fox Industries and had a busy week in front of him. He wouldn't be able to meet until Saturday. Taylor had his first med school test coming up on Friday and was going to be spending all week locked away by himself studying. And Lance was having to take on more White Knight duties this week to make up for the other two being so busy. With all that, plus Sam working the Dutchmen's Thursday night game that week, the next step would have to wait a few days.

Sam spent the next day trying to find more packing peanuts to use for the Thursday night game. First, he walked down to the shop where he'd bought his most recent camera.

"Um, sure. Let me check on that for you," the col-lege-age clerk told him after he explained what he was looking for. The clerk disappeared into the back and a few minutes later returned with an older man.

"How can we help you today?"

"Hi, yes, I was hoping to buy some of your packing peanuts off of you and maybe see where your store gets them from. I'm needing to ship a few fragile items, and the packing peanuts that were in the box with the camera I bought from you were high quality," Sam explained.

"Well. We don't usually sell those, but I guess there's nothing wrong with it. I can sell you a box this size,"—he motioned with his arms creating a box two feet long on each side—"full of them for, say, twenty dollars?"

"You've got a deal." Sam smiled as he pulled his wallet out.

"Oh, right now? Yes, of course. Run to the back and get that order filled real quick," he told his clerk as he rang Sam up at the counter.

Sam carried the box back to his apartment and began separating the peanuts into piles. Larger piles were for game days, and smaller piles were for practices. He was able to get a breakdown he was content with: three game-day piles and five for practices.

Sam spent the rest of Tuesday and Wednesday holed up in his apartment. The last few days had been incident-free, but with his powers being so new and the chance to finally find some control being so close, he didn't want to risk a catastrophe by being too eager. Using a couple of peanuts from a practice pile, he turned on his TV and found a station running a marathon of an old sitcom all day Wednesday that played as he rested.

Thursday afternoon, Sam arrived at the stadium early to set up for that night's game against the Burnett Bandits, traveling in from Nevada. The Dutchmen were undefeated while the Bandits had yet to secure a win, or even a loss by single digits. The game went according to script with the Dutchmen jumping out to an early lead and never looking back. Sam was able to get a handful of good shots without any issues popping up aside from the jokes about his packing peanuts from some of the other photographers on the sidelines, but he just ignored those.

After the game, he left the stadium and walked the mile north to Fran's to meet Jason, Hailey, and Gwen. The diner was overflowing with the postgame crowd, but Darlene greeted him with a smile and pointed to the booth on the far side where the other three were waiting.

"It's about time you got here," Hailey chided as he sat down next to Gwen. "We're already on our second plate of nachos."

"Fran's doesn't have nachos."

"Apparently, they do for Hailey." Gwen shrugged as she bit into another chip.

"We got here before the rush, and she talked Dennis into making an exception," Jason explained.

"She's been doing it a lot lately," Darlene laughed as she walked up to the table with a cup of soda for Sam.

"She really has," Sam answered. "And thank you."

"Anytime, sugar." She smiled and patted his shoulder as she headed back across the diner.

"These are really good," Sam said after eating one of the nachos. "Maybe Dennis should add these to the menu."

"They haven't changed that menu in twenty years. Dennis isn't going to update it for some nachos," Hailey laughed.

"How's your week been?" he asked Gwen.

"It's been fine. As busy and stressful as usual. I knew social work was difficult coming into it, but it's hard to really prepare yourself for how draining it can be."

"That makes sense. At least you had the energy to have fun at the game tonight."

"Ha!" she laughed, shaking her head. "I woke up from my daily nap a little after halftime and just came straight here. I certainly do not have the energy to go to a football game on a work night."

"Well, I'm glad you're here, at least."

"Me too." She smiled back.

"What about you, Jason? What's your week been like?"

"Hectic. We should've finished making things for the holiday season months ago, yet here we are three months away, and we still haven't gotten that taken care of." He shook his head. "This is the one night I'm not working overtime this week, and next week will be the same. Luckily, next Friday is the last day to get the holiday products finished, so one way or the other it will ease up after that."

Sam knew that wasn't everything. He didn't like lying to Brooklyn at work, but he hated that he now had to lie to Gwen and Hailey about this, too. Even if he wasn't telling them something untrue, he knew his mom would tell him that a lie of omission is no better than any other kind of lie. He knew they meant well when they'd told him about their secret as a show of trust, but as fun as being in on the biggest secret in the city was, he'd take not having to lie to Gwen and Hailey over knowing a hundred times out of a hundred.

"How about your week, Sam?" Gwen asked as one of the college waitresses handed out their food.

Sam laughed. "My week pretty much started and stopped today. I got back from Sanders early Monday morning, took care of a few things, then worked tonight. There weren't even any practices to go to with the short week."

"My week has also been pretty busy," Hailey said. "Three White Knight sightings on top of my usual two articles. Like, we get it, man. You're a hero. Take a night off every now and then. I'm overworked."

"We all see you regularly. Everyone already knows how your week was." Gwen tossed a fry at Hailey.

"It's still nice being included," Hailey retorted, jabbing the fry at Gwen before biting into it.

"Where are Taylor and Lance tonight?" Sam asked, looking around the table, wondering if Taylor was at the warehouse and Lance was in his suit as the rest of them sat in the diner.

"Taylor has that big test tomorrow, so he's been locked in his room all day," Jason answered.

"And Lance can't afford to not work game nights. The rates for drivers go up after big events, and he usually makes more after games than he does the rest of the week. So, after he took people to the game, he picked me up and dropped me off here during the lull before people started heading home," Gwen added.

"It's too bad. It's been a while since we've all been in the same place at once," Hailey said.

"I'm sure we'll make something happen soon," Jason assured her, wrapping an arm around her shoulder.

They talked and laughed as the diner thinned out. The two girls hopped in Jason's car as Sam walked home, another incident-free day under his belt.

EIGHT

"Okay, let's do it," Sam responded as Jason finished outlining the plan.

Other than his post-gameday morning meeting with Barry, Sam had stayed in on Friday. Taylor wanted everyone to meet at the warehouse by seven Saturday morning, but Jason, Lance, and Sam convinced him that ten was early enough.

Sam stretched out his arms, still waking up, as he waited for Jason to finish setting up. Jason had explained that he'd brought a number of materials of differing strength from Fox Industries and that he had two identical pieces of each material. He also brought a machine that Fox Industries used to determine how much pressure an object could withstand before giving in. Jason's plan was to have Sam apply varying levels of pressure to the materials and then use the machine to determine how much force was required to achieve the same impact as Sam had. Taylor was busy catching up on crime charts and incidents that had occurred throughout the week while he'd been studying. Lance had yet to arrive, telling his roommates that he would be in by eleven since he wasn't needed before then.

"Alright." Jason stood up straight and took a step back from the desk. "I think it's ready to go."

Sam rolled his shoulders and stepped up to the table, awaiting Jason's next instructions. He tapped his fingers on the side of his legs.

"I've spent so much energy the last week trying to not use any of this strength," he said to Jason as he rocked on the balls of his feet. "It's weird to now be purposefully using it. I haven't really done that since Taylor ran his tests, other than jogging to places a bit quicker."

"It's going to be fine," Jason assured him. "We're running simple tests in a controlled environment. There's nothing to worry about here. I know you and Taylor have measured what you can, and I have those results here, but I'm looking at how your strength manifests in a different way than he did. Now, the first thing I want you to do is step up to the table and, as lightly as you can, push down on that slab of Styrofoam, like you would when you take a picture. This is the weakest material, and we need to figure out the floor of your strength."

"Got it," Sam said, setting his hand over the block. As gently as he could, he pushed down on the Styrofoam. It immediately gave way to his finger, leaving an indentation of two and a half inches.

"That's as soft as you can press?" Jason asked, to which Sam nodded. "Okay." Jason measured the imprint and made a note on his own clipboard. "Now let's do halfway between that and what you would normally do to take a picture before your new strength."

Sam nodded and set his hand back on top of the block. Doing as Jason had instructed, he tapped the block, and his finger shot through the Styrofoam, stopping another four inches below the previous mark as the Styrofoam under his finger compacted.

Jason measured the block again before stepping back. "Now push like you would to take a picture."

Sam once again pushed down on the block, a little harder this time. The Styrofoam crunched as Sam's finger ripped all the way through the block, leaving a small imprint on Jason's metal worktable.

Jason's eyes widened, but he didn't say anything as he made another note on his clipboard. He removed Sam's destroyed Styrofoam block and replaced it with the next material.

"We'll do the same thing again," Jason said as Sam placed his hand over the new material. This continued as they worked their way through all of the blocks of material Jason had brought with him. As stronger materials made their way to the table and the lightest push no longer did anything, Jason would have Sam start with the second push and add a third stronger push. They continued to cycle through Sam's forcefulness as the stronger materials required, but even the strongest materials that Jason had brought failed to resist Sam's strength, as each block broke by the third press without Sam ever pushing his limits.

"I might bring some even stronger materials in the future, just to see what the limits of this are, but for building you some household and everyday items that won't shatter by normal use, I should have what I need here. I'm going to prioritize getting you a new camera shell, so you aren't worried about that, and then I'll start work on the other items."

"I really appreciate that, Jason," Sam thanked him.

"Of course, man! This is the coolest thing I've ever gotten to make. It's like a dream project."

"And you thought building super suits was cool," Lance quipped as he walked in with his coffee.

"Also cool," Jason answered, "but not as cool as working with someone to build things that will withstand their superstrength."

"Don't get too attached to his praise, Sam," Lance warned, "next year he's going to find a new project that will be his favorite."

"But until that day, this will be the coolest thing."

"I'm just thankful to think there is a day coming where I won't have to worry about breaking everything,"

Sam told them. "I mean, still most things, but at least I'll have a few things that shouldn't break."

If I could just get my apartment and camera Sam-proofed, that would be a good start. The packing peanuts are a hassle, and it would be nice to be able to turn off the "don't break whatever you touch" warning in my brain, at least in my own home.

"That second part is where I come in," Lance said. "Take a break if you need one, then meet me over on the sparring pad. We've got some work to do." He set his coffee down before he walked over to the pad.

Sam followed him across the room, coming to a stop at the edge as Lance sat down just past the midway point. Lance lifted his eyebrows as Sam hesitated, gesturing for him to join him on the pad. Sam lowered his large frame to the ground and sat with his legs crossed like Lance.

Lance rested his arms on his legs and closed his eyes. Sam watched him, waiting for instruction before realizing he was probably just trying to get him to meditate. Sam rolled his eyes and let out a deep breath, then he, too, rested his arms and closed his eyes. Ten minutes passed as they sat there in silence, the only sounds being their breathing and the distant sounds of Taylor and Jason working across the warehouse.

"Okay," Lance said, finally breaking the silence. "Let's stretch." He stood, letting his body hang so his fingers dangled near his toes.

Sam followed suit. "So, I get why Taylor had Jason help me with creating stronger items for everyday use. He's a brilliant mechanical engineer with a gift for inventing things and access to a surplus of materials from Fox Industries. But what about you? What are your qualifications for helping me 'learn self-control'?" Sam asked, using air quotes around the last two words.

Lance silently shifted to a new stretch before answering. "My qualifications are that I have free time. Taylor and Jason do a lot more White Knight work than I do during times when I'm not in the suit. Taylor is a medical student. Jason has a full-time job where he often has to work overtime. So, what qualifies me is that I have the time to do this with you, and Taylor felt like our shared secret would make it easier for everyone to trust everyone by keeping the circle tight rather than bringing someone else in."

"So, you have no real training in this area at all," Sam stated. "I thought Taylor said something about yoga or martial arts or something."

"Something like that," Lance answered, shifting into a new stretch. "My father had this dream of turning me into the perfect cop, just like he saw himself. So, my childhood was spent differently than most people's."

"How so?"

"I was signed up for every kind of class you can think of. Varying martial arts, fencing, yoga, different boot camps, and a new summer camp every year until high school, when I joined a traveling baseball team. The best part is that his determination to raise a cop backfired in the most incredible way, with me being the most wanted criminal in two cities."

"Wanted criminal? I thought people saw you as a hero?"

"The public does. That's due in large part to Hailey's coverage of me. But the city government? The police department? There's no one they'd rather have behind bars than me."

"That's gotta be tough," Sam said. He hadn't pushed back when they told him they could somewhat understand what he was going through, but he hadn't fully bought it. Maybe there was more to it than he realized, though. Lance, looking over his shoulder and waiting to see if he was going to get caught every time he did a job, wasn't the same as being afraid that anything you touch might shatter, but it was at least analogous.

Lance shrugged. "It comes with the territory. In high school, there weren't too many people whose opinion I really cared about. Mainly Gwen. Four or five others. In college, it shrank even further to this group we have now. That's part of the growth that came from all those classes, and it's the actual reason I'm the one over here with you right now. Taking those classes trained my body and mind. It taught me how to control my body and mind and focus on those things. We don't lose control of our mind and body when all we are focused on is our mind and body. It's only when we start focusing on things out of our control that we can no longer control ourselves either."

"That's deep."

Lance averted his eyes, leaning away from Sam into a new stretch. "One summer was spent at some boarding school for a summer program where all we did was read classic literature, poetry, and philosophy. It was one of the better summers, if that gives you any indication of what my childhood was like," Lance laughed.

"So, you've got training to make you a hero, but how does that translate to helping me with my problem?"

"Yoga, martial arts, fencing, meditation, all of those are about connecting the mind and body. Most people take for granted that they aren't just a body, but a whole made up of a bunch of smaller parts. You're being forced to consider that every second of the day now. I've been trained to be aware of that distinction my whole life. That's why I'm the one training you. I think that's enough for today."

"We only stretched, though."

"And that's day one. And part of the lesson. Your homework is to do three different ten-minute meditations before we're back here tomorrow. Think you can handle that?"

"I can do that," Sam answered.

Lance slapped his shoulder and walked back to Jason and Taylor to grab his coffee.

They had agreed to meet again the next morning at eleven. Taylor and Jason picked Sam up on their way to the base and arrived fifteen minutes before eleven. Lance showed up an hour and a half later. He hadn't gotten in until four from White Knight duties the night before, so no one questioned his bleary eyes or his lateness.

"Saturdays are rough for you, huh?" Sam asked as the two of them set up on the sparring pad again. Lance nodded in response, his eyes still not fully open all the way.

"Thursday through Saturday are the toughest nights. Things happen throughout the rest of the week, but those three nights it feels like things never stop happening," Lance answered.

Lance sat down in the same position as the day before and motioned for Sam to do the same. Once again, they could faintly hear Taylor and Jason working across the warehouse. After ten minutes, they transitioned to stretching, the two of them still sitting in silence.

"Alright," Lance announced after ten minutes of stretching. "We're going to try some yoga."

"Yoga?"

"That's right. We're trying to train you to fully control your body, and nothing is going to make that happen as well as yoga will. We'll start light today, but it's still not going to be easy."

"Then let's get to it."

When they finished forty-five minutes later, Sam was drenched in sweat and panting. Lance's forehead glistened, but other than that, he seemed to be okay. Sam was in decent shape but hadn't felt strains like this before.

Lance tossed him a towel and headed to the bathroom as Sam walked back to the front.

"Why didn't my new abilities keep me from getting drained doing that?" he asked Taylor, leaning against the wall next to the computer. "I haven't so much as worked up a sweat doing anything else."

"My guess? It's because your body is only working against itself in yoga. You can tire yourself out at the same rate when you're focused on manipulating your own body in a way you don't when you're working against outside forces. But I can't be sure." He shrugged as he leaned back in his chair.

"Well, isn't that great." Sam shook his head and rested it against the wall.

"We thought you all were probably getting hungry, so we brought everyone lunch," Hailey said, dropping the food on the table.

"A little Sunday picnic," Gwen added, following her with a bag of her own as the door closed behind them.

"Perfect timing, I'm starving." Jason hopped up from his workbench and walked to the table to see what they had brought.

Sam and Taylor sat slack-jawed as they stared first at the two girls, then at each other, and then back at the girls. Hailey gave them a wave as Jason sat down and helped Gwen pull containers out of the bag.

"Hey," Lance's voice called out across the warehouse as he returned, his head buried in his towel, drying off his sweat. "So I've been thinking. What if—" his voice cut off as he removed the towel and saw the girls. He froze, staring at Gwen and Hailey as the towel hit the floor.

"What if what?" Jason asked, looking up from the food at Lance. He traced Lance's stare back to the girls as his eyes widened. "What are you two doing here?" he gasped, almost falling out of his chair as he finally realized where they all were.

"Lunch," Gwen answered, gesturing at the food.

"Were you not listening?" Hailey asked.

"No, I mean yes, but how did you know we were here?"

"I just looked at Sam's location on the phone," Hailey answered.

Everyone looked towards Sam, who put his hands in the air.

"Jason told me to bring it, and I can't use it right now."

"We, uh," Taylor started, "we just like to come hang out here sometimes on the weekends. There's room to study and work out. Jason has room to work on his stuff."

"Yeah, just like a man cave. A bro spot. You know, guy stuff," Jason added.

"Yeah, we just like having a space to come to." Taylor nodded as he talked.

"You mean a space to come to for being superheroes," Hailey finished for him.

"What are you talking about?" Jason's voice had gone a full octave higher.

"She's talking about you being Ironside. And Lance," Gwen turned to look at him, as he hadn't moved a muscle, "is the White Knight."

Sam's heart raced as his gaze moved from the table where Hailey and Gwen stood to where Lance stood, staring at Gwen. Had he done something to give them away?

"What are you talking about?" Jason repeated while Taylor said at the same time, "No, he's not."

Lance tossed the towel from one hand to the other before slinging it over his shoulder and burying his hands in his pockets. "How long have you known?"

Hailey and Gwen looked at each other and then back at him. "Probably a couple weeks after these two found out," Hailey answered, pointing at Jason and Taylor. "They went from being equally worried about you to defending you and seeming more distant themselves.

From there, I started piecing it together along with what I was picking up reporting."

"I didn't believe her at first," Gwen added. "But when she started laying out her theory, I realized it was obvious all along. And it explained a lot."

"Why did you never say anything?" Taylor asked from his desk.

Hailey shrugged. "You guys clearly wanted to keep it private and while we would've loved to be a part of it we understood why you wanted to keep it between the three of you and we wanted to respect your decision. Since we had figured out what it was causing you to all act weird, we weren't as worried about you anymore."

"But then Sam got powers," Gwen interjected.

"And that changed the dynamic." Hailey nodded. "My cousin getting powers that we don't know anything about meant I had to help him get in contact with Taylor, who I figured would bring you two into it as well. Pretty soon, it would've been impossible for me to keep up with his health and how he was doing without being a part of this team. So, we decided to take advantage of the opportunity when we saw Sam's location come out here."

"Plus, we were also hungry," added Gwen, who'd taken a seat at the table and now brandished a carton of fries.

"Are you mad?" Lance asked, his voice soft.

"No," Gwen answered, shaking her head with a smile. "We understand why. I understand why. It took me a while to get there, but I did. I was pretty upset for some time after we found out. It's one of the reasons I wanted space in the spring. But Hailey helped me understand why you were doing what you were doing. I'm not upset anymore."

Lance smiled. "Then I'm glad the secret's out. It hasn't been the same not having you two be part of the team."

"Ooh! Part of the team!" Hailey ribbed. "Do we get cool jackets?"

"Nope," Taylor said, sitting down across from Gwen. "Apparently, Jason only makes clothes for people who physically fight crime. Like what I do here isn't as important."

"How many times do we have to go over this?" Jason groaned. "You don't need a suit because you're not in danger. It's not because you're less important, it just wouldn't help you in any way."

Lance sat down next to Gwen and took a fry from her lunch. She slapped at his hand and laughed while Taylor and Jason continued to bicker as Hailey stoked the flames. Sam sat next to Taylor and laughed along as they enjoyed their Sunday picnic, relieved they had pieced out their secret long before they brought him in on it.

NINE

"That's enough for today," Lance said, lying face-first into his towel on the pad as Sam sat down and lay on his back.

The two panted, trying to recover from their two-hour training session. In just the week since they'd started doing yoga, Sam had come a long way in building both his stamina and the control he had over his body.

"Mmmruuughh," Lance groaned into the towel. "I feel like every part of my body was hit with a hammer. This is worse than the time the car hit me on campus."

"You got hit by a car?"

"Yeah. The White Knight did. Or I guess technically I didn't have a name at that point. But yeah. It was a couple of nights before Jason and Taylor figured out my secret. It wasn't pretty."

"I'm not going to test it," Sam replied, "but I'm pretty sure if I got hit by a car right now, the car would be in worse shape than me."

Lance chuckled into the pillow. The difference in him in just the last week was remarkable. He'd gone from being moody and distant to outright cheerful and friendly since Gwen and Hailey had shown up the previous Sunday.

"I need to go take an ice bath so I can make sure I'm good to go out tonight. Fridays are usually a busy night. In the future, I may not do all the exercises with you. I might just stand here and coach you instead, so I'm not dying on rounds. You've come a long way, though. I'm really impressed."

"Thanks, Lance, that means a lot."

"No problem, man," he said, getting to his feet. "Can you lock up behind you whenever you're ready to leave?"

"Sure thing."

"See you tomorrow, Sam," he called as he walked off towards the door. Sam closed his eyes and stayed lying on the pad for another ten minutes before getting up, locking the door like Lance had asked, and heading out himself.

He made his way back downtown for a late lunch at Fran's. He liked coming in after the normal lunch rush when he could because it gave him more time to talk to the staff and other regulars. With his self-imposed semi-quarantine the previous few weeks, he hadn't really had the opportunity to just sit in the diner and talk, and he had missed it.

"Sammy!" Darlene called out as the bell above the door rang as he walked in. A chorus of "Hey Sam" echoed around him as he smiled at the group before sitting on the barstool next to Harry.

"How's life treating you lately, Samson?" Harry asked as Sam settled in.

"Oh, you know, nothing too crazy," he lied.

"That's good, that's good!" Harry slapped his shoulder and smiled. "It's been a while since you've been in here alone. I've missed our chats."

"Me too, Harry. What's been going on in your life? Catch me up to speed."

"Samson, when you get to be my age, speed doesn't really accurately describe my day-to-day life anymore," Harry laughed. "What I've done lately is sit at this bar and talk, watched TV at home, and gone to church. The only remotely different thing I've done was go to visit my sister in her retirement home right outside the city. Darlene and I don't get out much these days. And there comes a point where you'd rather stay in together anyway."

"Hey, that sounds pretty good to me," Sam said. "I don't think I knew you had a sister."

"Two of them: Mary and Christina. Both of them are older than me, I'm the baby of the family. Christina still lives in Sanders, but Mary moved out here twenty years or so ago when Dad died. Christina usually comes out here a couple times a year, and we'll head out and see her usually for an extended stay around the holidays."

"That's so cool. I don't have any siblings. Me and Hailey are close but growing up, she lived in St. Lawrence while I lived in Oklahoma, so I never really got to experience that bigger family thing as a kid."

"There are definitely hard parts of having siblings," Harry laughed, "especially when you're all young, but once you get older, it's a really sweet thing."

"It sounds like it," Sam answered as Darlene sat his usual in front of him—a burger and fries basket with a sweet tea. Sam cautiously wrapped his fingers around the cup and lifted it to his mouth to drink. Fran's glasses sloped outward at the top, allowing Sam to let the cup rest on his fingers rather than actually holding onto it. He'd learned the hard way that cups without that slope weren't as easy for him to drink from, and now he had all but run out of cups in his apartment as a result. Hailey had gotten him four identical metal water bottles that he could swap out, and those could mostly withstand his normal grip, though they each had a growing collection of dents.

"How often do you go back home to Oklahoma?" Harry asked, bringing Sam back to the moment as he gently set the glass down and cupped his burger to avoid crushing it.

"Um." Sam finished chewing before answering. "Not really at all since I moved here. My dad passed away almost seven years ago, and then my mom died two years ago. Most of my friends moved off after college, and so there's not really much to head back home to."

"I'm really sorry to hear that, Sam. I didn't realize your parents had both passed."

"Yeah, I don't talk about it much. It's just not really the kind of thing I want just anyone to know."

"I'm honored you would share it with me then." Harry smiled at Sam as he rested a hand on his shoulder.

Sam smiled back before returning to his burger in silence, and Harry excused himself to talk to another regular who had just entered.

When Harry returned, the conversation shifted back to their normal sports talk as Sam ate his fries. Harry was excited about the Dutchmen's undefeated start and peppered Sam for any info he'd been able to pick up being around the team and watching practices. After an hour at the diner, a little before five in the evening, Sam's eyelids began to grow heavier, and he said his goodbyes before heading home.

The diner was close to Sam's apartment, but he still struggled to make it home, stumbling up his stairs from his exhaustion. After a few tries, he was able to pull his keys from his pocket and unlock the door. After locking the door behind him, he walked to the couch, unable to make it to his bed, and collapsed into the cushions, falling asleep immediately upon his head hitting the pillow.

"Alright, good job," Lance told Sam as he finished the yoga workout. "Now do it again from the top and really push yourself. Hold each pose for an extra five seconds, ten if that's not pushing you." Sam panted, covered in sweat, but nodded. He took a long drink of water from his bottle beside the pad and started the workout.

Taylor and Jason sat across the room at their work-stations. Taylor had scanners and video running on the computer but wasn't actively monitoring them. He had his medical school books open on the desk, and he had been lost in those since they'd arrived an hour ago at one. Jason worked at his table, tinkering with some of Sam's new equipment. The shell of a camera rested in front of him as he worked.

Sam worked fluidly from one position to the next. His stamina and ability to hold positions were far greater now than they were when they started, and his flexibility had steadily increased, too. He grabbed his bottle from the bench and sat down on the pad. The halfway point of the routine marked the transition from standing poses to the ground poses and, with it, a short two-minute break to catch his breath. Setting the bottle down, Sam prepared to get in position when Taylor's voice cut across the warehouse.

"We've got a situation!" he called as Lance ran across the room and Jason jumped up from his table. "We've got a shooting in front of the downtown Peak First Bank.

Looks to be at least five gunmen. There are hostages in the bank right now, and police were just dispatched to back up the one car there now that's taking fire."

Without another word, Jason and Lance sprinted to two lockers along the wall that Sam hadn't noticed before now. Taylor followed and helped them strap into their suits. Lance's White Knight suit looked the same as it had in the pictures in the Daily, as well as what he had seen in Franklin four months ago. It was a bit bulky up top, but it allowed for a pretty decent range of movement. He hadn't seen Jason's Ironside suit before, but the red armor was much more streamlined than Lance's. The helmet seemed similar, but his suit lacked the plates that Lance's had on his torso and limbs. It looked more movable but also less protective.

The two grabbed their weapons, Lance buckling his sheathed sword to his belt and Jason grabbing his javelin and walked to their motorcycles—white for Lance and red for Jason to match their suits. Jason placed his javelin into a groove on the bike and they both revved the engines before peeling out of the warehouse, headed downtown.

"Your ETA is three minutes," Taylor said into the headset he had donned, the first words spoken since he had finished briefing them.

Sam stood behind Taylor's chair with his arms crossed as he watched them race towards the bank on the monitors in front of him.

"I'm going to circle the block and hit them from the opposite side," Jason said. "Lance, slow down just a bit to give me time to get in position."

"Copy that," Lance and Taylor answered simultaneously. Their voices were surprisingly clear through the mic. Learning his friends had been living double lives as the local superhero team had been a shock, but what had surprised him most since learning their secret was how professional their operation was. They were less than a year in, and already they each had defined roles, top-tier equipment, and procedures to make everything work together efficiently. He shook his head in amazement that three recent college grads in a warehouse had already gotten this far.

Sam stared at the monitor, where Jason took a sharp left on the next street, darting in front of an oncoming car, as Lance held his course.

Taylor had four monitors up, one each for Lance and Jason's video stream, one of the bank's security feed, and the last a street camera on a pole across the street from the bank.

"In position," Jason updated as the standoff came into view on his screen.

"I'm coming straight in for the two outside gunmen," Lance said. "Increasing speed now. Once they're cleared, you get inside. I'll join you soon."

"Copy that," Jason and Taylor answered, and the gunmen entered the screen as Lance rapidly approached.

"Come on," Sam whispered to himself as he watched the gunmen come into focus from Lance's point-of-view camera.

Slowing down slightly as he approached, Lance swept his rounded-off sword into the legs of one gunman before pulling back and swinging at the gunman on the other side of the bike as well, sending both of them crumpling to the ground, grasping at their legs. Jason had leapt from his bike and sprinted into the bank before the second gunman hit the ground. Lance drifted to a stop. A cry of agony was called through the speakers as Jason used the end of his Javelin to pierce the first doorway gunman's calf.

The man fell, and the gunmen stationed at the other two doors both turned and opened fire. Jason crouched and extended his retractable shield out of his arm to help cover his upper body. The gunshots paused as they reloaded, and Jason stood to his feet. Gripping the javelin, he hurled it at the gunman to his right, catching him in the shoulder and forcing him to drop his gun.

"Don't move!" the last gunman demanded as he ripped a small boy from his mother's grasp and pointed the gun at him. "Make a single move and I'll kill him."

Sam gripped the chair in front of him instinctively as he watched the kid get yanked around through Jason's helmet cam, realizing a second too late the consequences it would have on the metal. *Where is Lance?* His camera feed showed running through the alley. Taylor spoke, but Sam couldn't hear him over the roaring in his ears and the mother's sobs in the speaker.

Jason opened his hands and raised them slightly. "Just let the boy go. We can work this out."

"I'll let him go once I'm outside of the city and there are no cops around."

"No deal," Lance growled as he shot through a side door and delivered a blow with the hilt of his sword to the gunman's head, causing him to fall to the ground.

Jason jogged over to retrieve his javelin as a chorus of "thank you, White Knight" and "thank you, Ironside" echoed throughout the bank.

"We're always here to help," Jason answered with a wave.

Lance and Jason ran out the side door where both bikes were parked. There were cop cars parked at either end of the alley, each with four officers pointing guns at the two as they continued to mount their bikes.

"You are under arrest. Place your weapons on the ground and raise your hands," an officer commanded over one of the car's PA systems.

Lance and Jason had started their bikes while the announcement was made. Lance had left the side door propped open, and Jason motioned to the small boy inside to push open the other door with hand signs, which the boy excitedly ran to do in order to help.

"This is your last warning before we open fire," the PA declared.

"It's open. Turn left when you get through." Taylor said through the headsets.

Without another second of hesitation, Jason drove into the bank with Lance close behind as gunshots sounded in the alley behind them. After two high-fives for the boy at the door, they peeled off to the left and raced up the unoccupied alley on the other side of the building, quickly leaving the police behind.

"That was incredible!" Sam shouted as Lance and Jason shot out of the alley. He let out a breath he hadn't realized he was holding, putting his hands on top of his head as Taylor slumped back into his chair, laying his headset down. "This is what y'all do every day?"

"Feels like it," Taylor answered. "Not quite, though. Most weekdays, Lance doesn't do much. Jason rarely even goes out between Sunday night and Wednesday night. The weekends, though, usually make up for that."

"Is it always that cool? Like, obviously it's not a bank robbery every day, but is it usually something that exciting?"

"Not at all. It's usually muggings that Lance stops, and we're on edge the whole time, hoping he gets there in time. There are more, um, glamorous days like today, but those are a lot more rare," Taylor explained before turning his headset back on.

"Looks like you've lost them. I'll keep my eye on the monitor but go ahead and head on in," Taylor said into the headset.

"Copy that," their two voices answered in unison.

"Sorry about the chair," Sam said.

"Huh?" Taylor glanced away from the monitor briefly to see the metal Sam had warped in his panic. "No biggie. Everything here is excess. Either Jason can fix it, or we'll throw it out. Don't worry about it."

With Taylor still locked in on the monitors, Sam paced behind him for the two minutes it took for the warehouse to come into the camera feed. Taylor hit the button to open the dock door, and Lance and Jason rode in under it. They dismounted their bikes and removed their helmets as the door closed back behind them.

"What happened after we left?" Lance asked as he put his helmet back in the locker, swiping his shaggy hair out of his eyes.

"All five gunmen were arrested and taken in. There were no serious injuries to civilians, though one did get hit by a bullet that ricocheted off Jason. Four different cars took off in pursuit of you two."

"That's more than last time," Jason observed as he pulled off the top of his suit.

"It is. They seem to be getting more intent on catching us than they are in catching the bad guys." Taylor had turned his chair to face them.

"We just have to keep being smart," Lance told them. "With Taylor watching it all from here, we're always a step ahead of them."

"Great work out there today, guys."

"Thanks, Sam," Lance answered with a smile as he began to remove his suit, too. "You know, with your, uh, skill set, you could really be an asset for the community if you wanted to join the team."

"I don't know about that. I'm still new to all of this," he laughed. While seeing the child in danger had made him wish he was there to help, breaking the chair without realizing it at the same time had immediately reminded him why that would never be an option, even if he wanted to be a hero.

"So are we," Jason laughed as he finished taking off his leg armor, sitting in the locker in a visibly damp burgundy sweatsuit. "We've got, what? Six months on him? And with your abilities, your learning curve would be a lot different than ours."

"They're right, Sam," Taylor added. "What the White Knight and Ironside do is important and heroic, but you could be a real-life superhero."

"I appreciate it, really, I do, but that's just not the life for me. I just want to learn how to manage this until I figure out a way to get rid of it. I'm much more comfortable behind a camera than in front of one." Sam tried to keep the smile on his face but could feel that familiar itch on his skin as anxiety rose as he realized they weren't just being polite, but actually trying to recruit him.

"That might be so," Lance said, "but sometimes we have to be a bit uncomfortable to really have an impact. I've never been a person comfortable with attention, but it's a small price to pay when I look at the good we're doing."

"Lance chose this life. Taylor and I chose it, too." Jason stood from the locker and walked to stand next to Sam and Taylor while Lance continued changing. "And I think all of us feel like it was the right choice, but we can go back to not doing that at any point. You may not have chosen the life, but it's chosen you. It's obviously up to you what you do with these gifts, but you're going to have to make those choices intentionally now. You can't just stay behind the camera. You'll have to make a choice to stay behind the camera instead of using your gifts."

Sam snorted and shook his head, trying to keep the anxiety from turning into anger. He could feel the polite smile he had worked so hard to keep on his face turning into a smirk to match his scoff.

"Okay. Yeah. Cool. Done. That's my choice. I'm going to stay behind the camera. I don't want these "gifts" as you call them. Those "gifts" are deformities that are wrecking my life. I don't want to be afraid of crushing everyday objects or hurting someone if I bump into them. And I don't want to go out there and play hero and end up sending someone to their grave because I hit them with three percent of my strength instead of two percent." Sam balled his fists to try and keep his voice from rising to match his increased pulse. "That's the kind of consequences we'd be talking about here. If either of you misjudges something by an inch, you might miss a bit. If I miss by an inch, someone dies."

"Sam," Lance interjected as Jason opened his mouth to respond, standing and walking from the lockers to join them. "We're not talking about throwing you out there and asking you to fight tomorrow or this weekend. We wouldn't encourage you to get in the field until we were sure you had your powers under control, and no one would get hurt."

"And maybe," Taylor added, "we're out of line here. Maybe we're so focused on the mission we've chosen that we're having a hard time seeing that it's not for everyone. That it's not for you. And that that's okay. I think it's just hard for us, especially Jason and Lance, to be out there struggling and to imagine what they could do if they had your strength."

"Yeah, well, I'll make sure to remember the struggle you face next time I hurt someone because we reached for something at the same time and my hand brushed up against theirs." His face felt feverish, and his stomach turned just imagining how much he could hurt someone just shopping at the grocery store. "I'll remember how lucky I am when instead of focusing on doing my job, which I loved, I have to now focus instead on just not crushing my camera."

Jason shook his head. "You know that's not what we mean."

"Whatever, man," Sam answered, grabbing his water bottle from the table, the dented metal giving way as he squeezed it in his hand. "I need to head out anyway. I've got stuff I need to do. I'll see y'all later."

"We're sorry, Sam," Taylor told him. "We didn't mean to overstep and upset you. Take some time, and if you still want to, we'll keep helping you train, and we won't bring it up again."

"I'll see y'all around," he answered as he left the warehouse, slowing down to turn and back out the push door to avoid breaking anything else.

chapter

TEN

Gifts, Sam snorted to himself and shook his head. *Not exactly what I had on my Christmas list.*

Sam looked out the window of the plane as it descended over Cameron City, the Colorado mountains rising up in the distance. The Miners were the Dutchmen's biggest rival and the defending champions. They were also undefeated coming into the first matchup of the season between the two teams for a Monday Night Showdown.

Sam grabbed his carry-on and stood up once everyone else had already exited the plane. He liked to wait until the other passengers had gotten off to stand anyway because of his size, and, with his new strength, it just wasn't worth the risk of hurting someone to get off the plane a couple of minutes early. He exited the terminal and was surprised to find a driver holding up a card with his name on it. Handing his bag to the driver, Sam followed him to the town car and got into the backseat.

"Hey Sam!"

"Brooklyn?"

She was sitting in the backseat. Her brown hair was down tonight which Sam had learned meant she had been working in public today. Whenever they were traveling or going to be in the paper's office, she'd have her hair pulled back in a ponytail and when she was covering a game or practice and needed to be "on" she'd let her shoulder length, wavy hair down.

"They flew me out yesterday to cover the practice today and I figured I'd come pick you up tonight since I was already in town. We can stop by the hotel to get you checked in then we can go grab a bite to eat. CC has the best steakhouses."

"Uh, sounds great," Sam answered as the driver closed the door and started the car.

The maître d' sat them down at a table near the back and left the two of them alone with their menus.

"So, Nick's is the best steakhouse in town, but it's closed on Sundays. The Stringer House is a close second, though, and their sides are better anyway."

"Uh, everything here looks pretty expensive," Sam said, looking at the menu. *The cheapest steak is thirty dollars!* The anxiety that the menu's prices gave him was almost as severe as the super strength-induced anxiety.

"That's the beauty of the *per diem,*" Brooklyn laughed. "We get sixty-five dollars a day, no matter what time we get in. The first rule of traveling is to eat somewhere nice on the first night in town when you can spend all your per diem on one meal. I'm getting the forty-five-dollar New York strip and a glass of the red for eight because I had to eat something earlier, you can go up to sixty or sixty-five if you want to. Compared to a lot of other steakhouses, Stringer is a bit cheaper for their quality."

"We get a *per diem?*"

"You're kidding. They didn't tell you about that? I'm going to have to talk to Barry about that when we get back. Yes, we get sixty-five dollars per day when we have to travel for work, for food, and for transportation. I have a card from the paper, so I'll put the whole meal on that."

"Well then, that's a game changer," Sam smirked and looked down at the menu with fresh eyes now that the anxiety had passed. "Let's see what this fifty-five-dollar steak tastes like."

"That's the spirit!" Brooklyn laughed again as the waiter walked up to take their order.

"I'm glad you were able to come out tonight," she said as they started working on their salads.

"Yeah, of course, thanks for inviting me."

"When I started working here ten years ago out of college, my photographer took me under his wing and taught me the ropes and helped me get comfortable with the job. It feels nice to get to pass that on. He retired last year after forty-five years with the paper."

"It sounds like you two were close."

"We were. He was like a fatherly mentor for me. Being a young woman in a male-dominated field could lead to some, shall we say, unwanted attention. But, from the beginning, Matthew defended me. And pretty soon, I didn't have to deal with that kind of harassment for the most part. He was a really good man. We'd get dinner like this every time we would travel. I was disappointed when you weren't able to make it to the first away game, but I'm glad we're getting to hopefully start a tradition of our own now."

"That would be nice." Sam smiled at her.

"Are you feeling better? I haven't really seen you the last couple weeks with home game press being different. I know you weren't feeling great in Sanders."

"Um, yeah, I'm feeling a bit better. I've been trying some new things that have been helpful, giving me some more energy."

"That's good to hear, Sam." She smiled back at him as their meals arrived.

Sam steered the conversation back to the Dutchmen and how well their star quarterback, Dante Sparks, had played the first three games, eager to stay far away from the topic of his health. Their dinner lasted almost two hours, and Sam was surprised at how sad he was when he got back to the hotel and they went to their separate rooms. It felt like it had been so long since he had been able to talk to someone else without having it be about what was wrong with him, or to at least have that weight hanging over the conversation. Tonight felt like he was normal again. And it was a nice feeling, even if it only lasted a couple of hours.

He set up in his usual spot in the end zone for the game the next night. He set his bag down next to him, ensuring his packing peanuts were ready to go. It was only a few minutes into the game when the first action happened in his end zone. The Miners were driving on their first possession and had second and four from the sixteen-yard line when they completed a pass into the end zone. The catch was further down from where he was sitting, but he still managed a couple of good shots from the play.

That was the last scoring play until late in the second quarter. The two teams had switched sides, and now it was the Dutchmen trying to get into the end zone near Sam. An incomplete pass on second and goal from the three-yard line stopped the clock at fourteen seconds. They broke from their huddle, and Sparks walked up behind the linemen. He called out his cadence and hiked the ball. He faked a handoff and dropped back five steps to survey the field in front of him. Stepping up in the pocket as a defensive end rushed him from the outside, he threw a strike to his favorite target, second-year receiver Sterling Lee, streaking across the end zone for a touchdown. Lee caught the pass right in front of Sam, taking two toe steps to stay inbounds before running out of the back of the end zone. Sam's adrenaline spiked as he took the photos, knowing he had gotten at least a few great shots.

Sam still had his camera to his eye when he heard a chorus of shouts and gasps happening around him. He lowered his camera and looked around. Sterling Lee was lying on the ground a few feet away, screaming and holding his leg. Sam looked up and watched with the rest of the sixty thousand in attendance as the scoreboard showed the replay. It showed Sparks stepping in to rifle a pass to Lee, Lee catching it and tiptoeing as his momentum carried him out of bounds, and then-

Oh no.

He watched on the screen as Lee's momentum carried him right into Sam, and then he immediately hit the ground and grasped at his leg. Sam had never even felt the contact, and with his camera lifted, he couldn't see Lee getting closer. All the photographers were asked to clear the area as they brought out a stretcher to remove him from the field. He gave a thumbs up to the crowd as they wheeled him off, but Sam still felt nauseous. The Dutchmen kicked a quick field goal to tie the game, and the Miners took a knee to go into halftime with a score of seven to seven.

How could I be so careless? Sam sat alone during the break while most of the other photographers had walked back

to the complimentary snack bar. He slowly rocked back and forth where he was sitting, trying to get his stomach to settle down as bile threatened to crawl up his throat. The stadium had quieted down with the break, but it felt like a roar to Sam as his heart pounded faster. *How could I not have realized I could also hurt people while I'm on the job?* Sam jogged over to the nearest trash can and vomited, unable to fight off the nausea any longer. *Sterling's career might never be the same now because of me.* Sam vomited again and wiped his mouth with the back of his hand.

He washed the taste out of his mouth with a soda and reluctantly returned to his spot in the end zone. There was nothing happening on Sam's side of the field until a big Miner's gain got them to the goal line at the end of the third quarter. On their first down play, they ran a quick slant that was broken up by the Duncan defensive back.

The two players collided as the ball fell to the turf, and they tumbled out of bounds towards the photographers. Sam jumped to his feet to move out of the way without hitting anyone, but in the process, he shattered the camera. *His* camera. The best sports camera he could ever hope to afford. The Blickon Z 2600, his dad's brand of choice, was a camera he could only afford because his mom had passed away, and the money she had saved after years of working two jobs couldn't make a dent in what the insurance wouldn't cover for her cancer. The camera was the physical embodiment of all the hopes and dreams his parents had for him. Broken beyond repair. Just like him.

The SIM card was ruined too, along with all the pictures he had taken that night. The roar of the stadium seemed to grow in volume until he felt like he was drowning in the noise as waves of sound crashed down on him from every direction. The cameras around him all seemed to be shuttering louder than a fireworks display. The in-stadium music and constant murmur of the crowd were even worse. He tried to shake his head to reset or cover his head with his hands, but none of it helped. The overhead lights, the scoreboard, and flashing camera lights all around him were suddenly brighter than he could tolerate. He tried blinking it away and squinting, but that just made him feel like the stadium had tripled in size as he stood there petrified by the sensations until he couldn't take it any longer. He tossed the remains of his camera into his bag and walked away from the end zone.

He walked through the stadium, out the doors, and back to the hotel to pack. Every nerve in his body had been numbed until he couldn't feel anything. Not the Colorado cold, not the shame of causing Sterling Lee's injury, not even the fear that had been so overwhelming moments before. He didn't realize he was at the hotel until he stood in front of his bed, the hotel room's door handle crushed in his hand. He didn't know if he had walked or run if he had taken a sidewalk or cut through a park. All he knew was that he had been at the stadium, and now he was in the room.

He dropped the piece of metal onto the bed, threw all of his luggage into his duffle, grabbed his bag, and jogged the seven miles to the airport in twenty minutes, getting there four hours before his plane was set to leave. Then he sat down and waited, rocking back and forth on the edge of his seat, waiting for the day to be over, knowing that consequences would come tomorrow but willing to speed those along if it meant ending this day any sooner.

Breathe.

Just breathe.

ELEVEN

"What good is a photographer who can't turn in a single picture to me?" Barry yelled in his office the next morning. The door was closed, but the walls were thin, and everyone in the small sports department could hear every word their editor was saying. Sam sat in the chair across from the man, staring at the floor as the words swept over him. "You think these are just vacations we're sending you on? Little getaways with free flights where you can expense a nice steak? I'm not sure if the problem is some kind of generation gap or that you haven't had to work a real job before, but if you want to keep this one, you better learn real quick how to do the job we're paying you for. I'll send the janitor with a flip phone next time if I have to. It's not like he would come back with anything less than the nothing you have for me today. If I send you to another game, which I'm strongly considering against doing, and you come back without a single picture again, you can go ahead and get your resume prepped. And I would advise against putting us down as an employer unless you want the recruiter to get my full opinion on your work, or lack thereof. Plan to be at a game on Sunday with your camera unless you hear I've changed my mind. Now get out of my office."

Everyone turned back to their computers and began typing again as Sam walked out of Barry's office. Everyone else office, but Brooklyn came up to Sam as soon as the door closed behind him.

"I'm so sorry, Sam," she said as soon as she got to him. "I'll talk to him. The steak thing was on me, and you shouldn't have that thrown back at you. I know he's angry now, but he'll calm down."

"Thanks, Brooklyn, but he wouldn't care about any of that if I had turned in those pictures. I really appreciate the offer, but I don't think there's anything you can really do to help. Nothing he's mad about had anything to do with you. I just need to go home and get some rest. I'll see you at the game as long as I'm still on the payroll come Sunday, if I'm not, thanks for everything you've done. You've been great."

"Everything will work out, Sam. I'll see you at the game on Sunday."

She rested her hand on his arm and Sam remembered how her former photographer had mentored her and how excited she was to pay it forward just two days before. Now, who knew if Sam would even make it to the next game, much less hang around long enough for Brooklyn to get to mentor him. Sam gave her a small smile and she patted his arm once before stepping aside to let him pass.

Sam grabbed his bag off the table that all the part-time photographers shared and walked to the elevator. The back of his neck prickled as he approached it. He could feel everyone in the bullpen watching him.

If I push that button, it's going to break. My heart rate is way too high to manage my strength right now. But if I take the stairs from the ninth floor, that will also look weird. I think if I jumped out the window, I could survive the fall. This isn't that much higher than how high I jumped with Taylor. I'm probably fired anyway, so I could just leave and never come back.

Sam lifted his finger and tried to take a deep breath as he reached for the button.

Ding.

The door opened as one of the basketball writers walked in. Sam stepped to the side to let him pass before taking his place in the elevator. He reached his finger out and hit the button for the ground as lightly as he could. A small crack appeared on the button, but the G lit up and the doors began to close. Sam looked up to see everyone still staring at him as the silver doors shut. He let out a deep breath and closed his eyes as the elevator started down.

It stopped three more times on the way to the ground floor. Sam tapped his legs as his eyes darted from the door to the little screen above the buttons displaying the floor they were on. He lifted himself onto his toes to stretch his calves before setting his feet back down as gently as he could. The elevator still shook under his movement, and the lights flickered, though it continued its descent. The elevator was still rocking when they reached the ground, and all four of the other passengers got off as quickly as possible while Sam exited last.

He walked through the automatic sliding door at the entrance and out into the windy fall day. Sam turned and started making his way up the sidewalk back to his apartment. He was halfway there, walking in a trance, zoned out, through the park, when a shout shook him back to reality.

A woman in front of him was shouting something about her purse. He looked to his side, and a man not much younger than him sprinted past with a bag in his hand. Instinctively, Sam reached out and grabbed the bag by its strap and pulled it back towards himself.

Pop.

A scream pierced the sky as everyone stopped to look for its source. The thief's fingertips dangled from his hand. A hand that hung limply off his wrist. His wrist was held up loosely by his forearm, which dangled off his elbow and upper arm, which had popped out of its socket in his shoulder. His arm swayed in the wind, looking boneless as everything had detached from the joints where they belonged.

The thief stared at his arm in disbelief for one second and then another before a bone-chilling howl escaped his lips. His scream continued as the people around him also began screaming. Some ran towards him to check on him, but most ran away.

Sam ran too. The panic rose so quickly and violently that his senses didn't have time to take in all of the stimuli before narrowing to the point where he could only see directly ahead and could only hear the sound of his heart pounding in his chest, desperately trying to escape from the monster he had become. He dropped the bag and took off through the park and back out onto the street the way he had come. He ran until the stores and shops turned into apartments. He sped up, and the apartments soon gave way to neighborhoods. He kept increasing his speed. He ran under the interstate overpass and was outside of the city limits in just ten minutes. And still, he kept running. The city turned into suburbs, and the suburbs turned into the countryside as he ran. Ran away from his job, ran away from the vigilantism, ran away from the man whom he had all but dismembered. He ran for thirty minutes and then thirty more. He crossed the state line and kept running. An hour and a half after he started, when he could run no more, he finally stopped.

It was the middle of the day in mid-September, and the Kansas air was heavy with humidity. Sam hadn't seen any cities or towns for miles and had only seen a couple of houses in all that time. There was a barn off the road with nothing else around, and Sam approached it cautiously. He called out as he approached the barn door, but there was no answer. Slowly, he crept in and looked around. There was hay against one wall and some equipment along another, but there wasn't anyone else there. He found the water spigot and stuck his head under it, cooling off from his run and drinking as much as he could get in his mouth. Returning to the barn, he sat in a corner covered in hay and lay down.

The moment he stopped moving, everything that had happened over the last three weeks overwhelmed him, and sobs shook his body as he cried. He'd been so caught up by how poorly everything had gone since he got his powers, he had never thought about how much luck had gone into not having caused even more pain and suffering. Every broken handle or dented piece of furniture could have been to a person instead. Sterling had only bumped into him, and he had to be rushed to the hospital. What if he had been moving too? Would Sterling be in a coma? In a morgue? He'd tried so hard to find a way to get back to normal, and he struggled through tremors of tears to wrestle with the selfishness of that focus, of putting everyone in danger so that he could try to get back something he had lost. What if he had hurt Hails? What if it had been Gwen or Taylor? Could Darlene, Harry, or Dennis have even survived a mishap? He tried to say his mantra, the one his dad had taught the anxious little boy so many years ago, but he couldn't.

Every breath he took wracked his body with shudders as he fought to inhale through his panic. He had lost every ounce of control he had ever had, unable to even control his breathing. He lay down as the short, clipped breaths refused to slow until the fatigue overtook the panic, falling asleep in the hay with tears still flowing from his eyes.

TWELVE

"Sammy, you have to get up. Sammy."

"Come on, Sam. We have to get you out of here, buddy. Let's go."

Hailey and Jason continued shaking him, but nothing worked. After five minutes without a response from being shaken, Hailey slapping his face, or Jason throwing water on him, Jason lifted Sam up from under his arms and dragged him out of the barn and back to the car. Hailey opened the back door, and Jason was able to get his torso into the backseat. He had to walk around the car to pull in the rest of him. It had been almost four hours since Sam had started running.

Thirty minutes after his meeting with Barry, one of the sports journalists filled Hailey in on what had happened. She tried texting and calling Sam but couldn't get an answer. She figured he was just upset and didn't want to talk. So, she went back to work. Then, twenty minutes later, she overheard a couple of the crime journalists talking about how a purse snatcher almost got his arm ripped off by some guy who took off immediately after the incident. Her heart dropped, knowing that only one person could have caused that. She tried Sam's phone again, but it went to voicemail. So, she tracked his phone. He was almost to the Kansas state line by that point. She immediately called Jason and told him what happened, and he left work early to take care of a "family emergency." By the time Jason picked her up and they were able to get on the road, it had already been almost two hours since Sam had started his run. The barn he'd stopped in took them another two hours to reach by car from Duncan.

Once they had arrived, Jason pulled off on the side of the road while Hailey jumped out and ran to the barn, her head whipping around looking for her cousin. She had just finished searching the outside when Jason caught up to her, and the two of them started searching the inside. Five minutes after they had split up to look, she found him curled up in the corner on a bed of hay. Jason had sprinted over to try and help wake him up before they finally gave up and loaded him into the car.

Hailey kept looking back over her shoulder at him, still asleep in the backseat, as they drove back to Duncan.

"I'm worried about him."

"I know you are, babe."

"No, like I'm really worried about him. This isn't like him. He's always been calm and reserved, and he's hurting someone and then running away like this." She shook her head, turning back to look at Jason while he drove. "It's not like him. And who knows how long he's been unconscious? We can't get him up. What if something is really wrong with him?"

"I wish I had answers for you, honey. I really do. But we're in uncharted waters here. There's no way to know what exactly is going on with his body right now, or with his mind. Taylor can guess, but that's all he's got. Whatever is wrong, we're going to try and find the answers, and I'm going to be by your side every step of the way."

He put his right hand over hers as he held the steering wheel with his left, offering her a quick smile before turning back to the road.

"I know you will," Hailey whispered as she hugged her arms around his right arm and leaned against him.

They drove in silence as Sam slept in the backseat. After crossing back into Missouri, Jason pulled off to get gas first, then to grab some lunch from a fast-food place next to the gas station. In their rush to find Sam, they hadn't had time to get lunch until now and it was already two-thirty in the afternoon. Jason ordered a meal for himself and Hailey and got a couple of extra burgers in case Sam woke up.

"Is there something I could be doing for him that I'm not?" she asked as Jason merged back onto the road. "Like, should we be taking him to someone with more experience to look at him?"

"I'm not sure," Jason answered while staring out at the road. "I don't think that's your decision to make. It might be worth bringing that up to Sam, but at the end of the day, that's going to have to be his choice."

"I just feel like I pushed him into going to Taylor and working with your team. What if that wasn't what was best for him?"

"Then he could have chosen somewhere else to go. I know it's hard not to put that weight and pressure on yourself, but you've got to trust that he's doing whatever he feels is best for him."

"I guess." She tucked her feet up under her and stared out the window as the countryside rushed by. Jason rested his hand on her knee as he drove.

They pulled into the warehouse parking lot at five-thirty that afternoon with Sam still asleep in the backseat. Lance was standing outside to meet them as they came to a stop. Together, they worked to get Sam from the car, into the warehouse, and onto a bed for Taylor to examine him when he got back from class.

Jason took Hailey to get her laptop from the office. She was going to hang out at the warehouse until Sam woke up and needed to catch up on some of the work she had missed during the drive. Taylor would be there by the time they got back to check the White Knight monitor and take a look at Sam. After Hailey filled Gwen in on what had happened, Gwen insisted on bringing dinner to the warehouse.

Everyone was there when Hailey and Jason returned. Taylor stood at the bed next to Sam with his clipboard in hand while Lance helped Gwen unpack the takeout. With Sam hanging out at the warehouse more and the girls now being in on the secret, Taylor had searched the warehouse and found a second couch being stored and brought it out into the area they used along with a couple of coffee tables, a tv, and DVD player that had been left.

"Is he okay?" Hailey asked as she joined Taylor by the bedside while Jason walked over to where Gwen and Lance sat on the couches.

"I think so," Taylor answered, laying his clipboard down. "His heart rate is slow with him being asleep, but other than that, all his vitals are where they were the last time I looked at him. Hopefully, once he wakes up, I'll be able to get some more answers. Until then, there's not a whole lot we can do."

"Okay..." Hailey's voice trailed off as she rested a hand on Sam's arm while Taylor walked to join the others. After a moment, she walked over to join them, too.

Gwen left to meet a client not long after they'd finished dinner, and Lance had to work a concert for a couple of hours before returning to be the White Knight. Taylor and Jason watched the monitors as Hailey sat by Sam's side. Lance showed back up at the warehouse at one in the morning to check for updates, but the White Knight monitor had been quiet, and Sam still hadn't woken up. Lance helped Jason move the two couches by Sam's bedside so that Jason and Hailey could sleep on them before Lance and Taylor left for the night.

Jason curled into a ball under one of the blankets Taylor had given them and was asleep not long after they'd locked up, but Hailey couldn't sleep. She sat in the dark listening to Jason's snores and Sam's shallow breathing for hours until she finally fell asleep just after four in the morning.

chapter

THIRTEEN

The clipboard clattered to the ground as Sam woke with a start and knocked it off the table next to him. Hailey jolted upright as he sat up in the bed, his head whipping around to take in his surroundings. Jason sat up, rubbing his eyes.

"Sammy, it's okay," Hailey whispered as she walked over to rest her right hand on his arm. "Jason and I brought you back to the warehouse. You're safe now."

Sam started crying as she spoke, holding his head in his hands. Hailey put her arm around his back and held him as he shook. Jason waved to catch her attention and motioned that he was going to go get them some food. She nodded before turning back to Sam as Jason backed away towards the door.

"You're safe now, Sammy," she told him again, squeezing his arm.

"But no one else is," Sam responded. His voice was hoarse and dry after sleeping for eighteen hours straight.

Hailey handed him a bottle of water that Gwen had left on the table the night before.

"What do you mean?"

"I mean that no one is safe from me," he croaked, taking a big drink of water. "I almost took a guy's arm off yesterday by just trying to grab a bag out of his hand. Two nights ago, I ended the season of a professional football player whom I didn't even realize had run into me until he was lying on the ground holding his leg. Who knows who I am going to end up hurting today or tomorrow? You, Gwen, or one of the guys could be next. Or what if it's Darlene next? Or Harry? Or Dennis? Could they even survive that? I'm a walking hazard to everyone around me. I can't live like this."

Hailey shook her head. "Sammy, that's not true. You c —"

"It is true, Hailey," he sobbed. "You can't deny it. If I bump into someone or forget that I shouldn't shake anyone's hand, I can't even sneeze, or people might get hurt. One hundred percent of my focus and concentration has to go towards making sure I'm not killing someone. I'm a weapon with no safety lock. That's my entire life right now. It's too much. It's exhausting and I just can't keep doing it."

"Samson Hall," Hailey said as Sam buried his head in his hands again. "You are the gentlest person I know. You are not a weapon. Yes, your new strength has its drawbacks, but you are still you. You're still my favorite cousin, Sammy. I've known you my whole life. We're going to figure out how to help you manage your strength better. It's going to be okay."

"No, it's not," Sam sighed, lifting his head back out of his hands. He lay back down on the bed and balled his hands together, resting them on his forehead. "I'm broken, Hails. I can't control this. It's too much. I'm a danger to everyone. I need to leave. To go far away, alone, so I won't hurt anyone. It's the only way."

"It's not the only way, Sam. We can figure this out."

Sam exhaled. "Too many people would get hurt while we figured it out. It's not worth it."

"Of course you are worth it, Sammy."

Sam clenched his eyes shut, and Hailey's heart ached as she watched the tears make it to his eyelashes but no further. The door slammed as Taylor walked into the warehouse.

"How are you feeling, Sam? I'm going to have you take a couple of the tests we've done in the past so I can see if your sleeping so long had a cause," he said, walking up to the bed.

"Fine," Sam answered with his hands still on his forehead.

"Not fine," Hailey said without taking her eyes from Sam. "He thinks he has to leave to protect people."

"Absolutely not," Taylor answered, looking over at Sam. "You need to stay here where we can make sure your body doesn't continue to change and be a support group for you. We have no idea if the changes will continue. You could put yourself and others in even more danger if you go somewhere else."

"I won't be going anywhere where there are other people. And if something is able to actually hurt me, then at least I'll know I can still feel something." Sam stood up and took the cup from the table next to him before walking to the bathroom.

"I'm worried about him, Taylor," Hailey said while she watched Sam walk away.

"The last couple of days have been traumatic for him. He needs some time to process. He'll be okay."

"I hope you're right," she sighed as Taylor started preparing the area to do his tests on Sam.

Jason walked in with two bags of takeout as Taylor swabbed Sam's mouth, his last test.

"Perfect timing." Hailey smiled at Jason as he set the bags down on the coffee table. Sam and Hailey walked over to join him while Taylor made notes on his clipboard.

"Here's your French toast, Hailey," Jason said, pulling a box out of the bag. "This one is Taylor's pancakes. Sam, I asked Darlene what you usually got, and she said you switched between two, so I just got you both since I figured you'd be hungry. Here's the waffles," Sam took the box from Jason as he reached back in for the other, "and here's the sampler."

"Thanks." Sam took the boxes from Jason and immediately began eating.

Jason looked up at Hailey and tilted his head, furrowing his eyebrows. Hailey gave a small smile with her lips, but her eyes were still misty.

"Where's your food?" Hailey asked as she picked up her box.

"I got a breakfast burrito that I ate on the way," he answered. "Only at stop lights, I promise!" he added after Hailey raised her eyebrows at him.

"How are you feeling, Sam?" Jason asked as Sam put down his empty sampler box to grab the waffles.

"I'm okay."

"Really? That's good. We were a little worried about you, what with running a hundred and fifty miles away and then sleeping for eighteen hours."

Sam lifted his eyes to stare at Jason without lifting his head from where he had been eating. After a couple of seconds, he went back to his waffles without answering Jason.

Hailey tilted her head towards Sam and widened her eyes at Jason, signaling him to keep pushing.

Jason sighed before asking, "What happened yesterday, Sam? How did you end up in a barn off the road in the middle of Kansas?"

Sam set his empty waffle container back down on the table and leaned back into the couch.

"A guy stole a lady's purse when I was walking home yesterday. I was already pretty upset after getting yelled at by my boss. Anyways, I saw the guy running by with the purse and instinctively reached out to grab the purse from him. Pretty much everything in his left arm was disconnected from what it was supposed to be connected to. All I did was grab the bag; I hadn't even been trying to hurt him, and I caused that much damage. I dropped the bag and started running until I couldn't run anymore. The last thing I remember was drinking water from a spout outside the barn, then falling asleep in the hay.

"You know that's not your fault, right?" Jason asked. "If that guy hadn't stolen the purse, he would have never gotten hurt. That's not on you."

"He might never be able to use that arm again, Jason. That hardly seems like a fair price to pay for a stolen bag."

"Maybe so, but it was his action that caused it to happen. You were only doing the right thing."

"You don't get it, man. The right things aren't the same for me anymore. If I can rip someone's arm off by grabbing a bag, then it's not the right thing now. The only right thing for me to do is move far, far away where I can't hurt anyone else."

"You're being too hard on yourself," Jason told him.

"Jason's right, Sam," Taylor added.

"I need to go for a walk and clear my head. I'll see all of you later." Sam stood and gave Hailey a small smile before walking out the door.

He didn't have a plan in mind for where he would go, so he just started wandering. *I have to leave,* he thought. *It's the only way to protect everyone. I'm sure I can make it alright, living away from people. Put that scout training to use. Live up in the woods and just live off the land somewhere in the north. Run into towns nearby to get supplies or books to keep me entertained. Better than having to constantly worry about killing someone.*

Sam had been locked in on his thoughts and hadn't realized he had already walked out of the city. He turned around to start walking back as an old truck came up the road towards him. The truck slowed to a stop as it neared, and the passenger window slowly rolled down.

"Need a ride?" Lance asked from the driver's seat, sitting back up after cranking the window down.

"I think I'm alright," Sam answered as he began walking back. Lance turned his car around on the empty road and caught up to Sam.

"It wasn't really a request. Hop in. I want to talk to you."

Great.

Lance leaned over and pushed the door open so Sam didn't have to put any effort into not ripping the door off, which was good because he wasn't sure if he'd have put that effort in or if he'd had to open it himself. He stared out the window as Lance started driving again.

"I heard that you feel the best way to keep people safe is to push everyone away and go off on your own."

"Something like that." It was one thing to have this conversation with Hailey or even Taylor, but he didn't particularly care to have to explain himself to Lance.

"I've been there. Before anyone knew my secret, I tried really hard to push everyone away. Jason, Taylor, Hailey, even Gwen. I thought if I could do it by myself, then they wouldn't have to worry about me, and they wouldn't share the danger I was in. No one would get hurt because of me. But as you can see, that didn't work. They knew the risks. They saw all of that. But they still stayed. We can't do this by ourselves. We can't do this alone. You've got to let people in, Sam."

"You don't get it." He shook his head and closed his eyes as Lance talked.

"I think I can understand it better than most. I may not have your strength, but I definitely get the feeling that I'm dangerous to those around me and thinking the only way to keep them safe is to distance myself. I've accidentally hurt criminals worse than I intended to, too. I dislocated a guy's elbow with my nightstick before I even had the sword. But he was going to hurt someone else if I didn't. That's not on our conscience. We have to be able to brush those things off."

"No, Lance, you don't get it." Sam turned away from the window to stare at Lance while he drove. "There is no we. We are not the same. You deciding to throw on a mask and beat people up doesn't make you understand what I'm going through right now. You can stop at any time. You can choose not to hurt people. I am a danger to everyone I come in contact with, whether I want to be or not. Stop the car."

"What? Hold on—"

"Stop the car. I'm getting out."

"No. Let's just talk th—"

"It wasn't a request. Stop the car." He turned away from Lance as he started to talk again.

"No, we—"

Lance's thought was interrupted by the wind rushing into the cab of his truck through the hole where his passenger door had been. Sam stood up and dusted himself off as the wheels of Lance's truck squealed to a stop behind him. Sam ignored the chorus of honking horns as he walked down the nearest side street, leaving Lance, and Lance's car door he had broken off in his escape, in the street behind him.

chapter

FOURTEEN

The bell above the door rang as a couple walked out of Fran's. Sam thanked the man who held it open for him and, after seeing the bar was crowded, walked to a corner booth.

"What can I get for you today, sugar?" Darlene asked, walking up to the table.

"Burger with fries and a sweet tea. Thanks, Darlene."

"No problem, honey. It's good to see you."

"Always good to see you, too, Darlene." Sam smiled back at her.

"You doing okay?"

"Eh. Not really. It's been a tough stretch these last few days. Have you ever felt like the best thing for everyone is for you to just leave?"

"I can't say I have. Harry and Dennis would be lost without me. This place wouldn't last a week. But I can understand how sometimes those feelings can block out the facts. You're right where you need to be, Sammy.

We'd sure miss having you around." She patted his arm and took his order back to Dennis.

Harry walked over to the table as Darlene ducked behind the counter with his order.

"Sam the man," Harry growled as he sat down in the booth opposite him. "How was Cameron City? Did you try any of the steakhouses?"

"Actually, I did," Sam laughed. "One of the writers, Brooklyn Jones, took me to one of our first nights in town. It was incredible."

"That's good! Nothing like a Nick's steak. Stringer House is great too."

"We went to Stringer on Sunday. I guess—"

"Nick's is closed on Sundays." Harry shook his head. "But Stringer is great too. They have the best potatoes you'll find."

"I didn't realize you knew so much about Cameron City."

"When I was a younger man, I traveled a lot for my job; I was in sales. Cameron City was one of my favorites."

"When you were traveling, did you ever feel like everybody was better off when you were gone?"

"Course not," Harry growled before laughing. "Most times, I was much more worried that I was gone too long. As much as I love traveling and being in new and different cities, if Darlene weren't with me, the only thing I wanted was to get back home. All those other things don't mean much at all if you don't have people to come back and share them with."

"Yeah, I guess you're right," Sam mumbled.

"Course I'm right. I don't have a head full of grey hair for nothing," Harry laughed again.

The door rang as an older man walked into the bar.

"Sam," Harry said after looking at the door, "you'll have to excuse me for a bit. That's an old friend from out of town. But we'll catch up on everything soon. Love ya, kid." He patted Sam's hand and walked over to embrace the man.

Sam rested his head on the table while he waited for his food. *Hailey will let them know I'm gone,* he thought as the door rang again. *At least I can't hurt them if I'm gone.*

"Mind if I join you?"

Sam lifted his head to see Gwen standing at the table.

"Be my guest." He motioned at the end of the seat. "I assume you've talked to the others this morning."

"I have."

"Well, let's hear your speech telling me why I can't leave. I've heard everyone else's."

"I don't have a speech." She said sitting down. "I just came to say goodbye."

She didn't have her bag with her, but Sam knew she had just finished work. Locks of sandy hair had fallen out of her braid, and her eyeliner had been slightly smeared. He'd heard Taylor point it out to her one day, only for her to tell him that it happened every day and that if she ever went a full day of work without tearing up, it would be the first. And yet, she was sitting across the table from him without even stopping at home.

"You're not going to tell me you understand what I'm going through or that if I'm patient, everything will just happen to turn out okay?"

Gwen furrowed her brows and shook her head. "I'm not. Of course, I don't understand what you're going through. As far as I know, no one has ever really understood what you're going through right now."

"Lance might disagree with you on that," Sam scoffed, looking out the window.

"Lance"—Gwen paused, lifted up the saltshaker, and twirled it in her hands as she chose her words. "Lance is an incredibly sympathetic and compassionate person. He cares about people a lot. But" —she set the salt back down—"he has basically no empathy. As hard as he tries, he has a really difficult time seeing things from others' perspectives. And that's a flaw that is highly visible whenever he gives advice, because if he can't relate it to something he's been through, he can't even really process how to go about helping. So, he tries to shoehorn it into something he has experienced. He means well and wants to help, but it often ends with his foot in his mouth."

"That's an understatement."

Sam saw a smile tug at the corner of Gwen's lips, and his shoulders relaxed, if only slightly. "And sometimes things don't turn out okay. As patient as we can be, some things are wrong and broken, and that's just part of life. They don't always get better."

"You really didn't come here for a pep talk, did you? I didn't believe what people were telling me earlier, but at least they didn't also think I was hopeless." It was bad enough having those thoughts in his head. Hearing Gwen confirm them aloud made his stomach feel like he had swallowed a bowling ball.

Gwen tilted her head to stare at him, furrowing her brows again. "I don't think you're hopeless, Sam. That's not what I was saying at all."

"Then what were you saying?"

"That your feelings are valid, and the attempts to convince you to stay weren't super helpful or true. Especially since they all miss what the problem is."

"And you know what my problem is?"

"More so than the others? I think so."

Sam lifted his eyebrows and couldn't fight the small smile on his lips as he answered. "Then tell me, what's the problem that everyone else missed?"

"They all missed it because they were focused on your strength and how that power is causing you to think you have to leave."

"And that's not the case?"

"I don't think so. I don't think you having too much power is the problem. I think the problem is that you feel powerless. Broken. Like nothing about your body or life is in your control anymore. And I think that scares you because you don't know how to live when you can't even control your own body."

"Oh." Sam looked out the window to the side as a couple passed with a kid sitting on the dad's shoulders. Sam reached for the saltshaker Gwen had played with earlier, but thought better of it. He didn't like being misunderstood by everyone else, but being understood might have actually felt worse. All the insecurities and fears hiding in his inner monologue were now out in the open, and he wasn't even the one saying them.

"Am I close?" Gwen asked, her voice forcing him to look back at her.

"How did you know?"

"Two reasons." She picked up the saltshaker again, pointing it at him to emphasize points as she talked. "One is that I've actually been listening to what you've said the last couple of weeks whenever you've talked about it. I'm not a hero or someone who covers them. I didn't immediately start thinking about possibilities when I heard you talk about your strength, so I was able to hear what you were actually saying. Secondly, I know what it's like to feel powerless, broken. To feel like I have no control over my body."

"What do you mean?"

"Last December, I was assaulted while walking home from studying at the library. I had to be taken to the hospital. I felt like I was broken. That other people could choose what happened to my body without me having a say. I felt lost and powerless."

"Gwen, I'm so sorry." He hated how Lance had thought he could relate to Sam's problem because he chose to be a hero, but he also didn't feel like he could compare what he was going through with what Gwen had endured. He had lost control, but he didn't have someone take that from him the way she did, and for the first time in a month, he felt forced to really take a step back and to remember that all of life was not, in fact, orbiting around his problem. "I didn't know that had happened to you."

"I don't like to talk about it," she answered quietly with a soft smile, glancing over her shoulder at the door as the bell rang when a customer walked in.

"That's what you meant when you said some things never become okay, wasn't it?"

"In part, yes. That's certainly one of those things. Sometimes people want to talk about the bright sides or good things that come from something bad, like that, as if that makes it okay that the thing happened. No matter what comes of it, it will never be okay what happened to me. And I understand if you feel the same about what happened to you. Only you can choose how this makes you feel. And only you can choose how to handle it."

"What about you? How did you handle it?"

"A few ways." Gwen gestured with the saltshaker in her hand again. "Therapy for starters. I took some self-defense classes, so I didn't feel as powerless. Luckily, I went to therapy early enough that my initial instinct to push people away was stopped before I had a chance to go through with it. Without Hailey, without Taylor, Jason, and Lance, I would've spiraled. Having them to lean on has been really important. And it's something I'm still working through. And it's not linear. But I'm better than I was three months ago, which was better than I was three months before that."

"So, what you are saying is you think I should stay?" Sam felt the bowling ball in his stomach lighten a few pounds. What she went through filled him with anger and sadness, but it also reminded him he wasn't the only one who had problems. His ability to be compassionate had always been important to him, and he'd been completely numb to everyone else's problems since he got his powers, because he had been so focused on himself. That realization came with a deal of shame, but that was also something he could address. He might not be able to change his power problem, but his compassion problem? That he could fix.

"I think only you can really know what is best for Sam right now." Gwen set the saltshaker in his hand.

"You asked what worked for me. But it's up to you what to do next."

Darlene set Sam's food down in front of him and turned to Gwen.

"What can I get you, sugar?"

"Thanks Darlene, but I was just about to leave. Just wanted to talk to Sam real quick," she answered, standing as Darlene walked back to the kitchen. "Just think about it," she told him before turning to leave. After a couple steps she stopped and turned back. "And if you decide to leave, just know it's been really nice being your friend, Sam Hall." She gave him a smile before turning back to the door.

It took a concentrated effort, but Sam set the salt-shaker back on the table unharmed and watched through the front window as Gwen walked past.

Sam opened the door to the warehouse later that afternoon to find the five of them there, a movie playing on the TV. Jason and Hailey were curled up on the couch. Gwen sat on the floor, leaning against the sofa in front of Hailey. Taylor was sitting at his computer, one screen cycling through security feeds while he used another to study. Lance closed the door to the old fridge they had set up behind Taylor's computers and was walking back towards the TV when the door closed behind Sam, and everyone turned to look.

After his conversation with Gwen, he finished his lunch and went for a walk to think about what she had said. She had been the first one to make him feel seen since his strength had changed. She was the first one to actually vocalize what he was feeling back to him. *If Gwen could make it through what happened to her,* he thought to himself, sitting on a hill in the park next to his apartment, looking out on the pond, *maybe I can too.* He shook his head. Gwen might understand his brokenness, but she wasn't putting everyone around her in danger by staying. *There may be a few people I could help with my strength, but how many more would I end up hurting?*

Sam had leaned his head back on the grass and let out a deep breath. *Breathe,* he'd reminded himself, *just breathe.* He had sat back up and felt something on the back of his hand. Looking down, he saw a caterpillar crawling across his hand. Gently as he could, being mindful of his breathing, as he had practiced with Lance, he'd reached over and picked up the caterpillar, placing it in his palm as he leaned back onto his other arm.

The caterpillar crawled around on his hand, unharmed. As it had crawled up his thumb, Sam secured it with his pointer finger and set it back on the hillside where it crawled away. He had smiled as he watched it inch away unharmed.

"I'll stay," he announced to the warehouse as everyone watched him.

"You will?" Hailey exclaimed, jumping off the couch and shouldering Jason in the process.

Jason rubbed his jaw while patting the couch to find the remote to pause the movie. He stood and joined Gwen, a few feet behind Hailey, who had buried her head in Sam's chest with a hug.

Sam smiled as his cousin squeezed him, but didn't dare to hug back. Lance sat down on the table separating Taylor's area from the couches, and Taylor rolled his chair over next to Lance to join the group.

Hailey finally released Sam from her hug and wiped at her eyes.

"What changed your mind?" Jason asked, wrapping his arm around Hailey's shoulders as she lay her head against his chest, still beaming at Sam.

"Just realizing that I don't have to be alone in this, I guess. I never wanted to be alone, but I thought that was my only option. A friend helped me see that wasn't true." Gwen returned his smile as he paused. "Here, where I have people I can lean on, is where I should be. That's what's right for me."

"We're glad to still have you around." Lance smiled, standing from the table, and he and Taylor stood to join the others.

"I'm really sorry about your truck, Lance."

"Don't be," Hailey and Jason responded at the same time.

Lance laughed, "It was just as much my fault. I was being stubborn, and I should have stopped to let you get out. It was probably time for a new car anyway. My Hoppin' rating was pretty low because people always complained about my car. I'll just ride the White Knight motorcycle until I get a new one."

"Speaking of the White Knight, I've been thinking. I keep thinking of my strength as destructive, but I want to bring healing with it instead and start viewing my strength through that lens. So, if it's still on the table, I'd like to join the team. Even if I don't want these powers, now that I have them, I guess I have a duty to help those in need. So I'm in."

"Yes!" Jason shouted. "That's what I'm talking about! I just finished up your everyday protective equipment, and now I can start to work on my favorite project: making some new hero gear."

"What Jason is trying to say is that we'd love to have you on the team, Sam," Taylor said, reaching up to put a hand on Jason's shoulder.

"So." Sam let out a deep breath. "What's next?"

"We keep practicing with you to control your new strength," Lance answered. "We're thrilled to have you on board, but there's still a lot of work to be done before you're ready to go into the field. You know better than we do that what happened with the thief the other day can't be the norm."

Sam nodded, but didn't say anything. Taylor picked up where Lance left off.

"You and Lance will keep working through those self-control exercises. Jason will work on making you some gear that will hopefully make it easier for you to go out without being afraid of killing someone. I'll show you how our systems work, though now that I think about it, we may need Jason to also make you a reinforced before we do that."

"And," Hailey said, "Gwen and I will make sure they don't go overboard on you."

"We're glad you changed your mind, Sam." Gwen smiled.

"Me too. And I'm ready to start with those exercises whenever you are, Lance."

"The two of you can start that tomorrow," Hailey asserted. "Tonight is movie night."

"When she's right, she's right," Jason laughed as the two of them returned to their spot on the couch. Gwen squeezed Sam's arm and then returned to the floor in front of Hailey. Lance sat at the end of the couch, in the chair he'd pulled from in front of the locker.

"You gonna join us or not?" Jason asked Sam as he picked up the remote.

"On my way." Sam smiled, sitting in front of the couch and leaning back against it a few feet away from Gwen.

"You too, Taylor," Gwen called out to Taylor, who'd gone back to his computer already.

"I have to study and watch the monitors, " he answered without looking over his shoulder.

"You study too much. You could use a break," Gwen argued.

"And," Lance added, "the White Knight rarely sees any action on a Wednesday night. We have the alarm set up. We'll know if something happens. Come on, Taylor."

"Taylor, come on," Gwen said.

A chorus of "Taylor" and "Tay" and "come on" filled the room as all five tried to convince him to join them in front of the tv.

"Fine," he sighed as the rest of them cheered, "not like I'd be able to remember anything while you all harass me."

"That's the spirit," Jason laughed as he picked up the remote to hit play, and Taylor rolled his chair up to the side of the couch.

The movie began playing again as Taylor came to a stop, and the sound from the speakers filled the silence that had fallen between the six of them as they all settled in for movie night.

FIFTEEN

"That's enough for today," Lance panted. He grabbed a towel to wipe the sweat that was dripping from his hair and clinging to his forehead.

"If you say so." Sam shrugged. A week had gone by since he decided to stay, and the constant training had greatly improved his stamina. While Lance collapsed on the bench, drenched in sweat after their training session, Sam didn't have a single bead of sweat on him. His body was adjusting to the strenuous exercises much quicker than it would have before the change.

He walked over to the water fountain as Lance sprawled out to lie across the bench, his groan causing Sam to laugh as he walked away. The game on Sunday had gone well enough. He used his camera from his first post-college job. It was still a Blickon, but the X 2100 was far less sharp than the Z 2600. Still, Barry was cordial in their meeting that morning and hadn't threatened to fire him, so that was something. After getting a drink, he walked over to Taylor, who sat at his computer.

"How's studying going?" Sam asked, pulling up a chair and sitting down.

"Oh, it's going," Taylor sighed, leaning back in his chair and pinching the bridge of his nose.

"That good, huh?" Sam chuckled.

"I studied in college, but not like this," Taylor answered, sitting back up and swiveling to face Sam.

"What do you mean?"

"I mean that in college, I studied hard to make sure I had every last detail memorized. I knew I wanted to go to med school, and I didn't want to leave anything to chance, so I made sure I was as close to perfect as I could be. In four years, I had one final grade that was lower than a ninety-six. It was a ninety-three in my understanding music class. I could have studied half as much and still graduated with at least a 3.8 GPA, which would have been good enough. But I didn't want to be good enough, I wanted to be the best. But now"—Taylor sighed again and gestured at his textbook—"now I'm studying more than I did as an undergrad, and I feel like I'm barely keeping my head above the water. I don't know if this is harder than I thought it would be, or if maybe I'm just not as smart as I thought I was, or both. No matter which one, it's kind of a shock to my sense of self. Everyone always thinks I'm humble because

I'm quiet, but I've just never felt like I had to say that I was the smartest in the room for everyone to figure that out. That pride has always been a major source of confidence, but now I don't know that I'm the smartest person in the room anymore, and it sounds silly, but it kind of scares me. Like, if I'm not the person I thought I was, what am I? You know?"

"Do I know what it's like to be the smartest person in every room I've ever walked into, then feel like that's taken away from me? No. I graduated with a 3.1, and I was super proud of that feat. I could have studied five times as much as I did and still not gotten a 3.8, let alone a 4.0. But do I know what it's like to think of yourself one way and then suddenly have that perception forced to radically change sometime in the last two months? I mean." Sam reached his arms out and shrugged, causing Taylor to laugh.

"Yeah, I guess you do know about that."

"Taylor, you're still the smartest in every room. Part of why you're struggling is that you're a superhero now and don't have the same time and energy to dedicate to your studies."

"I'm not the hero. Those guys do all the superhero things. I just sit at a computer."

"Nonsense. Both of them would literally be dead without you. Lance alone would have found a way to somehow die four or five times by now."

They both paused to turn and look as Lance groaned again at the sound of his name, still face down on his towel on the bench.

Turning back to face Taylor again, Sam continued, "You are one hundred percent the same level of hero that those two are. And look at the free medical attention and research you're using to try and help me. None of those other med students are also trying to figure out an unprecedented change in the human body like you are right now. You have to give yourself some more grace, man. You're doing incredible, and everyone who sees you working would agree."

"He's right," Lance added, finally getting up from the bench. "About all of it. You're just as much a part of everything the White Knight and Ironside do as Jason and I are. We'd be toast without you. You're doing great, bud. And if you ever feel like you're overextending and not focusing on your school enough, let us know. Jason and I can switch off going in the field and watching the monitors. Once Sam's ready, he can join the rotation. I'm sure Gwen and Hailey would love to fill in for you to give you a breather to study, too, now that they're part of the team. We're all here for you." He clapped Taylor on the shoulder as he finished.

"I appreciate that, but how have you sat on that bench for ten minutes with a towel and are still sweaty enough for it to seep through my shirt when you touch me?" Taylor asked, pulling the wet fabric away from his skin.

"Well, it was a nice moment," Lance said, turning away. "I'm going to take a shower and take a nap to get ready for tonight."

Lance walked towards the door with a half-salute to Sam and Taylor.

"I should probably head out too," Sam said. "I'm still on a short leash with the paper, but I'm getting another shot this weekend, and I fly out in a few hours. I should finish packing. And I'm here for you if you ever need to talk or process, seriously."

"I appreciate that, and I'll keep it in mind. Thanks for listening."

"Of course, dude. Anytime."

They looked over to the door, which closed behind Jason, who had carried in a box.

"Lance looks and smells like he swam through a sewer," he joked as he set the box down.

"He put his hand on my shirt before he left, and I think there's some fungus already growing on me."

"I was just about to head out," Sam said, grabbing his bag.

"Well then, I'm glad I caught you. I come bearing gifts." Jason beamed, setting the box down.

"What do you mean?"

"It means I've made some new toys." Jason bounced up and down on his toes as he reached into the box and pulled out the first item. "To start, here's a new phone case that should be able to withstand your new strength without breaking while still responding to the touch screen." He handed the small box over for Sam to look at before going back into the larger box. "Next is a new remote for you to use to watch TV without fear. Then I have new fixtures and gadgets for everything in your house to make it usable for you. New sink and shower handles, doorknobs, microwave button panel, even a grip for the fridge and reinforced hinges for every door."

"Jason, this is incredible." Sam stared at him. His eyes glistened, but hadn't started watering. Not yet, at least.

"I saved the best for last." He beamed again. Taylor coughed, and Jason rephrased. "Sorry, we saved the best for last." Reaching back into the box, Jason pulled out a perfect shell for his camera. "This covers the entire camera without obstructing the lens in any way. If you so much as dent or scratch your camera with this bad boy on it, I'll give you your money back, guaranteed."

"Jason. It's—it's amazing. It's perfect. But I don't have the camera this was made for anymore, that's what I crushed two weeks ago. I don't think it'll fit around the 2100 I'm using. I'm so sorry for making you go through all of that work for nothing."

"That's where I come in," Taylor said, standing from his chair and grabbing a box from behind the computer. "I didn't want to give it to you until I knew Jason had finished the shell." He handed the box over to Sam.

It was a Blickon Z 2600, the exact same camera Sam had broken. The camera he'd saved for and dreamed of for so long. His parents' dreams for him in physical form. He didn't even try to stop the tears now as they poured down his face at his friend's generosity.

"I don't know what to say. You have no idea what this camera means to me. I-I would hug you, but I can't."

"We'll hug you then," Jason laughed as he and Taylor wrapped their arms around Sam. He laughed and wiped at the tears on his face as they let go.

"Thank you, guys, so much. I can't begin to describe what you did for me," he told them again, still wiping his eyes.

"Of course!" Jason answered again, clapping his shoulder. "You're back, baby!"

SIXTEEN

"We're going to try something new today," Lance said as they walked to the mat for their training on Tuesday. Sam had gotten in early Monday morning, and Lance had taken a couple of hard hits Sunday night, stopping a mugging, so they decided Monday would be a rest day. Sam's weekend trip had been a success without a single issue coming up as the Dutchmen tallied another win. He didn't even have to use the packing peanuts. Jason's shell worked as promised. Barry had still been cold towards him during their meeting on Monday, but Sam was scheduled to work this week's home game, so that was something.

"Today, we're going to actually start working on fighting."

"You sure that's a good idea, Lance? I'm getting better at controlling my strength, but I don't think I'm ready to fight someone. I could really hurt you."

"Oh, you're not fighting me. No way. Absolutely not. I like living. And you're not going to be doing any offensive moves anyway. No, I'm going to use the dummies we have to teach you some defensive maneuvers you can use until you have enough control over your strength to do more."

"Okay, let's try it then," Sam answered, settling into the center of the mat.

Lance nodded and walked a few steps away, towards the bench. He turned and stared intently at him. Before Sam could figure out why, he was engulfed in a cloud of sand as a dummy bag hit his back and exploded. He coughed, waving his hand in front of his face to clear the air of the sand.

"Lance!" Taylor yelled from across the warehouse, jumping up and walking towards them while Sam's vision was still obstructed. "Why didn't you talk to me about this? I could have saved the punching bag and the money it'll cost me to replace it by telling you how dumb your idea was."

"I had to see what would happen."

"This was the only thing that could have happened!"

The sand all settled around Sam as Taylor walked back to the computer, shaking his head.

"First lesson is to always be aware of your surroundings. That dummy had been up there since before you got here. Next lesson is on stances."

Sam watched as the dummy, or the little canvas that remained of it, swayed from the wire Lance had used to secure it to the rafters. Lance walked him through a series of poses, pausing each time to demonstrate and talk through the benefits and scenarios where each would be helpful.

"The big thing with you," Lance explained, "will be letting them hurt themselves by hitting you. You're strong enough that they're not going to be able to inflict any pain on you, but when they try, you'll be able to hurt them without being afraid of dismembering them. And, if a situation comes up like a couple weeks ago where you need to stop someone, you're fast enough to cut them off, beat them to the spot, and again let them do your work for you. It'll be like they ran into a wall. Painful, sure, but not life-threatening."

Sam nodded along as Lance talked. After they had walked through a handful of positions, Lance told him to choose one and get ready. Lance retrieved a pole with a boxing glove on one end and feinted with it, having Sam react by changing his stance before swinging it into him, snapping the pole.

"Give me a sec," Lance told Sam, lifting a finger and jogging off towards the other side of the warehouse. Sam walked over to take a drink of water while he waited.

"Absolutely not!"

Sam stood back up from the water fountain as Taylor's voice boomed through the warehouse.

"It's fine," Lance answered. Sam began following the sound of their voices. They were back at the lockers, and he couldn't see them from the mat.

"It's not fine, and I'm not going to pay for you to be an idiot. And I'm not going to have Jason fix it either. Find another way."

"There's not another way without me getting hurt."

"Well then, if that's true, I guess you'll just have to get hurt," Taylor said as Sam walked around the corner to see Lance with the bottom half of his White Knight suit while Taylor held the top half away from him. "You're not going to destroy your suit for no good reason. Literally nothing will come from you doing this."

"Fine," Lance huffed, unstrapping the bottoms. "Sorry, Sam, training is over today. Not much more we can work on like this. You did great. I need to go get some rest to be ready for tonight. I'll see you at dinner." He grabbed his bag and walked out the door.

"Is he okay?" Sam asked as he followed Taylor back to the computer.

"He's fine. When he's in the field, he's patient and makes wise and thoughtful decisions. When he's not in the field, he's impatient and impulsive. For some reason, he and Jason switch personalities when they put on the suit. Probably just to make it harder for me," Taylor chuckled as he sat back down. "No, he'll be fine tonight.

Sometimes he gets worked up, but he doesn't hold grudges against anyone but himself."

"I can understand that." Sam looked over at the locker where the white suit sat in sharp contrast to the dark stained wood. He was causing Taylor to spend enough money and making Jason to fix enough things without adding a super suit to the tally.

"I think he's mainly frustrated because he can't figure out how to best train you. Your strength has incredible benefits in helping people, but it also makes it incredibly difficult to practice without breaking whatever is being used for practice. He thought his suit could withstand your strength enough to test out some of what you two were working on, but that's too expensive a gamble to take on a hunch. We'll talk with Jason and try to bring him in to help train. A fresh perspective should help."

"That'll be good. It feels like you three really complement each other well. Skills-wise and personality-wise."

"Skills-wise, definitely. Personality can be a bit trickier. Sometimes our differences work great and function as a checks and balances system that keeps everything running smoothly. Other times, it leads to tensions that can take a few days to settle down. Luckily, we've all been together long enough that there's a trust between us that can weather a few days of tension."

Sam nodded as Taylor talked. *Must be nice.*

"I'm going to head back to the house to rest as well. These training sessions always drain me afterwards, even if I'm not working up a sweat for some reason. I'll see you at dinner."

"Sounds good, Sam. See you then." Taylor turned back to his computer as Sam walked into the bright afternoon sunlight, preparing himself for a warm jog.

Fran's was livelier than usual as Sam arrived for dinner. The diner was packed, and everyone there did their best to talk over the other tables around them so they could be heard, causing the room to buzz. He turned to the right and found Hailey and Gwen already at their usual table, sitting on opposite sides of the booth.

"Hey Sam." Gwen greeted him with a smile as he walked up and slid further into the booth for him.

"Sammy!" Hailey turned her head to see his approach.

"I'm glad y'all got here early. This place is packed," Sam said as he sat down next to Gwen.

"Darlene knew we were coming tonight since I swung by for some afternoon coffee, so she conveniently didn't clear the table until she saw us come in," Hailey laughed.

Sam smiled and shook his head as Darlene caught his eye from across the room and gave him a thumbs up which he returned.

"How's your world going?" he asked Gwen as Darlene began taking another table's order.

"Exhausting," Gwen groaned, throwing her arms out on the table and putting her face down in between them.

"She's had a tough week," Hailey said, patting the back of Gwen's head.

"It's Tuesday?"

"I've had a tough week," Gwen repeated, her voice muffled by her arm.

"Fair enough. You've had a tough week." Sam lifted his hands in surrender as he spoke.

"Hey guys." Jason crawled into the booth next to Hailey. Lance followed him in as Taylor took the spot next to Sam.

"We've been waiting for thirty minutes," Hailey scolded him as Gwen sat back up and scooted in more to make room for Taylor.

"We're three minutes late," Jason laughed. "If you've been here for thirty minutes, that's on you."

"He's gotten a lot better at being on time since college," Taylor pointed out.

"Having a grown-up job has helped with that," Jason said.

"Speaking of college, have you heard about the new vigilante at Franklin?" Hailey asked, leaning in and looking around to see if anyone else was listening.

"No, what do you mean?" Lance asked, leaning forward.

"Apparently, there's a new crime fighter filling the void left by the White Knight's departure."

"What can I get you all tonight?" Darlene interrupted.

Each of them ordered and passed down their menus, and Darlene took the order back to Dennis.

"Tell us more about this new vigilante," Jason said as Darlene walked away.

"So, all I know is that last week there was a blonde woman in a mask who stopped a backpack theft, and they wrote a short article about her."

"What did the article say?" Taylor asked.

"Nothing good. The guy assigned to my old beat is a huge misogynist. And also something of a shock jock. He took some shots at the White Knight but saved most of his stuff for the new girl."

"Man or woman, whoever it is, is in over their head. You can't just jump into something like that." Everyone stared at Lance without saying a word as he finished talking. After a few seconds went by, Lance spoke again. "It's not the same."

"It's absolutely the same."

"Same. Same same. Same same same."

"It's the same thing, Lance."

"You're kidding, right?"

Everyone but Sam immediately chimed in. He hadn't been there when Lance had started out, but it wasn't too difficult to piece together what they were talking about. Lance waved his hand and looked away.

"And that's all you know about this new vigilante?" Jason asked, returning to the point at hand.

"Yep. She doesn't appear to have been on the scene very long. I'm trying to find out more."

"Taylor can help," Lance said, returning to the conversation. "We should still have access to all the security feeds as well as a few of our own cams on campus. He should be able to pick up on our new friend if she keeps going out, so we can figure out who it is. Might be good to keep tabs on that situation in case we need to stop them or help them."

Taylor was already nodding as Lance finished. "Yeah, I can check on that."

"We can help with that, too," Hailey said. "We want to be more involved with the team now that everything is in the open and we're all on the same page. We can help."

"That would be great." Taylor smiled. "I was just talking to Sam and Lance about how I feel overextended doing med school and all my White Knight duties. If I could teach you two how to man the monitor so that you could just do it a couple times a week, it would help me a ton."

"Wait, really?" Hailey asked.

"Makes sense to me." Jason shrugged.

"I think it would be really good for Taylor, which means it would be really good for the team. This is hard enough without inviting burnout," Lance said.

"What do you think, Sam?" Gwen asked, looking up at him. "Would you mind us stealing some of your new team member attention?"

"I'm just along for the ride. I'd love having people around who are also new to this. Would help me feel less out of place."

"So, it's settled." Hailey lightly slapped the table with her hand. "Gwen and I will begin training on the computers this week."

"And also training to fight," Gwen added.

"Now hold on a second—" Lance started before Gwen cut him off.

"We don't want to go fight crime or anything. But we want to make sure if us being around the team puts us in danger that we can defend ourselves. We need to learn self-defense to feel safe, now that we all know. And who better to teach us than some superheroes?"

"It would probably make them safer," Jason responded while Lance shook his head.

"I'm still not sure it's wise."

"Well, it's not really your call, Lance. If you and Jason won't train us, we'll just find someone else to train with," Hailey said. "I promise we won't try to become the White Knight and steal your role."

"Or any other color of knight," Gwen added.

"I think we should train them," Jason repeated.

"I agree," Taylor added.

"Well then, I guess it's settled," Lance sighed. "We can start this week. I didn't realize that being a superhero would come with a class to instruct. I'm not sure I'm cut out to be a teacher."

"You'll figure it out." Gwen smiled at him from across the table.

Darlene returned to their table with a tray full of food and began passing out their orders.

That Friday night, the six of them all met at the warehouse. While Jason and Lance suited up to go on rounds, Taylor had Sam, Hailey, and Gwen each pull up a seat to learn how to run the monitor. Lance and Sam had continued their training throughout the week, but differing availability meant the others hadn't been there at the same time until tonight.

"If you have all of this video feed, what's the point in having them go out on patrols when you can just see what's happening and then send them out once something happens?" Hailey asked as they got settled.

"Usually that's what happens," Taylor answered, turning in his chair to look at the three of them crowded around him. "Most nights, they're here, and if something normal happens, Lance will go out, and if it's a bigger incident, Jason will join him. But a lot of times on Friday or Saturday nights, there's so much happening that can be missed on here, but they can see patrolling. It also allows them to get places faster when they're already out in the city."

"Plus, it's good for the brand for us to just be seen out in the city looking cool," Jason added, walking up. Other than his helmet, he wore his entire Ironside suit and grinned from ear to ear.

"Good for my brand, at least," Lance said, walking up. "Your brand has never really overcome that whole Ironside name thing."

Everyone but Sam turned to stare at Hailey.

"I said I'm sorry. Move on," she said with a shove to Jason who was shaking his head and smiling.

"Well, we're off. Keep an eye on us while we're out there," Jason said, following Lance to the bikes where they each put on their helmet, completing the look they were known for. The motors coughed to life, and the two of them rolled out of the warehouse, with Jason giving a little wave as he pulled out behind Lance.

"So now what do you do?" Gwen asked Taylor as everyone turned back to the monitor.

"Now I usually study. The video feeds will cycle through different security cameras, but there's rarely anything just happening. While I was out of school over the summer, I spent time creating a program that could latch onto disturbances in front of any of the video feeds I have access to in the city, which is most of them. Those disturbances will then show up on the feed with a red box around them. A lot of the time, it's not anything worth the White Knight's time, but most of the time, things the White Knight responds to first popped up here in a red square."

"That's incredible," Sam said, shaking his head. "If you're this good at computer stuff, why aren't you doing that for your career?" he asked while Hailey and Gwen looked at each other through the side of their eyes.

"It's complicated," Taylor answered before turning back to the monitor. Sam looked to Hailey and Gwen, but Gwen gave him a small shake of her head and turned back to Taylor. "That's when I alert them. I give them the location, a summary of what's happening, and any other details I think can help. Once they get close to finishing, I call the police to let them know that the White Knight just stopped someone. They get there faster if they think there's a chance they can catch him. And that's about it. I help them avoid cops and make sure they aren't tailed as they get back here."

"It feels like you're not giving yourself enough credit," Gwen said as Taylor swiveled his chair to face them again.

"That's all I do for the monitoring. I also doctor them if they get injured, and when we were at Franklin, I would have to do more work when we were trying to catch hackers and hack into things ourselves. A lot of my current role was simplified because I put in the work on the front end to create this program. In the spring, I was just having to cycle through video feeds constantly."

"This is all so impressive, Taylor." Sam shook his head again, staring over Taylor at the screen. He was really good with technology related to photography, but could do little else with computers. Taylor might as well have been performing magic tricks.

"You are pretty great at what you do," Hailey said, patting his shoulder.

"Thanks, guys. I've worked hard to do my part for the team."

"You're doing great, Tay." Gwen smiled at him.

Taylor smiled back and stood up from the seat. "Hailey, Gwen, would one of you like to take a spin on it? I can show you how the different programs work. Sam, Jason is finishing up a new reinforced keyboard and mouse for you, and once that's finished, I can go back through all of that with you."

"Sounds good," Sam replied as Hailey sat down.

They all laughed as she stretched her arms out in front of her and cracked her knuckles. She shook her shoulders out and placed her hands on the keyboard.

"Ready," she said as Taylor shook his head, though he couldn't conceal his smile.

The next twenty minutes was spent with Taylor explaining how to make one of the small feeds take up the whole screen, how to manually cycle through the video feeds, and how to do other things within the program like open a map inset in the video feed that can help whoever is in the field navigate. Once Hailey had gone through it all, the next ten minutes was spent with Gwen working through everything. She was able to make it through faster, having just watched Hailey do it.

"So, what do you think? You feel comfortable running the show every now and then?" Taylor asked as he replaced Gwen in the chair, as she sat back down next to Sam and Hailey.

"I don't know that I'm ready to run the show yet," Hailey laughed, "but I think I could definitely get there."

"Me too," Gwen answered with a nod. "I just think I need to watch a bit more before I'm ready."

"Well, here's your chance." Taylor pointed at the red box in the bottom right quadrant of the screen. He enlarged it so that the entire screen showed the single video feed outlined in red.

"Lance, Jason," Taylor said into the mic on his desk. "We've got a situation on Sixth and Porter. Man and woman being held at gunpoint. Pushing back into an alley."

"On it," Lance responded.

Taylor pulled up a map that was inset into the bottom right corner of the screen mapping Lance and

Jason's course to the holdup. Estimated time to arrival: thirty seconds.

Sam, Hailey, and Gwen all sat on the edge of their seats to better see the second inset Taylor put on the screen, a video feed from Lance's helmet in the lower left-hand corner.

Cars flew by in the opposite direction while Lance and Jason, behind him, blurred past pedestrians and buildings. Twenty-two seconds away.

In the big picture, both man and woman had their hands above their head as the mugger waved his gun through the air, periodically checking his surroundings with quick jerks of his head. Sixteen seconds out.

Lance's video jerked as he had to skid and swerve to miss a man walking his dog across the street through traffic. After the swerve, they'd lost a few seconds according to Taylor's map. Seventeen more seconds.

The man fumbled in his pocket with one hand as the woman slowly set her purse on the ground beside her. The man retrieved his wallet. Ten seconds.

The mugger came into view in the distant right part of the feed as Lance and Jason rapidly approached. Eight seconds left and his gun was being raised as he stood up straighter. Six seconds away and the man and woman came into view. The woman kicked her purse to the mugger as the man tossed his wallet in turn.

Lance unsheathed his sword, rounded on the edges to serve more as a blunt weapon, and held it in his right hand as he approached, steering with his left and pulling his sword arm back. Two seconds left as the mugger stood, purse and wallet in hand.

Taylor cleared the map and had the two feeds share an equal part of the screen. The man fell to the ground as Lance swept the sword through his legs, buckling his knees. On the security feed, they saw Jason skid to a stop and roll off his bike, stopping directly between the mugger and the couple, who had turned and covered their heads as the chaos started.

The gunman sat up and fired a shot towards the couple, but Jason had extended the shield on his arm and took the impact from the bullet. Those few moments were enough for Lance to circle back and engage the shooter again, making quick work of him as he slumped to the ground.

"Officers dispatched," Taylor said into the mic. "Forty-seven seconds out."

"Got it," Lance grumbled. He picked up the purse and wallet and joined Jason where he was talking to the couple.

"No injuries to report," Jason said through the speakers. "Looks like our part is done, and the cops can take it from here. We're out."

The speakers went silent as the mics were muted and Lance and Jason returned to their bikes, jetting off from the scene.

"And that," Taylor turned from the monitor and smiled, "is what we do. So, the monitor role is really important to the team, but I've made it to where it's not difficult to perform. Most weeknights, Lance doesn't even get involved with a single incident. The weekends are a bit busier, but we wouldn't ask for anyone to cover those until you all had a lot more practice. Any questions?"

Hailey laughed. "When can I start?"

chapter

SEVENTEEN

Sam continued to train with Lance throughout the following week, and, after Jason had given him the new reinforced mouse and keyboard, he was able to spend one night walking through the monitor process with Taylor.

That Sunday, after the Dutchmen won their noon game to improve to seven wins and one loss on the season, Sam returned to the warehouse to join the team. The new shell worked wonders, and even after just one week without it, using his new Z 2600 felt like being whole again. Sundays were typically just Taylor and Lance, so he was surprised to find Jason sitting in front of the monitor, throwing a football back and forth to Lance, who sat on the couch. The last football game of the day played on the TV next to Lance.

"I thought Sunday was your day off?" Sam asked as he sat down across from Lance.

"Usually is," Jason answered as he caught the next pass. "Taylor's got a test in the morning, so I'm covering for him while he locks himself in his room to study. Plus, we've been wanting me to stay back here while Lance goes out one night to show you what it is we do in the field and why. Figured this would be a good opportunity for that." He threw the ball back to Lance.

"Oh, okay. What do I need to do now?" Sam asked.

"Right now, we're just hanging out and waiting for something to happen," Lance said, tossing it back to Jason. "We've got some food in the fridge. Game's on if you wanna watch that." He caught a pass from Jason and threw it before resuming his thought. "Obviously, the mat is open if you want to train. Up to you."

"Okay, cool." Sam turned to watch the game while Jason and Lance kept playing catch. *Maybe Jason can somehow make a reinforced football someday,* Sam thought as he listened to the sound of the ball thud from one hand to another. *Not that I'd be able to throw it back without hurting someone.*

With the game still tied and five minutes left in the fourth quarter, they stopped tossing the ball in order to focus. Lance was a Duncan Dutchmen fan, growing up less than an hour away. He and his father would go to one game a year while he was growing up —one of the few activities he did with his dad that he actually enjoyed. Jason, though, was a Harrison Badgers fan, having grown up in Harrison, Wisconsin. His family could never afford tickets growing up, but they would go to the stadium for every home game to tailgate with the rest of the fans and try to watch the game on the scoreboard from outside the stadium.

The Badgers were playing in Cameron City against the still undefeated Miners, and they had them on the ropes, their offense driving as time ticked off the clock. Sam walked over to the monitors and sat down as Jason moved closer to the TV for the stretch run.

"Hey guys," Sam called from the monitor.

"Huh?" They both responded without turning.

"There's a red box. Looks pretty serious."

Jason sighed but got up and jogged over to the monitor. "Yeah, Lance, you need to suit up."

Lance hopped up and jogged to the locker to get ready while Jason's eyes flicked over the screen.

"Three guys in a convenience store with guns. Two cashiers at the counter. Four customers were all seated against the far-left wall in a line facing the gunmen. Fifty-three seconds away. Thirty seconds have passed so far. Cashier still fumbling with the register."

Lance already had his base layer on, and with the efficiency borne of muscle memory, he had the rest on within a minute and was slinging a leg over his white bike. Without another word, he took off.

"Cashier is putting money into a bag from the second cash register. One register left. Twenty-five seconds out."

Jason split the screen between the security feed and Lance's feed as the store came into focus.

"Okay," Jason whispered to Sam as he kept his eyes on the monitor. "We got lucky, this convenience store was closed. Lance was ready to go within a minute, but they're still already almost finished. That's why no matter what's happening here, we always have to be ready to drop whatever and go."

Gunshots fired as Lance slid to a stop in front of the door, hopping off the bike and ducking behind it.

"The suit and helmet are basically bulletproof, so he's not going to get pierced by anything, but it still hurts getting hit. We try to avoid that if we can, even if it won't kill us."

Lance pulled open the door as the glass shattered around. A lull followed as the gunmen reloaded and Lance leapt to his feet and rushed in.

"It takes about four seconds to get those reloaded. That's all the time he has, so he has to make decisions based on instinct or he'll miss the opportunity. Once you have a little more control over your strength, Lance will start working on situational strategies with you. It has to become muscle memory to respond in the time we have to make decisions."

Lance had unsheathed his sword as he approached and swung it into the nearest gunman's arm, leading to an audible crack, even through the mic, and the gun falling to the floor as the man let out a cry. Lance kicked the gun away and jabbed the second man in the thigh with the end of his sword and lunged at the third to take him to the ground.

"He decided a good strategy for one on three would be the acronym D.I.E. that he came up with. I think he had the d and the e and just wanted to make a word out of it. It stands for disarm, impale, and engage. He disarmed the first man, stabbed the second in the leg to get him otherwise occupied, and tackled the third guy before he could get a shot off. When you're outnumbered, you have to find ways to shift the balance of power."

Lance knocked the third man out with the hilt of his sword as gunshots rang out on the feed. Lance groaned as the bullets rattled to the floor. The second gunman had fired with one hand while holding his leg with the other. Lance knocked him out as well and spotted the first man, who was scrambling for his gun, and knocked him out too.

"Cops are forty seconds out. Leave the way you came," Jason said into the mic.

Lance talked quickly to the cashiers and customers, then hopped on the bike and tore off. As he left, Jason reached under the desk and pulled out a binder.

"Taylor says if he's not here, to call in case of a medical emergency that's not in the binder, but non-piercing gunshots are definitely in here. Lance is going to be sore, but other than compression, ice, and painkillers, there's not much we can do about it but have him rest."

He walked to the freezer, pulled out a few ice packs, and put them on a cart that he wheeled over to the medical bed. Lance pulled in and stumbled off the bike. He took his helmet off, and Jason helped him get out of the suit and into a pair of shorts.

"I'm not getting into the stupid bed," Lance said, pulling his arm away from Jason as he tried to help him walk that direction.

"The binder says to put you in the bed, so I'm putting you in the bed whether you like it or not. Or should I call Taylor?"

Lance mumbled under his breath but walked with Jason to the bed, where Jason helped to wrap the ice packs on him and gave him some medicine. Sam couldn't hear the conversation from the computer monitor but could see them talking animatedly, and then Jason started pushing the bed towards the TV.

"Are you happy now?" Jason panted as he got Lance next to the couch.

"I'm less mad."

"Good enough."

Jason walked back to the monitor.

"Taylor fills out a report every time the White Knight responds to a situation. So I've got to do that now."

"Do y'all not usually tip Hailey about situations?"

"We do. There's a button we can hit that sends an alert to the police, and it just says the White Knight responds to a situation at whatever location the map has Lance at the time. Hailey gets a text from that alert, too."

"Oh, that's smart."

"Trust me, if there's a thing to make this work better, Taylor's thought of it," Jason laughed, pulling out his phone. "I've got like four missed calls from my family trying to talk about the game. Can you watch the monitor while I take this?"

"Sure thing," Sam answered, and Jason rushed to hook up Sam's equipment before walking to the locker area to call his family back.

Sam watched the monitors the rest of the night for practice, but Sunday night was quiet after the earlier excitement. At three in the morning, the three of them walked out into the cold fall night, where Jason and Lance left in Jason's car and Sam jogged home.

EIGHTEEN

"I've been really impressed lately, Sam."

He and Brooklyn had just sat down at the restaurant after the Dutchmen's afternoon win. They'd improved to eight and one, undefeated since the game in which Sam had destroyed his camera in Colorado. "You could have been shaken after the incident in Cameron City, but you've been doing your best work ever since then. Each week, you've improved. I know Barry has still been a bit curt with you, but I promise he sees it, too."

"I appreciate that." Sam smiled as she finished. "That was definitely something I wanted to be able to learn from and not have happen again. I know I'm on a pretty short leash after that game, so I want to make sure I don't give him any other reason to move on from me."

"No one's moving on from you, Sam," Brooklyn laughed. "You're a great young talent, and Barry knows how lucky we are to have you with us." The waiter interrupted to take their order and returned to the kitchen.

Brooklyn continued as he walked away, "I wouldn't be surprised if here in a few years you're the one moving on from us."

"That's kind of you to say," Sam laughed, "but I'm pretty content with where I'm at right now. I'm not too interested in leaving any time soon."

"That's good to hear," she smiled at him, "but we'll see. Looks like with a couple more wins, they'll clinch a playoff berth. You excited to cover your first playoffs?"

"I am." Sam nodded. "I covered some postseason games in college, but the atmosphere in the regular season games is already so different at this level. I can't imagine what that's like in the playoffs."

"It can definitely feel a bit overwhelming at first," Brooklyn laughed. "But you'll have an experienced team around you showing you how it all works. The way the team is playing lately, we may even get to cover a championship run."

"That would be amazing to see that year one here," Sam said as the waiter returned with their food.

"With Dante having this breakout year, this might just be year one of many to come for title contention."

They finished their meal, grabbed their bags, and left for the late flight back to Duncan. After landing, Sam jogged back to his apartment and collapsed into his bed as soon as he got home, drifting off to sleep immediately.

Bang. Bang. Bang.

Sam groaned as he lifted his head off the pillow and walked to the door. He raised a hand to shield his eyes from the light that flooded the room as he opened it.

"I was starting to get worried." Lance was standing in the doorway wearing shorts and a hoodie.

"What do you mean?" Sam yawned and gently leaned against the wall.

"You didn't show up for training, and you weren't answering your phone. I've been banging on the door for ten minutes." Lance pulled out his phone and started typing as he talked. "Sorry, I have to cancel the search and rescue team. I sent everyone a text five minutes ago when you weren't responding to my knocking."

"What time is it?" Sam asked, patting his pockets, looking for his phone as he asked.

"It's two-thirty. We were supposed to meet four hours ago."

"I must have slept through my alarm." Sam scratched his head as he yawned again.

"Probably. I'm finally getting my new truck this afternoon, so I won't be able to meet now. I just needed to make sure you were alright. Just make sure not to sleep through tonight."

"I'll try my best," Sam laughed.

"Sounds good. See you then, Sam."

"See ya, Lance." Sam closed the door as Lance headed towards the stairwell. He walked back to his room to retrieve his phone and found fifteen messages and seven missed calls. Four calls and seven messages were from Lance. He had one message each from Jason and Taylor, two messages and a missed call from Gwen, three messages and two calls from Hailey, and an unrelated message from Brooklyn.

He sent an explanatory text to each of the crew and left Brooklyn's unread to come back to once he was more awake. After washing his face and brushing his teeth, he felt nauseous from hunger and walked to Fran's for lunch.

"Burger and fries coming up." Darlene smiled at him as the bell above the door rang out when he walked in.

"Thanks, Darlene," he responded.

"How's it goin', Sammy?" Harry asked as Sam sat down next to him at the bar. Since it was the afternoon lull, there were only two other tables being used at the moment.

"It's going," Sam chuckled. "Got in late last night on the flight back and just woke up not too long ago."

"Cross country flights are one thing I do not miss from my salesman days," Harry laughed with a pat on Sam's shoulder. "Loved visiting all the cities, but the flights were a different matter, you know what I'm saying?"

"I know what you're saying, Harry," Sam laughed as Darlene slid him a tea and went to wait for the other customers.

"That was some game yesterday," Harry said as Sam took a sip of his tea. "This is shaping up to be a special team."

"I said at the beginning of the year that Dante was going to break out this year. I always knew he had potential that was just waiting to be tapped into," Dennis called out through the kitchen window, causing Harry to let out a laugh from deep in his belly.

"You said no such thing. You wanted him cut at the beginning of the year."

"I never said that. I knew he could do it; he just needed to be held accountable, and that's happening this year. I always knew he was a special kid."

Harry chuckled and said softly to Sam, where Dennis couldn't hear, "In the decades I've known this man, he has never once been wrong about a prediction he's made. All you have to do is ask him and he'll tell you it's the truth." Harry's eyes were bright, laughing at his friend.

Dennis came out of the back with two plates, a burger with fries for Sam, and a piece of cobbler for Harry. "Don't listen to a word he says, Sam," Dennis grumbled as he set the plates down in front of him. "The man doesn't have a truthful bone in his body." Dennis walked back to the kitchen as Harry giggled like a little kid.

Sam talked and laughed with Harry, Dennis, and Darlene until the first of the evening crowd began to trickle in at four-thirty. With a pat on the back from Harry, Sam headed home to change and take a nap before meeting Lance at the warehouse.

He woke up to his alarm this time and, after running back in to grab a hoodie after initially leaving without it, began his jog to the warehouse. Taylor was already at the monitor, talking to Jason, when he walked in.

"I'm fine," Taylor insisted.

"You've pulled three all-nighters in a row and are just barely getting by on power naps. Go home and rest. We can handle a Monday night."

"I haven't been pulling my weight for the last week because I was busy studying. I need to make up for that."

"You don't need to make up for anything," Lance walked over from the lockers. "You do more than anyone else here. Go get some rest. Let us shoulder some of the weight."

Taylor sighed. "I am pretty tired. Promise you'll call if you need anything? I'll leave the ringer on."

"I promise." Jason nodded in response.

"Okay. I'll see you all in the morning." Taylor got up and headed to the door, giving Sam a smile as he walked by, but not much else as he dragged himself to his car.

Sam joined Jason and Lance at the monitor.

"What's the plan for tonight?" he asked.

"We're going on a patrol," Lance answered.

"Okay, so I'm watching the monitor tonight?"

"You and Lance are patrolling tonight," Jason said. "I'm on the monitor."

"I'm going in the field?"

"Yep." Lance nodded. "We're still trying to figure out how to make a suit work for you, so for now you'll start out like we did and go out in a hoodie."

"You sure I'm ready?"

"Only one way to find out." Lance shrugged.

"You're ready, Sam," Jason said, rolling his eyes at Lance. "You're not going to get involved in anything tonight. You're going to walk with Lance and see what he does when he's on patrols. Learn his process. If anything happens, Lance will engage while you watch. This is step two. Step one was showing you stuff from here, now you get to see it firsthand."

"Okay." Sam nodded, Jason's talk giving him more confidence. "Let's do it."

Lance and Sam went on patrols each night that week to give Sam the experience of being out in the city. Other than a couple fights that dispersed as soon as the White Knight showed up, nothing too exciting happened on their patrols. Taylor took back over monitor duties on Tuesday after catching up on sleep, but nothing that demanded the White Knight's attention came up on his monitor either.

Friday, the six of them (or at least Hailey, Gwen, and Jason) decided to have their own Halloween party at the warehouse since the White Knight team couldn't be off duty on Halloween weekend to go to any other parties. Even though Halloween wasn't until Sunday, they knew that the whole weekend would be all-hands-on-deck with the holiday.

Hailey and Gwen showed up early to decorate the warehouse for the party: hanging spider webs, setting up skeletons, and doing their best to put costumes on the dummies. When Lance, Sam, and Taylor walked in, Gwen was holding a ladder still while Hailey stood on her tiptoes to put the last corner of a spider web in place.

"Place looks nice," Sam said as Hailey stepped off the ladder.

"Thanks!" She smiled at him.

"It should look good," Gwen laughed, "we've been here two hours trying to set it up."

"You two really didn't have to do all this," Taylor said.

"We know," Hailey answered, "but we wanted to go to a Halloween party, and since we didn't want to go without the team and the team couldn't leave, we decided to go all out on our own little party."

"What exactly is your costume, Hall?" Lance asked, his arms crossed.

Hailey had on a white dress with a gold satin belt around her waist, gold armband, and a gold sash that went across her body.

"Wait, it's not finished." She ran over in her gold sandals to the couch and put on a gold helmet with white wings on the side. "What do you think?" she asked, beaming, as she walked back to the group.

"I still don't know what you are," Lance replied.

"I'm the Roman god Mercury!"

"Wasn't Mercury male?" Taylor asked.

"It's a Roman god, Taylor. It's not real. I think it can be used as a woman's costume too."

"You're right," Taylor answered, raising both hands in the air.

"Besides, I always miss cross country this time of year and since Mercury is the god of speed," Hailey ran in place as she talked, "I figured it worked well!"

"Are you and Jason doing some weird couples costume again?" Lance asked.

"Nope, not this year. He's been really secretive about what he's dressing as. Said it's a surprise." She shrugged. "I see you went all out this year," she said, rolling her eyes.

"I wear a costume every night and will probably be in it again in a few hours," Lance said, wearing a hoodie with his jeans. The other four all booed him.

Lance shook his head but laughed along with the rest of the group as they made their way to the couches.

Sam had dressed as the giant from his favorite movie, wearing an oversized collarless button up, blue flannel pajama pants, and boots. Taylor had slicked back his hair, put on a suit, a fake mustache and a monocle, and walked around with a cane talking in a Mid-Atlantic accent. Gwen had on a flowing, sage green, velvet dress and a tiara.

The group talked for another ten minutes before a knock came at the door.

"Jason must need help with the pizza." Lance hopped up and jogged to the door. When he opened it, the pizza was there but it was a delivery man and not Jason. Lance thanked him and walked back to the couches, setting the boxes down on the table with the other snacks Hailey and Gwen had laid out.

"Where's Jason?" Gwen asked.

"Beats me." Hailey shrugged. "He said he'd meet us here with the pizzas."

As her voice trailed off, the lights flickered in the room, and the sound of thunder echoed through the warehouse. A chorus of voices began singing the words "This is Halloween" through speakers around the room over and over as the lights flickered back on revealing a man swinging from a rope into the sitting area, hitting the ground and somersaulting to his feet, Jason stood up wearing a skeleton costume and a black blazer, stretching his arms wide before giving a bow.

"How-how long have you been up there?" Gwen slowly asked after a few seconds had passed, while the rest just stared at Jason.

"Three hours," he answered, bouncing on the balls of his feet. "I have to pee so bad."

"You freak," Hailey deadpanned.

"Absolute weirdo," Taylor added.

"Imbecile." Lance shook his head at the same time as the other two.

"Worth it," he responded, still bouncing.

"Dude," Sam said, "go to the bathroom."

"Yeah, good call. It takes a while to get in and out of this thing, so it might take a bit." He bounced again before running to the restroom as they all laughed at him.

The rest of the team got their pizza as Jason was in the bathroom. Sam was getting up for his third and fourth slices when Jason finally returned.

"Okay." Gwen sat up as Jason was finishing his plate. "We have some games to play," she announced as she pulled a bowl out from under her seat.

Pulling names out of the bowl, she divided the group into two teams. Gwen, Lance, and Sam on one team while Hailey, Jason, and Taylor were on the other.

"There are five games, and each team gets a point for every game they win. We have charades, pin the tail on the Minotaur, taboo, password, and bobbing for apples!"

"You're going down, Locke," Hailey said as she started writing down words for the game.

"Do I have to bob for apples?" Lance asked, ignoring Hailey.

"Yes!" everyone said in unison, causing Lance to roll his eyes.

Round one went to team one as Jason wasn't able to get a single point for his team while acting, which led to Hailey throwing a pillow at him as he made the same movement for the fifth time in a row.

"How is that supposed to be a pumpkin?" she yelled as the pillow hit him.

"I was making pumpkin pie!"

"That's the worst way you could have tried to get us to guess that!"

Round two went to team one as well, though there was controversy regarding how close Sam's tail was after he put his hand through the divider the poster was on. Taylor reluctantly sided with Team One and said that Sam should get credit for where the hole was because it wasn't his fault that his hand went through the divider.

"Traitor," Jason mumbled at Taylor as Gwen put another point up for their team on the whiteboard.

Rounds three and four both went to team two, though, leading the competition to all come down to bobbing for apples. Jason and Sam squared off first, with Jason winning five apples to none after Sam was unable to keep from biting through each apple in his thirty seconds. Hailey beat Gwen three to two, increasing their lead to a six Apple advantage.

Taylor was preparing to go next as an alarm blared through the warehouse.

"We got a hit," Jason said as the group rushed to the monitor, except Lance and Jason who ran to the lockers and began putting their suits on.

"Looks like we've got a car chase," Taylor called. Lance was already in his pants and was putting on the top of his suit as Taylor spoke. Jason was close behind, his skeleton costume at his feet.

"Where are we headed?" Lance asked as he secured his top.

"The interstate," Taylor answered. "I'm mapping it now to get you to an intersect point."

Hailey and Gwen stood behind Taylor, watching the screen. Sam went to Lance, who was mounting his bike while Jason finished getting dressed.

"How can I help?" Sam asked as he approached.

"You can't," Lance answered. "You're not ready to go out for something like this yet. We'll keep practicing, but tonight we have no margin for error. Hang tight here. We'll get you out there soon enough."

"I feel like I could help. Speed and strength seem like the two most useful things for stopping a car chase.

If there was ever a situation made for me to be helpful, it would be this one."

Lance started his bike and revved the engine. "Not tonight, Sam."

With that, Lance tore out of the warehouse. Jason gave Sam a slap on the shoulder, and then he mounted his bike and took off after Lance.

Sam rejoined the team at the monitor as Taylor put the video feeds up on the screen. A white truck was flying down the interstate followed by five police cars on one screen while a map with dots showing where the truck was and where Lance and Jason were blinked on the other. Taylor was typing away, trying to get information from the police system about the situation.

"Guys." Taylor picked up the mic to make sure they would be able to hear him. "There's a kid in the truck. Looks like his dad kidnapped him. You're going to have to find a way to get him out of there before something happens."

"Copy that," Jason responded.

"I can't watch this," Sam announced and walked outside. Ever since his talk with Gwen in the diner, he'd forced himself to be intentionally empathetic and not be so blinded by his own problems that he couldn't see other people's. That, combined with his new powers and being around the team's heroism, had left him perpetually frustrated that he wasn't doing more to help people.

Leaving a mugging or a robbery to Lance and Jason was one thing, but a kidnapped child in a car chase? He felt sick having to ignore that.

"Sammy, you okay?" Hailey asked, but he just waved her off. She took a couple steps towards him, but ultimately gave him his space and returned to the monitor, watching as he walked through the door into the chilly night air.

Lance and Jason caught up to the truck and merged onto the interstate right behind the first police car on its tail. The two motorcycles quickly left the patrol cars behind and pulled up alongside the truck, one on each side. Lance swerved out of the way as the driver veered in his direction. He motioned for the driver to roll his window down, but the driver just veered towards him again, going even further than before. Lance swerved again, this time barely able to stay on the road. A grassy hill was just beyond the shoulder, sloping down twenty yards before leveling out and meeting a train track that ran parallel with the road.

"What's the plan here, Lance?" Jason yelled, his voice only slightly muffled by the speakers in Lance's helmet.

"We have to get the kid out. Can you get the door open?" Lance dared a look through the truck's windows. looking past the disheveled man and crying child to see the red of Jason's suit on the other side.

"Don't open the door, Jason," Taylor yelled in their headsets. "Lance, that could kill the kid! And maybe Jason, too! You have to find a way to get him to stop or pull over."

"And how do you expect us to do that?" Lance snapped back, leaving the car's side to avoid tire scraps on the shoulder. The police had succeeded in one thing; the truck, motorcycles, and patrol cars were the only vehicles on the road at the moment. What they hadn't thought through was the train that Lance could feel rumbling behind him, even without the horn blaring every three seconds.

"Maybe try to pop a tire with the sword or spear? Wait until there's a ditch that's more level and bait him into veering into you again?" Taylor looked over his shoulder to see if Hailey or Gwen had any ideas, but they just shook their heads no.

"Popping the tires won't work," Jason answered. "Not from this angle with the car going this fast. We'd have to have spikes."

"Well, here goes nothing, I guess," Lance mumbled as he drove up closer to the truck again.

"Lance, not here!" Taylor shouted but it was too late, the truck saw Lance approaching and took no chances with the swerve this time. Turning almost ninety-degrees, the truck connected with Lance's bike and sent Lance and the bike skidding down the grass hill with the bike flipping over on top of Lance, pain searing through his surgically repaired shoulder as he came to rest a few yards shy of the rushing train that had fully caught up to them.

The truck, meanwhile, had lost control and was flipping end over end in his, and the train's, direction.

"Lance!"

"No!"

"Locke!"

"Look out!"

Taylor's, Gwen's, Hailey's, and Jason's voices tore through the speaker, but there wasn't time for Lance to do anything as the truck left the ground and soared above him, almost hovering. The airbags had already deployed as the truck careened towards him, the two white circles in the windshield looking like eyes that had rolled back into someone's head. Lance closed his eyes with that haunting last sight and waited.

A thud swiftly followed by the sound of crunching metal sounded right above Lance. He opened his eyes to find the truck still hovering right above him, not even a foot away. The child's arms were still over his face as the airbag deflated. The driver seemed to have been knocked unconscious by the impact. Standing behind Lance, his face scrunched up in concentration as he held the truck up over his head as the train thundered behind him, was Sam.

chapter

NINETEEN

New Hero in Duncan

Last night, a car chase took place on the streets of Duncan. Travis Gibson kidnapped his nine-year-old son after the boy got out of school. Laurie Taylor, the boy's mother, who has sole custody of her son, called law enforcement when her son did not arrive on the bus after school. Officers quickly located Gibson and tried to retrieve the boy before Gibson fled in his truck. Officers pursued the truck but had no luck in stopping the chase without hurting the child.

The White Knight and Ironside joined the chase and were able to quickly pull alongside Gibson's truck, but their presence led to Gibson's more aggressive and hostile driving. After the White Knight attempted to approach the truck, Gibson swerved to hit the hero, knocking him and his motorcycle into the grass shoulder. This turn led to Gibson flipping his truck, and the airbags deploying in the vehicle. The truck tumbled into the grass shoulder, careening directly at the White Knight, before coming to an abrupt halt when a new hero showed up and caught the truck midair.

Possessing what appears to be superhuman strength, this new hero saved the life of not only the White Knight, but also the child and his father, who were each treated for minor injuries but were not hospitalized. The young boy was reunited with his mother while Gibson was detained, awaiting a hearing to be set. A new hero in Duncan is a welcome addition to our team.

Hailey Hall

"Front page, boy!" Jason gave Sam a shove when he got to the warehouse Saturday afternoon after sleeping in.

Sam and Jason had returned to the warehouse after stopping the car chase while Lance went on "patrol" and was off comms the rest of the night as he sat on rooftops overlooking the city. Taylor wasn't happy about Lance getting hit by a car and not coming in to get checked out, but there wasn't much he could do about it. It wasn't Lance's first time being hit by a car. He checked Jason and Sam when they got back, but neither of them had any injuries. Jason couldn't stop talking about how cool it was to see the truck come to a complete stop midair, only to see Sam holding it up. Gwen and Hailey were also excited to talk to Sam about his heroics.

Hailey had excitedly told him how, as soon as they saw what happened and were able to see they were safe, she had gotten on social media to see if anyone there had gotten a photo of him. There were a number of screenshots from the news helicopter's feed that clearly showed a man holding up a car, but none close enough to see Sam's face. She messaged the person who posted the best one to get permission to use it, and she had already sent in her first draft of the article while they waited for them to get back to the warehouse.

Sam smiled quietly as the group talked about that night's events. After thirty minutes, though, he needed a break.

"I'm still not sure yet how my powers all work, but that took a whole lot out of me, and I'm exhausted now. I think I'm going to try and make it back home to get some rest," he had told them.

Taylor insisted that someone drive Sam home, given how tired he was. They had each offered to drive him, but with Taylor watching the monitors and waiting for Lance to return for his checkup, he couldn't go. Jason needed to be on hand in case any situations arose since they didn't know if Lance would be able to get anywhere in time, and Hailey was suddenly on a deadline to post about the new Duncan superhero. So, Gwen took him home and helped him up to his door. He fell asleep as soon as he crawled into bed and hit the pillow at 11:00.

He woke up to the sunlight shining bright in his room at 12:30 pm the next day. Hailey, Gwen, and Jason had all texted him about Hailey's article making the front page of that morning's paper. Taylor had sent him a text letting him know they were planning on eating and having a team meeting at 2:00 pm that Lance had called.

Sam showered off and got ready, walking at a leisurely pace to the warehouse but still arriving by 1:30.

Sam laughed at Jason's greeting and shook his head. Hailey rushed up to him and handed him a copy of that morning's paper.

"I took a whole stack to make sure we were able to save some." She beamed up at him.

"Thanks, Hails." He smiled back.

"Did you sleep well?" Gwen asked as Sam sat down on the couch next to her.

"I just woke up not long ago, so I'd say so," he laughed. Jason and Hailey joined them in the sitting area, taking their spots on the opposite couch. Hailey threw her legs over Jason as they got comfortable. "Turns out catching a two-ton truck over your head takes a lot out of you, even with super strength."

"Next time you tell the story, the truck should be at least five tons," Jason told him, swinging his hands out to his side to make a "bigger" motion.

"And who exactly do you think he's telling this story to next time that's not already here?" Hailey asked.

"I mean, that's about as great of a pickup story a guy could have," Jason answered.

"He's not using that to flirt with someone. He's got to keep it private so people don't know who he is. And why are you giggling like that?" Hailey looked over at

Gwen, who hadn't stopped laughing softly to herself for ten seconds.

"Pickup story," Gwen giggled.

"Nice," Jason laughed and gave her an air five as Hailey rolled her eyes at the two of them.

The door opened, and Lance and Taylor walked in with bags of food from Fran's.

"About time, I'm starving," Jason said, flinging Hailey's legs off of him to go get the food. The other three joined him in grabbing their containers before returning to the couches.

"What's this meeting about, Lance?" Jason asked through a handful of fries.

Lance chewed on a bite of his burger in silence until he swallowed. "It's about a couple of things," he said, leaning back in his chair. "The first thing is I need to apologize to all five of you, but especially Sam, for my behavior last night. I acted like a child and went and sulked, and that wasn't fair to Sam's moment, and it wasn't fair to the safety of the city for me to respond like that. I minimized my friend's achievement and put the city in danger because of how I responded, and that's not okay."

"It happens to us all," Sam said softly, remembering how he had just gone weeks so wrapped up in his own problems that he had forgotten other people were struggling too.

"I appreciate that, Sam, but I still need to apologize. You saved my life last night and the lives of two others, and I responded by going off the grid. I was annoyed that you hadn't listened to me telling you to stay here, and that the situation hadn't unfolded in reality like it had in my head. I was prideful, and I put the mission of the team at risk. That's unacceptable, and I'm sorry to all of you."

Lance took another bite of his burger, and the group sat in silence as he chewed and then took a drink of his water.

"The second reason I called this meeting was to make sure everyone was on the same page and let everyone know I'm going to take a short hiatus from the White Knight."

"Now hold on a second," Jason started before Lance cut him off with his hand. Sam and Gwen had both sat up on the edge of their seats at Lance's words.

"I'm not leaving because of last night," Lance assured Jason. "I'm not leaving permanently or anything else. A few weeks ago, Hailey told us about a new vigilante in Franklin. Hailey, Taylor, and I have been keeping tabs on that situation since then, and we have reason to be a bit concerned. I was planning on going down to pay the new vigilante a visit, but before I could, she went off the grid completely, and we're worried about her. As soon as she comes back on the grid, I am going to go down there for a time to work with her and train her. I brought the White Knight to campus, and when I left, I created a void that threw the campus into chaos. She's trying to fix my mess, and I need to go down there and help clean it up and put her in a better position to succeed."

"You two knew about this?" Jason turned to look at Hailey and Taylor.

Hailey nodded. "We've been trying to figure out what obligations we have to give her space and privacy versus what we feel the team is responsible for in continuing to keep the campus safe. We didn't feel comfortable giving away her identity previously, and we didn't know if we could bring it up without revealing who she was."

"And what's changed to make you comfortable with that now?" Sam asked.

"She's been off the grid most of the time we've known about her, and we're getting worried," Taylor answered. "She hasn't shown up in a hospital or anything else during this time. She just recently started going to class again, and we're concerned for her well-being to the point that we feel we have to intervene. And once we decided on that, we knew it was right to bring the whole team in on the discussion."

"Who is the new vigilante?" Gwen asked, turning from Taylor back to Lance.

"Ashley Adair. Sophomore soccer player I saved last year," he explained to Sam. "She's the one who gave me the name White Knight. She also became our friend towards the end of the year."

"And that's why Lance is going back," Hailey added.

Lance nodded. "I'm going to go down there to try to train her. She has a ton of potential, but I'm afraid that she's going to get hurt the way she's doing it. Hopefully, some of the experience we've gotten this year can help her protect the campus even better than we were able to. While I'm gone, it'll also give Sam an opportunity to get reps in on the A-team. One of the reasons I struggled last night was because after not being able to figure out the right way to train Sam, he showed up and saved the day by doing the exact opposite of what I said."

"Sorry about that," Sam mumbled, lowering his head. He had been able to help, but he still felt like he had over-stepped. This was their team, and he had blatantly and intentionally disregarded what they had said, even though they were just trying to keep him and everyone else safe.

"Don't be," Lance responded, shaking his head but smiling. "It's the only reason I'm still alive. There's not much I can do to train you in here anymore." Lance gestured at the warehouse. "You need to be out in the field getting experience. That's the best way to learn. You and Jason will be working as a team to protect the city while I'm gone. If I thought the city was less safe with you two on hand than it was with me and Jason, then I wouldn't leave, but I have full confidence in your abilities."

"With all of the different factors, we just thought now was the most opportune time for Lance to do this thing we think is important," Taylor finished as Hailey nodded along.

"You still should have brought us in sooner," Jason said, looking at each of them in turn. "Sharing this information with us up front would have saved us from being blindsided. If half the team already knew, where was the harm in telling the other half? You have to have more trust in us."

Gwen nodded along while Sam sat there quietly.

"Maybe we should have," Taylor conceded. "But we wanted to make sure we were doing right by her first and foremost. The three of us needed to figure out what was going on, and we wanted to respect her privacy as long as we could. We brought this to everyone as soon as we felt it was right."

"It was only about protecting Ashley," Hailey said, resting a hand on Jason's knee. "It had nothing to do with a lack of trust in you. Any of you."

"Hmph," Jason snorted but didn't argue further.

"I see where you're coming from," Gwen said, "but Jason's right. We're all on this team together. There has to be more transparency."

"We'll do better at that going forward," Lance promised.

"Are you sure I'm ready?" Sam asked, finally speaking up. The anxiety he felt was different from what it had been in the past, less all-consuming, but he could still feel it rising. He saved the day last night, but the previous time he had tried his hand at heroism, he had turned a man's arm to jelly. This wasn't without risks. "Last night was the first time I had really responded to anything, and it was uniquely suited to my abilities. Y'all weren't wrong to tell me to sit out. I could really hurt somebody in a different setting."

"You're not giving yourself enough credit. The headline said it clearly," Lance smiled, walking over and putting a hand on Sam's shoulder, "Duncan's got a new hero. I think it would be good for the city to see more of him going forward."

chapter

TWENTY

A week after their team meeting, Taylor got an alert on his monitor while Jason and Sam were in the field. Ashley was out as the vigilante again. Lance grabbed his go bag and left for Franklin in his truck. He had stayed in the base with Taylor all week, watching the monitor and running comms so he could leave for Franklin as soon as there was another Ashley sighting.

The rest of the Halloween weekend had been busy; Jason and Sam were constantly responding to one situation or another, but none of the incidents were the same level as Friday night's car chase. Then, the week after Halloween had been a dead period—people had apparently gotten it all out of their system over the weekend. Or the weekend had tired everyone out too much to have the energy for shenanigans during the week. For whichever reason, Jason and Sam didn't leave the warehouse again the rest of the week.

Sam walked into Fran's on Saturday afternoon at 2:30. With his new habit of staying up late and sleeping in, his meal schedule had shifted back a bit. He would eat a small breakfast when he'd wake up, usually eat lunch around three, and then wouldn't have dinner until he was at the warehouse around ten. Luckily, his job afforded him the flexibility to handle this new schedule. He couldn't understand how Jason was able to be up all night and at work again by eight the next morning. One unexpected benefit of his new schedule was how much quicker service he got going in during the lulls at restaurants, not that he ever had to wait long at Fran's regardless of what time he came in.

As the bell above the door announced his arrival, Gwen looked up from her book and waved Sam over. She sat in a booth next to the counter with her back to the wall, one leg straight out on the seat with the other tucked up close to her. A cup of coffee and a half-eaten slice of pie already sat on the table.

"What are you doing here?" he asked, sitting down across from her.

"You're not the only regular here," she laughed, putting her open book face down to hold her place and taking a bite of pie.

"I just didn't expect to see you here, that's all." Sam smiled back.

"It's a nice place to read when it's not crowded. I like being here in the heart of the city. Everything feels alive around you as you sit, you know? All the other coffee shops around here have a different vibe. They're all dark and moody, which is fine, just not what I'm looking for to read."

Sam nodded as she talked. "I get that."

"Plus," Gwen said, smiling up to Darlene who had shown up with a tea for Sam and a pot of coffee to refill Gwen's mug, "I get to have good conversations about books with people who love them as much as I do."

"Anytime you want it, sugar," Darlene responded as she filled up her cup.

"Darlene, Harry, and Dennis each read more than all of our friend group combined," Gwen explained. "Jason and Lance aren't big readers at all. Hailey prefers reading articles over books, and Taylor was a big reader in the past, but he's been so busy with med school that he's left me without a book buddy. But here,"—she swept her arm across the diner —"there are people to talk about whatever kind of books you want to talk about."

"What's your area of expertise, Darlene?" Sam asked.

"I like a good crime or legal thriller," she answered with a smile. She set the pot of coffee on the counter and sat down in a chair next to the booth. The diner was empty of customers other than Gwen and Sam.

Gwen nodded and added, "Harry loves anything science-fiction, fantasy, or fairy tale. And Dennis —"

"War books?" Sam interjected, looking over his shoulder at the kitchen, looking for Dennis.

"As a matter of fact, yes," Dennis said, drying his hands with a towel and stepping out of the kitchen. "But Gwen and I usually talk poetry."

"Poetry?" Sam asked, looking at Gwen and Darlene to see if it was a joke before turning back to Dennis.

"Poetry," he repeated. "What's it to you?"

"Nothing at all, Dennis. Just wanted to make sure I heard you right."

"Hrmph," Dennis snorted before returning to the kitchen to continue cleaning.

"He also writes poetry," Gwen said, lowering her voice. "It's really beautiful stuff. We've been trying to convince him to publish it."

"A losing battle I've fought for my whole life." Darlene sighed, standing back up and wiping the counter down.

"How do you feel about Lance taking off?" Sam asked Gwen as Darlene left.

"I understand it. I wish they had communicated it with us better instead of just dropping it on us like that last week, but their hearts were in the right place. It's not like it's permanent or anything, and he's not too far away."

Sam nodded along. He'd been blindsided by the news, too, but he had a different relationship with Lance than she did.

"I just know the two of you are close," he said.

"Yeah, it's hard. Lance has never been the best at letting people in or communicating what he's feeling and thinking. That's been a consistent tension in our relationship, especially since my assault and his"—she paused and looked around before continuing—"new hobby."

"If you don't mind me asking, what exactly is y'all's relationship? I've been trying to figure out exactly what it is, but I'm not sure I've figured it out." He'd been trying to figure out their dynamics for months. Sometimes it would seem like they had been a couple for years, and other times it seemed like they were almost avoiding each other. Having said it out loud, he felt almost rude, though. Luckily, Gwen removed the stone of anxiety he felt moving to his stomach before it had even arrived.

"That's fair," she laughed. "Honestly, I don't think we know exactly what it is. I feel like we're on the same page with everything, but it's kind of a gray area as far as labels are concerned. We've been friends our whole lives, you know? There have been times he's liked me, but I wasn't interested, and vice versa. There have been times when we were both interested but didn't know how to move into anything new or different than friendship. A year ago, it was all starting to come to a head before"—Gwen gestured with her hands —"well, everything. Right now, we're still rebuilding trust and learning how to navigate a different season of life together in more ways than one."

She took a drink from her coffee as Darlene brought Sam's lunch out.

"Sorry if that doesn't clarify much," she laughed as he dug into his fries.

"No, no, I appreciate it. Thank you for sharing with me. I just kept feeling awkward around the two of you without knowing that dynamic. Plus, I'll take any additional information I can get to try to figure out what Lance's whole deal is."

"Well, that makes two of us." Gwen smiled and shook her head. "I'd gladly take any insights you get if you don't mind."

"Sounds like a deal." Sam smiled back as the bell above the door rang out again, followed by Harry greeting them.

"My two favorite regulars. It's a good day indeed!"

"Told you," Gwen smirked before taking another sip of coffee, causing Sam to laugh.

"Hey, Harry," Sam said, waving a fry at him.

"What are we talking about?" he asked, taking his stool at the end of the counter closest to them.

"Books!" Gwen answered.

"And young love," Darlene said with a wink at Gwen before giving her husband a kiss and pouring him a cup of coffee.

"Two of my favorite subjects," Harry smiled. "You know, our love was young once. Matter of fact, still is most days."

"Just most?" Darlene asked, stopping her coffee pouring to look at him.

"Some days I don't love like I should, but I'm getting better with age." He smiled back at her.

"Smoother too." She rolled her eyes and put the pot back on the burner while Harry winked at Sam and Gwen.

"Thirty-seven years married, thirty-eight together, and we still got it." Harry laughed and patted Darlene on the hand as she returned to the counter.

"How did the two of you meet?" Gwen asked, pulling both legs up to her chest.

"This hotshot salesman came in one day trying to peddle something to Mama, but she wasn't interested in talking to him. Lord knows why, but I let him talk to me for a couple of minutes, and then that turned into a first date, which turned into a second date, and here we are now."

"I swept her off her feet," Harry laughed from deep in his stomach. "I was in Duncan on a sales trip from Sanders, walked in to grab a bite to eat, and my heart just stopped when I saw her. I didn't even have anything of use to sell to a diner, but next thing I knew, I was trying to spin it so I could come back again. Took her on a date that same night, called my boss in the morning, and requested a transfer to the Duncan office. Told my family I was moving to Duncan when I got home and never looked back." Harry was smiling from ear to ear as he took a sip of coffee.

"And he ain't stopped talking in those forty years either," Dennis hollered from the back without stepping out of the kitchen, eliciting another belly laugh from Harry.

They continued talking for another hour before the early dinner crowd began trickling in, and Sam and Gwen said their goodbyes.

They walked together back towards the warehouse for the Saturday night excitement. Gwen was bundled up with a scarf and coat over her sweater while Sam just wore his flannel and khakis on the brisk fall day.

"How are you not freezing?" Gwen asked, her teeth chattering as she hugged herself as tightly as possible.

"I'm not sure," Sam answered slowly. "I've never cared for colder weather before, but until you mentioned it, I didn't even think about it being cold. I guess with the way my body has changed, the cold doesn't bother me as much anymore."

"Lucky you," Gwen muttered, yanking at her scarf to cover more of her face.

"I'll switch places with you," Sam laughed. He walked a bit faster to get in front of her to block the wind. "Did that help any?"

"Actually, yeah!" Gwen answered from behind.

"Alright then, keep up," Sam said as he led the way to the warehouse.

TWENTY-ONE

"Jason, suit up," Taylor called from the monitor as the three of them sat in the warehouse a week later. Sam still didn't have a suit, just the hoodie for now, so he didn't need to 'suit up.'

"What's the sitch?" Jason asked as he jogged to his locker.

"Lance isn't here, so now you think you can start saying that again?"

"Taylor."

"Right, right, we've got a break-in at a jewelry store downtown. Cops were just dispatched. You've got a seventy-five-second drive, and officers should be there in three minutes."

"How do they not already have officers downtown?" Sam asked.

"Duncan PD is sometimes weird about who handles which situations," Jason answered while buckling his suit up. "They have a specific squad that handles high-profile B and Es stationed at headquarters. They don't even like uniformed officers responding until they're on the scene, which is incredibly dumb but great for us. Let's head out."

Jason mounted his bike and tore out of the warehouse with Sam sprinting out behind him.

"Sam," Taylor said into the earpiece. "Take the short-cut I'm sending you. You'll go through the park while Jason stays on the road."

Jason hadn't had time to make Sam a suit yet, but he and Taylor had created a mask for him to wear with lenses so that Taylor could project things into his vision via the screens. Sam veered off and ran through the grassy area, his shortcut cutting twenty seconds off his time to the jewelry store. He stumbled to a stop in front of the broken window.

"What's the plan?" Sam shouted into his mic.

"Stop the bad guys!" Jason yelled back over the roar of traffic.

"Jason is still fifteen seconds out, Sam," Taylor's voice cut in. "You need to go in and keep them occupied until Jason shows up so you guys can take care of them before any cops show up."

"Copy that," Sam answered, climbing through the broken storefront window.

Occupy them, he thought to himself. *That shouldn't be too hard.*

He turned a corner and found himself in a room with five armed men, two of whom were standing guard while the other three loaded jewelry into bags.

"Everyone st —" Sam started before the sound of gunshots filled the room.

Sam instinctively threw his arms up and turned away as the bullets flew around him. The silence that followed was broken by the clatter of the bullets falling to the ground, unable to penetrate Sam's skin.

"Sam!" Taylor yelled through the earpiece. "You're bulletproof!"

I'm bulletproof.

Jason showed up, spear in hand, as the two guards frantically tried to reload. It was too late. Jason had already crossed the room and engaged them, quickly disarming and incapacitating them both.

The remaining three tried to escape out the back with their bags, but Sam sprinted to cut them off at the door, easily overtaking them with his speed, even with their head start. The first one lowered his shoulder and tried to run through Sam before crumpling to the floor, howling in pain. The other two took off the other way before Sam again cut them off.

Jason came upon them and, with an assist from Sam, who was keeping them in a small area, quickly finished them off. The two of them raced out of the building as red and blue lights appeared in the distance.

They were already headed back to the warehouse, Jason on the street and Sam through the park, when the police finally arrived on the scene. The adrenaline rushing through Sam got him back to the warehouse faster than he had ever gone before. He pulled at the door and ripped it off its hinges, the first incident he'd had in months.

"Oops," he said as he gently set the door down on the wall next to the door frame.

"Sam!" Taylor yelled, running over and pounding his hand on Sam's chest. "You're bulletproof!"

"I know!" Sam yelled back.

"You scared me to death when they started shooting; I thought you were going to die!"

"I thought I was going to die! But I could barely even feel them when they hit me!"

"Glad you're okay, Sam." Gwen smiled from the couch.

"Gwen!" Sam said, still yelling. "When did you get here?"

"Hailey and I just missed you, it sounds like."

"Yeah, they walked in while you were en route to the jewelry store," Taylor added.

"Hailey's here?" Sam looked around as he asked.

"Not anymore," Gwen laughed. "She wasn't here thirty seconds before she headed to the jewelry store for the scoop."

"When were you two going to tell me he was bullet-proof?" Jason asked, walking in and tossing his helmet at his locker.

"We just found out!" Taylor exclaimed.

"You mean to tell me Sam could have died tonight?" Jason said, pausing between words.

"Yeah, but I didn't! Because I'm bulletproof!" The adrenaline coursing through his body wouldn't let him stop yelling, but he didn't even care. This was a high he'd be on for hours.

"That's great, but irrelevant." Jason glanced at Sam but turned back to focus directly on Taylor. "Taylor never should have sent you in without me there. Especially with you not having a suit of your own and not having experience with situations like this."

"That's not really fair," Sam said, looking from Jason to Taylor and back again, confused by how quickly the energy in the room had shifted. "He was just trying to help. And I'm really fine."

"You're fine because of luck." Jason didn't even look Sam's way this time. "You'd be dead right now if it weren't for your powers. If Lance or I had been in that position, we'd be dead. Stopping a burglary isn't worth Sam's life, Taylor."

"I never said it was," Taylor answered, but his heart wasn't in it.

"You didn't have to. Your decision said it for you."

"Take it down a notch, Jason," Sam tried again, but Taylor shook him off. The high that had just made him feel like he was walking on the moon had flipped completely, making him feel like he was wading through molasses now instead. His body had stopped the pleasant buzzing, and his mind had slowed to a crawl as he watched the exchange.

"No, Jason's right." Taylor sank back into his chair and ran a hand through his sandy hair. "I wasn't thinking about you not having a suit and being able to withstand being shot at. I took it for granted that you'd be fine going in because Lance or Jason would be fine going in in their suits. I'm so used to them being bulletproof that it never even crossed my mind that you weren't wearing protective gear, and my job here is to be aware of things like that. You could have died tonight, and it would have been my fault."

"That's not true," Sam said, shaking his head. He could have been more careful tonight. He could've been smarter about how to delay them. He couldn't let all the fault fall on Taylor. He opened his mouth to take the blame before Jason stopped him.

"We can't do what we do without holding each other accountable, Sam," Jason said, his posture softening as he finally turned to face Sam. "These are hard conversations, but we have to have them. I've been on the receiving end of them. Lance has been on the receiving end of them. Taylor too. I'll go ahead and tell you right now to get ready because you're going to get them sooner or later. It's part of the gig. We're all on the same team, which means we want to see each other succeed. To do that long term, we have to point out where people are falling short. Lives are in the balance. Taylor is a genius, but he's not infallible. Still, there's no one I'd trust more to be in this seat than him. One bad call doesn't change that."

With that, Jason gave Taylor a slap on the shoulder and walked to his locker to undress. Taylor began filling out his incident report while Sam walked over and sat down next to Gwen.

"That was intense," Gwen said as he sat down.

"I know, I can't believe Jason was talking to Taylor like that." Sam was still dealing with the emotional whiplash the conversation had given him.

"I mean, it makes sense. They have to put a lot of trust and faith in each other to hold up their end of the deal. If one of them isn't doing what they need to, they could die. That's what you're getting yourself into. You may be bulletproof, but Lance and Jason aren't."

"I guess that's true. Still," Sam ran both his hands into his hair and leaned back into the couch, "I wasn't expecting something like that. I'm not used to people communicating that way, so up front about conflict."

"I'm not sure that translates to their other relationships. I think the pressure of doing what they do—of doing what you do—brings that out a bit more."

"Yeah, I guess." First the lying, now this. Sam had spent his entire life trying to keep the peace. How was he supposed to just accept this level of confrontation as a new norm? He had no say in how his powers changed him physically, but how much could he let being a hero change him mentally before he wasn't even the same person anymore?

"Hailey just called," Jason announced, walking back from the lockers, jolting Sam from his thoughts. "She's heading home to work on her story on the attempted burglary. She asked if we could postpone movie night. And also, if someone could take Gwen home. I told her yes on both."

"I guess that's my cue." Gwen smiled as she stood up and grabbed her coat.

"We should all call it a night," Jason said, patting Taylor's shoulder again as he talked. "We'll see you tomorrow, Sam."

The four of them walked out into the cold night together, Gwen, Jason, and Taylor piling into Jason's car while Sam began his run home in the dark November night.

He spent the jog thinking about what had happened. *I was so caught up thinking about how I was putting others in danger, I never really thought about the danger I was in too*, he thought. *Gwen is right, being out in the field like this is life and death for everyone involved. I have to be more aware of those consequences. I should have waited for Jason, even after Taylor told me to stall. I have to do better next time too.*

He spent the rest of the jog wrapped in his thoughts. He was still struggling with how openly confrontational it all was and what it meant for his sense of self if he had to adapt to existing in that confrontation. He was so distracted, he overshot his apartment by a mile and had to backtrack home. When he finally made it he fell asleep as soon as he hit his bed, the adrenaline from the night wearing off and leaving him exhausted.

The movie night went as planned the next evening. They waited until Sam had time to change after working the afternoon Dutchmen home game, which Duncan won, improving to 11-1 and clinching a playoff bid with four games to go.

Taylor brought food for everyone from the Tex-Mex restaurant a block from the warehouse. They had eaten more Tex-Mex while Lance was out of town since he always complained about it when it was suggested. It was Gwen's turn to pick the movie, so they watched a murder mystery from the forties.

Taylor had the monitor up all night, but it never interrupted. It was a quiet Sunday night in Duncan.

The next few days were quiet as well, relative to their normal workload at least. Sam and Jason went out a couple times during the week, but there weren't any major issues. Still, it was a good opportunity to build their connection in the field.

And then Friday came.

"Sam, you busy?" Taylor asked over the phone at two in the afternoon.

"Not really, just taking care of a few things at the office. What's up?"

"There's an incident downtown, and I can't get ahold of Jason. There's a standoff outside a bank. I know you haven't gone out on your own before, but it's not looking good for the people out there. Are you up for it?"

"I'm on my way," Sam answered, already heading for the stairwell, bag slung over his shoulder.

Sam took off for the warehouse where he dropped his bag and grabbed his mask and hoodie before heading right back out the door, sprinting towards the bank.

The scene was tense when he arrived, with helicopters circling the area and a number of heavily equipped police vehicles parked on the street. Officers tried to maintain boundaries and push onlookers back, but the crowd had grown so large they struggled to make any progress.

"Sam, can you hear me?" Taylor's voice cut into his earpiece.

"I thought you were in class?"

"Took a bathroom break. Now listen. It looks like there's just one man, but he's threatened to shoot if anyone approaches the building. You can get through a window and to him before he has a chance. I can see him through one of the police's video feeds. He keeps walking back to the office whenever they call him. I'm going to call the number. The moment he starts walking towards the office, I'll give you a signal, and you take off. The office is about thirty feet beyond the front door and fifteen feet to the left. You're going to jump through the front window and run straight back to the office and take care of it there. Got it?"

"Yeah, okay, I got it, I'm ready." Sam rolled his shoulders and bounced on the balls of his feet as he waited for the signal.

"Now, Sam! Go!" Taylor's voice was still coming through the earpiece as Sam began his sprint.

The wind raced by as he picked up speed, passing people, cars, and buildings on his way. He leapt as he approached the front of the bank. Mindful of his abilities as he was, he still almost overshot the top of the window. He lifted his arms to cover his face as he braced himself for impact. The glass shattered, cascading to the floor around him as he hit the ground running. Three steps and he had crossed half the room. Two more, and he was almost to the office door when bullets came flying out of the office. Sam took the bullets to the chest and entered the room. The sound of gunshots was followed by metallic clattering as they fell around Sam.

"Wh-what are you?" the man whispered as the last of his bullets fell to the ground. He looked to be in his late forties. White, a hat on to cover his balding head. He looked small next to Sam.

"Someone trying to make the most of a bad situation," Sam answered, striding across the room.

The man cowered as Sam approached. Sam reached over and took the gun, crushing it in his hand as he set it down on the desk. Then, picking the man up by the back of his shirt, Sam walked him out of the building and dropped him to the ground as he stood over him. His hoodie was riddled with bullet holes, and his long hair had been let out after a bullet had caught his hair tie.

The officers present stood in shock as Sam waited only a second before sprinting away from the scene, heading back to the warehouse.

It had only been fifteen minutes since Taylor's call when Sam got back to the warehouse. With Taylor in class and Gwen, Hailey, and Jason all at work, he was on his own at the base. He sat down on the couch to change into a new set of clothes without bullet holes before heading back to work.

"Sammy." Hailey's voice sounded distant to him. "Sammy, get up," she continued.

He felt himself being shaken and slowly opened his eyes.

"How long have you been asleep?" she asked as he looked around the room, blinking to adjust to the light.

"I don't remember," he mumbled, rubbing at his eyes. "I don't remember falling asleep. What time is it now?"

"Eight-thirty," Jason said, entering his frame of vision and handing him a bottle of water. "We've been trying to wake you up for two hours; everyone took turns. Hailey's been over here five or six times at this point."

"I remember getting back from the standoff and sitting down to change clothes," he said before taking a deep drink of water and shaking his head. "That's the last I remember."

He looked down to find himself still wearing the bullet-ridden hoodie.

"I'm glad you're up. We were all getting worried, Sammy."

"I'm okay," he said, giving a smile to reassure his cousin, though her expression didn't change. "Where are Gwen and Taylor?"

"We sent them after food," Jason answered. "None of us had eaten, and we figured you'd want to eat when you got up. Plus, it got Taylor out of here for a bit. He was starting to freak out a little, thinking he had somehow done something to cause this. After our conversation last week, I think he's a bit jumpy, making sure he's not being careless."

Sam took another drink and nodded, but he didn't say anything. He still thought Jason had been too hard on Taylor.

"Wake up a bit," Jason said, slapping Sam's leg and standing up. "Walk around or something to get those cobwebs out. Food will be here soon."

Jason walked back to the monitor, and Sam sat up next to Hailey.

"I'm okay, I promise," he told her. She hadn't looked away from him since he had woken up, and he could tell she was still concerned.

"I'm just still getting used to this new schedule," he laughed, but that didn't seem to ease Hailey's concern either. "I'm going to step outside and get some air to wake up. I'm good."

"Okay," she sighed, still unconvinced but not pressing him on the subject.

He got to his feet and walked to the door. Jason had put it back on its hinges the same night he had torn it off.

Sam stepped outside and took a deep breath of the crisp fall air. He walked in circles in the parking lot, swinging his arms in and out as he went. Five minutes went by before headlights pulled into the parking lot and drove directly towards him.

"Sam!" Taylor yelled as he put the car in park and hopped out of the driver's seat. "How are you feeling?"

"I'm okay. Just still getting used to this schedule, I guess."

"We're going to run some tests just to be safe," Taylor answered.

"A little help here," Gwen called from the car as she stacked to-go boxes in one arm. Dennis still had a no-takeout rule at the diner, but for their group, enforcing that rule was no longer even attempted. He'd gone so far as to start keeping to-go containers on hand since one of them came in with a big order for the group at least once a week.

Taylor jogged back over to help Gwen unload the Fran's takeout and the three of them returned inside. It took some time, but Gwen, Jason, and Sam finally convinced Hailey and Taylor to let Sam eat before they started running tests.

"You're kidding," Hailey muttered as Sam took his first bite of his burger. Everyone else had already opened their containers, but Hailey was staring at her phone. "What an absolute rat."

"What is it?" Jason asked, leaning over to look at her phone.

"Remember the guy I told you about that had taken my place on the paper at Franklin? The one who was trashing Ashley?" She waited for hesitant nods from the group before continuing. "His name's Jasper Saunders, and he's apparently decided to take a break from Ashley to write about Sam instead."

"Let me see," Jason said as she handed him her phone. "The Duncan Devil? I guess it really could have been worse than Ironside. Says here that Duncan's new hero is an abomination, an atrocity, and an affront to God himself. You'd think he'd have made it out of the A's in the dictionary by now."

"Jason, this is serious," Hailey said as she swiped her phone back from him.

"The dude's a hack," Jason answered as he went back to his sandwich. "You've said so yourself, he's just trying to rile people up. This is just as unserious as he is."

"That doesn't make it okay that he's saying these things about Sam, though." Hailey put her phone down and covered her face. "I'm sorry, Sam. I should have pushed for them to get rid of him when I was still at the paper."

"It's not your fault," Sam shrugged. "Besides, I'd rather him come after me than y'all's friend. I'm sure there's a lot more pressure on her with the articles being written about her at her own school than there is on me being up here in Duncan."

"You really don't mind?" Hailey asked, tapping her finger on the back of her phone.

"I really don't. I've had my entire life flipped in the last few months, and I've been on both sides of near-death experiences enough now that some jerk with a column isn't going to take too much of my headspace."

"Okay, that's a relief," Hailey said, exhaling a long breath before opening her container. "But I'm still going to give the people at the paper a piece of my mind for letting Jasper talk about both you and Ashley like he has been."

"I support that," Sam answered with a smile. She pushed at her eggs with her fork, but could tell she wasn't okay even after he assured her he was fine. And he was. He didn't like having someone talking about him like he wasn't human, but that had grown all too common even without factoring in unprecedented superpowers. The hatred drove clicks, and clicks drove the business. Jason was right, it was hard to take people like Jasper seriously enough to let them get under your skin. As far as he was concerned, it was a non-issue, though he could tell Hailey didn't feel the same way, especially since it was from her old paper. "And you're already doing your part, covering all of us in a positive light. Don't take the blame on yourself because this Jasper guy sucks."

"Okay, okay," Hailey said with a small smile. "You're right. But I'm still calling the paper tomorrow."

"Deal," Jason answered after swallowing. "Now eat. Please. Your food is going to get cold, and you refuse to eat cold eggs, and I don't want to lose my sandwich."

They finished eating by nine and Taylor immediately began putting Sam through all the tests. Taylor had the results from previous tests pulled out as he went, so he could check for any discrepancies. A little after ten, Taylor finally finished and let Sam join the others.

"I want to run a couple of these again to make sure we got the right results," Taylor said as he walked up with his clipboard ten minutes later, causing Sam to groan.

"That's going to have to wait, Taylor," Jason responded from the monitor. "We've got a break-in at Armstrong Enterprises. Department of Defense contractor. We need to check this out."

"No, there might be something wrong with Sam," Taylor said, shaking his head.

"I'll watch him," Jason answered, putting a hand on Taylor's shoulder. "We need to check this out. This isn't a bank or a jewelry store. Whoever is breaking into a place like this is after more than a quick score. He'll be okay." He turned to Sam. "Let's roll."

They waited for Jason to get suited and then took off for the factory, Jason on the motorcycle and Sam running alongside him.

"Okay." Taylor's voice was terse as it came through his earpiece. "Armstrong Enterprises has the most sophisticated security system I've seen. I can't get in, so I'm only going to have the body cam on Jason's suit and the small camera on Sam's mask once you're in. I'm rewinding the outdoor feed Jason spotted them on, and it looks like there are twelve armed men in the factory. I'll speak up if I see anything that's helpful, but I'm flying blind for this, so I won't have too much to say. Be careful in there."

"Anyone on patrol?" Jason asked as he killed the engine and glided into the parking lot.

"Not that I can see," Taylor answered. "It looks like everyone in the group went into the building."

"Copy that." Jason hopped off the bike and motioned for Sam to follow him.

They walked up to the door and Jason turned the handle. Locked. Jason stepped aside and made room for Sam. Sam obliged, and the door opened with a loud crack as the lock broke off.

They stood still, waiting to see if the noise had sounded an alarm, but the hallway before them remained empty. The two of them crept through the building, looking in each room for the burglars. They didn't see another person until they got to the large double doors leading into the main factory at the end of the hall. Unlike the other doors in the facility they had passed, these had no windows.

"We're going in blind," Jason mumbled as he slowly pushed one of the handles down.

The silence erupted as gunshots tore out before they could even see into the room. Jason screamed out as the bullets pierced first the door, and then his suit. Sam stared as a mixture of horror and dread threatened to overwhelm him. The roar of gunfire. The blood. He hadn't been doing this long, but this was the first time he had felt real fear for Lance or Jason.

"Jason!" Taylor yelled through the headset as he saw the scene play out on their suit cameras, shocking Sam back into the moment. "Sam, get him out of there!"

Without another second's hesitation, Sam scooped Jason up and sprinted back out the way they had come as bullets continued riddling the door behind them. Once out of the building, Sam slowed as he approached the bike.

"I can ride back," Jason said through gritted teeth, climbing onto the motorcycle.

"You sure about that?" Sam asked as they heard the sound of the door behind them opening.

"Yes," Jason answered before tearing off. Sam stayed close behind him as gunshots sounded around them, narrowly missing them as they escaped into the night. He had taken it for granted that they would continue to be fine with their suits and with Taylor running the show. But now?

TWENTY-TWO

"Get him to the bed!" Taylor yelled from across the room while he prepped his supplies.

Jason had been able to ride back to the base but had struggled to drive in a straight line the whole trip. Sam had to lift him up off the bike so he could get off. Jason walked in on his own two feet, but only by using Sam's arm for support.

Hailey and Gwen both rushed up as they walked through the door.

"J, are you okay?" Hailey asked, her usual cool demeanor shaken.

Jason managed a single nod but couldn't get any words out. Gwen reached one hand up to Hailey's shoulder and wrapped the other around her for a hug as Sam kept Jason moving across the warehouse.

Sam lifted him up and gently laid him down on the bed. Hailey and Gwen began working to take off Jason's suit, with the exception of the left arm guard, where the bullets had hit.

"Everyone give me space," Taylor said, returning with his cart of supplies. Sam and Gwen walked back to the sitting area, but Hailey refused to go more than a few feet away while Taylor worked.

"What happened out there?" Gwen asked as she sat down on the couch, looking back over her shoulder at Jason as she talked.

"I don't know," Sam sighed, sinking as deep into the couch as he could and pinching the bridge of his nose. "One moment everything was quiet and fine, and Jason was opening the door, and the next he was screaming, and gunshots were echoing around. That's all I know. Adrenaline kicked in, and I got him out of there. That's all I know." Sam shook his head as he repeated himself. He opened his eyes after Gwen rubbed his back and gave her a small smile, which she returned. Adrenaline still coursed through his body, but he had no release for it. He wasn't going to leave until he knew Jason was alright and there wasn't anything he could do in the warehouse to expel energy like this without bringing the whole place down. So the two sat in silence for the next twenty minutes, save a few short questions with shorter answers, before Taylor called them over to the bed.

"I've never seen anything like this before," Taylor said softly, a few feet away from where Jason was sleeping. Taylor had given him pain meds and put him under while he worked. Different equipment surrounded the bed, stuff Sam hadn't seen but Taylor must have still been dragging out as they'd returned. "These aren't like any kind of bullets I've seen before. Jason might know more about this stuff once he's up, but for now, I have no idea what we're dealing with. He got lucky. Only three bullets actually hit him. Two grazed his arm, and the third was a through-and-through without too much damage. He'll be fine in no time, but he's going to have to fix his suit. And we might want to be extra cautious if the suit can't protect him from these bullets. Jason's suit isn't quite as strong as Lance's, but we've never seen anything pierce even his suit like this. I'm going to stay with him overnight, but you all should go get some rest."

"Absolutely not," Hailey said immediately. "I'm staying."

"I figured." Taylor shrugged, and Hailey walked over to sit next to Jason, using her sleeve to wipe some of the sweat that was still sitting on his forehead.

"You two should go rest though," Taylor said, turning back to Sam and Gwen. "We'll let you know if there's any updates."

The two of them nodded as he spoke. Sam walked away, and Gwen followed shortly after, taking a moment to talk to Hailey before leaving.

Sam showered off when he got home and made himself a sandwich, hungry again after the night's activities. Even after his long nap earlier in the day he was exhausted when he got to bed and fell asleep with the faint glow of his lamp still shining.

Sam woke up and rubbed at his eyes, groaning as he sat up in bed. Five new messages were on his phone. A long one from Hailey detailing how Jason was doing, one from Taylor giving a more condensed message of how Jason was doing, and three from a group chat Jason had created with him and Gwen. The first text read *I'm fine!* The second was just a selfie of him smiling while making a hang loose sign with his arm bandaged and Hailey asleep next to him on the base's hospital bed. The third message was Gwen liking the photo.

Sam smiled as he stretched his back out, glad Jason was feeling better. His phone buzzed again, and a new message popped up from Brooklyn.

Where are you?

The text bubbles popped back up.

We're about to start boarding.

Sam frantically scrolled up and found the message Brooklyn had sent a few days earlier, which he had forgotten to read.

Game flexed from Monday to Sunday due to incoming weather. Leaving Saturday at noon.

Oh no. Sam grabbed his camera bag and threw a change of clothes in his duffel bag and ran out the door. It was 11:43 when he began the seven-mile run and he got through the doors of the airport at 11:49. He ran up to the express security line and was rushed through in ten minutes, arriving just before the gates closed. Sam stepped on the plane at 11:59 and hadn't even had time to sit down before it turned to 12:00.

"Cut it close enough," Brooklyn said as Sam sat down next to her.

"Sorry about that," Sam answered, breathing heavier than usual. He leaned into his seat and let out a long sigh. *That was close.*

Brooklyn put her headphones on and looked out the window as the pilot made his announcements.

Sam closed his eyes as the plane started moving. Takeoff never got easier for him.

"Sir, sir." Sam opened his eyes. A stewardess was shaking him. "We've landed. You have to get off the plane."

Sam looked around. The plane was empty. He apologized as he grabbed his bag and continued saying sorry the whole way out the door. Brooklyn was gone when he got to the baggage claim area. He already had everything he had packed in hand, so he stepped out the door into the freezing rain. He pulled his coat tight around him and began the jog to the hotel.

He looked for Brooklyn when he got to the hotel but couldn't find her and she didn't return his texts, so he ordered delivery for his dinner. He sent an explanatory text to the team detailing why he was gone so abruptly and then lay down in the hotel bed, remembering to set an alarm this time.

Brooklyn had already left for the game when Sam got to the lobby on Sunday morning. He ate the free breakfast at the hotel and began his jog to the stadium. He arrived ahead of schedule and made his way to the press room.

Brooklyn began walking towards him as soon as he entered the room.

"We need to talk," she said as she walked past him into the hall.

Sam turned around and followed her to an empty room.

"What's up?" Sam asked as she closed the door behind them.

"I like you, Sam, but you have to start communicating better and prove to me I can count on you. You're late a lot, you're hard to get a hold of, and nobody ever knows where you are. You never responded to my message about the game time changing, and then you almost missed the flight. I've put my neck out on the line for you with Barry. I staked my reputation on you being worth it. And lately, I don't think you're holding up your end of that bargain."

Sam stood there, staring at the ground. He scratched his head and took a deep breath as she stood there with her arms crossed.

"You're right," he said softly. "I didn't know you had put your neck out for me, but you're right that I haven't been carrying my weight here. I've been preoccupied by other things, but I haven't been communicating well with you, and it's a fair criticism to say you're not sure you can count on me. I'm sorry." Sam's eyes stayed on the floor until the last sentence. "You've had my back from day one, and I let you down. I'll be better."

Brooklyn's face softened, and she rested a hand on Sam's arm. "Thank you. It means a lot that you owned up to it. I'm sorry for giving you the cold shoulder yesterday. I was frustrated, but I should have gone about it differently. I could have communicated better, too. I just wanted us to have this talk and be on the same page."

"I appreciate that." Sam nodded as he answered.

"Now let's go get ready for this game." She slapped his arm, and he followed her back out into the busy hallway.

chapter

TWENTY-THREE

"I'm ready to go back out," Jason insisted as Taylor stood with his arms crossed, shaking his head.

It had been a slow week after the incident at Armstrong Enterprises. A lucky break with Jason's injury and Lance still being in Franklin. Gwen had lunch with Lance early that week and caught him up to speed with what had happened. She seemed to think he'd be returning soon.

Taylor repeated the same refrain he had used every other night that week when Jason begged to return to the field. "You're not fully healed yet. If you go out before you're a hundred percent, you'll only cause a setback for yourself and prolong your hiatus."

"Just take it easy and get some rest, babe," Hailey called from the couch where she was sitting with Sam and Gwen. "You'll have plenty of time to get back out there once you're healed."

"It's okay, Hailey, Taylor is babying me enough for ten people, you don't have to jump on too."

"Fine." Hailey threw her hands in the air and turned to the TV. Gwen and Sam exchanged a quick look. Jason had been more irritable than usual since his forced hiatus, but he had reserved that irritability exclusively for Taylor. His snapping at Hailey seemed to surprise Gwen just as much as it did him.

Jason sighed and walked over to the couch, sitting down next to Hailey.

"That was out of line. I'm sorry. I'm just frustrated about being sidelined. Lance is out of town, and I have the chance to kind of take that mantle, and now I'm hurt and feel like I blew that opportunity. Everyone in the city thinks I'm just the White Knight's sidekick, and I wanted to use his absence to prove them wrong. I know you're only looking out for what's best for me, and I appreciate that." He kissed the back of her head since she was still facing the TV.

"You do appreciate that?" She was still facing the TV and her voice stayed flat, but it had softened slightly.

"Of course." He smiled, reaching over to hold her hand. She sank back into him and rested her head on his shoulder.

"Okay," she answered after a moment, tilting her head back to look at him as he kissed her forehead. "That's good."

Gwen had picked the movie. The four sat and watched in silence after that while Taylor watched the monitors.

Snow fell outside of the warehouse, the first snowfall had started the day before and was still going steady, causing some issues with travel for the post-Thanksgiving traffic, but nothing the team could do much to help.

Hailey explained to her family that, because she was a first-year student at the paper, she had to work the holiday and couldn't make it to them. Jason had the week off, but he wasn't much in shape for traveling, so he told his family he wasn't feeling well and that he didn't want Hailey to be alone for the holiday. Taylor's dad didn't care much for celebrating holidays, and he expected Taylor to be studying the whole break anyway. Gwen had driven down to her parents' house outside of Franklin Wednesday night and came back Friday afternoon.

"Everyone is welcome to join," she had told them on Wednesday before she had left. "It's a short drive, and my family is happy to have others join us."

No one had taken her up on the offer, though, and they had takeout in the warehouse for Thanksgiving like they did most other nights. Gwen had only been back in town for a couple of hours when they started the movie.

"Okay, we have a problem," Taylor called from the monitor. Sam, Jason, and Hailey immediately joined him at the monitor, and Gwen followed shortly after, pausing the movie.

"Another break-in. This time at Goldfinch Incorporated. Same M.O. as the last group. Twelve guys all looking the same. Their security system is top of the line, so I can't get any of their cameras pulled up. These guys have to be either pulling inside jobs or be well beyond professionals."

"Let's go get them," Jason said, turning to walk to the locker.

"Absolutely not," Taylor said. "I'm passing this tip to the police and hoping they actually act on it for once."

"Really, Jason." Hailey shook her hand, her arms crossed across her chest. "Do you have a death wish?"

"We can't just let this go. The same group hits two defense contractors a week apart, which means some big stuff is in the works. We need to check it out."

"Jason's right," Sam spoke up. "These people already have too much firepower. Who knows what else they're getting from these factories? I'll go check it out." If they already have guns that can tear through Jason's suit like it's paper, whatever they're after has to be bad news. This is what he signed up for when he decided to be a hero, and there's no one else to go. Ready or not, it had to be him.

"You can't go rushing in by yourself, Sam," Taylor said, shaking his head no.

"Then let me go with him," Jason tried again. "I'll be careful and just there for support.

"I don't know." Taylor was still shaking his head as he talked. "I don't think you're healthy enough to be in the field.

"I'll manage. But we need to go now or we're going to lose our chance."

Taylor ran his fingers through his hair and tapped his fingers on his forehead.

"Okay, fine," Taylor sighed. "But you're following Sam this time and avoiding any unnecessary risks. We don't know anything about these bullets, so both of you try to stay out of sight. Don't take any risks you don't have to take. Go in, see what they're after, and get out. Reconnaissance only tonight, do not engage."

"Deal. Let's get ready, Sam." He patted Sam on the arm and jogged to the locker. Hailey didn't say anything but walked over to the lockers with him, and they spoke while she helped him suit up. He had put some sort of metallic patches on his suit during the last week, but hadn't been able to fully repair it yet. Three minutes later, he had mounted the bike, and they were pulling away from the warehouse while Hailey wiped at her eyes and rejoined Taylor and Gwen at the monitor.

"Okay." Taylor's voice came through their earpieces as they approached the factory. "All twelve are inside. No lookouts again. Remember the plan. Sam leads the way, and Jason is just there as backup. Be smart. Be cautious. Be safe."

"Copy," Sam and Jason both replied as Taylor finished.

Jason came to a stop on the bike as they arrived, and Sam slowed to a walk while Jason dismounted.

The two of them slowly approached the building. Sam broke the lock on the outside door, and they crept inside. The hallways were dark, the only light being a dim line that stretched across the center of the ceiling. Sam took the right doors and Jason the left as they ensured each room was empty.

As they came to the end of the hall, it branched out to the left and right. They crept to the point where the halls intersected. Sam motioned for Jason to stand back while Sam checked the halls. Jason nodded and Sam moved, quickly looking both ways before diving back the way he came.

"All clear," he said, standing back up as Jason swore.

"Then why are you diving around? About gave me a heart attack. Come on, man." Jason shook his head as he walked past Sam into the intersection.

Down the left hall, the walls were lined with doors leading to another intersection further down. To the right, the walls were bare before ending in two large double doors at the end of the hall, about fifty yards away.

"I'm thinking we go to the right," Jason said as Sam joined him in the intersection.

Sam nodded and began leading the way to the doors. Like at Armstrong, these were solid metal with no windows. There had been different noises coming from behind the doors in the other halls, hummings, whirrings, and the like, but the hall leading to the double doors was silent beyond the muffled noises Sam and Jason made as they approached. The silence as they came to a stop at the end of the hall made the hairs on Sam's arm stand up under his hoodie. He motioned for Jason to stand back and then tried to open the door slowly.

The moment the door creaked open, the crack of gunshots tore through the silence. Sam made it back behind the wall without being hit, but just barely.

After the gunshots subsided, they waited to see if any gunmen would come out like they did last time. After twenty seconds of silence, Sam stood back up.

"What's the plan here, Sam?" Taylor asked as Sam walked in front of the door.

Without answering, Sam kicked the door open, using as much of his strength as he could to send the door flying through the air, striking two of the gunmen. "Reconnaissance only" had gone out the door when the bullets started flying. Before anyone had time to respond, Sam kicked the second door too, striking another two gunmen, diving back behind the wall as gunshots echoed through the room.

"Sam, what are you doing?" Taylor screamed into the earpiece.

Sam didn't have time to answer before two more gunmen came into the hall, raising their guns at him.

He kicked the closest one in the leg, feeling the bone snap effortlessly on impact and causing the attacker to fall to the floor. Jason lunged with his spear across the hall, piercing the shoulder of the one in the rear and sending an electrical current through the spear, causing that gunman to also fall to the floor.

Gunshots flew through the door as the second man was still falling, his body riddled with bullets from his own team.

"Now what do we do?" Jason yelled from across the doorway.

The fire alarm began blaring, and the sprinklers went off as the gunshots stopped and were replaced with yelling. One of the gunmen yelped before more gunshots sounded. These weren't directed at their door, though. Sam and Jason peeked into the room to see a glint of white dive behind a wall, narrowly missed by more bullets.

Sam ran into the room, using the chaos as cover. His hair had quickly become drenched from the sprinklers, and any loose hairs were now plastered to his face. Lifting one of the doors he'd knocked in earlier, he threw it at the remaining five gunmen, knocking each of them over. The white blur they'd seen earlier reappeared from behind the wall.

Lance!

Sam and Lance ran from the room as the gunmen who weren't unconscious or unable to stand scrambled to their feet. Jason joined them as they sprinted down the hallways and back out the doors to their bikes.

Sirens blared as they tore out of the parking lot and headed back to the warehouse.

"Welcome back, Lance," Taylor greeted as the three of them came into the warehouse, Jason and Lance on their bikes and Sam on foot. Taylor, Gwen, and Hailey were all still sitting at the monitor watching the scene at Goldfinch's factory unfold as the flashing lights of cop cars filled the parking lot.

"Good to be home," Lance answered, slumping into his locker and beginning to take off his suit.

"How was Franklin?"

"It was a good time. Got a lot done down there. But clearly, I've been missing some stuff up here."

"This is still a pretty new development," Jason said while sitting down in his own locker.

"And after two near-death run-ins for Sam and Jason, we still have no idea what they want or what these weapons of theirs do," Taylor sighed.

"Well, that's half true," Jason said, leaning up with a grin. He reached behind him and pulled out one of the guns from the factory. "Grabbed this on the way out from one of the guys we fought in the hall. Thought I'd take a look at it and see what we're up against."

"Jason, that's brilliant," Lance said, looking over at the gun.

"Yeah, it's late tonight, but starting tomorrow, I'm going to see what I can figure out about this piece. That might help us figure out what they want to do."

"Please be safe messing with that thing," Hailey said. "We've already seen what it can do to you."

"I'll be safe," Jason reassured her with a smile.

"Lance, how did you know to go to the factory?" Sam asked.

"I had gotten back and came straight to the warehouse. I had just missed you two leaving, and so I suited up to serve as backup or reinforcement if you needed it. Taylor was talking me through everything he could see on your cams and keeping me up to speed."

"Guess that's why Taylor hardly said anything to us all night," Jason remarked.

"Sorry, I was trying to help you not get killed." Taylor shrugged. "If you remember, it was supposed to be reconnaissance only, so I was trying to stay off your comms as much as I could. Once the bullets started flying, I was trying to get Lance in position to help."

"Fair enough," Jason yawned and leaned back into the locker. He had taken the top part of his suit off, but the leg pieces were still attached.

"So, what's the plan now?" Sam asked, hoping that engaging after the bullets started flying wasn't going to lead to him being on the receiving end of one of those confrontational lectures Jason had warned him about. After the experience last time with the gunmen chasing them down, he'd figured trying to retreat down that long haul with bullets flying would've been a death sentence for

Jason. Still, he'd jumped right in and completely disregarded the plan without running it by anyone. Luckily, no one seemed to be too concerned with calling him out tonight.

"Jason will take some time to look at this new weapon, and he and Taylor will come up with some ideas about what it is and what it means," Lance answered. "Then we'll reevaluate. For tonight, though, you all should call it a night. I'll take the late shift."

"Sounds good to me," Jason yawned again. He took off his leg pieces and stood up, putting his hoodie on as he did. "I need some rest to be able to examine this bad boy tomorrow."

"I'll stay here with Lance in case someone needs to watch the monitors," Gwen said as Hailey and Jason began walking out.

"You don't have to do that, Gwen," Taylor said. "I'm good to stay."

"I know you are. But you're always having to stay. And I want to spend some time with Lance anyway, after not getting to see each other much these last few weeks. You and Sam go get some rest. You've earned it."

"I'll see y'all tomorrow," Sam said, walking out the door with a wave. He jogged back to his apartment in the brisk November night air, then crawled into bed and fell asleep immediately.

TWENTY-FOUR

The sun was bright when Sam woke up. As was becoming a habit, he had a slew of missed messages on his phone after oversleeping again.

He showered and ate before leaving for the warehouse. When he arrived, Jason was there examining the weapons, but no one else was around.

"Any luck so far?" Sam asked as he fell onto the couch in the sitting area.

"Just getting started," Jason answered without looking up from his work. "I'm hoping to have an update tonight before anyone goes into the field."

"Cool, cool. Where is everyone?"

"Hailey and Gwen are at some sort of event that Hailey is covering this afternoon. Taylor is studying right now, and he'll be there this evening for dinner. No clue where Lance is."

"Did he go back to Franklin?"

"No, that trip's done. This is just typical Lance being off grid."

"Gotcha. Anything for me to do that can help?"

"Not really, not right now. Just hang out until everyone else meets back up tonight."

"Sounds good," Sam answered as he turned the TV on and got comfortable on the couch.

"Hey Sammy." Sam opened his eyes as Hailey shook him softly. Gwen sat on the couch opposite them while Jason still worked on the weapons at his table.

"Hey." Sam stretched out his arms and yawned as he sat up. "What time is it?"

"A little after six. How long have you been asleep?"

"Just a couple of hours."

"It's been four hours," Jason called from his table without looking up.

Snitch.

"I'm fine," Sam said as he saw the worry cloud Hailey's face. "Just a little nap."

"Mhm," Hailey hummed. Sam could tell she didn't believe him, but she didn't press it any further, and for that he was thankful. The fatigue was starting to worry him, too, but it seemed a pretty logical tradeoff for his powers. He did more, so he needed to rest more. Until Taylor told him he should be more concerned than that, he was going to keep on with business as usual.

Another hour passed before Taylor and Lance showed up with dinner. They each carried two pizzas that they sat down on the table.

"Eat up," Lance said as he stood back from the table, apparently having reappeared on the grid.

Everyone stopped what they were doing to fill a plate before gathering on the two couches.

"What's the update on that tech, Jason?" Taylor asked before taking his first bite of pizza.

Jason swallowed before answering. "It's top-of-the-line stuff. I know Fox has been working on something similar, but I don't have the clearance for that type of stuff. I think there's currently an arms race between a few different manufacturers to see who can develop this next-generation gun first."

"Let me guess," Lance said, "Armstrong and Goldfinch are two of those companies?"

"Bingo." Jason nodded. "Duncan has a lot of weapons manufacturers between Armstrong Enterprises, Goldfinch Incorporated, Fox Industries, and Fulmer Tech."

"But they already hit Enterprises and Incorporated, so we can rule those two out, right?" Sam asked.

"Maybe." Jason took another bite while he chewed on his words. "It could be a fake to cover their tracks, but I doubt either of those companies is behind it. It could still be their weapons, though. We can't be entirely sure it's one of those companies that are behind the break-ins.

Someone could have gotten their hands on the weapons and is just trying to find more. But if it is a company running these raids, then it's probably Fox or Fulmer."

"My money is on Fox," Lance said, shaking his head and scrunching up his nose, as if saying the name had the same effect as smelling sewage.

"I assumed it would be," Jason laughed. "I'll see what I can find out when I get back into the office. Like I said, I don't have that level of clearance, but I can poke around and see if there are any clues to be found."

"I can touch base with some of my sources too," Hailey added. "I might be able to turn something up that will get me a promotion instead of getting me fired." She batted her eyelashes at Jason.

"A true power couple," Gwen said, elbowing Hailey. Jason laughed and took a bow as he stood up to get more pizza.

The conversation turned to Lance's time in Franklin. Sam had never seen Lance as animated as he was now, talking about working with Franklin's new vigilante.

As ten pm had hit and the monitor hadn't sounded any alerts, Lance stood up and walked over to the lockers.

"What do you say we go on a patrol, Sam?" he asked as he walked away. "I've missed being out in Duncan."

"Sounds good to me," Sam answered as he stood up as well.

"Well then, let's get to it."

The two of them left the warehouse, Lance on his bike and Sam on foot as usual.

They got to the outskirts of downtown and came to a stop when they saw crowds of people up ahead.

"This is what makes patrols in Duncan so much harder," Lance complained as he got off his bike and pushed it as he talked to Sam. "There are people everywhere. It makes it impossible to go anywhere."

They skirted around and found a building with a fire escape and climbed it to the top.

"I missed this," Lance said, staring out at the city lights from atop the building.

"Yeah?"

"Being in Franklin again, being low-tech, doing patrols, running around rooftops. It took me back to the spring when I was just starting and knew even less than I do now. It wasn't a job then. It didn't feel this weighty. I was just trying to help people, you know? That feeling is more present when you're out here patrolling than when you're sitting in front of a computer waiting for something bad to happen."

"That makes sense. You're more of an active player in everything when you're out here."

"Yes, but it's not just that. Being in the fresh air, being in the heart of the city, you get to feed off the energy around you. You feel connected with what's happening in a way you can't just sitting in a warehouse. I really enjoyed being able to experience that again these last few weeks in Franklin, and I'm glad we're out here tonight."

"Me too, Lance. Me too."

They stood in silence as the city buzzed beneath them. They watched as city employees strung up Christmas lights overhanging the street. With Thanksgiving having passed, the downtown area was being transformed into a winter wonderland before their eyes.

An alarm blared out from below as gunshots cracked from behind them. They rushed to the opposite ledge to see a man tossing shots behind him as he fled the building they were on.

"Go. I'll catch up," Lance rushed to the fire escape even as he spoke.

Sam took a few steps back and then sprinted towards the ledge, leaping off into the night sky.

"Sam, no!" Taylor's voice broke in over the earpiece as Sam floated through the air.

The building they were on was ten stories high. Sam had never practiced or tested anything like this before—it was solely his gut instinct that he could make it. As he drifted towards the ground, he watched as the gunman ran out in front of him a few yards. Sam braced himself as he landed, stabilizing himself with his fist in the ground as he made contact. The earth shook beneath him, and the gunman fell to his knees at the force of the tremor. Sam rushed forward and lifted him off the ground, shaking the gun out of his hand as he did so.

"Looks like a normal gun," Taylor's voice came over the earpiece. "Still better not to take chances with it."

"Copy that," Sam answered and kicked the gun away.

"P-p-please," the man begged. "I was just trying to get some food for my family."

"Next time, don't bring a gun on your grocery trip," Lance said as he walked up and joined them.

"Cops are dispatched. ETA forty seconds."

Sirens blared down the street right as Taylor's voice cut out. Sam and Lance secured the man before taking off into the night, taking different paths back to the warehouse.

"That wasn't safe, Sam," Taylor said as they walked through the door. He'd been standing behind his chair with his arms crossed, waiting for them to return.

"I'm fine," Sam assured him. "You can give me a checkup if it would make you feel better."

"I plan on it."

"You have to admit, Taylor," Lance said as he took off his suit in front of his locker, "it was pretty cool."

Taylor pinched the bridge of his nose and sighed before conceding. "Yeah, okay, it was pretty cool."

"I'm glad to hear you say that," Jason said, hopping up from the couch. "I've been wanting to watch it again, but wanted to wait for Taylor to cool off. Everyone, come gather around."

Jason pulled up the video of Sam's jump from three camera angles, two security feeds, and Lance's suit, and the six of them critiqued the jump through laughter until Hailey and Gwen excused themselves to turn in for the night. Lance sent Jason, Sam, and Taylor home as well, as it was already pretty late, and he said he could handle anything else that popped up that night.

TWENTY-FIVE

As much as Lance wanted to continue going out on patrols every night like he had in Franklin, even he acknowledged that wasn't the best use of their time and energy. With Christmas approaching, they needed all-hands-on-deck for the crime wave taking place. It was the busiest they had ever been, with multiple break-ins happening every night. Luckily, while the volume of incidents was up, they had very few incidents that were more serious than a burglary, so Lance, Jason, and Sam could split up and cover more ground.

This strategy worked for a few weeks, with the team never sending more than one person for any assignment. They'd also avoided any more issues with the new weapons, though neither Jason nor Hailey had been able to turn up much useful information on the subject.

Both streaks ended the Saturday before Christmas.

"We've got an incident at the mall," Taylor called from the monitor.

It was two o'clock in the afternoon and everyone was in the warehouse. Sam, Hailey, and Jason sat on the couch watching football while Gwen and Lance were propped against the wall. Gwen was reading a book, and Lance was on his phone.

"Whose turn is it?" Jason asked without looking away from the TV.

"I think it's probably mine," Sam answered, also without looking away from the TV.

"Not that kind of incident. Everyone suit up," Taylor said.

Jason and Lance immediately got up and jogged to the lockers to get ready. Sam walked to the monitor to see what was happening. Gwen and Hailey joined him.

"Shooters in the mall," Taylor said, loud enough for Jason and Lance to hear from the lockers. "Looks like they may have gotten ahold of those new weapons."

"Wait, what?!" Jason yelled from the lockers.

"Judging by the damage the few shots they've taken have done, I'd say to expect the worst."

"Why are they attacking the mall?" Sam asked. "Going from defense contractors to a shopping mall doesn't make sense."

"The guns are on the street now," Jason answered, fumbling with his suit trying to get dressed faster. "Those aren't the people we've gone up against before. How many gunmen, Taylor?"

"Five."

"Different crew," Jason said, strapping his helmet on. "We need to get there now. Can't imagine what kind of chaos and destruction those things could cause in a public space."

Jason peeled out of the warehouse on his bike with Lance and Sam hot on his heels. The mall was further than where they usually responded to calls; it was almost five minutes from the warehouse with Taylor able to direct traffic out of their path.

"These aren't professionals," Lance said into the headset, "and they're not in an empty factory. We don't have the time to be any more cautious than necessary. Get in, take out the gunmen as quickly as possible, and get out. Everyone understand?"

"Copy that," Jason and Sam both replied.

"Good. Taylor, what kind of eyes do we have inside?"

"All cameras are running. I can see it all. When you're a minute out I'll give instructions on where to go."

"Copy," Lance said before the headsets went silent.

"Okay," Taylor's voice cut back in as they got closer to the mall, "they're at the second-floor jewelry store. Three outside guarding the store, two inside loading up bags. Three security guards are down, severity unknown. Police are on the north end and dispersing. You should be able to make it in the south door before officers block it off."

"Copy that, Taylor. Approaching now," Lance answered as the mall rushed towards them.

Sam sped up to take the lead, lowering his shoulder and shattering the glass leading into the mall. Jason and Lance rumbled in behind him and headed straight for the empty escalator going up, both riding their bikes to the second floor. While they rode up the escalator, Sam leapt up to the second floor, overshooting the jump and stumbling a bit as he landed.

He dove behind a pillar as gunshots sprayed around him. They didn't know if the new guns could hurt him yet, but they could definitely hurt Lance and Jason, even with the suits, so he was more than happy to be the one drawing fire. He peeked around the side and saw Jason leap off his bike, allowing its momentum to run it into one gunman while he tackled another nearby. Lance swung his sword through the legs of the third man guarding the door as he rode past, dropping him to the ground. Sam sprinted over and captured all three weapons before the gunmen could retrieve them.

More gunshots fired from inside the store as the two remaining gunmen opened fire. A scream echoed through the mall as the man Jason had been tangled up with was hit by a bullet.

"Taylor, I need eyes!" Jason yelled into his headpiece.

"Both behind the glass counter."

A crash sounded from inside the jewelry store as Lance's bike crashed into the counter and rolled to a stop outside next to Jason. Sam rushed in to take advantage of the distraction and secure the other two weapons. Sam's speed allowed him to get to one of the gunmen's weapons before he had time to react, but a shot fired as Sam was picking up the other gun.

"Aaaahhh!"

The still-intact glass cases erupted at the sound of Sam's cry. The windows to the stores surrounding the jeweler's shattered as well. The two gunmen screamed, clawing at their bleeding ears.

Sam's ears rang as glass fell to the floor around him, his hand gripping his right arm where the bullet had hit. Someone tugged on his back. He turned to find Jason above him, yelling words Sam couldn't hear.

Lance was mounting his white bike that was scratched up from crashing into the counter. Jason communicated with his hands for Sam to get on the back of his bike. Sam obliged. The three of them raced back down the escalator, exiting through the hole Sam had created earlier and passing through throngs of officers shouting unheard words.

Sam kept shaking his head, trying to regain his hearing and stave off the darkness he felt threatening his consciousness. If he slipped under now, who knew what kind of damage he'd cause lying in the road. On the other hand, if he lost consciousness the pain would finally stop, he thought, grinding his teeth as Jason hit a bump.

Taylor met them at the door. Hailey and Gwen stood up in the sitting area as Taylor and Jason led Sam across the room to the hospital bed. Sam rested his head on the pillow as Taylor began doing whatever it was he was doing.

Everyone swarmed around him, their mouths moving, but Sam couldn't hear any of them. He felt his breathing slow down as he sunk into the surprisingly comfortable bed. Taylor tried to say something to him. Sam stared at his mouth, trying to read his lips, but he couldn't make sense of it and his eyes began to glaze over. The pain dulled. Numbness spread, his entire body becoming less sensitive.

He blinked once, then twice for a bit longer, and then closed his eyes for a third time and drifted off to sleep through the pain as an overwhelming fatigue gripped him.

Sam blinked his eyes open and reached his hand up to rub his face. His muscles were stiff, but he did just get shot, so that was to be expected.

"He's up!" Jason yelled jumping from his seat next to Sam as footsteps sounded throughout the room.

Too loud. Sam groaned as Jason's voice hurt his ears. *At least I can hear again, though,* he thought.

"Sammy, are you okay?"

"Give him space!"

"Is there anything I can get him?"

The voices all mixed in with each other to where Sam had a hard time understanding what anyone was trying to say.

"Sam," Taylor's voice cut through the others', "I need you to look at me."

Sam blinked, trying to focus on Taylor. He had his glasses on and a bit of stubble on his chin.

That's a first.

"What's up, doc?" he croaked. He tried to smile but could tell he made more of a grimace. "Water?"

A hand held a bottle of water in front of his face, and Sam gratefully took a sip. He grimaced as it slid down his dry throat.

"How are you feeling?" Taylor asked.

"Like I just got shot," he croaked again. The water had only increased the burning in the back of his throat. He took another sip and winced as it burned going down again.

"Sam," Taylor said, his face hard, "you've been asleep for four days. I need you to chill with the jokes so I can figure out what's wrong."

Four days!

"There's no way I've been asleep that long. I just rested my eyes for a minute!"

"It's true, Sammy." Hailey reached out her hand and rested it on Sam's shoulder. "We've all been worried about you. Taylor hasn't left since the incident at the mall, and there's been at least one more of us here at every point since then."

Four days.

He breathed a sigh of relief that this had happened on the Dutchmen's bye week and he hadn't missed a game.

"I feel fine," Sam said, shaking his head. "Really, I mean my throat is dry and hurts, and my arm is a bit sore, but I feel fine other than that."

"Well, I'm just glad you're up." Taylor let out a deep breath as he pinched the bridge of his nose. "I'm going to run some of our tests on you, and then I'll probably go home and rest for a bit, leaving you in the capable hands of these three."

"You deserve some rest. Thanks for keeping an eye on me."

"What are friends for?" Taylor gave him a small smile and picked up his clipboard. "Everyone else go back to the sitting area. I need thirty minutes with Sam and then he's all yours."

Jason and Gwen headed towards the couches. Hailey hesitated a moment before she turned and walked back too.

"Okay," Taylor sighed, "you know the drill."

TWENTY-SIX

"I'm fine," Sam insisted. "I can help."

Gwen and Hailey just stared at him and shook their heads.

"You're not winning this one, bub," Jason laughed as he walked past carrying a box. "You're going to have to accept you're sitting this one out."

They were decorating *Fran's* for their Christmas party that Wednesday night. With Taylor catching up on sleep and Lance making Hoppin' trips back and forth to the airport, it was just the four of them left to decorate. Or rather three, since no one would let Sam so much as hang tinsel.

"How long am I going to be sidelined? I mean, if I can't help with Christmas decorating, how am I supposed to go back in the field?"

"You're not," Hailey answered flatly without looking away from the garland she was laying out on the bar top.

"I promise, I'm fine."

It was partially true. His arm was still incredibly sore, and lifting it caused considerable pain, but Taylor had done imaging on it, and nothing was broken or torn. Lance and Jason regularly went back out in the field with soreness. He understood why this situation was different, but that didn't make it easier to swallow.

"Just give it a few days, Sam," Gwen said, standing on top of a table to hang more garland from the ceiling. "We just want to make sure whatever was wrong is out of your system. Humor us." She winked at him as she stepped down off the table.

The bell above the door rang out, and Dennis and Harry carried in a medium-sized pine tree. Both of them were bundled up from head to toe in snow-dusted winter gear. Darlene walked in behind them, a thermal cup in hand.

The two men leaned the tree up against the wall. Dennis put an arm down on the counter to hold his weight while Harry put both hands on his knees.

"How'd us old farts get stuck doing the heavy lifting?" Dennis asked, breathing heavily.

"No, no, no," Jason laughed. "Don't start with that. I begged you to let me go take care of it." Jason bent over, made his voice gruff like Dennis's, and wagged his finger, "You don't know the first thing about picking out a tree, young buck. It's not about flash or pizazz, it's about substance that only an experienced eye can see."

"Why you little—" Dennis stood up straight and stepped towards him as Jason laughed and danced away.

"Come on, I'll help set it up," Jason offered, grabbing the tree and walking it over to where the stand was set up.

"That's what I thought," Dennis mumbled as the two of them walked over.

"Won't hear any complaints from me," Harry laughed, slapping Sam's non-injured shoulder as he sat down next to him. "Darlene sure picked out a handsome one. And the tree's not half bad either." Harry laughed as he watched Jason and Dennis trying to set up the tree.

"You're never at a loss for words are you, Harry?" Gwen laughed.

"Only every time I look at my wife." He kissed Darlene's hand as it rested on his shoulder.

"Why don't you ever talk about me like that?" Hailey called across the room to Jason.

"You're not my wife yet."

"And who's fault is that?" She cocked her head to the right and stared at him with eyebrows raised.

Jason stared at her for a moment and took a deep breath before turning back to the tree without answering.

"That always shuts him up," Hailey chuckled, softly enough that Jason couldn't hear her from across the room. "He'd propose right now, but he knows I'm not ready."

"That's good the two of you are communicating about that," Darlene said, slapping Harry's shoulder.

"She turned me down probably a hundred times before she agreed to marry me," Harry laughed. "I just kept the ring in my pocket and would ask again every so often. Sometimes a couple weeks would go by in between. Sometimes I'd ask her three or four times on the same day. She just kept saying—"

"Not yet," Darlene filled in the gap Harry left with a smile.

"I would have asked a million more times."

"That's why I finally said yes." Darlene gave him a soft tap on the head and walked back behind the counter to start a pot of coffee.

"Anyone give you guys any trouble with the closed sign out front?" Dennis asked as he and Jason came back from setting up the tree.

"None at all." Gwen smiled. "Are you sure you don't want any company for Christmas with Harry and Darlene going to Sanders? I hate for you to be all alone for the holidays."

"That's mighty sweet of you, but I'm looking forward to a couple weeks without having to see these two every day. Besides, I leave in the morning for Minnesota. Me and a couple of old buddies go up there to ice fish this time of year. It's the only time of the season where it's not too crowded."

"Well, I hope you have a good time," Gwen responded as Dennis gave her a pat on the shoulder.

"I gotta go start on the sweets," Dennis said as he walked back to the kitchen.

An hour later, they had just about decorated the entire diner when the bell rang, announcing Taylor's arrival. He brushed the snow off the shoulders of his sweater and joined the group around their table.

"Perfect timing," Jason jeered as he sat down.

"I was out hard," Taylor yawned, "I'm still half asleep."

"He earned it," Sam laughed as Taylor put his head down on the table.

"You're kidding," Gwen said as the bell rang again.

Standing in the doorway, decked head to toe in a Santa suit complete with a bushy white beard, was Lance.

"Ho ho ho, merry Christmas!" he bellowed, holding his stomach.

"We're closed," Dennis called from the kitchen window as everyone laughed.

"Go ahead, hyuck it up," Lance said, turning the chair between Taylor and Gwen around to sit in it backwards. "This bad boy more than paid for itself in tips today. People loved being driven around by Santa Claus."

"Since when are you a Christmas lover?" Gwen asked, poking his arm.

"Since it paid better than being a grinch," Lance laughed. "Though I guess I could also buy a grinch costume and find out which pays better. Really put it to the test."

"You're too much." Gwen shook her head as Dennis and Darlene brought out plates of food.

Sam stared in wonder at the platters piled high with ham, turkey, stuffing, mashed potatoes, corn, green beans, glazed carrots, gravy, cranberry sauce, and dinner rolls. He had never had a Christmas with so much food before. His grandparents had all died before he was born, and Christmases growing up had always just been him and his parents, so they'd always had simple meals. He wouldn't have traded those Christmases for anything, but he'd be lying if he said he wasn't excited for this big Christmas meal with Dennis pulling out all the stops. The group had pushed a few of the tables together so that everyone could sit around one large table together.

Harry stood up as the platters all got set on the table. He reached a hand out in each direction, one to Darlene and one to Jason. Everyone else followed suit as Harry closed his eyes, bowed his head, and prayed over the meal.

"Amen," Harry finished, sitting back down as a chorus of mumbled amens followed his.

The table erupted with noise as everyone began filling up their plates.

"You should really add some of this stuff to the menu, Dennis," Jason said through a mouthful of turkey.

"Absolutely not." Dennis shook his head. "Takes too long. Not worth the effort to sell."

Darlene retrieved the sweets and lined them out on the counter as everyone finished eating. Drawing teams out of a hat, they split up into three groups for Gwen's 'reindeer games': Sam, Gwen, and Taylor on one; Lance, Jason and Darlene on the second; and Harry, Dennis, and Hailey on the third.

The first game: a gingerbread house competition.

Each team took their ingredients to their respective tables and began working on their house. Sam wasn't able to help much with the construction of the house even with how much better his control had gotten. Admittedly, he'd broken his fair share of gingerbread houses before the super strength entered the equation. He offered ideas, though, as Gwen and Taylor worked together on the construction. Their house wasn't perfect, but given that it was the only one standing at the end, everyone had to agree they had won the first game.

For game number two, Darlene handed out a pair of reindeer antlers and a pack of candy canes to each team.

"The object of the game," she explained, "is for two of the people on your team to hook as many candy canes as they can on the third team member's antlers."

With Sam still not the best choice for fine-motor-skill games, it was decided he would join Lance and Hailey in wearing the antlers.

Still dressed in a full Santa costume, but with antlers instead of his red hat, Lance won the reindeer game for his team, hooking seven canes on his antlers, leaning as far in each direction as he could from his chair to make sure as many as possible found their mark.

Thanks to Harry and Dennis's movie knowledge, Hailey's team won the Christmas movie trivia handedly, leading to a fourth game winner-take-all.

"The last game will be—" Gwen looked around at each group as everyone waited to hear what the event would be . "—charades! Each person should write down three Christmas-related nouns to be put into—Lance's Santa hat." She grinned as he handed it over. "Whichever team guesses the most on their turn wins!"

As the buzzer went off, Lance threw the hat on the ground signaling the end of his time—and the game.

"How was I supposed to act out Figgy Pudding?" Lance complained after losing to Hailey, Harry, and Dennis.

"Just act like you were eating pudding!" Jason yelled at him. "There aren't that many Christmas-themed puddings! We would've gotten there!"

Sam laughed at their bickering with everyone else, but he was glad the games portion of the night had ended. He liked games, but his shoulder had gotten more and more sore throughout the night, and charades had almost been too much for him to handle.

"This gold champion stocking will look great hanging from our mantle some day," Hailey ribbed Jason, holding the stocking up in the light in front of his face.

"I'm sure it would." Jason rolled his eyes and walked back for another cookie.

"Now for the final event," Gwen announced as everyone gathered around the tree, "white elephant!"

The tree had nine presents under it. Each of them had brought a present that met three criteria: it cost less than twenty dollars, its main function was practical, and it was something they considered at least somewhat absurd.

Everyone drew numbers, and Jason stood up to grab the first present.

"I'm going straight for this big boy," Jason said as picked up the large box Dennis had brought in.

Ripping the wrapping paper off and opening the box as everyone watched, Jason's jaw dropped as he reached inside to pull out the gift.

"Where do you even find something like this?" He asked, pulling a large cookie jar out of the box. The jar was a purple ceramic alien, doing a handstand. The lid came off by pulling the legs and removing the butt to reveal a jar full of cookies Dennis had baked.

"There's no way that's under twenty dollars," Hailey said, shaking her head.

"Garage sale," Dennis giggled, "cost me ten bucks last summer."

"Incredible," Jason said, marveling at the jar.

"Well," Lance said, standing up, "it's mine now." He walked over to Jason and handed him his slip of paper that had a number two on it.

"Sleep with one eye open, Locke," Jason warned as he got back up to grab another gift.

Other presents included a mini bake oven found at a thrift shop, a landline phone shaped like a frog, and a loaf of bread that Lance got stuck with after Hailey stole the cookie jar away from him.

"This cookie jar is all you're getting for Christmas," Hailey told Jason as they cleaned up after the party.

"It's all I need," he laughed.

"You sure you don't want to meet us in St. Lawrence for Christmas, Sammy?"

"Yeah, I'm good. Taylor and Lance will be around, and Gwen will only be gone a couple days. I'll be fine." He smiled at her.

He could tell Hailey was disappointed, but he really didn't want to go to his aunt and uncle's house yet; not with this strength. He was getting better at controlling it, but it still scared him. He knew she'd tried to convince him it would be fine, and she'd probably be right, but he felt more comfortable sticking to his own apartment and the warehouse.

"You could even leave for Harrison with us tomorrow, if you wanted. I'm sure the plane's full, but you could make it in a couple hours running I'm sure," Jason added with a wink.

"I appreciate it, but really, I'm okay," Sam laughed.

It was almost ten o'clock when they'd finished cleaning the diner. Darlene and Harry had an early flight to Sanders the next day, so they had already left. Dennis put out a sign that read "Closed for the Holidays - re-opening Jan 5," then retired to his apartment above the diner.

Hailey gave Sam a hug before she and Gwen headed home. Hailey and Jason also had an early flight in the morning to visit his family in Wisconsin.

"Merry Christmas, Sammy," she whispered as she let him go.

"Merry Christmas, Hails. I'll see you next week."

Jason, Lance, and Taylor had already jogged to their cars to get out of the cold by the time Hailey and Gwen drove off. The snow picked up, falling harder as Sam walked through the city and back to his apartment alone.

TWENTY-SEVEN

"Should auld acquaintance be forgot," Lance and Jason sang into the karaoke machine Gwen had found at her parent's house and brought back to the warehouse. The two of them had their arms around each other's shoulders singing into the only mic she'd been able to find. Hailey, Gwen, and Sam sat on the couch watching New Year's Eve coverage while Taylor had set up on the hospital bed across the warehouse trying to study as far away from Lance and Jason as he could.

The snow had stopped abruptly Christmas Eve, and all traces of it had disappeared other than the sogginess of the ground. Gwen returned the day after Christmas, and Jason and Hailey got back to Duncan three days later.

Sam, Lance and Taylor had kept busy stopping crime, but thankfully there hadn't been any run-ins with the new guns in the past week. They didn't know how to safely handle those, even with a full team, and with Sam out of commission and Jason gone, Lance would have had to take it on solo.

It was still early. The little box in the corner of the broadcast on the TV said it was still an hour and a half before the ball would drop in Calvin, NY on the East coast, meaning it was just now nine-thirty in Duncan.

"Hey, Sam," Jason called from the locker area after he and Lance had finished their performance, "come over here! We've got a couple of late Christmas presents for you before the night starts to get wild."

Sam walked over, confused but curious. Gwen and Hailey stayed on the couch until Taylor came across the room and waved them over.

"What kind of presents do y'all have for me?" Sam asked, stopping in front of the locker that Lance and Jason stood in front of.

"Ta-da!" Jason said, stepping aside, "Your own locker!"

"My hoodie will look great in there," Sam joked as Lance handed him a box.

"Open this one, too," Lance said as Jason crossed his arms and smirked.

Sam unwrapped the paper and opened the box underneath to find a leather jacket inside. At least, it looked like leather.

"I've been working on it for a bit," Jason told him. "Wasn't sure on the color scheme, so I went with a classic dark brown leather look. We can always make a new one later if we need to rebrand."

Sam lifted it and flipped it around in his hands before trying it on. It fit perfectly.

"I don't have material to stop these new bullets, and normal bullets don't affect you anyway, so I didn't worry too much about that part of the equation," Jason continued after Sam had gotten the jacket on. "What I focused on instead was flexibility, making sure that the suit would move with you even at your higher speeds and increased strength. I'm sure you could rip it if you tried, but hopefully normal wear and tear for you shouldn't affect it too much. I've seen how many hoodies you've gone through these last few months."

"I appreciate that," Sam laughed. "I'd hate for you to have to make me a new suit every other week. I imagine that would cost more than the hoodies Taylor bought in bulk for me."

"You and me both, pal. Your pants are made of the same material, but I went with black for those. I made you ten black T-shirts that are even more flexible than the jacket, and pants for you to wear under the jacket. Even made them Henleys, just like you like them."

"My man." Sam reached out a fist for Jason to dap.

"You'll see a half circle on either side of the zipper," Jason continued. "If zipped, they create a single white circle in the center of your chest. If you don't like the logo, it's an easy change. We brainstormed for a while before coming up with two pillars, one on either side. Paying homage to your namesake, Samson."

"No, no, I love it. Until this moment I hadn't even thought of a logo."

"That's why you have this marketing team behind you," Taylor quipped from behind Sam.

"I upgraded your black mask to where it has the full range of features Lance's and mine have. Also made you some hair ties out of our bulletproof material since that's been an issue before."

"Haha," Sam laughed, "that's a definite need. I appreciate all of this."

"One last thing," Taylor said, handing him another box for him to open. "Shoes that should withstand the beating you put on them better than your sneakers. Another Jason engineering feat."

"It was nothing," Jason waved his hand dismissively. "Just some everyday fashion technology breakthroughs. Pretty average attempt by my standards. I was already working on another suit and weapon anyway. Sam only needed the suit. No big deal."

"Well, I really appreciate it," Sam said, lifting it up in front of his face to admire the jacket.

"I'd go ahead and put that on," Lance said as Sam admired the jacket. "I'm expecting us to have a busy night."

"Does that mean I'm not sidelined anymore?"

There was still a slight soreness in his shoulder, but he felt a lot better than he had a week ago. He'd barely even noticed the pain while photographing the Dutchmen's latest win on Sunday.

"Yes," Taylor sighed, "but be careful. No unnecessary risks."

Forty-five minutes later, they had their first incident.

"Hey, guys, I think we have a situation," Gwen called, bringing the festivities to a halt as everyone gathered around the computer. Taylor took Gwen's place in front of the monitor.

"Looks like gang activity just East of downtown," Taylor said, prompting Jason and Lance to begin suiting up. "Looks like the algorithm picked it up a bit over a minute ago now. About fifteen people involved, and a few dozen bystanders on top of a parking garage."

"Any new guns?" Jason asked as he finished securing his suit.

"Doesn't look like it, but don't find out the hard way."

Jason and Lance rode off, and Sam ran after them as Taylor continued talking into the mic.

"Computer has hits on some of their logos. One group is the Five Aces. The other is the First Sons. Looks like there are a lot of hits on the Five Aces in Duncan, but I'm not seeing anything from the First Sons here before. They've been active in other cities, but not here."

"Guess New Year's Eve is as good a time to make an entrance as any other," Jason responded over his headset.

"Looks like it," Taylor muttered as the three of them closed in on the parking garage.

"See y'all at the top," Sam yelled, gathering himself and leaping to the top of the three-story parking garage.

"Show off," Jason laughed as he and Lance raced up the ramp.

The garage rumbled slightly as Sam landed on top, drawing all eyes to him. The two gangs stood in front of him, staring at one another across painted parking spaces. Seven men stood on each side, while at least three times as many sat on top of cars an aisle over.

"Hey, how'd he do that?" one of the guys from the gang on the right asked.

"Welcome to Duncan," one of the guys from the left answered as the rest of the Five Aces laughed. The Aces each aimed their weapons at Sam and began firing. He sprinted around the top of the garage as the First Sons began firing too.

"How is he that fast?" a voice cried as Sam looped behind all the onlookers, who dove off their cars while bullets pierced the sides of the vehicles and shattered the windows.

"Looks like normal guns," Sam said into his mic. Motorcycle engines revved, and Jason and Lance roared out of the tunnel, weapons drawn. They headed straight for the gangs.

Jason leapt off to engage two Aces while his bike bowled over three others who were still focused on Sam. Lance took out three First Sons members with his sword on his first pass before turning his bike around and reentering the fray.

The onlookers who could start their cars were trying to leave. Those who couldn't were either hopping in other cars or racing for the stairwells as sirens began sounding nearby.

"Cops ETA is eighty seconds," Taylor announced as Jason and Lance fought and Sam drew fire.

Lance had left his bike after taking out two more First Sons on his ride back through, leaving only two who'd fully focused on him. Jason had taken out one of the two Aces he had engaged, but was still outnumbered three to one. Jason caught one of the remaining Aces with the tip of his spear, drawing a shout from the man with the electric current.

The man didn't go down. He opened fire at Jason and continued screaming. Jason turned and lifted his shield, his suit taking most of the fire, but more bullets flew past in the direction of the fleeing onlookers.

Three men and two women were standing outside of the stairwell when the gunshots were fired, waiting for a path for them to clear so they could exit. None of them turned to see bullets headed their way; gunshots had been going off the entire time they were fleeing.

They jumped as first one car slammed down behind them and then another landed on top of the first. Bullets riddled the side of the cars but didn't make it through, and the group stumbled safely into the stairwell as bullets continued to bounce off the cars.

"How—" a voice began as Sam ran back into the fight. The speaker was cut off as Lance finished off the last of the First Sons. Lights filled the tunnel leading to the roof.

With Lance and Sam joining him, Jason quickly finished off the Aces. Jason and Lance mounted their bikes as cop cars arrived.

Sam jumped into the air once, cratering the garage on his landing. Jumping again, he broke a hole in the garage, allowing Jason and Lance to drop through and ride onto the exit ramp, avoiding the swarm of police on the entrance ramp and escaping into the night.

The three of them were en route to the warehouse when Taylor's voice cut through the silence.

"Two women walking home on Berry Street are being harassed by a group of three. One of you should check that out."

"On it," Lance answered as he veered away from Jason and Sam.

Thirty seconds later, Jason and Sam arrived back at the warehouse. Sam slowed to a jog and then to a walk as he came up behind Taylor, Hailey, and Gwen at the monitor while Jason was getting off the bike.

"Lance there yet?" Sam asked as he looked up at the monitor.

"Should be in three, two, and there he is," Taylor said as he closed out the tab with the map open.

The three men had surrounded the two girls moments before Lance arrived. Before Lance had entered the frame, one of the men had taken off in a sprint in the opposite direction. The other two didn't see him quick enough. The first landed on his back as Lance swept his legs out from under him with the rounded off edge of his sword. He caught the remaining man across the back as he tried to escape, sending him falling to his hands and knees.

Lance sped to catch up to the one who had fled and swiped him across the back as well, sending him tumbling to the ground. He picked the man up by his jacket and held him up off the ground as he rode the bike back to where the other two were still trying to stand.

Lance tossed the third man into them as lights appeared in the distance on the screen. He said something to the two women with his mic off before speeding away as the cop lights got closer.

"Just another day in the office," Jason said, slapping Sam's back as he joined them at the computer.

Jason, Sam, Gwen, and Hailey all returned to the couches while Taylor monitored the video feed. Five minutes after he had left the scene, Lance pulled in on his motorcycle.

"This is the first New Year's Eve we've done this, and I already hate it," Lance said as he took off his suit.

"I'm sure something will still happen tonight to get you on the news. Keep your head up," Jason told him from the couch before taking a long drink out of his water bottle.

"Ha ha ha," Lance mocked as he collapsed in a chair next to Taylor at the monitor.

"I think I might need a bullet proof jacket, on second thought," Sam said, looking down at himself after landing on the couch. "Bullets may not do anything to me, but they can still tear through this material. Sorry for already getting the suit messed up."

"I can fix those holes much easier than I can make a new suit every time, though I should probably make a couple extra to buy me time on fixing them," Jason laughed as he looked at Sam's bullet-ridden jacket.

The three of them stayed busy the rest of the night, but nothing as exciting as the gang fight happened again. Hailey and Gwen went home at two in the morning, and Jason and Sam headed out at four. Taylor left an hour after them, but Lance insisted on staying all night, "just in case."

Jason sent a text and a picture to the group the next morning that he came in and found Lance asleep at the monitor at eleven and carried him over to the couch so he could sleep a bit easier before shutting everything down and heading to meet Hailey for a New Year's brunch.

TWENTY-EIGHT

A few days later, Sam was on the monitor as ten o'clock hit. Taylor was sitting on one couch, and Gwen and Lance were on the other while a movie played on the TV. Jason had early morning meetings on Thursdays, so Wednesday was his day off from suiting up. Typically, he and Hailey would take advantage of that and have a date night for themselves. That was not the case this Wednesday.

"You won't believe it!" Jason yelled into the room as he threw the door open, the sound of the door hitting the wall causing Gwen to jump a few inches off the couch.

Jason was almost jogging to the table with a folder in his hand as Hailey came in behind him and closed the door. The folder thudded against the table as he slammed it down, and everyone gathered around to see his discovery.

"I found the specs on these new guns. They're a Fox prototype." Jason pointed at the top sheet of paper as he shook his head. "We're the ones who have been making these monstrosities. They're even more heavy duty than I had originally realized. We're experimenting with plasma bullets in a way that most people think is only possible in sci-fi movies. But that tech is here, and Fox is weaponizing it as we speak."

"Geez," Taylor breathed as he stared at the papers.

"And that's not all." Jason pulled three sheets out of the folder and laid them side by side before jabbing his finger at each one. Sam studied the faces of the men and their titles as Jason went on. "I had Taylor run the names of any faces he could pull from the two raids, and I ran those against the employee directory at Fox. I've already connected seven Fox employees to the raids, and each of them are in the same classified division of the company, which means I can't get any more info on them."

"I told you Fox was behind this." Lance spat the name out before he crossed his arms and shook his head.

Jason rolled his eyes and continued talking, "Yeah, great work on that, Sherlock, because it caught the rest of us so much by surprise that the evil billionaire we've been working against was behind it all. But I've got more. I was doing some research on who the company feels is our closest competition, and the two places that have been hit so far are numbers two and three."

"What's number one?" Sam asked as Jason paused.

Jason was unusually animated tonight. The guns that had hurt the two of them so badly coming from where he worked had clearly hit a nerve.

"Fulmer Technology. There's a big gap between number three and four. There's a bigger gap between one and two. Fulmer is known for having the best corporate security on or off the market, but I have to think Fox has a plan to get his men in there."

"Wait," Gwen interrupted, "you think Fox himself is orchestrating this?"

"He has to be," Lance answered immediately.

"They could be working outside of his direct vision to give him deniability, but I don't think this many of our prototypes could make it onto the streets without him being aware of it," Jason said. Gwen nodded along.

"So, what can we do to help protect Fulmer?" Sam asked.

Best corporate security on the market or not, that hadn't stopped Fox's team at Armstrong or Goldfinch. Fulmer would need support to keep Fox from getting his hands on whatever he was after.

"Well, we haven't exactly done a great job anywhere else," Jason answered, scratching at his chin as he leaned back in his chair.

"I'll make sure we have surveillance on the facility, and that we're alerted if there's any suspicious movement,"

Taylor said. "We'll keep trying what we've been doing and hopefully that plus Fulmer's security will be enough."

"What do you mean you'll keep trying what you've been doing?" Hailey asked, drawing her words out slowly. "Last time you ran into these guys, Sam got shot. Before that, Jason got shot. There wasn't a thing his armor could do. Nothing else has been able to get Sam's attention when it hits him, much less pierce his skin. You guys can't just keep facing these guys like you are."

"Well we have to do something," Lance said, shifting his weight from one foot to the other.

"Lance is right," Taylor agreed, "there's too much at stake to not do anything. We understand where you're coming from, Hailey, but we have to keep trying. The police have never listened to us before, and I don't think they're going to start now. We're the only thing standing between Fox and his prize at Fulmer, whatever that is."

Sam knew they were right. They had to do something, and they were the only ones who could. But Hailey made some good points. What good would trying to stop them do if they still couldn't defend themselves against these new guns?

"You can't just admit you're in over your heads." Hailey shook her head and laughed. "You know I've always supported this mission, but you haven't even been doing this for a year yet. Now you're trying to stop a billionaire with guns that don't even sound real, on your own, even when you have no defense against these weapons. You're being reckless, and someone is going to get hurt because of it. I don't want it to be my family or my boyfriend taking a bullet they can't heal from next time."

"There wasn't a draft for this," Lance answered, placing his hands on the table hard enough to echo in the large room. He leaned forward. "Everyone who is here is here because they want to be. We're all adults. No one is forcing anyone else to take part in this."

"Lance is being a bit too confrontational about it, but he's right." Taylor nodded, side-eyeing Lance. "Everyone knew the risk involved. That's nothing new."

"I mean, it's kinda new," Sam said as Taylor finished.

They still weren't wrong that they might have no choice but to be involved, but they were wrong to brush off Hailey's valid concerns as if it was just business as usual.

He cleared his throat before continuing. "Like, it's new to find out that Jason's armor can't stop these bullets, or that my skin won't deflect these like typical shells. The circumstances have changed, and honestly, I'm not sure I feel comfortable being out there right now. It was one thing when we didn't know what was going on with me, but I could be an asset since I was indestructible. When I am definitely destructible, it's a different story."

"Well if that's how you feel, then leave." Lance shrugged, jerking his head at the door as he recrossed his arms over his chest.

A wave of heat crawled up Sam's neck as he worked his jaw, trying to stay calm. He had crossed his own arms to keep himself from hurting something if he got overly animated.

"Lance," Gwen said softly.

"What? We've been working with him to try and get his powers under control for months, and now—when, for the first time, things aren't easy—he wants to leave? Then he can go." Lance's tone stayed flat and his features stayed relaxed, which made what he was saying all the more frustrating. "Jason and I have been definitely destructible since we started. If him not being immortal anymore is going to make him hesitate in the field, then he's a liability. It's better for everyone if he just hangs it up if that's the case."

Sam scoffed and just shook his head, unable to stop a smirk from showing his disbelief at Lance's audacity.

"Lance," Gwen repeated with more force this time.

"Maybe everyone should take five." Jason pushed his chair back away from the table.

"We don't have time to take five," Lance responded shortly before jabbing his finger at the door. "Every moment we waste, Fox is getting closer to realizing his next step. I don't know what it is yet, but I know if it's part of his plan he needs to be stopped."

"Lance is right. We need to stop having this discussion and get to work," Taylor agreed.

"You two are unbelievable." Hailey shook her head as the slightest chuckle left her lips. "I'm out."

"Not like you do anything around here anyway," Lance mumbled under his breath.

"Yeah, I'm out too." Jason stood up and walked out after Hailey. "Good luck figuring it out though!" he called out over his shoulder as he left.

"Dude, Jason, come back," Taylor pleaded, glaring at Lance before walking after Jason. "We'll figure out a compromise!"

"I'm out too." Sam followed a few steps behind Jason and Hailey.

"Sam, wait!" Taylor called, but Sam didn't turn back around, he just kept walking out of the warehouse and into the brisk January afternoon.

Sam lifted his head up towards the sky and let out a long sigh.

Great. Just what we needed right now, he snorted.

He didn't want to leave the team, but Taylor and Lance were going overboard. Lance and Taylor may have had good points about needing to stop Fox, but Lance's complete disregard for everyone else was more than Sam was willing to swallow. Especially in talking to Hailey like that.

Everything will work itself out when tempers cool, he thought to himself as he began his walk home.

He would usually jog and be home within ten minutes, but took a more leisurely walk that afternoon. Thirty minutes later, he locked the door behind him and, after eating a handful of snacks, collapsed on his bed and fell asleep.

Everything did not work itself out when tempers cooled.

Thursday and Friday passed without Sam hearing from Taylor or Lance. Jason had packed a bag and was staying on Sam's sofa for the time being.

"I just can't stay there right now," Jason explained Thursday afternoon when he showed up outside Sam's door with two duffel bags. The two of them had moved to the couch, where Sam had gotten Jason an extra sheet and a blanket. "Lance going overboard and crossing lines isn't new; you've been around him long enough now to know he'll just be like that sometimes. I usually just roll my eyes and wait it out because he's my best friend and his good qualities far outweigh him occasionally being a headstrong jerk, but what he said about Hailey was too far for me to put up with. And it's not like Taylor to just agree with him when he gets like that. I think they've both made this White Knight business their entire personality, and it's not a good look."

Sam sat there and nodded along as Jason talked, but didn't say anything. He wasn't so sure Lance's good qualities weighed as much as Jason claimed, but he trusted him, Hailey, Gwen, and even Taylor—despite him siding with Lance the other night—enough to take their assessment at face value.

"And then there's what Lance said about you." Jason shook his head as he continued. "I'm sorry you had to hear him say those things about you. I don't think that's how he really feels, and I know it's not how anyone else feels, but that definitely crossed the line too. This thing with Fox is consuming him. It consumes him every time the name even comes up. I thought his trip to Franklin had helped recenter him, but it seems to not have lasted too long."

"I could care less about what he said about me." Sam shrugged. And he meant that. Trusting the other's assessment of Lance didn't mean he had to give any weight to what Lance had to say about him. "I was most upset about how he was treating Hailey. She's made the White Knight into a hero when others would have made him a villain. She's given him tips and scoops to make his life easier. And then she has the audacity to disagree with him on whether or not he should be putting people in life or death situations and all of a sudden it's 'you don't even do anything here'?" Sam made a face as he mocked Lance before shaking his head. "No, that's not going to fly."

Friday night, Jason and Sam met Hailey and Gwen for dinner at *Fran's*.

"I don't know." Gwen shook her head as she talked. "He's refusing to budge. You know how stubborn he is."

"And Taylor?" Sam asked, more confused by Taylor than Lance at that point.

"He'd apologize, but he still thinks that he and Lance are right about pushing forward, and he figures that as long as he and Lance are on the same page, it's kinda out of his hands with how Lance is acting. I've told him that's stupid and cowardly, but it hasn't changed anything."

"Where are you at in all of this, Gwen?" Jason asked. "What's your opinion?"

"I think both sides make good points about whether or not the team should push forward or wait it out and think some more. I understand why both sides think the way they do. But the way Taylor and Lance specifically are handling this is awful, and I don't blame any of you for walking out. I just don't get it…" Her voice trailed off and she shook her head again as Darlene walked up with their food.

"Wish I could stay and chat," Darlene said, handing out plates. "Pre-concert crowd has us stretched thin."

"You're fine, Darlene." Jason smiled at her.

"Absolutely, don't worry about us," Hailey added, and Darlene smiled at them and went back to work.

"So where do we go from here?" Sam asked as Darlene left them.

"I'm not going back until Lance apologizes to Hailey and to you." Jason shrugged. "Until then he's on his own as far as I'm concerned."

"Yeah, I definitely think he owes both of us an apology, but I doubt we'll get that," Hailey said, taking a drink of her tea.

"I'll keep trying to work on him and Taylor," Gwen added softly.

"I hate to say it—" Jason shook his head, "—but it may have to get to the point where Lance is on the receiving end of these new bullets before he admits he's wrong. I don't know that anything short of that will persuade him. He's so hyper fixated on Fox that as soon as he found out for sure that's who was behind this, he flipped back to how he was acting last spring."

"I hope it doesn't come to that," Gwen answered.

"Don't we all," Jason snorted as he took a bite out of his burger.

Sam got to the stadium early on Saturday for the Dutchmen's first playoff game. They had finished the season with fourteen wins and only two losses, and had secured a bye in the first week of the postseason. Their quarterfinal game against the Calvin Comets wasn't until seven pm that night, but Sam was there wandering the halls at noon, getting shots of anything that could be useful for the articles that would come out over the next week whether they won or lost.

Three hours before the game, he ran into Brooklyn during a stop he made in the press box.

"Are you excited? Do you feel the energy?" she asked, bouncing on the balls of her feet as she talked, slightly faster and louder than normal.

"I am," Sam laughed, and he meant it. As much adrenaline as being a hero provided, the buzz of tens of thousands of people in one place hoping to see something spectacular was a different feeling entirely. "I made sure I got here early today to get those nerves under control. How do you feel?"

"I feel great! The playoffs always get me extra energized, but it may have been a bad idea to have already had three coffees since I got here two hours ago."

"Yeah, that'll do it to you," Sam agreed with a smile.

"Alright, I'm off to interview some front-office types before the game. Let me know if you need anything!" She started walking down the hall, and Sam chuckled and shook his head. She turned back after a few steps and looked over her shoulder to call back to him. "And Sam?"

"Yeah?"

"Have fun today! Take it all in! You only get your first playoff game once!"

"I'll remember that!" Sam shouted back with a smile and received a quick over the shoulder thumbs up as she turned back around and kept walking.

Sam made his way down to the field as players began to warm up for the game. He pulled his Blickon Z 2600 out of his bag and began snapping photos of the kickers launching field goal after field goal as they kept scooting back further with each successful kick. The defense came out next and performed their calisthenics. Then the offense followed suit before running some passing drills against the defense.

Sam took a quick break in the press box before returning to his spot behind the end zone for the national anthem. The Comets were the league's most successful franchise over the course of the league's history, but their 10-6 season had gotten them back to the playoffs for the first time in five years. And from the opening possession, the Dutchmen outclassed the Comets. Duncan jumped out to a fourteen to three lead by the end of the first quarter and never looked back, winning the game with a final score of 41-17. Dante Sparks passed for three hundred and twenty yards and ran for another eighty, continuing his momentum from an MVP-caliber regular season into the postseason.

Sam got a great photo from a touchdown celebration early in the third quarter after Dante passed to Dexter Caleb for a twenty-two yard touchdown and sprinted to the end zone to celebrate with him. Caleb ran and jumped into the air, and Dante caught him and held him up as Caleb spread his arms wide, football palmed in one hand. That photo landed Sam on the front page of the next morning's edition, along with three other photos he'd taken from different articles in the sports section. It might have been the best shot he'd ever gotten, and it was a welcome gift after a long and frustrating week.

chapter

TWENTY-NINE

A week went by, and Jason was still living with Sam. Jason had gone back a couple times when he knew Lance and Taylor wouldn't be home to grab things as he needed them. Sam had gotten his spare key back from Hailey so Jason could use it while he was living there. None of them had heard from Taylor or Lance since they had walked out. Gwen was functioning as a middleman, trying to broker peace, but with little luck.

"You're sure you're cool with me staying here while you're gone?" Jason asked as Sam sat his duffel bag on the coffee table and tucked his camera bag on his back.

"Positive," Sam answered, tightening the straps.

"I appreciate it. Don't worry, it'll be clean when you get back, and I won't have anyone over."

"Jason, dude, I'm not worried. It's fine," Sam laughed and shook his head. "You can relax."

Sam had a flight to catch for that weekend's game. After the victory over the Comets last week, the Dutchmen were playing the Hamilton Highlanders on a neutral field for the semifinals. The game was being played in Winchester, TX, in their new, state-of-the-art stadium. He would go to the press conferences that night after landing, and then cover the game the next evening before flying back in.

"I'll see you on Monday," Sam said, tossing the duffel bag over his shoulder as he walked out the door.

He set off on a light jog to the airport, leaving early enough to get to his gate an hour before takeoff. His pride was still a bit hurt from the conversation he had to have with Brooklyn a few weeks earlier, and he wasn't going to make that mistake again.

He spent the entire flight from Duncan to Winchester asleep in his seat. A stewardess had to wake him up after the short flight once all the other passengers had deplaned. He'd been using his powers less frequently since stepping away from the team, and his fatigue had lessened as a result, even though he still slept longer and harder than he ever did before getting his powers. Sam retrieved his duffel from the overhead compartment and got off the plane himself.

Brooklyn gave him a wave from across the room at the press conference, but that was all he saw of her that night. He grabbed dinner at a restaurant next to the hotel on his way back in, and fell asleep as soon as he hit the bed in the room. He knew she had wanted to build more of a relationship throughout the season, and he'd been looking forward to that as well. But with everything going on with his body and joining the team, they hadn't had a chance to build that rapport. Hopefully his break from the team coming during the playoffs would belatedly give him the chance to spend more time with her and earn back the trust he had lost earlier in the season.

The next morning, the hotel buzzed as reporters, photographers and others in the journalism community mingled about the hotel. With this being the conference finals game, there were more journalists than usual as other locales without teams playing sent reporters for a story and the National outlets could focus all their talent on just the two games.

Sam found Brooklyn eating breakfast with another reporter, a stocky, balding man in a bomber jacket he recognized from *SportsNow*, Jerry Burns. He was also a legend in the field. Sam could remember reading his column fifteen years ago, back when he still had dreams of playing in the playoffs instead of photographing them.

"Good morning." Jerry greeted him with a smile as Sam sat and pulled his chair in.

"Hey Sam!" Brooklyn smiled. "We were just talking about today's agenda. With everything going on at the stadium today, we think we're going to head over around noon. You're welcome to join us!"

"Yeah, I think that would be good," Sam answered as he picked up his fork. "I'll get ready whenever I finish eating and head over with y'all."

"Great! I hate to leave you alone, but I think we were just finishing up," Brooklyn apologized as she gathered her trash. "I need to take care of a few things before we leave so I'll see you in the lobby at noon?"

"Sounds good." Sam nodded between bites as Brooklyn and Jerry each returned to their rooms.

He loved the playoffs. He didn't get to meet people like Jerry Burns during the regular season. Now he was eating breakfast with him, even if he had left as soon as Sam sat down.

The conference finals game was a much tighter contest than the quarterfinal. Even with Hamilton barely squeaking into the playoffs and barely winning in the quarterfinals after a controversial no call, the game came down to the final minutes. The Dutchmen were up three, with one minute and forty-seven seconds left and a third down and three from the Hamilton fourteen-yard line.

Dante snapped the ball and rolled out to the right side of the field looking for a receiver, but without any luck. With a defensive end closing in on him, he scrambled, juking a linebacker for the first down and getting to the second level of the defense. All of the secondary were occupied with receivers when he began his run, and they were late responding to him. He left his feet as he dove for the end zone. His legs got hit while he was in the air, and he completed a front flip with the ball barely staying in bounds as it passed over the pylon for the touchdown right in front of Sam.

The stadium erupted as Dante leapt back to his feet in celebration. His teammates mobbed him as the PA announcer screamed, "Touchdown Dutchmen!"

After four quick incompletions and a turnover on downs, Duncan was able to run out the rest of the clock and secure the team's first trip to the championship game in nineteen years.

Sam moved around taking shots as the celebration unfolded around him. He uploaded all of his photos to their internal server in the press room afterwards, including a shot of Dante completely flipped and facing him as he scored the touchdown to seal the win. That picture would get Sam back on the front page in that week's paper, as well as in other papers and websites across the nation.

He leaned back against the wall he'd been working against and let out a sigh of relief after another big win for the Dutchmen. As he finally let himself relax after the day, he pulled out his phone to find a number of missed calls and a couple texts to go along with one voicemail. The voicemail was from Gwen, and Sam covered his left ear as he raised the phone to his right ear.

"Hey, uh, Sam. Sorry to bother you." He sat forward at the sound of worry in her voice. "I know you're busy and all with the game and photos and everything. I, um, was just calling to let you know that Lance is, uh, in the hospital right now." Her voice shook a bit as she spoke the last three words. "Taylor's dad is performing surgery after he took a plasma bullet to the chest. There was an incident at Fulmer tonight, and he took off to try and stop it by himself. He was doing well until he got shot in the, um, chest. Taylor and I are here now, and Jason and Hailey are on their way. I just, uh, thought you would like to know what happened."

Sam closed his laptop and hopped to his feet. Without making a stop on the way, he returned to the hotel and packed his bags. Grabbing them, he walked out the door and jogged to the airport to catch a plane that left in an hour instead of the next morning. Before the plane departed, he sent a quick text to Brooklyn to let her know where everything was if she needed it and let her know he'd left due to an emergency.

He felt the all too familiar itch and burn of anxiety as the plane taxied to the runway.

Breathe. Just breathe. He repeated his mantra three times in his head as he steadied himself. The hurt and fear in Gwen's voice in the message was enough to get him to rein in. He wasn't going to do anything to increase her stress.

He tried to keep his eyes open on the plane, but had no success and finally succumbed to sleep as they left Texas.

THIRTY

"How is he?" Sam asked as he found Taylor, Jason, and Hailey sitting in the waiting area. It was eight in the morning. Sam had dropped his gear off at his apartment, showered, and changed clothes before coming over.

"He's doing okay," Taylor answered, rubbing at his eyes and yawning. "Broke a couple ribs. The bigger issue is he has a punctured lung, and they're having a hard time dealing with that because of the nature of the plasma bullets. They didn't just pierce them; they ate away the walls of the lung where they went through. Dad couldn't sew them shut, he had to patch them at both the entry and exit points."

"Long story short," Jason offered, "he'll live, but he's going to be out of commission for a while."

"It must be serious, though, for you to bring him to the hospital instead of doing this yourself."

"It is." Taylor nodded. "We avoided it as long as possible, but it was necessary. I only told my dad information he needed to treat Lance, so he doesn't know what Lance was doing when he got hit or anything else. But he's the best there is when it comes to stuff like this, so it was worth it for something we've never seen before."

Sam nodded as Taylor talked, but stifled a yawn as he finished. His adrenaline began crashing, and he sat down on the couch next to Hailey.

"Sam, wake up."

"Come on Sammy, we have to go."

"We're getting looks, dude."

Sam blinked his eyes open to find Jason and Hailey above him. It was dark outside now as the sounds of the hospital came into focus.

"What time is it?" He yawned through a stretch as he sat up on the couch.

"Six forty-five pm," Jason answered as he pulled on Sam's arm to help him up. "Visitor hours are almost over. Taylor's dad pulled some strings to let us stay last night, but since Lance is stable now, we're being asked to leave."

Sam nodded as Jason talked, hearing the words come out of his mouth but having a hard time processing what he was saying. He followed them out to Jason's car and sat down in the passenger seat.

Jason drove the three of them out to the warehouse and helped Sam out of the car and inside. Sam tried to convince him that he was okay, but the truth was he was so tired he couldn't walk more than a few feet in a straight line.

"They're going to discharge Lance in a bit and Taylor is going to set up an observation area here where Lance will have to stay for a while so Taylor can report back to the hospital—a requirement from Dr. Jansen to let Lance leave. We'll run shifts here, but Taylor will run point most of the time. He said he'd have more info when he got here."

"Do we have any food?" Sam asked as he sat back down on the couch.

"I'll check," Hailey answered, getting up to go check the kitchen.

"Hey Sam, it's time to wake up."

Sam blinked open his eyes after a gentle push to see Gwen sitting on the edge of the couch next to him.

"I fell asleep again?"

Gwen nodded and patted his arm. She reached over and handed him a container from *Fran's* with a burger and fries in it.

"They said you were hungry, so I stopped on the way back and grabbed this for you."

"Thank you, I'm starving." Sam took the burger and began eating. Hailey and Jason were sitting at the table, and Taylor was at the bed they'd set up for Lance.

As Taylor returned to the group, Hailey and Jason made their way over to the couches to join Gwen and Sam.

"Okay." Taylor dropped into a chair with a sigh as he pinched the bridge of his nose. "I promised I'd fill everyone in once he was stable and now we're there. Last night around nine, our cameras picked up movement at Fulmer and we saw a team move in. Lance suited up and headed that way."

Taylor paused as he took a sip of water.

"He got there and there were twelve people there again. They were waiting for us this time, though. He never had a chance. He turned a corner and tripped a wire. A gunman got three shots off at him before Lance fell. One missed, one grazed his arm, but the other caught him square in the chest and went all the way through. Jason created a safety measure in the suit to compress if it ever got punctured, and that saved his life."

Taylor shook his head and slunk back deeper into the chair.

"By the time I got there, even with the safety measures he was in tough shape. The gunmen had just left him there. I got him out of the suit and was able to drag him back to the sidewalk. I called an ambulance and told them we were out for a walk when he got hit by some weird bullet. They took him to the hospital, I retrieved his suit and got in my car to follow them. I called my dad on the way to let him know I needed him to be ready.

They fixed up his lung and got his ribs taken care of, but he'll be in bed for a couple weeks. It will probably be two months before he's able to even start training again, much less be ready to fight."

"I tried to tell you —" Hailey's voice broke a bit as she talked. "Lance could have died, Taylor. I know this is important, but him getting himself killed isn't going to help anything."

"I know," Taylor whispered, looking down at his hands and not at Hailey.

"I want to say I can't believe he was stupid enough to go by himself but that's not true. I believe it." Jason shook his head.

"He's going to be okay, though, right?" Gwen asked.

Taylor nodded. "No telling yet if there will be long-term limitations on him, but he's going to live. They got him fixed up pretty well."

Gwen flashed a fleeting smile and gave a slight nod as she resumed staring at the far wall.

"So," Sam started, pausing to think about his words. "What do we do now?"

Lance's behavior and his own health had brought in new complications to consider, but he still believed in the mission. And with these new guns on the street, the mission was more important than ever.

"That's up to you." Taylor shrugged. "I know that there were valid reasons you walked away. I don't blame you; it looks like you were right, but the choice is yours. You can jump back in and get out there, or you can walk away from it. Can't say I'd blame you if you chose the second option, but it's all your call."

"I'm still in," Jason answered. "I was never out, I just needed Lance to stop being a jerk to people about it."

"I'm in too," Sam added.

"But no going after these guns until you know more," Hailey said, her arms crossed on the couch.

"I think that's a good call for now." Jason rubbed her back in circles with his hand.

"Okay, well, I'm going to be here for the foreseeable future with the patient, so whenever you want to be on, I guess just hang out here and we'll try to go back to how we operated when Lance was in Franklin."

"I missed this," Jason admitted with a small smile that faded as he looked around the room and his eyes fell on Lance. "I guess we should get to work."

He kissed Hailey's shoulder once and got to his feet, walking to the monitor to go through Taylor's notes from the last week and a half. Times Lance had responded to something, what the situation was, how it went, etc. were all recorded in Taylor's logs.

The rest of the group also stayed at the warehouse. Sam laid back down on the couch, still trying to recover from his fatigue, Taylor returned to Lance's bedside, and Hailey and Gwen sat on the couch opposite Sam and turned on a movie. Thirty minutes later, Gwen offered to watch the monitors for a bit, so Jason brought the report binder over to the couch.

Jason was still working through the first week's logs fifteen minutes later when Gwen interrupted the silence.

"Hey guys, something is happening," she called from the monitor.

Hailey, Jason, and Sam got up from the couches to walk over while Taylor came over from Lance's bed.

"Let me see," Taylor said as he switched places with Gwen. "Looks like another gang incident between the same two groups from last time. You two should both suit up."

"Sam, you head that way as soon as you're ready and I'll leave as soon as I'm dressed," Jason told him as they jogged over to the lockers. "Guns, Taylor?"

"None are out yet so look sharp. We need to prevent this from escalating, but we also need the two of you to get back in as few pieces as possible."

Sam pulled his pants over the shorts he was wearing and, after putting on his jacket and mask, he was out the door in less than two minutes.

"It's in a parking lot outside a superstore south of downtown," Taylor said through Sam's headset as a map projected into his vision. "ETA thirty-five seconds."

Sam ran through the slight drizzle falling around him in the dark. Taylor tried to send Sam on routes without cars as often as possible.

The parking lot quickly came into view, and Sam slowed a bit to survey the situation as he approached.

"Looks like about fifty people total, Sam. Maybe a slight split between the groups. Like 27-23 maybe? Not too big a difference."

"Copy."

Sam walked up to the parking lot as the rain began to fall a little harder.

"Everything good here?" Sam shouted as he walked up.

A few of the people shifted on their feet, but none moved or answered.

"Just heard something was happening out here and thought I should check it out," Sam continued. "I think if everyone just went back home, it would be in everyone's best interest."

"Jason is thirty seconds out, Sam," Taylor said through the comms.

"How 'bout you go home and let us handle our business," one of the Five Aces members yelled back. A chorus of agreement from his group followed.

"Afraid I can't do that." Sam shrugged as he inched closer.

"Well that's just too bad." The man smirked as he said the words. "By the way, sorry to hear about what happened to the White Knight. We're all big fans of his." Another chorus of laughter followed. "Let him know the Jack of Clubs sends his regards."

"Mighty kind of you, Jack," Jason responded as he came to a stop on his bike next to Sam.

"Your friend was just leaving," Jack responded. "You should run along too."

"Not going to happen," Jason answered, pulling out his spear, the head glowing and sizzling as the rain fell on the electrified tip.

"Your funeral." Jack smirked again, shrugging.

He pulled out a gun and fired twice at Jason. The first bullet pierced through the bike next to his hand and the second hit the back. Jason was flung forward and up into the air as the bike exploded underneath him.

"They've got plasma bullets!" Sam exclaimed as he watched Jason float through the air, seeing the scene in what felt like slow motion.

"Sam, get Jason and yourself out of there ASAP!" Taylor yelled into the comms, snapping him back into focus. "Forget everything else."

Sam ran ahead under Jason's trajectory to catch him. Bullets began firing between the Five Aces and First Sons. The First Sons tried to retreat after seeing what the plasma bullets were capable of. Sam jumped and pulled Jason out of the air, then took off sprinting away from the scene. Bullets peppered around him, some plasma and some normal. Luckily if any hit him, they were regular bullets that didn't leave a mark.

He sprinted across the street and through the park on the other side before he dared to slow down and take stock of what was happening. No one had followed them, and the gunshots were a distant noise now.

"Will you *please* put me down now?" Jason asked from his shoulder.

"Oh, right, sorry," Sam answered, setting him down.

"I guess fifth time's the charm, huh?" he grumbled, brushing at his arms.

"What?"

"Guys," Taylor's voice cut through their headset. "You need to get back here now. Sam will need to carry Jason."

"Here we go again," Jason mumbled as Sam picked him up and took off.

Forty-five seconds later, they made it back to the warehouse. Hailey met them at the door. Sam set Jason down and headed towards Taylor at the monitor.

"It's just a bit humiliating," Jason told Hailey as he took his helmet off and followed Sam. "Being carried like a child."

"I know, baby," she responded, rubbing his back.

"Take a look at this."

Taylor pulled up a live broadcast of helicopter footage of the parking lot they had just left. Cops hid behind cars with bullet holes visible on the feed. Bodies of cops and members of the First Sons were strewn about the area.

Gunshots sounded on the screen, followed by the helicopter beginning to sway before the screen shut to black.

Gwen gasped as Jason and Hailey simultaneously reached for their faces —Jason covering his eyes while Hailey covered her mouth.

"Ladies and Gentlemen, it appears we've lost our feed. We hope to update you later that our staff is unhurt from the incident. We're going to break as we try and figure out what is happening."

The five of them sat in silence for a moment.

"I'm glad you two got away in time," Gwen said softly, breaking the silence.

Hailey nodded in agreement. "Me too."

"If these guns are really hitting the streets now, everyone is in real trouble, including us," Jason said.

"We need to find something that can withstand these bullets," Taylor added. "Otherwise, we have no shot and might as well pack it all up."

Sam nodded. These guns were a trump card now. Without something to protect them, it wouldn't matter what they tried; those bullets would stop them before they even got started.

"Let me look into the files at work," Jason said. "They have to have done some sort of testing on these weapons. Surely I can find something to give us a lead."

"I think that's a good place to start." Taylor nodded.

"Hey, what was he talking about with that Jack of Clubs stuff?" Sam asked. "With everything that happened after that, I didn't have time to really process what he was saying, and I have even less of an idea now."

"I can actually answer that. It's a title," Hailey said. "I did some digging after your first run in with the Five Aces. They started when Duncan was one of the final stops for those settling the west. The people here got tired of outlaws coming through, so the five most powerful people in the community teamed up to create basically a neighborhood watch group that took on a life of its own. Each family had its own suit, with the two Tillman brothers both taking the suit of spades. Ace is the title for the head of the family. King and Queen go to the next highest rated man and woman respectively. I think there are usually a couple of Jacks per suit before they start being numbered. Basically, this guy is one of the five most important members of the 'Club' family."

"So, everyone in the gang is part of a family?" Sam asked, trying to follow along despite fatigue replacing his adrenaline at worrying speeds.

"Well," Hailey put two fingers in the air on both hands to do air quotes, "a 'family.' That's what they call each suit. In the past, a lot of people who weren't able to make it as pioneers would stick in the area and join the Aces as a way to make a living in the community, because each of the heads would provide jobs for anyone on their roster.

Now I think it's largely a result of location in the city. There's a lot of information available on how the gang was started, but very little on how it currently operates. They mostly seem to be white collar, at least at the top. They also usually operate in the shadows. For them to come out into the open to confront the First Sons like this, they must be either really scared or really mad."

"That makes sense."

"So what's next?" Gwen asked, her eyes still locked on the muted screen, which was showing commercials.

"I'm going to work on finding a material to give us some protection against these new weapons," Jason answered. "Until then, everyone should carry on as normal—except we won't be going into situations where these guns could be. There's no positive outcome from that. If we're not sure, Sam can check it out and update us if it's safe or not, since he'll be able to get out of danger more easily."

"Sounds good to me," Taylor said, and Sam nodded.

"Well, if that's it for tonight," Sam stood up and stretched as he stifled a yawn, "I'm going to head home and get some rest. It's been a long couple days."

"See you tomorrow, Sammy." Hailey gave him a soft smile and a wave as he left before turning her attention to the TV that Gwen had unmuted with the return of the anchors.

chapter

THIRTY-ONE

The next three days passed without anyone seeing Jason other than Hailey, who took him dinner at work on Wednesday and Thursday and earned a total of twenty-five minutes over those two visits.

"Is he okay?" Sam asked Friday afternoon as he sat on the couches with Gwen and Hailey.

"He's fine," Hailey laughed. She had just gotten there from a meeting at the paper. Gwen had a long break in the middle of the day before having to leave to meet with some clients later in the evening. "Every now and then he gets like this. He'll hyperfixate on a project and will be MIA for a few days. Luckily, he's a genius, so it doesn't usually take him too long to figure it out."

"And at least now you know what he's working on, unlike the spring where he ghosted you for four days making his and Lance's suits," Gwen said.

"Gah, don't remind me." Hailey rolled her eyes, but smiled. "How's Lance today?"

"He's doing okay." Gwen nodded as she talked. "He was conscious for a bit earlier and was able to recognize me. We talked for about five minutes. Taylor says he's reducing his medication, and that his head should clear up soon."

"Did Taylor have a timetable for that?"

"He said it just depends on how his body reacts. It could be in ten minutes, or it could be another day or two. He's just not sure."

"At least he's getting closer." Hailey shifted in her seat.

"And now we wait!" Jason yelled as he threw the door open and walked over to sit down on the couch next to Hailey.

"Hey you," she laughed as he sunk deeper into the couch. "What are we waiting for?"

"I think I figured out a compound that will work to stop the bullets. I need it to harden before I can test it, but if my calculations are right it should hold up. Then we'll be in business."

"Jason, that's incredible!" Sam shook his head in awe. "How did you do that in such a short amount of time?"

"The specs on the bullets I found in our system gave me a good starting point. After that it was just a matter of putting in the time to get it completed. I worked myself pretty hard the last few days, but it paid off. We have a shot now. Where's Taylor?"

"I finally convinced him to go home and shower and rest," Gwen said. "He hasn't left in four days."

"I can't believe you got him to leave. He definitely needed to get out of here a bit."

"When do you think your prototype should be ready?" Sam asked.

"Hopefully in twenty-four to thirty-six hours. I'll test it out and, if it works, I'll figure out a way to incorporate it into our suits."

"I'll feel a lot more comfortable going out there again once we have that." Sam felt the anxiety in his stomach at least loosen, if not lighten, at the thought of better protection.

"You and me both, Sam," Jason laughed.

"I can't believe you're here so early. It's just now three," Hailey said, turning to face Jason. "No one said anything about you leaving early?"

"After putting in back-to-back sixteen-hour days? They were happy to see me leave."

"I still can't believe you're able to just work on these side projects while you're at work."

"Most people don't know what I'm supposed to be doing anyway." Jason shrugged. "We all kind of work on our own projects and keep to ourselves. As long as I'm working, they assume I'm doing my job. Besides, you know what they say. Boss makes a dollar, I make a dime, that's why I set about bringing his plan for world domination to demise on company time."

"Not a saying."

"Pretty sure it is."

"Definitely not."

"Okay." Gwen stood up. "While you two figure out if it's a saying or not, I'm going to see how Lance is doing."

"I'm going to get up too to check the monitors," Sam said, leaning forward to stand from the couch.

He shook his head, amused, as Hailey and Jason argued over which of them caused him and Gwen to leave.

Sam settled into the chair and surveyed the screens to find, well, not much. A couple of the screens showed footage of traffic in a standstill, one showed a view of the city maintenance team finally taking down Christmas decorations, and the rest cycled through shots of people walking down sidewalks or driving through streets. Even for the early evening it was slow; there was not even a car wreck in sight.

Not that Sam was complaining. With the recent run-ins all including the plasma guns, the last few slow days in a row had been nice.

He sat back. Jason and Hailey seemed to have either come to a consensus or at least a truce, because their conversation seemed a lot less confrontational than when he had left them. Gwen sat next to Lance reading a book, glancing over at him every few minutes.

Sam turned back to the screens and flicked through them again. *Wait.* He scrolled back two frames as he clicked through the feeds.

There.

Sam leapt to his feet and sprinted out of the warehouse, the reinforced door groaning in protest as he threw it open.

He weaved around people and through traffic when necessary as he ran downtown. Ninety-three seconds after he jumped from his seat, he slid to a stop at the back of a crowd of people all looking up in horror.

Two of the cables from the scaffolding that the maintenance workers were using had split. A man had tried to catch himself as he fell, and one of his arms was hanging limply at his side while the other held the railing, straining against the weight of his body as he dangled in the air.

Sam's head shot back and forth as he surveyed the scene. A glass wall of windows was on one side of the man, and the road was on the other. There was a crowd of people on the ground seven stories below him. None of the other scaffolding crews were close enough to help.

I really hope there's not a desk there, he thought to himself as he took a deep breath and bent his knees.

Pushing off, Sam flew through the sky as he jumped, clearing the crowd and the first four stories with ease. He turned his head and lifted his arms to cover his face as he crashed into the fifth-floor window. The glass shattered as it gave way. He tumbled to a stop four feet into an office.

"Hi," he said to a terrified woman who had stopped mid-keystroke to stare at him in silence. He pointed at the empty spot where he'd landed. "I was really hoping there wasn't going to be a desk there."

She didn't say anything. She didn't move. She just continued staring at him.

"Well, gotta jet. Thanks again for your interior design choices."

Sam walked to the ledge, turned to where his back faced the street and bent his knees again, this time jumping straight up along the wall. He threw out his hands as he reached the seventh floor and held onto the ledge as glass cascaded down around him. Once the glass had stopped falling, he lifted his head towards the now-open room.

Of course there's a desk now, he sighed to himself as he saw the wooden table right above his hands.

Reaching up, Sam pushed at the leg of the desk and sent it sliding across the room. With it out of his way, he pulled himself up into the room and turned back towards the street.

The scaffolding was swaying five feet out from the window ledge and another four feet to the side of the opening Sam had created with his jump. The man's torso was even with the ledge.

"Try and swing yourself over to me!" Sam shouted over the sound of a helicopter that had just arrived on the scene.

Without turning to face Sam, the man shook his head vigorously and clutched the railing tighter.

"Come on, dude, you can't hold on much longer. Let me help!"

The man still refused to turn, but began slowly rocking his body back and forth to create some momentum for the scaffolding to swing. Inch by inch the platform got closer to Sam's outstretched hand. It stopped just shy of Sam's fingers and drifted back away. He lowered into a stance to catch it on its next swing.

CRACK

The crowd below cried out with a chorus of shouts and gasps as one of the two remaining cables snapped, hurling the man and the platform into the window on the fourth floor. The window cracked in an elaborate spiderweb.

The platform was now resting against the wall of windows and swinging side to side, but was still just out of reach of Sam when—

CRACK

The last cable snapped, and the platform was in free fall.

Sam lunged for the cable with his left hand and buried his right hand into the wall as his feet left the ledge. Wrapping the cable around his left hand, he held himself up with his right as the platform once again came to a stop.

He loosed a howl as he clung to the wall and the cable. The two competing forces left him suspended in the air.

His strength didn't ease the pain of his arms pulling in opposite directions. He lifted himself back up onto the ledge with the cable still wrapped around his left hand, and began pulling the platform up to him, reaching one hand over the other. The cable couldn't damage his skin, but it still burned as it tried to saw itself out of his grip. Ten seconds later, he was able to pull the entire platform into the office and remove the man from the railing.

The man had passed out at some point in the fall, but had gotten his arm stuck in the railing, so he hadn't fallen off. Sam lowered his ear to the man's mouth and heard a faint rattle of breath. He let out a long sigh of relief and laid out on his back.

The sound of cheers and applause cut through the sound of the helicopter, and he allowed himself a small smile. Getting up to his feet, Sam walked to the back of the office and sprinted forward, leaping off the ledge at an angle and clearing the crowd. He hit the ground running and took a few detours on the way back to the warehouse, only returning when he could no longer hear the helicopter that had tried to follow him back.

"Sam!"

"Sammy!"

"Dude!"

Hailey, Gwen, and Jason were all standing around the monitor waiting for him when he returned.

"That was incredible, man!" Jason shook his head as he talked. "We thought he was a goner after the third cable snapped, much less the fourth. I've never seen anything like that!"

"That really was amazing, Sam." Gwen beamed at him.

"I appreciate it guys," he answered with a smile of his own. "You couldn't tell it was me without the mask, could you? I was in such a hurry to get there it never occurred to me to grab that."

"Nah, I think you're good. It was a far shot and you were out of the shot in the office most of the time."

"That's a relief," he sighed. "I think I need a nap after that. Wake me if you need anything."

He stumbled over to the couch and collapsed into the cushions, falling asleep as soon as he landed.

THIRTY-TWO

Sam opened his eyes but immediately slammed them shut again to shield them from the bright lights.

"So he got back in and immediately fell asleep?" He heard Taylor asking someone.

"Yeah," Gwen answered. "I mean, he talked to us for like thirty seconds but then he just walked over and collapsed on the couch. We tried to wake him up when Hailey and Jason were leaving, but we didn't have any luck. Since I was already staying, we decided to just let him sleep."

"I'll check into that when he wakes up. I think I know what's happening, but I want to talk to him before I come to a conclusion. How's Lance?"

Gwen's answer grew faint as their footsteps carried them across the warehouse to where Lance was. Sam tried to open his eyes again, but the lights were still too bright.

I'll just let them rest a bit longer, he thought as he let out a deep breath.

"Come on, Sammy. You're starting to worry me again."

He blinked his eyes open to see Hailey's face hovering over him. He reached up to rub his eyes as she let out a sigh.

"I'm glad you're up." She smiled at him and rubbed his shoulder before standing up.

As she walked away, Taylor took her place. Sam had to squint as the overhead lights Hailey had been blocking hit his sensitive eyes.

"Hey, Sam. I know you're tired, but I need to ask you a few questions."

Sam didn't say anything but slowly bobbed his head up and down before Taylor continued. Crawling out of the post-sleep fog was even harder when he pushed his powers like he did downtown.

"How much do you sleep each night?"

"Umm, I'm not sure." He rubbed the left side of his face and pinched the bridge of his nose. "I guess it just kinda depends."

Taylor paused as he wrote something on his clipboard. Sam looked past Taylor and saw Gwen, Hailey, and Jason sitting on the other couch. Gwen was on one end leaning against the armrest while Jason leaned against the other arm rest with his arm around Hailey's shoulders. All three were watching his and Taylor's conversation.

"How often do you find yourself feeling like you need to nap?"

"Uh, it kinda just depends again. I just try and listen to my body when it's tired."

More writing on the clipboard.

"How long does it typically take you to fall asleep once you lie down?"

"Hmm." Sam stared at the ceiling for a beat before looking back at Taylor. "A couple seconds honestly."

"Okay." Taylor looked up from his clipboard. "One last question, do you tell a difference in how tired you are or how much sleep you need on days you use your powers or exert yourself more?"

"I mean, yeah. The more I push myself, the more tired I feel. But, I mean, that was the case before I got my powers too. I'd feel more tired on days that I worked out more or was up doing things than on days that were slower, you know?"

"Yes, but I think this is more serious," Taylor answered while he wrote, looking up once he had finished. "Sam, I tested some of the blood we got when you were shot, and I'm worried. I think that your energy output level has been increased, but how that energy affects your body has stayed constant. So when you push yourself to run four or five times faster than you used to be able to and do that four or five times longer, your body is responding as if you were doing that with your old body.

"I'm afraid that every time you use your powers, your body is aging a bit faster. Not always rapidly, but I think each time you do it, there's an impact. Maybe jogging downtown would've been ten minutes of your life, but doing it twice as fast makes it twenty. You responding to an incident by sprinting for a minute, using your strength, and sprinting back may take fifteen minutes now, but it could be costing you two hours of lifespan. I obviously can't be sure of the exact effects with the data I have to work with, but it's clear your body is responding to your new strength differently than normal bodies respond to energy outputs."

"Wait," Jason interrupted, "are you saying when Sam uses his powers, he's killing himself?"

"Possibly. Very slowly. It's like his biological clock is sped up, but it's dependent on how much he exerts himself. I don't have nearly enough expertise or data to know much more than that."

"So he's done, right?" Hailey asked, looking around at everyone. "Sam obviously can't keep using this strength if it's killing him. We need to find a way to reverse this."

"I'm trying," Taylor said. "I don't know how, and I don't even know where to look to find someone who does."

"But he's off the team, right?" Hailey asked again.

"That's up to Sam."

All four of them turned to look at Sam.

"I just woke up," he told them as he sat all the way up. "I don't know what's best right now. That was a lot

I just got dumped on me. I just need to go for a walk to clear my head and we can talk more about it later."

Sam stood up and gave Hailey a small smile as he walked out the door.

Normally he would jog to *Fran's*, but after Taylor's reveal, he decided on a more deliberate pace.

How much time have I ticked off my biological clock just trying to get places a couple minutes faster? He wondered as he strolled along.

What could have taken him four minutes took closer to twenty as he made it to the diner. The bell rang out over him as he walked in and sat down next to Harry at the bar.

"Well good afternoon, Samson," Harry greeted him with a slap on the back. "How's it going?"

"Oh, it's going."

"That good, huh?" Darlene asked as she poured him a glass of tea.

"It's just been a long week I guess," he answered with a shrug.

"I bet." Harry nodded. "It's been a long week for a lot of people. Did you see the story of the city worker who almost died taking down Christmas decorations? Had to have been a long week for that guy. Probably for whoever saved him, too."

"Yeah, it must have been. Not every day you almost die."

"Or save someone from certain death." Harry pointed out.

"Yeah, that too, I guess."

Harry nodded as he stared at Sam. "Well, the city is lucky to have him, whoever he is. The White Knight and Ironside too. Hopefully they give this new guy a better name though."

"Hopefully," Sam chuckled.

"You look tired, sugar." Darlene sat his tea down in front of him. "Everything going okay?"

"Yeah, just haven't been getting enough rest. Playoffs and everything."

"Mmm," Darlene hummed, nodding. "That must be it. How about some cobbler on the house?"

"That always picks me up," Harry laughed and slapped Sam's shoulder again.

"You don't have to do all that," Sam started, but Darlene cut him off, shaking her head.

"Nonsense, honey, I'll bring it out once you finish your dinner. Dennis'll have that out shortly."

Darlene patted his hand and smiled as she took her coffee pot to a table by the window.

"What do you think about the Dutchmen's chances next week?" Sam asked Harry, pausing to take a sip of his tea and hoping to steer the conversation away from heroes and powers to try and clear his head. "Both their losses came to the Miners, but beating a team as good as Duncan three times in a season isn't an easy feat."

"No, sure isn't." Harry sipped his coffee. "Win or lose, though, Cameron City doesn't have superheroes like we do. So at least we've got that on them!"

He slapped Sam's arm again as Dennis came out with his burger.

"Order up," Dennis said as he put the plate down in front of him. "Darlene said to have some cobbler ready for you too. Said you looked like you could use a pick me up. Can't we all."

"I'm really fine. You don't have to do that." Sam had hoped his trip to the diner would make him feel less under the microscope, but the focus had been fully trained on him since he walked in there, too.

"Forget about it, kid. Family discount, dessert is free."

"Since when is that the case?" Harry chimed in.

"You get free desserts sent home every day."

"Only when it's going bad."

"It's not bad yet so what's the issue?"

Harry sipped his coffee and shook his head, a smile breaking out across his face.

"You see that new hero this week?" Dennis asked, turning back to Sam.

"Yeah, we were just talking about that," Sam reluctantly confirmed, looking down and picking up his burger. He'd wanted a distraction from thinking about what he needed to do, but it didn't seem like the world was going to let him put it off.

"Lucky to have him, that's for sure. Proud to have that kinda person representing our city. Real life superhero that one is."

"That's what I was saying," Harry added.

Sam was already halfway through his burger as they talked. He took another sip of tea as Dennis slapped the counter and gave him a nod before walking back to the kitchen.

After finishing his meal and his cobbler, he headed back to the warehouse, again walking slowly, with another cobbler in a to-go container. The conversations at the diner about the new hero—about *him*—swirled around in his head.

He could do real good, but what was the cost? He had finally accepted the risk that potentially hurting someone else was less than the benefits he could provide as a hero, especially with him being hyperaware of that possibility. But now that he could be killing himself doing this? He'd known the fatigue was connected to the powers, but he'd thought the fatigue itself was the consequence, not just a symptom of something much bigger. As the warehouse finally came back into sight after returning at the same slow pace, he made a decision. The absence of good choices didn't absolve him of still having to choose.

Gwen, Hailey and Jason were watching a movie when he made it back. Taylor sat at the monitor. Jason hit pause as Sam walked over.

"How you feeling, Sam?" Gwen asked as he came to a stop next to the couch. Taylor got up from the desk and joined them in the sitting area too.

"Okay. Still a lot to take in and process. I'm not sure exactly what all this—" he motioned around at the warehouse, "—looks like going forward. I want to stay helpful, but I can't keep doing it how I've been doing it."

"Before you make a final decision on the subject, can I say something first?" Lance asked, his voice gravelly, as he limped to the sitting area carrying his IV stand.

THIRTY-THREE

"Lance!" Gwen gasped, leaping up from the couch as he walked up.

"You shouldn't be out of bed," Taylor scolded him, also standing.

"I'll go back in a minute," he said, raising a hand to stop Taylor from going any further, "but I need to say some things first. I know I messed up."

Lance paused. Everyone stared at him. He looked directly at Hailey.

"My first apology is for Hailey. I was out of line in how I talked to you. You are a huge asset to the team, and saying you weren't was wrong. Even if it wasn't, you're one of my best friends, and I can't imagine life without you. I shouldn't have talked to you like that. The White Knight wouldn't be what he is without you. I'm sorry."

"I forgive you. I'm just glad you're feeling better," Hailey answered him, nodding at him while she rested her hand on Jason's arm.

"Sam." Lance turned his head to look at Sam. "I owe you an apology too. It was fair for you to have second thoughts. The situation changed completely once you were affected by the new bullets, and you deserved to be able to make a revised decision based on the new information. Your being on the team is completely voluntary, and it wasn't okay for me to act as if that was my decision to make. Whatever you want to do is your choice, and you being part of this group and welcome here isn't dependent on you making a specific decision."

"Thanks Lance."

It had been hard enough to hold onto any of the anger he had felt for how Lance had treated them after his injury. Sam still didn't trust Lance as much as the others, but he wasn't going to hold their last interaction against him. With the genuine apology and his own health now at risk, it didn't feel worth trying to fight to hold onto the resentment or animosity he'd felt, not when there were so many bigger things at stake. What had happened, happened, and it was in the past now as far as Sam was concerned.

"Now to all three of you, I completely lost my head when we found out it was Fox. I let my desire to bring him down push me to be willing to get myself hurt as well as put you in danger of being hurt, and that's not okay. I hope you can forgive me."

"You're forgiven. Just don't be a jerk about it next time," Jason said as Lance finished.

"I wish I could tell you it won't happen again, but let's face it, it probably will. I'll try my best, though. My last thing is a suggestion. I've heard you all talk off and on about Sam's situation. It's obviously one-hundred percent Sam's decision, but one additional option would be Sam staying part of the team but being more selective on when he goes out on call. Not using him for every little thing, and instead only having him exert that energy when it's needed. We could also get him a strength-proof bike that he can ride to scenes instead of running. No reason to make him lose time unnecessarily."

Lance rested a hand on the couch to steady himself as he finished. Gwen took two steps over to help him balance himself.

"I think I need to lie back down. I really am sorry again for how I acted to all of you. It shouldn't have taken me literally getting shot and almost dying to apologize for that, and I'm sorry that's what it took."

Gwen held Lance by one arm and Taylor held the other as he hobbled his way to the other end of the warehouse.

"So did that change what you were going to say any?" Jason asked Sam as they waited for Taylor and Gwen to return from helping Lance back to bed.

"No, not really," he answered. "That was pretty close to what I was going to say, actually. That it might be better for me to be a 'break in case of emergency' option instead of an every-situation answer. I was probably going to quit before I went to *Fran's*, but they kept talking about how great it was that there was this new hero and how proud they were to have him represent them, and I realized just how much what we do means to people."

"Well, I'll certainly feel better knowing if things go south, I can still count on you to have my back," Jason laughed as he punched Sam in the shoulder.

"How is he?" Sam asked as Gwen and Taylor returned.

"Tired," Taylor answered. "Just that short walk and speech took everything out of him. I'll stay and watch him tonight. Sam, I think you should go and try to be proactive in getting some rest. I don't think it's good if your rest is usually coming when you collapse from exhaustion."

"Yeah, that's probably smart. See y'all in the morning," Sam called as he walked out of the warehouse.

He walked slowly back to his apartment and went and laid down on his bed, but didn't immediately crash. He hadn't thought of it before, but this was the first time in a long time he had laid down in bed and had just thought. Normally he fallen asleep too quickly to think about anything. He let his mind roam as he slowly drifted off to sleep.

Sam opened his eyes and let out a yawn. Reaching for his phone, he checked the time. Eight thirty-five. He couldn't remember the last time he'd woken up without an alarm—or person—waking him up. At least not before noon. He sat up and stretched his arms before getting ready for the day.

He stepped out into the brisk late January morning and headed to the warehouse. What could have been a five-minute jog previously was now a thirty-five-minute slog when not using his powers. The change was going to force him to find some kind of transportation that he wouldn't break with his strength because he couldn't walk everywhere anymore.

When he finally got to the warehouse, he found Taylor asleep on one couch, Lance asleep on the bed, and Gwen sitting up on the other couch reading a book. She sat the book down on her lap and waved to him as he pulled the door closed behind him.

He sat down at the opposite end of the couch from her.

"Long night?" he whispered, looking from Taylor to Lance and back to Gwen.

"You know them." She jerked her head at Taylor then Lance. "Pushed themselves until they couldn't go any longer. Jason called it a night two hours before they did. There wasn't even anyone around to respond if anything did happen."

Sam laughed with Gwen and shook his head.

"Where are Jason and Hailey?"

"They said they were going to try out a church this morning and that they'd see us afterwards for lunch."

"I didn't realize they went to church."

"They haven't been. I guess Jason grew up with that being a big part of his life and wants to get back into that, especially with him and Hailey talking about marriage more."

"Huh. Interesting. It's so weird to me that Hailey is talking about marriage."

"Me too," Gwen laughed.

"It just feels like it wasn't long ago we were kids." Sam shook his head but smiled. "Well, I got some good sleep last night at least. Turns out Taylor might have been on to something about my fatigue being tied to my exertion."

"Don't you hate it when he's right?"

"Ha! Not at all. I'll take any information I can on all this."

"Fair enough," Gwen laughed as she picked her book back up.

Sam grabbed a book of his own out of his bag, and the two of them sat in silence reading for an hour before Taylor woke up. Another hour after that, Lance got up. And a little over an hour after that, Jason and Hailey returned with bags of barbecue.

"I'm starving," Lance said as Gwen helped him to his feet. He hobbled to the table as fast as he could to eat.

"How was church?" Sam asked as he walked over as well.

"Long," Hailey answered.

"It wasn't too bad for our first time going. We'll see," Jason said with a shrug.

The six of them gathered around the table and began eating. Hailey pulled out her phone as the group ate.

"Sorry, I got a few emails this morning but was told not to check my phone during the service."

"It's bad manners." Jason shrugged again, causing Hailey to roll her eyes.

"Oh, you all might find this interesting," she said as she cleared her throat to read the message.

"'Dear Miss Hall, I'm afraid I'm in too deep and I didn't know who else to contact. I came to Duncan a few months ago with other First Sons brothers. We weren't informed what we were getting into with superheroes and guns that tear through people like this. I don't want to do this anymore. There's a buy set up for us to get some of these guns too, but I'm afraid that's just going to make it all worse. It's happening Wednesday at the railroad sometime at night. That's all the information I have right now. There are murmurs about a war for the city. Please don't reach out, I don't want to risk anyone else seeing that I spoke to you.'"

"Whoa." Jason set his rib down as Hailey finished.

"Whoa is right." Taylor shook his head. "How did they know to contact you?"

"She's the one writing about us the most." Lance scratched at his chin as he spoke. "Probably assumed she'd have the best chance at getting a message to us."

"We'll need to find a way to be more careful with that in the future. We can't let Hailey become a target to get at us," Jason said.

"I agree," Taylor answered. "Right now, though, we've gotta stop that buy from going down."

"By telling the cops, right?"

"Hailey—" Taylor started before she cut him off.

"By telling the cops, right?"

"We don't have much evidence of the cops helping us or going off our intel. And we can't afford to let these guns hit the streets."

"Unbelievable." She shook her head. "Lance is eating his first meal not through a straw, and you're already planning on how to get someone else hurt or killed."

"Babe." Jason reached his hand over to touch Hailey's arm. "I get that you're worried. I am too. But I should have our suits updated by Wednesday, so we will be protected by then. It's a risk, but we'll be prepared. We can't let these get out there."

"I know, it's just—"

"I know. But we'll be okay. We just need to start coming up with a plan for Sam and I to stop this."

"You're going to need more help for something this important," Lance said. "Make a plan for three."

"Lance, you're nowhere close to ready yet," Gwen cautioned, but Lance shook his head.

"I'm not talking about me. I'm going to put in a call."

"I'll get the whiteboard." Taylor dropped his food and hopped to his feet to retrieve the board. He talked as he started writing. "So here's the train station and the most logical layout for a buy would look like this."

They continued eating as Taylor mapped out the first draft of their plan, taking feedback from the table as he went along.

THIRTY-FOUR

Hailey had her feet propped on the arm of the couch while she wrote on her laptop, leaning against Sam, who was editing pictures he'd taken earlier in the day at the final press conference in Duncan. That weekend, the Dutchmen would leave for the championship game being played in St. Lawrence, Missouri, two hours northeast of Duncan.

Gwen had stopped by during lunch before leaving for work and Taylor said it was the one day that month he had to actually show up to class. No one had heard from Jason yet, not that it was unusual on days he worked. Lance was pacing around the warehouse, trying to will himself back to being healthy enough to help the team.

Knock knock knock

Hailey and Sam froze as the sound echoed off the tall warehouse walls. Neither of them had heard anyone knock on one of these doors since the pizza guy came on Halloween. All six of them had a key, and no one else had been in the building in the six months since Taylor had set it up as the new base.

Lance was by the monitors when the knock sounded, and he hobbled over to the door to answer it.

"Lance, what are you doing?" Hailey asked as he approached the door.

"I'm expecting a friend," he answered as he pushed it open.

"Oh good, I wasn't sure I was in the right place, what with the seemingly abandoned warehouse and all. Although, I guess this is pretty on-brand considering the base I was left. Wait, are you hurt? What happened to you? Why are you limping? Hailey!" Ashley Adair didn't stop for breath as she entered the warehouse.

Her blonde hair was pulled back into a braid. In place of the suit Jason had recently made her, she wore a pair of black jeans and had a blue denim jacket over a grey T-shirt. She rushed to the sitting area without waiting for Lance to answer any of the questions she'd asked as she sprinted to hug Hailey, every bit as tall as Hailey's five-foot-ten.

"It's been so long!" Ashley exclaimed as the two rocked back and forth, squeezing each other.

"I know! I'm so proud of you though! The new hero of Franklin! How did you like all of your gifts?"

"They were great! Don't tell the others, but your article was my favorite gift."

"Oh, I'm definitely telling the others," Hailey laughed as the two sat down. "You hear that, Lance? Your weapon, Jason's suit, and Taylor's tech all came in second to my article on the new hero."

"She's just still mad at me from our training sessions when I was down there a couple months ago," Lance answered from the monitor.

"That's got to be it," Ashley laughed as she rolled her eyes to Haley.

"Hi," she said, turning her attention to Sam, "I think we met at Taylor's party, but I'm Ashley. Hailey adopted me last year when I was a freshman at Franklin, and the White Knight helped me out one night. So now I'm the new vigilante on the campus. You must be Sam."

"Um, yeah. Nice to meet you."

"Big fan of how you can catch cars and whatnot."

"Uh, thanks. I think." He tilted his head trying to figure out what was happening as Ashley kept going.

"Anytime! Gwen!"

"Ashley!" Gwen had just walked in the door as Ashley hopped off the couch to run to Gwen. "What are you doing here?"

"Lance called me yesterday! He said there was some freelance hero work available if I wanted to come up and help. Which reminds me—" she turned back to Lance "—you never said what happened to you."

"You never gave me a chance. I just had a little run-in during a situation, that's all."

"He got shot by a new kind of bullet that went straight through his suit and would have killed him if Taylor's dad hadn't performed emergency surgery," Hailey corrected him.

"Oh." The smile left Ashley's face, and her body stilled.

"And that's who we're up against with this freelance work he told you about," Hailey added.

"Jason has a new material figured out that will stop the bullets, though," Lance said. "You know I wouldn't put you in a position to get hurt."

Ashley nodded as he talked, her excitement still visible, even after finding out what they were up against. "Well okay then. When do I start?"

"We're still waiting for the buy to go down on Wednesday, but I think the whiteboard is still up with the plan if you want to look over it with Lance and I?"

"Absolutely!" She walked over to the whiteboard with Hailey while Lance hobbled behind to join them. Gwen sat down with Sam on the couch.

"I'm not sure dragging her into this is a good idea," Gwen said, her voice soft as she looked over at Ashley. "She just healed from her own catastrophic injury two months ago. Throwing her into this fire after she's just been on campus seems like too much."

"I don't really know her, so I'm just going off whatever y'all tell me." Sam followed her line of sight to see

Ashley actually bouncing on the balls of her feet as Lance pointed at the board. "She seems really excited to be here."

"She's great, and I know she's picking all this up fast. Lance says she's more gifted than him or Jason out there, but still. She's twenty. She's been doing this for a total of four months. It's a lot to put on her shoulders."

"That's the gig, though, right?" Sam asked. "I mean, I've been doing this just a few months myself. Lance and Jason aren't even to a year yet. We're all new at this. But the status quo wasn't working, so we're all kind of flying blind in some way with this."

"I guess you're right. I just don't want to see her get hurt like she was a few months ago. Or like Jason was two months ago. Or you a month ago. Or Lance now. This hobby just seems to get you all hurt a lot."

"That's true." Sam conceded as he watched Hailey pointing to the whiteboard. Ashley nodded along. "But we've saved a lot more than four people from getting hurt or worse over that time. This is just the trolley problem every day, except with us on the diversion track. We can save a bunch of people, but we have to risk ourselves to do it. It's worth it, but that doesn't make it easy."

"I guess that's true…" Gwen's voice trailed off as she watched Lance and Hailey talking to Ashley. She pulled her book out of her bag and started reading, though her leg never stopped bouncing as she read.

Sam pulled his laptop back out and continued to edit photos until Jason busted through the door an hour later.

"Everyone bow before my genius," he declared as he stood inside the door with his arms stretched wide.

"Oh babe, did you finally learn how the blinker on your car works? I'm so proud of you, honey," Hailey said.

"I just successfully created an entirely new material that will keep us from getting killed by these new bullets, but yeah, let's get those jokes off."

"I love how we're always on the same page." Hailey smiled back.

"Check it out. Lance, grab the gun." Lance did as he was told and retrieved the gun from the lockers. "Now shoot me in the chest."

Everyone spoke at once.

"Absolutely not."

"What?"

"Jason!"

"Dude no."

"I have the new armor on underneath my shirt. I've already tested it. Now let me show it off. If Lance doesn't shoot me, I'll just take the gun and do it myself. Now shoot me."

"Yeah okay." Lance lifted the gun.

"Lance, no!" Hailey shouted.

Too late.

Bang. Bang. Bang.

Lance fired off three rounds, all hitting Jason in the chest. Jason's knees crumpled and he fell to the floor, the gunshots still echoing around the warehouse.

"Jason!" voices cried out in unison.

"And that," Jason said, hopping to his feet, "is what would have happened without the armor. But with it I'm fine!"

He pulled his shirt off to show how the new armor had withstood the impact. Hailey stormed out of the room.

"The bit was probably too much. We'll talk more about this later. Hailey, wait up!" he yelled as he ran out after her.

"So what would that have looked like before this new armor?" Ashley asked, looking around at Gwen, Lance, and Sam.

"Jason would have died and there would have been three huge holes in his chest," Lance answered. "These bullets put a hole through Jason's suit and his arm, through my suit and chest, and through Sam's arm when nothing else has been able to hurt him."

"Whoa, that's a cool power. I could've used that a few times already."

"Trust me, the side effects make it something I wouldn't recommend," Sam answered.

"Okay, we're back," Jason announced as he and Hailey rejoined the group. Jason was rubbing at his chest where

Lance had shot him, but was still smiling as he spoke. "I'm on probation from doing dumb bits, but we can get started again. Tomorrow I'll go about adding the material to my suit, Sam's jacket and pants, a new helmet for Sam to wear so he's not vulnerable there, and apparently a new suit and helmet for Eagless. Hey there, Ashley."

"Hey Jason!"

"Good to have you on board. I trust they got you up to speed on the dumpster fire that is Duncan right now?"

"More or less."

"That'll play. Okay, now there's not much to do but wait and watch the monitors. Ashley, since you're here, do you mind responding to any incidents? With Lance out of commission, Sam on a minutes restriction, and me being busy with the suits, we could use another hero. What do you say?"

"I didn't come up here to sit around and hangout. I'm skipping class for a chance at the big leagues. Let's do it."

"There's that superhero spirit. Welcome aboard officially. Now let's get to work."

The next few days dragged by as they waited for the buy to happen. Ashley responded to a few minor situations, but with it being the early part of the week there wasn't much action.

"Hey Sam, come help me out," Jason called from the warehouse door before returning to his car.

He'd gotten in from work a little after six in the evening on Wednesday while the rest of the group, plus Ashley, had been there most of the day.

Jason had Sam carry in a big box that was too heavy for him to bring in himself. Sam sat it down on the table and Jason began unpacking it like a coach passing out new uniforms.

"This mission is going to be more of a covert type thing, so since I was already making new suits, I figured we would go darker for all of them. A nice alternate uniform, ya know?" He pulled out a dark navy-blue jacket from the box and tossed it to Ashley. "Here you go, Ash. And here are the matching pants, and I'll get you the helmet, gloves and shoes in a sec. All the new suit pieces will be able to protect you from the bullets piercing through, but they'll still hurt. I've added a little padding, but any more and you couldn't hardly move."

Ashley's navy-blue jacket and pants had black stripes running up each side, down each arm, and her black Eagless logo in the center of the jacket against the blue background. It had two slots on the back, one over each shoulder, for her weapons.

"You're next, Sam."

Sam caught the suit Jason tossed him and looked it over as Jason dug back into the box. A dark brown jacket with a black logo and black pants. Simple, like he preferred.

"And I found the new material worked so well in the jackets that I opted for a jacket and pants myself."

Jason pulled out a dark crimson jacket and the same color pants. Jason's jacket had a simple black shield in the middle where Ashley's and Sam's had logos.

"I'll let you know if I see any differences between this and the suit," Jason told Lance as he sat the jacket down on the table. "Might do a new uniform for us if it works well. I'm almost done with your version of this suit, in case these guns are still a problem when you're healed."

Next, Jason opened up the smaller box he had carried in. He pulled out three helmets and tossed one each to Sam and Ashley. All of Sam's pieces were black, while Ashley had all navy and Jason's were that same crimson.

"Helmets are reinforced everywhere but the face. Hopefully if you get hit in the head by a bullet it will just knock you out instead of killing you. Hopefully. Try not to find out. Same comms and tech that we're used to. Gloves and shoes are reinforced as well. Unless they get in some clean face shots, we should be able to withstand anything that they fire at us."

"You're sure these will work?" Hailey asked, her arms crossed.

"You want to grab the gun and test it? Sorry, sorry." He quickly retreated at Hailey's scathing look. "Won't happen again."

"Okay," Taylor said as Sam and Ashley admired their new suits, "here's the plan. Hailey is going to drive Ashley and Sam to the drop off point next to the train station. Jason will ride the one bike we still have running to meet them there. I'll be on the monitors, and once I see movement you three will move in, Jason and Ashley on the bike, Sam running. Sam, we're conserving your energy when we can, but when you're in a situation, you have to be one hundred percent engaged. Don't conserve while you're in the field or people will get hurt. Got it?"

Sam nodded. This was what he had decided on for his powers. Getting to the diner ten minutes faster or catching a pickpocket wasn't worth taking time off his life expectancy, but trying to keep the city from falling into a turf war with next gen guns was a cause worth a few hours on the back end. He could pull the level on the trolley problem for something of this magnitude.

"Okay good. It's already dark out, so you three suit up and head over. I doubt anything goes down for a few hours, but it would be better for you to be waiting on site when it happens instead of sitting around here."

Jason and Sam walked to the lockers while Ashley took her suit and bag to the restroom to change.

"And you're sure these will keep bullets from coming through?" Sam asked as Jason changed into a dry fit tee for under his suit.

"I wouldn't be going out there if I didn't. And I wouldn't send you or Ashley, either. Unless they've come up with a completely new weapon in the last few weeks, we're as protected as we can be."

"I trust you. Let's do it." Sam took off his shirt and began changing as well.

With everything but their helmets on, Jason and Sam walked back to the sitting area. A couple minutes later, Ashley joined them in her new suit with her duffel bag in her left hand.

"Alright." Jason clapped once and stood up as she walked up. "Let's go get in position."

"Lance and I will be on comms as soon as you leave," Taylor said. "Gwen will be standing by ready to hop in a car if someone needs to get picked up. We'll see you on the other side."

Jason gave Lance and Taylor a fist bump on his way to the bike, securing his new helmet as he sat and waited for Hailey, Sam, and Ashley to make it to the car. Gwen gave Sam and Ashley a hug, and Lance gave Ashley a few quick words out of ear shot. Less than a minute after Taylor finished talking, they crawled into the back seat of Hailey's car.

"How are we feeling, gang?" Hailey asked, looking at the two of them in the rear-view mirror as she pulled out. "We want music or silence tonight?"

"Um, I'd say silence," Sam answered after a beat.

"Same," Ashley said, staring out the window.

"Silence it is. Do you want me to talk, or are you both focused?"

"Focused," they answered at the same time, Sam staring up at the ceiling.

"Gotcha. That's cool. More of a nervous talker myself." She pulled out onto the road as a few drops of rain began to patter onto the windshield. "But I get that's not the vibe tonight. No doubt."

"Hails."

"Right, right, sorry." She waved to Sam through the mirror. "Just three people I care about doing something dangerous and, some might say—not me, but some— reckless. I'm just a bit on edge."

"We'll be fine," Sam answered, his head still leaned back and his eyes closed. He tried to give a reassuring smile.

He fully trusted that the suit Jason had designed would work as promised, but that didn't get rid of the memory of his last interaction with these guns. The suit might work against the bullets, but they couldn't stop his skin from burning as the anxiety made itself felt in every inch of his body.

Breathe. Just breathe.

"I know, I know," Hailey muttered to herself. "I know, I know."

The car slowed to a stop as Hailey pulled into the agreed upon parking lot. They were at the train yard, but out of sight of the old depot where the buy was taking place. All three of them jumped as the door flew open. Jason crawled into the passenger seat and removed his helmet.

"It's coming down hard out there," he said as he leaned back into the chair and looked at Ashley and Sam through the rearview mirror. "Why is everyone breathing hard?"

"Everyone there?" Taylor's voice cut through each of their comms before anyone could answer.

"I just got in the car," Jason confirmed.

"Okay good. Hang tight for now. I'll update you if I see anything."

"Copy that," Jason answered before the comms went silent again. He looked at Sam and Ashley again in the rear-view mirror and asked, "How are we feeling, gang?"

"A bit nervous. This is all more intense than what I've done before," Ashley answered, looking out the window again as she tapped her fingers on her knee.

"You and me both," Jason chuckled. "We'll be through it all soon, though."

No one answered him. The car shifted to the four of them sitting in silence as they waited for Taylor's voice to break through to alert them of movement. Eight o'clock came and went, and then nine. Jason attempted to make conversation a few more times, but Ashley and Sam weren't able to make it last longer than a few seconds. Hailey tried to humor Jason, but after a while she couldn't hold the conversation either. Ten o'clock passed, and Jason had finally had enough.

"Talk to me, Taylor. Is there anything happening?"

"Not yet. I'll let you know as soon as we see something on our end."

"Any chance our source lied to us?"

"He could have, but I don't think so. What would he have to gain from that? Let's hold tight a bit longer."

"Copy that," Jason sighed, sinking back into his chair.

Hailey reached over and rubbed his arm, but didn't say anything. The silence continued to drag on as eleven went by.

"Wait, we've got movement." Taylor's voice came through the comms at eleven forty-seven, spurring Jason to sit up straight. "Hold your positions, but we have one vehicle arriving. Looks like an armored van. Definitely a passenger with the driver. Could be more in the back."

"Probably early for a midnight meet," Lance added.

"Copy that. We'll be out of the car, stretched, and ready to go at midnight then to make sure we're moving as soon as we get your signal," Jason said into the comms before adding to Ashley and Sam, "I don't know about you two, but being in a car for five hours has me stiff. I'm going to stretch a bit."

"I'll join you," Ashley replied, already opening the door.

"I'm good," Sam answered, repositioning himself to get more comfortable.

He wanted to conserve as much of his energy as he could, and he knew he was too anxious to not try and dissipate that if he had to stand outside the car.

"Suit yourself." Jason shrugged before joining Ashley.

"You okay, Sammy?" Hailey asked once they were alone.

"I'll be better when this is over." He closed his eyes again and leaned back against the headrest, trying to keep his pulse as low as possible.

"Me too," she said while watching Jason through the rain smeared window. "Me too."

"Two more trucks just arrived," Taylor's voice cut back through the comms. "It's about go time."

Sam let out a deep breath and waited for Hailey to reach back and open his door for him so he could stand out in the rain next to Jason and Ashley. As he walked around the car, they had already mounted the bike.

"Please be as safe as you can," Hailey asked through her rolled-down window.

"You know we'll try our best," Jason laughed.

Hailey gave him a small smile and mouthed "I love you" to him.

"I love you too," he responded, cupping his hands into the shape of a heart over his chest as Sam lifted himself up and down on the balls of his feet as slowly as he could.

"Okay, we have eyes on the guns. Mission is live."

Jason revved the engine and he and Ashley tore off through the rainy night on the bike as Sam ran close behind.

The bike took a sharp right turn around a container, and they were thirty yards in front of the depot. They slowed to a stop as soon as they turned the corner. There wasn't a car in sight, only a single body swinging from the depot's entrance.

"Okay, it looks like all of the men from both trucks are taking part in the loading and unloading." Taylor's voice came over their speakers as they stopped. "Why aren't you engaging?"

"We got played," Jason said, unstrapping his helmet. "There aren't any trucks here. They have you watching a dummy feed."

"That's impossible," Taylor scoffed as the sound of keys rapidly being punched filled the comms. "It shows that this is the live feed, I've authenticated it twice."

"Well, I don't know what to tell you, man." Jason started walking forward. "The only thing here is a body strung up on the depot. Looks riddled with bullets. There's a sign hanging off of —oh."

"What's it say, Jason?" Taylor asked.

"Uh," Jason scratched his chin and turned to see Ashley and Sam standing where he had left them. "How about I just bring the sign in, and we talk about it there?"

"What's it say?" Hailey's voice was barely a whisper as it cracked.

Jason took a deep breath and read it aloud. "For our friends in suits. To the attention of Hailey Hall. A pet rat from us to you."

"Take the sign but don't touch the body," Lance's voice cut through the comms this time.

Jason used his spear to lift the sign up off the man and rejoined Ashley and Sam to head back to the car. Hailey's head was in her hands against the steering wheel as they returned. Jason and Ashley helped her get out of the front seat and into the back. Ashley climbed into the driver's seat as Jason crawled into the back with Hailey.

"Sam, hide the bike somewhere we can find it and hop in the passenger seat. We'll come back for it later," Jason said before closing the door behind him and letting Hailey collapse against his shoulder.

Sam did as he was told and returned to the car. Jason's eyes were distant as he held Hailey while she sobbed. Ashley's face was ghostlike in its paleness, and her hands were somehow whiter as she squeezed the steering wheel. Sam, gently as he could, closed the door behind him and they headed home, taking a short detour to avoid driving by the depot again.

Breathe. Just breathe.

THIRTY-FIVE

Between Taylor being bested on the tech front, Hailey feeling like she was to blame for the death of the First Sons' member, and Ashley being thrust into the big city crime-fighting waters by seeing a dead man almost immediately, the team was pretty shaken up when the four of them got back to the warehouse.

Gwen rushed to Hailey as soon as they walked in, and she and Jason switched projects as Jason went to try and encourage Taylor. Lance hobbled over to where Ashley was sitting and tried to lift her spirits. Sam walked to one of the hospital beds as everyone else was occupied and closed his eyes. Almost immediately, everything disappeared for him.

Sam blinked and sat up, letting out a yawn as he did so. He patted around for his phone but couldn't find it.

The lockers.

He was still wearing his suit from the mission, and his phone was in his jeans pocket.

He hopped off the bed and walked across the warehouse, slowing as he realized only Lance and Ashley were there—Lance on the monitor and Ashley on the couch.

"Where is everyone?" Sam asked as he rubbed at his eye with the heel of his hand.

"You're up," Lance said, spinning his chair around. "Jason and Gwen are at work. Hailey is at home taking a sick day, and Taylor is on Hailey duty currently. Taylor said we should let you rest as long as your body needed. It's three o'clock Thursday now."

"I didn't feel like I was sleeping that long." The sprint at the depot had taken more out of him than he had realized.

Lance shrugged and turned back to the monitor.

Sam changed out of his suit and back into normal clothes before joining Ashley on the couch.

"How are you doing? I know last night shook you up pretty good."

"Oh, it definitely did. I've never seen a dead body before, not even like a funeral or anything. Seeing one for the first time like that was chilling. Disturbing even. But I feel a bit better. Lance talked to me for a bit, and then Gwen talked to me after she talked to Hailey, and she always knows what to say. So I'm still a bit shaken, but better than last night."

"That's good to hear." Sam smiled at her.

"How about you?"

"Apparently I was just tired. And I'm worried about Hailey, but I'm not really sure what there is for me to do about it."

Ashley nodded along as Sam talked. "I feel the same way. I want to help her right now, but how do you possibly do that?"

"I guess we just show up. That's all we can really do."

The next two days passed without incident, but also passed without Hailey returning to work or Taylor going to class, albeit for different reasons. Hailey stayed home grieving Thursday and Friday as they all took shifts being there with her, with Jason and Gwen carrying the brunt of the load when they weren't at work. Taylor, on the other hand, spent every minute of every hour on the computer trying to figure out how he had been beaten so it wouldn't happen again.

As Saturday came, Sam left for a two-night stay in St. Lawrence after stopping by to tell Hailey bye. He had been commuting the two-hour-one-way train ride back and forth all week, much to Brooklyn's confusion, but now that the game was approaching, he would need to be present the next forty-eight hours.

Part of him was thankful to be away from the chaos going on in Duncan, but the rest of him knew it would be better if he was with the team. Still, he was in St. Lawrence and figured he might as well enjoy it. The final press conference before the game was Saturday afternoon, and he'd be there taking photos. Then, that evening, there was a big party for all the media attending the championship at a swanky downtown hotel.

Sam got dressed in some khaki pants and a flannel, putting on his boots to walk through the rainy streets, then left the hotel for the stadium at four o'clock. With him conserving his strength now, it took him a lot longer to get from place to place.

By the time he made it to the stadium, the atmosphere was buzzing. Staffers wearing PFL logos, team employees for the Dutchmen and Miners, stadium workers, and media members were all bustling up and down the corridors. Sam tried to make it to the press stage on the field without bumping into anyone but heard more than a few exclamations of pain as people ran into him.

"Hey Sam!" Brooklyn waved and walked over to him as he wandered onto the turf. "Can't believe all the parties you've missed going back and forth all week. Those are the best parts of the gig," she laughed.

"Yeah, I had some personal stuff to take care of this week, but I'm staying tonight. At least I'll make it for the big party."

"It's supposed to be crazy. The first couple hours are typical formal affairs but after that I've heard it's unlike anything else."

"I'm pretty out of practice when it comes to partying, so I guess we'll see how well I handle it."

"I'm sure you'll be fine." Brooklyn laughed again. "Hey I think they're starting. I'll see you tonight!"

She jogged to join the scrum of reporters around the stage while Sam walked to where the photographers were all huddled and got his camera ready.

Sam headed back to his hotel room after the press conference and showered before the party. He wasn't sure what to expect, so he opted for his usual: flannel and khakis with boots. He was in the process of tying his hair in a bun on top of his head when there was a knock at the door. He finished his hair and went to answer it.

"Whoa."

Brooklyn had a tan coat on over a floor-length navy satin dress, navy heels, and she had her hair up too, though in a more intentional manner than Sam.

"Well," she laughed, "since neither of us have been there before, at least one of us will be dressed appropriately."

Sam helped her into the car at their hotel and out at the party hotel. They walked into the ballroom together to find that Brooklyn was the one dressed appropriately.

Most of the men were wearing suits and very few were without a jacket. Almost all of the women were wearing dresses.

"Well now we know for next time, eh?" Brooklyn lightly elbowed Sam and gave him a smile. "You look fine, let's go find our seats."

They walked around the room looking at the name-plates on each table until they found their names.

"I'm going to mingle a bit before they get started. You want to come with?" she asked as she laid her coat across her chair.

"No, I think I'm good for now. I'm sure there will be some time later."

He was excited to be here, there weren't many bigger stages for him to photograph in the sports world, but he couldn't stop thinking about Duncan. The image of the man swaying at the depot had burned itself into Sam's mind, and he was still worried about Hailey. Being in a place like this with lavish clothing and fancy food after what he had seen earlier in the week felt jarring and wrong.

"Your choice." Brooklyn shrugged and walked away, leaving Sam alone at the table.

Twenty minutes passed before a speaker walked on stage and everyone found their seats. Their dinner was served as the man talked and, once he finished, another woman took his place. She wanted to acknowledge some of the guests for their careers, mostly older national reporters who were either scaling back in their coverage or retiring altogether. Then another man spoke on the importance of journalism as the dessert was being finished.

"I didn't think he'd ever finish," Brooklyn whispered to Sam as the last man walked off stage to a round of applause.

Sam followed Brooklyn and a crowd of journalists to the elevator as they all made their way to the rooftop party. The rain earlier had left the roof a bit damp, but the staff had cleaned it up well for the most part. Sam checked his phone as they got off the elevator. It was eight thirty-two. By the time he helped Brooklyn back to the elevator to head back to their hotel it was after one.

Sam helped Brooklyn get into her room before returning to his own room. Even without having used his powers today, he was exhausted. He laid down on the bed and quickly fell asleep.

Knock knock knock

Sam stared at the hallway ceiling the next morning as his knocks echoed loudly off Brooklyn's door even as he tried to hit it as lightly as he could.

Knock knock knock

The door echoed some more before it squeaked open. Brooklyn stood on the other side, rubbing at her eyes.

"I hadn't heard from you, and I was about to head to the stadium. Figured I should check on you before I left," Sam explained.

"Thanks, I'll see you there," she answered before closing the door in his face.

Sam shrugged and headed to the stadium. It was a beautiful winter day for the championship game. A few players were on the field either doing drills individually or with a partner as Sam snapped photos. Warmups came and went, and Sam was snapping photos of the stadium as the seats filled up and the entire place began to buzz.

Before the anthem played and captains were introduced, Sam slipped back to the press room for a snack to fuel up. He found Brooklyn along with a half-dozen other journalists all crowded around the coffee machine. Brooklyn gave him a nod and small smile but didn't move from her spot, so Sam just returned her nod and smile and headed back to the field to prepare for kickoff.

The Dutchmen received the opening kickoff and drove down the field before being stopped at the Miners twenty-five-yard line and being forced to settle for a field goal. That was the only points either team managed in the first quarter.

The second quarter opened the scoring up a bit as the Miners scored two touchdowns and the Dutchmen added a touchdown of their own to go with another field goal to send the game to halftime with a score of fourteen to thirteen in the Miners' favor.

Sam got some good photos of the halftime performance and was back in his spot in the end zone as the third quarter began. The Miners managed to hold the Dutchmen scoreless while adding two field goals to their score to take a twenty to thirteen lead into the final quarter.

The Miners started the fourth off with another touchdown to take a fourteen-point lead on the Dutchmen. The Dutchmen answered right back as Dante led them down the field for a touchdown of their own to cut the Miners' lead back to seven.

With four minutes to go and the Miners at midfield for a third down with seven to go, the Miners quarterback fired a ball to the outside that was intercepted before the defender got knocked out of bounds. After a quick celebration, Dante led the offense back onto the field and began driving again. With twenty-three seconds remaining and the Dutchmen on the Miners' seven-yard line, Dante fired a strike for a touchdown to bring the Dutchmen within one as the stadium erupted.

The field goal unit ran onto the field, but Dante was staying on the field next to the sideline talking to the coaches. Sam zoomed in and got a few pictures of Dante raising two fingers at the coach before the coach called a timeout. The stadium erupted again as Dante led the offense back onto the field out of the timeout. Faking a handoff and rolling out to his right, Dante made two defenders miss before sprinting forward, stopping on a dime, and jumping to throw a pass over the outstretched hands of a Miners linebacker. The two-point conversion was completed, and the roar of the crowd became deafening as the Dutchmen took their first lead since the first quarter.

Twenty-three seconds of game time later and the Duncan Dutchmen were the PFL Champions. Sam squeezed in and out of the crowded field to capture the euphoria on each of the Dutchmen's faces, getting the entire celebration on film.

Sam extracted himself to the press room, where he began uploading all of his photos to the newspaper server. Before he exited out of the server, a video caught his eye. His computer was muted, but he didn't need the volume to see that Duncan was at war. Civilians ran for cover as the Five Aces and First Sons destroyed the city with the plasma guns they were aiming at one another. He caught a glimpse of red as Jason came into the picture long enough to pull a child onto his bike before exiting the frame as quickly as he had entered it. The video had just been posted ten minutes ago. He could still make a difference.

Sam shut his laptop and ran through the stadium to find Brooklyn in the Dutchmen locker room.

"No time to explain," Sam shouted to her so she could hear him above the noise. "I have to leave. All the photos are uploaded onto the server."

Brooklyn opened her mouth to speak but he was already gone. By the time Brooklyn would get back to her place in the locker room scrum, Sam was out of the building, racing down the highway back to Duncan, running faster than he ever had before as he effortlessly passed cars returning to Duncan from the game. He could feel his energy waning, but he pushed through the fatigue and pushed his body harder. An hour and a half after he left the stadium, Sam had made what was a two-hour drive from St. Lawrence back to Duncan. He slowed momentarily before pushing even harder as the city lights came into view with smoke and flames rising up above.

THIRTY-SIX

Sam stumbled into the warehouse, out of breath for the first time in months, to grab his suit. Taylor was alone at the monitors.

"Give me a briefing while I get dressed," Sam panted, causing him to jump.

"Sam? What are you doing here?" Taylor asked as Sam walked to the lockers.

"I got Gwen's call. I immediately left the game. What's going on?"

"Aces and Sons have loaded up and made uptown a war zone. Gwen got *Fran's* emptied out before the fray moved that far. She and Hailey are working to clear out as many people as possible from areas that haven't been hit. Lance is trying to get people out who are still in the middle. Jason and Ashley are doing their best to break it up, but there are hundreds of people and hundreds of guns, Sam. Do you have enough energy to help after that run?"

"I guess I have to." Sam shrugged, putting his helmet on as he walked out the door and sprinted towards the flames.

Gunshots rattled off as he got closer to the area. The cracks from the guns mingled with car alarms, sirens, and screams to make a horrifying chorus.

There were flashing lights blocking off a street as he approached, so he started there.

"How can I help?" Sam asked the officer and firefighter standing behind their cars.

They both jumped and the cop pulled his gun as they turned around to face him. The officer lowered his gun once he saw who it was.

"Your friends are helping evacuate as many civilians as they can. I know the other two in suits are trying to stop gunmen when they can, but there are just too many of them."

"Not for me there's not." Sam looked at the chaos erupting around him and started walking forward past the two cars.

"We're not sure where the Aces have taken up a battleground HQ, but the First Sons seem to have holed up at St. Andrews Middle School."

"Then that's where I'll start."

Sam sprinted towards the school. He arrived in less than a minute, ripping guns away from three people on the way. He twisted the barrel of each gun so they couldn't shoot and tossed them into a dumpster outside the school. Two armed lookouts opened fire as he approached. He ducked behind his arm as the bullets bounced off of him. Jason's suit holding up as promised.

Leaping forward, Sam ripped the guns away from the guards, twisting the barrels again. Both lookouts visibly gulped as Sam stepped towards them again. He wrapped an arm around each of them and jumped.

The two men yelped as they flew through the air. Sam landed on the roof of the three-story building and dropped them to the rooftop before jumping back down and breaking through the door to the school.

Three men opened fire on him as the door fell to the ground. Once again, the bullets bounced off of him, clattering off to the side. Sam picked up the door and walked it towards the retreating gunmen. Jogging forward, he caught up to the three of them in two steps and pushed the door into them lightly, sending them all hurtling back into the wall. Sam rushed forward, slamming the bottom of the door into the wall on one side of them. Pulling and bending the top around them, he buried it into the wall on the other side, holding them in place.

He returned to where their guns had fallen and twisted the barrels of each, kicking them back to the wall under their owners as he finished.

Sam left them struggling against the door as he walked down the corridor towards two big doors with the word "cafeteria" over them. Taking a deep breath and pushing back against the fatigue, he relied on the adrenaline and the knowledge that if he let himself succumb to exhaustion, he would likely die and many more would too. So he pressed on.

He threw open the doors and was immediately pushed back by the sheer quantity of bullets that slammed into him. They couldn't pierce or hurt him, but the combined force of hundreds of bullets pushed him back out of the cafeteria and he took cover behind the wall as more bullets flew by.

"Well, I've found the First Sons' headquarters," he said through the comms.

"Do you need backup?" Jason asked, panting.

"No, eventually they'll have to run low enough on bullets that they can't push me back with them. After you complete the evacuation can y'all try and find the Aces' base?"

"I'm working on that now," Taylor answered. "I've got it narrowed down to a few buildings. I'll keep working and let you know what I find once you finish at the middle school."

"Copy that."

Sam took a deep breath and stepped back a few feet. Lowering his shoulder, he rushed forward, barreling through the wall. Debris flew through the air.

More bullets shot his way as hands began grabbing at his suit, trying to rip it open. He threw out his arms, sending four men flying into the others, but more came and took their place. Again and again, Sam flung people off of him and again and again more took their place. One got a hand on his jacket zipper and pulled it a quarter of the way down before Sam could remove him. Another got a hand up under the bottom of Sam's mask and was almost able to insert the barrel of a gun before Sam ripped it out of his hands.

Sam sprinted away from the mob, lowering his shoulder and going through the wall on the other side of the room, trying to catch his breath.

"Tell me things are going better out there," Sam panted into his comms, slumping back against the wall.

"Really wish I could," Jason replied. "Could use your help when you get out of there."

"Copy."

He straightened and re-entered the cafeteria and was again met with a cloud of bullets.

I thought they would run out of bullets, but I guess not.

He ran along the wall and dove back through to the other side. The building rumbled as he pushed through a column. Ceiling tiles crashed to the floor around him.

That could work.

Sam rammed his shoulder into the column three more times, then ran through the wall again, sprinting all the way through the cafeteria and through a wall on the other side as the one behind him collapsed in. He found another load-bearing column and set about knocking that pole out as well. The wall connecting the cafeteria to the hall he'd come in through faltered and fell around him as the building collapsed in on itself from above, trapping everyone in the room with no doors, and burying Sam under the rubble in the hallway.

Breathe.

Just.

Breathe.

Sam repeated his mantra to himself over and over for fifteen seconds before he was able to regulate his breathing. He was strong enough to break through walls, but lifting an entire building off of himself was a different challenge. He wiggled himself into a position to do a push up and was able to get himself a few inches off the ground. He threw himself forward a foot before the weight crashed back down on him. It took every ounce of will he had to not give in to the fatigue and just let whoever found him in the rubble at the end of all this do what they may. He repeated this process another four times before he was able to remove himself from the weight that had covered his legs and stand up in the dim light, surrounded by rubble. Hearing the muffled voices of the trapped gang behind him, he went to the opposite pile of rubble and began digging out a hole to climb through.

It took him longer to dig the hole than any other physical task had taken since he had gotten his powers, but ten minutes later, he had created a space big enough to get out.

"The First Sons' HQ and reinforcements have been neutralized. Where am I needed next?" he asked as he made his way back through the hall and passed the three men still pinned to the wall.

"Sam!" Taylor exclaimed through the comms. "We lost your signal when the building fell. We thought we'd lost you."

"Not yet. Where do I need to go?"

"Lance, Jason, and Ashley are pinned down inside of *Fran's*. Aces and Sons are both outside alternating between firing at one another and firing at us whenever we try to move."

"Should I go there next or to the Aces' HQ?" He was still pushing back against the fatigue that had grown stronger while he was extricating himself from the rubble. Taylor didn't say anything about Darlene, Dennis, or Harry, so Sam assumed they were safe. He had to. He wasn't sure he'd be able to stay standing if he thought something had happened to them.

"National Guard has been deployed, and I've already left them a tip of where the Aces are hiding out. I think all three of our people are hurt. Not sure how much longer before someone just goes in there and tries to take them out."

"Copy. I'm on my way"

Sam exited the school to find a group of five armed men standing outside staring at the fallen building. As they were still turning to face him, he was already moving, taking and twisting each of their guns before a single shot could be fired.

He turned without saying a word and left the newly unarmed men where he'd found them, throwing the guns into a dumpster as he walked away. He ran down the street that fed into the alley behind *Fran's*, which was usually reserved for delivery trucks.

There were two men standing watch at the back door, in case the group inside tried to escape, Sam assumed. They had their backs to him as he approached and didn't have time to scream, much less run or shoot, before Sam grabbed them by the back of their jackets. He hoisted them into the dumpster behind *Fran's*, sending a cloud of flies into the air. Pulling the dumpster onto its side, he trapped the lid up against the wall.

"Someone let me in the back door. It's clear out here," Sam said into the comms. A few seconds later, Ashley opened the door and let him in, locking it behind him.

"Nice to have you join us," Jason said as he walked in, giving a little salute.

The front of the store was cluttered with shattered boards and tables that they had piled up to have some protection against the plasma guns. Jason and Ashley stood by the bar with a bunch of crumpled sheets of paper around them. Lance sat on a barstool beside them, leaning on the counter. All three of them had taken their helmets off, so Sam followed suit.

"You okay, Lance?"

"The suits stop the bullets from piercing, but they still pack a punch," Jason answered for him as Lance just put a thumb up without lifting his head from the bar. "He shouldn't be in the field yet, but he insisted. Caught a couple to the chest where he was still healing, and now he's in a tough spot. He needs to get looked at by Taylor, but we have to finish this first."

"And how's the planning coming?" Sam asked, pointing to the crumpled sheets of paper.

"Not great," Ashley said.

"How many are out there?"

"There were probably around a hundred total earlier. There are different areas that turned into mini battlegrounds, and this was one of them. It's been an hour or so since we barricaded ourselves in, and there's been shooting the whole time, so unless they brought in reinforcements, those numbers should be lower now." She looked at Jason for confirmation, and he nodded.

"Well, I've taken care of the First Sons' HQ, so there shouldn't be many reinforcements coming from there. Taylor said he's given the National Guard info on where the Aces are, so they should be neutralized soon too. If we can clear out this group in front of us, we can end this without any more deaths or damage."

"And how do you suggest we 'end this'?" Jason asked, arms crossed.

"I go take their guns and break them where they can't fire. It's what I've been doing all night. Once I'm drawing the fire, you two can go around and take out people one at a time in a way I can't without killing someone. It'll take some time if there are still even half of that hundred out there, but it's something."

"I'm coming too," Lance said, wincing as he stood up.

"I'll take that gun you've been using and shoot you in the chest some more if you try coming out with us," Jason answered with a shake of his head. "Must be out of your mind."

"You need all the help you can get. I'm able to fight."

"Lance —" Ashley hesitated, choosing her words. "We know you want to help, and we appreciate it. But we need your help in the future too, and if you get yourself killed, it's going to hurt us more in the long term."

"What if he took that gun and just sat on the roof working as a sniper?" Sam asked.

"I'd be willing to do that," Lance agreed.

"Fine. We could use the cover anyway. So, what's the order we're doing this in?" Jason said.

"We all go out the back, I jump Lance up to the roof. I jump down to the front of the building and start taking fire and taking guns. Lance gives you two the sign when it's safe to come in after I've gotten a good amount of guns out of commission. We fight until there's no one else."

"Works for me." Lance secured his helmet back on and reached for the gun they had brought in. Ashley and Jason both put their helmets back on as well.

"Let's do it then," Jason said as they walked to the door.

The back alley was still clear when Sam led the way out. Sam picked up Lance and leapt to the top of the three-story building, dropping him off before jumping back down to the ground. There were still forty-something gunmen at this battlefront and they all opened fire on him as soon as he landed. Bullets fell to the ground around him as he walked through the chaos and began taking guns away.

Silence fell around him as he looked for the next gun to take. Blue and red blurs took out men left and right while others fell to the ground as single gunshots fired down from above. There were no more guns for Sam to disarm. Men continued to fall around him as the rest of the team took them out, until there wasn't anyone else left to fight.

Sam allowed himself a relieved smile, swaying a bit as his adrenaline slowed down. His eyes seemed to have grown much heavier in just the few seconds since he'd finished disarming the gunmen, to the point he could no longer keep them open. He couldn't fight the fatigue any longer, but he had fought it long enough. His mouth was still curved into a soft smile as he collapsed to the street.

chapter

THIRTY-SEVEN

Rising from the Ashes

The fires still burned this morning in the aftermath of last night's standoff between members of The Five Aces and First Sons gangs. Hundreds of men with high-tech weaponry took to uptown as part of an ongoing turf war. The First Sons tried to make a name for themselves in Duncan, where the Five Aces have long been entrenched.

These new weapons, a Fox Industries. prototype that has hit the streets, use plasma technology that cuts through people and armor much easier than normal bullets, a lesson Duncan PD learned firsthand as twenty-three officers were injured by the guns, and three were killed. Neither CEO Matthew Fox nor Fox Industries. returned requests for comment.

Though gunshots echoed through the streets and fires blazed all around, the citizens in the area were not alone. A team of heroes, including the White Knight, Ironside, Samson, and Eagless, were on the scene. The heroes helped contain the First Sons, break up a key battleground on Broadway, and evacuate civilians out of uptown before the fighting could move into more populated areas.

The city is scrambling to get these weapons off the streets and to find new equipment that can be used to combat these guns if they do surface again. In the meantime, Duncan has heroes watching over us to come in and do the job of protecting the city from harm.

Hailey Hall

Sam walked out of the Daily building and passed what was left of *Fran's* on his way back to the warehouse. His talk with Barry had gone okay; there was no anger or disappointment during the conversation. Barry understood when Sam explained that he'd panicked when he heard about uptown, since Dennis, Darlene, and Harry were basically family to him, and that's why he left abruptly from the game to go check on them.

And Sam understood when Barry laid out all the reasons that Sam was being let go as a staff photographer after his first year there. Brooklyn offered to try and talk to Barry to get his job back, but Sam didn't let her. He knew these were the results of his decisions. He and Barry had worked out a plan for him to leave on a good note, where the Daily would work to secure a media pass for him to do freelance work and that would allow him to not have to worry as much about working while also figuring out the hero stuff. It was a good deal, even if it meant his time as Brooklyn's coworker was coming to an end.

It was still early on Tuesday as he made his long walk back to the warehouse. After he'd passed out Sunday night, Lance had kept anyone from getting close to him from the rooftop while Ashley and Jason finished taking out the stragglers. The three of them were able to work together to lift him into Lance's truck and they wheeled out a hospital bed to get him inside.

Sam didn't wake up until after midnight on Tuesday, sleeping through a chaotic day of phone calls from work, Hailey's article making the front page, and the fallout for Fox Industries. The afternoon after Hailey name-dropped them in her article, Matthew Fox held a press conference promising to look into the accusations that these were Fox weapons and to have a full investigation into how they were leaked if they were indeed from Fox Industries. Regardless, he promised, his team would work to provide state of the art equipment for the city's law enforcement so that they would not be at a disadvantage in this new arms race.

When Sam woke up early on Tuesday, Taylor was asleep on the couch, Lance laid in a bed a few feet over, Hailey and Ashley watched the monitors, and Darlene sat in a chair next to his bed while Harry, Dennis, Jason, and Gwen all sat around a table playing dominoes, waiting for him to wake up.

"What are you all doing here?" Sam had asked, not sure if he had actually woken up or if he was still dreaming.

"Waiting for the hero to wake up," Harry laughed as he laid a tile, causing Dennis to mumble under his breath.

"We've been worried about you, sugar. Just wanted to make sure you were alright." Darlene patted his hand and gave him a smile as she sat her book down.

Sam had fallen back to sleep pretty quickly, and slept through the night, waking up just in time to make it to Barry's office to have their conversation before his nine o'clock morning meeting.

His walk back to the warehouse took much longer when he had to walk at this crawl of a pace instead of running at sixty plus miles per hour or even jogging at forty plus, but these were the doctor's orders. After what felt like an eternity—but was closer to thirty minutes—Sam made it back to the warehouse.

"Good, you're here," Hailey said when he walked in, waving him over to join her. Taylor, Dennis, Darlene, and Harry were with her in the sitting area. "We need your help."

"I don't think even he'll be able to help you," Harry laughed as Sam walked over.

"Help with what?"

"We're retiring," Dennis answered him shortly.

"We just think it might be time, sugar." Darlene smiled at him as his eyes grew wide. "We've been doing this a long time now. We don't have any kids to pass on the business to, and we really just don't have it in us to put all these pieces back together. Harry and I will travel more, but we'll still be around. Dennis thinks he'll move north, but you know he'll always be a phone call away and he'll visit regularly. It's just time."

"Wow." He shook his head in disbelief.

More than his apartment, more than the warehouse, more than anywhere, really, since his mom died, *Fran's* had come the closest to making him feel at home. He'd miss that, but he couldn't expect them to order their life around what he wanted, no matter how hard losing that place of comfort would be.

"I mean, if that's what y'all feel is best. It'll be weird without *Fran's*, but y'all have to do what's best for you."

"That's all you have to say?" Hailey asked with her palms up. "You're no help. *Fran's* is a Duncan staple! It can't close."

"We know sweetie, but we can't do this forever." Darlene patted Hailey on the arm as she spoke.

"Well, what are you planning to do with it?" Taylor asked.

"We'll probably just sell the building as-is," Dennis shrugged. "Place is trashed and would probably cost more to fix than we'd be able to sell it for."

"What if someone wanted to buy *Fran's* and keep it running?" Taylor leaned up on the couch. "Hailey's right, it's a staple, and I'm sure you could sell the business and even keep getting rent from the building."

"That's nice, honey, but I doubt anyone would want to do that. And I'm not sure we'd even want someone else we don't know running it," Darlene answered him.

"What if we bought it?" Taylor asked. "My dad is constantly talking to me about diversifying what I'm doing and not just having income from my job. I'm sure an investment like this would fit that bill. We could work together to keep it running."

"That's mighty kind of you, sugar, but all you kids are so busy. None of you have the time to run a restaurant."

"That's not entirely true," Sam said. "I just had a conversation with my boss, and it ended with me not having a job and moving into freelancing. I could freelance for big events but manage the diner as my day job. I'd probably need to hire more staff than y'all had to make everything run, but I could help run things there."

"That's not a bad idea," Dennis grumbled as he scratched his chin.

"We don't want you to feel like you have to do that, sweetie. You do what you need to do, don't worry about us."

"No, this is actually a great opportunity. I'd have a stable job, and I could just use the freelance work to supplement that. I don't have much experience with anything like this but I'm a quick learner and I'd love to keep the *Fran's* legacy alive."

Plus, though it'd be different without having them there since they were what had made the place feel like home, he would get to hold onto some of that feeling of having a place where he felt he belonged.

"I take it back. You are a help," Hailey wrapped her arms around Sam's neck as he talked.

"Let me talk to my father about it and then we can work out a contract if you're up for that," Taylor said.

Dennis and Darlene shared a look, and then Darlene answered, "I think this is a better outcome than either of us could have hoped for. You've got a deal." She laughed as Dennis shook Taylor's hand.

"Changing the subject now that that is taken care of—" Sam cleared his throat. "—how long have you known we were the heroes?"

"We've known it was you for a month or two," Harry laughed. "Ever since you started showing up in the paper. You were pretty recognizable to us. We weren't positive on the others until we got picked up Sunday night. We thought the rest of the group could have been involved, but we weren't sure until then."

"Don't worry," Dennis grunted. "Your secret's safe with us."

"I appreciate that, Dennis," Sam laughed.

"So, what's next for you all?" Harry asked.

Sam looked over at Taylor and raised an eyebrow.

"Well," Taylor shrugged, "probably more of the same. Jason will probably handle the brunt of the workload until Lance is healthy. Ashley has already had to head back to Franklin for class. And we'll try and keep Sam from overexerting himself too much when we can. Whenever Fox, the Five Aces, First Sons or anyone else tries to make their next move, we'll be ready."

"Just keep on keeping on." Harry nodded as Taylor finished.

"Exactly."

chapter

THIRTY-EIGHT

The whole team was busy the rest of that week. Gwen and Hailey both had heavier workloads as a result of the turf war, while the guys all worked to help clean up *Fran's*. Jason had the week off as long as he volunteered for city cleanup and reported his volunteer hours. Fox Industries. was trying to get any positive PR they could find after Hailey broke the story about their involvement in what happened. Taylor, Lance, and Sam all had their schedules pretty much up to them at the moment, so it was easy for them to help too.

Because Ashley, Jason, and Lance had holed up in *Fran's* and had fortified against bullets, the restaurant wasn't as big of a cleanup as other places along Broadway. They'd need new windows and tables, but there wasn't too much debris or damage on the inside.

By the time Saturday rolled around, they'd done about all they could do with the *Fran's* cleanup. Jason and Sam had even spent some of the day Friday helping other uptown businesses.

Jason had also been busy as Ironside throughout the week, as there was lingering unrest caused by the weekend's turf war. Sam had suited up a couple times to be backup, but Jason always took care of the situation before he was needed. The turf war was a reminder of not only the value Sam could bring to the team, but also what it cost him to do so. For him to be able to show up when it mattered most, he'd have to sit out most of the other missions or serve as an emergency reinforcement at most. It was going to be a hard transition, but it helped that everyone, even Lance, agreed it was in the best interest of both Sam and the team.

He was glad that he was still getting to play a part, though, even if he still held out hope that Taylor would find a cure. What they could do for the city as heroes made a real difference. Despite all that had happened to him, he was proud of what he'd turned his situation into.

On Saturday, with the guys having finished cleanup and Gwen and Hailey having received a much-needed day off after the week, all six of them were able to meet in the warehouse for the first time since everything had happened. Hailey, Jason, and Lance sat on one couch while Sam and Gwen sat on the other, waiting for Taylor to rejoin them.

"Paperwork should be finished by the end of the month," Taylor said, sitting back down and cracking open a can of soda. "*Fran's* will officially be ours to run then. I figure we can plan on having it back open no later than May."

"That'll give me time to learn how to run the place from Dennis and Darlene." Sam nodded. "Dennis said he'll stick around until April to show me the ropes and make sure I know how to run everything in the kitchen. Darlene said she and Harry would hold off on traveling until we got it up and running so they could be there for opening night and also so she could go through all the processes they'd come up with to keep things running smoothly."

"That'll be helpful," Taylor agreed. "Once you feel like you're in a place where you can run it, we'll start looking for employees."

"It's so exciting!" Gwen smiled at them.

"You know what's crazy?" Taylor asked the group before answering himself. "A year ago, we still didn't know Lance was the vigilante. The amount of things that have gone down in such a short amount of time would have been incomprehensible to me last February."

"I hadn't even made my first stop yet. I was just walking around with my nightstick this time a year ago," Lance added.

"And now we're all wrapped up in this mess of a world thanks to your foolishness, Locke." Hailey lifted her cup in a mock toast and everyone but Lance followed suit.

"To the fool!" Jason bellowed as everyone, including Lance, laughed.

"And two cities are safer because of it," Lance pointed out. "Four new heroes in twelve months; we keep this pace up and we're going to have to come up with some sort of membership. Dues and applications. Whole nine yards."

"Let's not get too ahead of ourselves," Gwen laughed and Lance just shrugged.

"I think we probably have enough heroes for a bit," Sam agreed as he laughed too.

"Never enough heroes; not when Fox is trying to put together an army and we have others like the Five Aces and First Sons causing problems too. I'll take all the help we can get."

"Hopefully we don't have too much going on that requires more help than we have." Taylor shook his head as he talked. "I think we've had about enough major situations to handle over the last year. We're due a lengthy break."

"I'll second that." Lance got a laugh from the group as he rubbed his bandaged chest and smiled. "But when the next situation does come up?"

He looked up and caught Sam's eye as Sam nodded.

"We'll be ready."

Acknowledgements

This is my second book and I still can't believe they exist. Thank you so much to everyone who has made it possible for these stories that have lived in my head for so long to actually find the light of day.

I first started thinking about what could come after The White Knight as soon as I finished the first draft. Samson has existed in different variations in my head since 2014 but it never appeared on paper until 2020 when I suddenly found myself with the time and mental head space to sit down with it. When I wrote The White Knight, I had no idea what I was doing and put out a first draft that reflected that. But after six years of tinkering with my writing, the first draft of Samson came so much more naturally. I always loved thinking about the stories I was creating, but I didn't love the actual writing process of making The White Knight. That changed in 2020 when I wrote Samson. The more character-oriented story, the superpowers, the relational dynamics through Sam's perspective, and of course the lovable new faces at Fran's made the experience feel less like a task and more like a release.

Whenever I talk about my characters, I talk about how all of them have pieces of me in their personality, but none are self-inserts. The more I've sat with Samson, though, the more I've realized that more of me is represented in him than any other character. Or at least the parts of me that sit closest to my identity are the ones that Sam represents. And I was not aware of that when I made him the character that would be from my home state of Oklahoma. Because of that, Samson holds a special place for me in the books I'm writing.

Diversity exists in both The White Knight and The Street Rat, but, at the end of the day, both are told from the perspective of white men like myself. While superheroes have grown more diverse as Marvel and DC have become more intentional in diversifying their characters and other creators have come into this space, superheroes have long been overrepresented by people who are white, men, and most frequently both. While I'm mindful that I can't understand what it's like to live as a different race or gender and don't want to tell stories that aren't mine to share, I think superhero stories have a universality to them and that having representation in these stories is important. For both narrative reasons and a desire to not fall prey to tokenism or to misrepresent cultures I'm not a part of, the focus of Sam's story is on the changes to his body, his decision to become a hero, and balancing all of these claims on his time and energy. Growing up in Oklahoma, I have always been around Native American art, stories, and landmarks which made me both aware and confused at how little representation there was in national popular media for Native Americans. I'm positive a more interesting story could be told by examining how Sam's body changes and decisions are impacted by his tribal affiliation, but my hope is that this story is respectful in how it handles the character's Native American heritage and that it is positive representation in the world of superheroes.

The first person I need to thank is my wife, Taylor. None of my stories would be out in the world without her support throughout this process.

Thanks to my parents and family for their support. Thank you to all my friends who have supported this journey and special thanks to my friends that have read my stuff before I could even think about publishing it, helped me navigate figuring out how to be a writer, and helping me learn to do all the marketing and design and everything else that comes with writing a book outside of the actual writing. So thank you Adara, Ashlyn, Brendan, Bronson, Emily, Haley, Jackson, Maddie, Matti, Nick, Steven, and Taylor. And a special thanks again to my friends at the University of Oklahoma on Muldrow 6, Muldrow 9, and the Couch RA staff which were all full of people who shared my love of superheroes and were instrumental in me starting to write The White Knight.

Finally, thank you to my editors. Megan Mossgrove did a manuscript assessment and the line editing for

Samson and it was such a great experience refining this book with her help and getting the affirmation that these characters and this story could connect with people in such a real way. Thank you to Haley Larkin on Fiverr for proofreading this book. And thank you to MIBLart for working with me on the cover design and interior formatting. Thank you to all of the people who signed up to be ARC readers and joined my Street Team, your support of this story before its release means so much to me.

Like The White Knight, I am self-publishing Samson. The reason I chose to self-publish these books is because these characters and this world are more than stories to me and it was important to me to have creative control over the final product. I also care a lot about the timing of the releases and having the ability to publish short stories in between my book releases. The cost of that creative control is that it's on me as the author to take care of all the logistics for the book's publishing as well as to pay out of pocket for the expenses that entails. I'm still working on writing future stories, but the speed at which they're published depends on the success of The White Knight and Samson selling so please encourage friends to buy a copy or to borrow from hoopla so that I can afford to continue the story as soon as possible. Lastly, thank you, reader, for your interest in this world I created and for supporting an indie author in this publishing journey!

About the Author

K.B. Kirtley is an author from Oklahoma writing the stories he always wanted to read. K.B. holds a lifelong love of superheroes and reading but has always struggled to fall into comics the same way he has with books. His debut series combines the kind of stories he loves in the format he most connects with in a collection of books and short story series introducing a new universe of superheroes.

To keep up to date on all news on upcoming books, find links to all social accounts, and for free access to The Street Rat and all future short story series, go to KirtleyBooks.com.

Turn the page for the first
two episodes of:

EAGLESS

Eagless is free to read at kirtleybooks.com

Eagless 101

Their rent house was only a block away from campus. It was just a small two-bedroom place in an old neighborhood, but it was nice. Every now and then, she glanced back to make sure she wasn't being followed. There hadn't been anyone else out all night, and that hadn't changed now. She leapt over the short gate to the backyard to avoid the squeak that would give away her position. Tiptoeing across the small yard, she made her way across to the bedroom window. Carefully, she raised it and slid in, closing the window behind her and locking it as quietly as possible to keep from waking up her roommate.

Her pale-blue eyes reflected eerily in her mirror, lit only by the moon. She took off the black mask she'd been wearing around her eyes and dropped it on the bed. Next, she took off her blue leather jacket and hung it back up in her closet. She switched out of her black jeans and back into a pair of grey sweatpants and laid down across her comforter.

She stared at the ceiling fan, making its slow rotations, following one blade and then the next as she sank into the bed. Then, with a sigh and a groan, she forced herself back up. She needed to shower off the sweat from patrolling the campus before letting herself get back into the clean sheets of her bed for the night.

"Stop any crimes tonight, Ashley?"

She froze at the sound of her name. Her roommate had the question ready as soon as she stepped out of her room.

"I was, uh, just studying," Ashley responded. She hadn't expected Nicole to still be awake when she got home.

"Did you wear your black mask while you studied? Is that a new focus tool?" Nicole answered without getting out of her chair or even looking up from her laptop. They lived in the house alone. Nicole Kirk had been her roommate in the dorms the previous year, and she was the first friend Ashley had made at Franklin.

Ashley crossed her arms and leaned against the door, not that Nicole could even see her masterful attempt at acting. "I'm not sure what you're talking about. I was just about to go hop in the shower to get ready for bed."

"So, you worked up a sweat walking around campus tonight?" Nicole still hadn't looked up from her laptop. Ashley clenched and unclenched her fists, annoyed that Nicole wouldn't stop being so certain that she was correct. Obviously, she was correct, but the fact that she didn't even have the slightest doubt after all the work Ashley had put into being secretive was frankly just rude.

"I don't know what you're talking about. I've had a long day, and my brain is fried from cramming for midterms. I'm going to shower and go to bed." Ashley had turned to walk down the hall when she heard the laptop close behind her.

"Talk to me, Ashley. Why are you doing this?" Nicole asked. She was standing now and had walked towards the hall. At 5'6", she was a few inches shorter than Ashley, but not so much that she seemed small standing next to her. "You've been acting weird for the last two weeks. I know you. You can't hide this kinda thing from me. I hear you coming back home late at night, and you do it through the backyard, which just makes it more suspicious. Plus, we have security cameras back there that clearly show you wearing a black mask and a leather jacket, I've never seen you wear other than in the video footage."

Ashley scrunched up her nose. She *might* have forgotten they had a security camera in the backyard. She'd never set up notifications for it, but apparently Nicole had. Maybe she hadn't quite covered all her bases like she'd thought. "Why do you think you have to be the campus's new hero?" Nicole continued as Ashley shifted her weight to her other foot. "Why do you think that the campus even having one at all is a good thing?"

"Why do I think it's a good thing?" Ashley was grateful for that last question since it let her shift from feeling chastised to frustrated. Frustration was, ironically, a less frustrating emotion than chastisement. "Because it's an undeniable need for this campus. You know that just as well as I do. Assaults are up sixty percent from last semester. Sixty percent!" she exclaimed, and Nicole's eyebrows went up as her volume rose. Ashley took a deep breath and continued with a slower and quieter inside voice.

"What the White Knight accomplished in lowering the crime was great, but he didn't fix anything. He was a deterrent. And now that he's gone, there's nothing stopping people. Nothing structural changed. Someone has to do something about it. Why is it me? Because no one else is doing it. The White Knight is gone. There have been plenty of sightings in Duncan, but no one has seen him here since May. He's moved on, and that's left a void here. I would love for someone else to have done something, but I'm not going to wait any longer for that to happen. People are getting hurt now. Somebody has to do something about it, and I am somebody."

"You're somebody that can get killed out there. You have no training for this! There are people who are being paid to do what you're trying to do. Just let them do their job!"

"They're not doing their job, though! That's the problem, Nicole! That's a sixty percent increase! Six—" she had started to emphasize it again, but Nicole's cocked head made her think better of it. "What I'm saying is if they were able to do it, then there wouldn't have been a need for the White Knight, and there wouldn't be a need for me. But they don't, and so that need is still there. I don't want to be a hero, but if no one else is going to do something, then I will. Doing nothing isn't an option."

"Of course, doing nothing is an option!" Nicole was smiling as she shook her head, but it wasn't the good kind of smile. It was the bad kind of smile. The Ashley-is-incomprehensible-and-overexcitable-and-needs-to-come-back-down-to-earth kind of smile her mother had perfected, and that Nicole was doing a horrifyingly good job at on her first attempt. "Doing nothing is the most sensible option!"

"I'm not changing my mind. I'm doing this. Because someone has to." Ashley wasn't backing down on this one, no matter how much Nicole channeled her mom. The White Knight was a hero to the campus—was a hero to her—but he was gone, and someone had to step up to fill that role.

"Fine," Nicole declared, throwing up her arms as she walked out of the hallway and across the living room to her room.

"Fine," Ashley sighed as she opened the bathroom door to finally shower. She turned the knob in the old bathtub and pulled the stopper, then sat on the toilet with her head in her hands, frustrated with Nicole for the conversation, with herself for not doing better to keep her secret, and with both of them for not being able to fully brush off Nicole's reaction. The room began to steam as the water heated. She grabbed her towel off the hook and draped it over the bar on the shower door.

Ashley showered longer than she had planned as she tried to figure out what to do about Nicole knowing. *Surely she wouldn't sell me out,* she thought. But as close as the two of them were, that could be the reason her friend would turn her over. This idea of saving her from herself. *I can't believe she doesn't see that this is what has to happen. Somebody has to do it, and no one else is volunteering. I'm doing the right thing. I mean, sure, I may not have any fighting experience, a weapon, or a real super suit, but I have moxie and enough athleticism to play collegiate sports. That's gotta count for something, right? And the campus can't afford to go back to how it was before The White Knight arrived. She'd only been there one semester without a hero, and that had been enough to force her to at least consider transferring. Who knows what would have happened to her and Nicole if the White Knight hadn't shown up when those guys tried to get them into that alley? If the campus needed a hero, then she'd step up and be a hero. No one else was going to do it.*

Ashley finished her shower and headed back to her room. All the lights in the house were off except for the one shining from Ashley's room. Ashley turned it off as she walked in and lay on the bed as a restless sleep overtook her.

SOMEBODY ONCE TOL-

Groaning, Ashley rolled over to turn off her alarm. *I hate that stupid song.* She didn't have soccer practice on Saturdays,

but if she wasn't consistent about waking up at the same time every day, she struggled to be as sharp competitively. She was a key reserve on last year's team as a freshman, but a starting spot had opened up when last year's conference player of the year graduated, and she wanted it.

After brushing her teeth and filling her water bottle, Ashley went for her morning run. Thirty minutes and four miles later, she returned to the house, panting. *I have to find a way to get some sleep during the day. I can't keep up this level of activity on the sleep I'm getting.*

Nicole was at the table eating breakfast as she walked in.

"Uh, hey," Ashley greeted as she set her water bottle down on the counter.

"Hey!" Nicole answered. "What's your Saturday look like?"

"I'm, uh, going to study for a while and then probably take a nap before I go to the gym. What about you?"

"I'm meeting with a study group at one, but that's all I have planned for the day."

"Sounds good. I'm going to go shower off."

"Okay! Talk to you later!"

Ashley shut the door to the bathroom and started the shower. *That was strange. Did I dream the conversation? No, but it was a nice thought.* She was too tired to try to figure out Nicole's response. That was a problem for future Ashley to figure out . . . once she had taken a nap.

"How can I help?"

She'd just woken up and was half asleep, putting on her gym shoes, when Nicole asked the question.

"What are you talking about?" Ashley managed through a yawn.

Nicole was teetering on the edge of the chair beside the couch. "I want to help! I want to help you be a hero!" Her red hair was bouncing as she rocked back and forth, and her green eyes lit up. "I've been thinking since we talked last night. I still don't think it's smart, but I also know you're going to do it regardless of how I feel about it. And I'm not going to let you do something important and cool on your own. So, I'm in. Whatever I can do to help."

"Okay," Ashley answered. She'd stared blankly at Nicole as she had talked. This was partially due to her only being somewhat awake, but mainly to do with her shock at Nicole's complete one-eighty-degree turn on the subject.

"Okay?" Nicole echoed.

"Okay," Ashley repeated. "I don't know what that would look like yet, because, well, I don't really know what I'm doing looks like yet, but yeah. Okay. Partners."

"Partners," Nicole responded with a smile.

Eagless 102

The bell above the library rang out twice, and students began to trickle out the doors, finished with another night of studying, as midterms were in full stride. Ashley sat perched atop the social sciences building next door, looking down on the students from above, hidden from those passing below by the dark sky.

Fifteen minutes later, an employee locked the doors from the outside and walked off, leaving her alone. The library had closed. Ashley had been sitting on the building for two and a half hours, making sure all the students made it out of the library and back to the residence halls safely. And for another night they did. Just like they had every other night since she started sitting up there. Climbing down from the rooftop, Ashley made her way back to their house, sticking to the shadows even though the campus was empty.

"I don't get it," she vented to Nicole who had to push pause on the show she'd been watching when Ashley had walked in. "I don't know where all this increase in crime is even happening. I sit and watch the library, and the students walk in and then walk back to the halls every night and nothing ever happens."

Nicole set her bowl of cereal down on the side table and turned to face Ashley, crossing her legs under her on the couch. "I'm sure if you check with wherever you got that sixty percent number you could figure out where it was happening. Maybe people are still wary of doing things in the open on campus after last year but they're more comfortable off campus or at their frat house."

"I guess that's true." Ashley collapsed into the over-sized and overused chair, sinking into the soft cushions as the little adrenaline from the night seeped out of her. "But what am I supposed to do to help prevent that? I can't be everywhere at once to watch what's happening. I definitely can't just hangout in frat houses waiting. I'm already working so much, and I can't afford to cut any more time from school or soccer."

"Maybe the issue isn't that you need to work harder. Maybe what you need to do is work smarter," Nicole answered, reaching back to grab her bowl from the table.

"What do you mean?"

"Well, right now you're just going and staking out the library every night, right? And you're not seeing anything." Nicole paused as she took another bite of cereal. "So, you're spending two hours a night where there aren't any problems. What you need to figure out is both where and when this uptick in assaults is happening. Find the records that say where arrests were made, or reports were filed, and check the time stamps.

Then you work from there to put yourself in the best position to succeed by going to the crime instead of waiting for crime to come to you."

"You're right!" Ashley tried to sit up as a new wave of energy and excitement hit her, though she struggled to escape the chair's comfy grasp for a moment before she was back on her feet, pacing. "I've had blinders on since it was that walk from the library where the White Knight helped us last semester. But clearly that's not where the current need is. Plus, he was spotted all over, not just in one spot. Great catch, partner."

"Thank you," Nicole laughed. "But there is something else I've been thinking of that I wanted to ask you."

"Go for it." Ashley picked up an apple from the bowl on the bar and tossed it from one hand to the other as she continued pacing.

"What weapon are you taking with you on your patrols? I've never seen you carrying anything."

"I don't feel comfortable with any kind of weapon. It feels wrong." She shrugged. "So, I just go out without one."

"You have to realize how dumb that is, right?" Nicole had the spoon halfway to her mouth but stopped and put the cereal back in the bowl. "You're putting yourself in danger by being a hero, and you're not taking even the most basic precautions against it. You're just putting on a mask you ordered online and a leather jacket."

"I don't want to hurt people, just stop them. Do you remember how the White Knight broke that guy's arm with his stick when he helped us? While I appreciated his help, I've been kinda scarred since then because of that. I just can't get the image of that arm dangling out of my head." Ashley shivered thinking about it again.

"Then you can't keep going out there. You have to commit to the whole thing if you're going to do this. And that means you're going to have to fight people and maybe hurt them. Would you rather the White Knight let those guys attack us instead of hurting them? No. And nobody you're going to try, and help is going to think 'I'm glad she didn't hurt that guy. I know he assaulted me because she didn't hurt him, but at least he wasn't in pain.' You have to make those tough calls sometimes, Adair."

"Look, you might be right, but I'm not comfortable with that right now. We can talk more later. I'm going to get too little sleep as it is, so I need to call it a night."

"Oh, we're definitely talking more later," Nicole called after her through a mouthful of cereal as Ashley walked to the bathroom.

The next night, Ashley looked up from the courtyard at the balcony. That's where the White Knight started. People staked it out for weeks after that first save. *It's worth a shot.* Ashley began climbing up to the balcony and settled into one of the chairs in the darkness.

Ashley clenched and unclenched her fists. It had been thirty minutes since she staked out her spot on the balcony, and the first cold front of the year came through earlier in the day. This was the first night since she'd started patrolling that the weather had made her uncomfortable. *I'll need some gloves. And probably a long-sleeved shirt to wear under the jacket going forward.*

"HEY!" The shout coming from the student union caused Ashley to jerk her head up and over, pulling her from her meditation. "Come back!" the voice yelled again as a guy sprinted into the courtyard with a backpack in his hands. Ashley darted to the ladder and skipped down the rungs.

A group of people had now walked out of the student union, watching the bag snatcher run. He was almost across the courtyard when Ashley landed and gave chase. He had a twenty-yard head start on her, but didn't know she was coming for him. Not that it would have mattered. She caught up to him after he'd only made it thirty more yards. Grabbing the bag, she planted her foot to stop her momentum and tugged. The man's feet went into the air as he fell and landed on his back, still clutching the bag. Scrambling to his feet, he tried to rip the bag from Ashley, but she wasn't letting go.

She yanked the bag, pulling the thief closer while also delivering a turning kick to his side. His grip released as he reached for his side, groaning in pain. Ashley toppled backwards as he let go, thankful for the leather jacket protecting her elbows in the fall. Jumping back to her feet, she saw the man scurry into the library. She hadn't gotten a good look at him. There was no way she'd find him in there. *But I got the bag back.* She smiled to herself as she turned around.

As she jogged back to the union, she noticed that a larger group had gathered in the courtyard as people watched her pursue the bag snatcher.

A loud cheer went up as she returned to the light of the courtyard with the bag in hand. Ashley smiled and gave a quick wave but quickly set the bag down and sprinted off when the crowd started rushing towards her. She darted between two buildings and up a fire escape, barely making it over the edge of the roof before a group made it to the alley.

Ashley lay flat on her back, trying to control her breathing. The group's muttering got further away as she panted. After waiting another ten minutes, Ashley sat back up and peered off the roof. The crowd had dispersed, and there were only a few passersby who weren't looking for anyone.

She descended the fire escape and put the mask in her pocket. No more heroism tonight. Ashley headed back to the house to call it a night. The smile had yet to fade from her lips.